MW01240614

# IMPRISONED

## BRIDES OF THE KINDRED, BOOK 22

## EVANGELINE ANDERSON

# Evangeline Anderson

BRIDES of the KINDRED

KINDRED TALES

ALIEN *Mate* INDEX

CyBRG Files

COUGAR-VILLE

BORN TO DARKNESS

www.evangelineanderson.com

*Imprisoned*, 1st Edition,
Book Twenty-Two of The Brides of the Kindred
Copyright © 2018 by Evangeline Anderson
All rights reserved.
Cover Art Design © 2018 by Reese Dante

This book is a work of fiction. The names, characters, places and incidents are products of the writers' imagination or have been used factiously and are not to be construed as real. Any resemblance to persons, living or dead, actual events, locale or organizations is entirely coincidental.

All rights are reserved. No part of this book may be used or reproduced in any manner whatsoever without written permission except in the case of brief quotations embodied in critical articles and reviews.

Cover content is for illustrative purposes only.
Any person depicted on the cover is a model.

IMPRISONED

BRIDES OF THE KINDRED, BOOK 22

**A girl dressed as a boy**
**In a Triple Max prison full of savage predators**
**A Kindred warrior undercover, trying to protect**
**What he thinks is an innocent boy.**
**Lathe can't understand why he is so drawn to Ari**
**But when her secret comes out, will it kill**
**them both?**
**You'll have to read *Imprisoned* to find out...**

Lady Arianna Blackthorn is a woman on a mission—she intends to rescue her brother, Jak, from the infamous BleakHall prison. BleakHall is a Triple Max Penitentiary where only the worst of the worst are sent--a males-only facility where not even female prison guards are allowed. So how can Ari infiltrate this fortress? With the use of a holo-projector that makes her look male (the important parts anyway) she's determined to get in and she has a foolproof plan for getting both herself and Jak out...or so she thinks.

Commander Lathe is a Blood Kindred who lost his younger brother to the horrors of BleakHall. He is on a mission to go undercover and collect evidence against the cruel and ruthless prison guards who run it and the Yonnite Mistresses who own it. He also has a plan to get out but it's going to take some time and while he's waiting, a strange new inmate comes to BleakHall—a boy called Ari.

Ari is in over her head from the minute she steps through the prison gates. She is immediately singled out by Tapper, Bleak-Hall's most ruthless sexual predator, as his next conquest. Only Lathe's timely intervention saves her from a fate worse than death...and death itself. Lathe moves Ari into his cell to keep her safe but he has no idea she is really a female and Ari doesn't dare to tell him.

Can Ari keep her secret from the big Kindred? Can Lathe sort through his confusing feelings for the "boy" he has taken under his wing? (Why does he smell like a female? Why can't Lathe stop thinking about him...stop wanting to touch him?) Can the two of them rescue Ari's brother and escape from the maze of sadistic guards, psychopathic prisoners, and ravenous lashers—the huge carnivorous cats that roam the corridors of BleakHall at night waiting to devour any inmates attempting to get away?

You'll have to read *Imprisoned,* Brides of the Kindred 22, to find out...s

## AUTHOR'S NOTE

A large part of this book is set in a prison and there are some scenes which may be disturbing to anyone who has experienced sexual abuse in the past. Please read responsibly.

## PROLOGUE

"My Lady Blackthorn, you cannot be serious—you must not do this thing!"

Arianna took a firmer grip on the shears and prepared to make the first cut.

"I am sorry, Hanna," she told her maid, "But I must. There is no other way to rescue Jak. Where he is, I must go."

"But not to BleakHall, my Lady! Surely not there!" Hanna protested. Her wrinkled hands fluttered about her face like distraught moths. "Tis said no one ever comes out of it alive! The Yonnites make sure of it."

"Don't speak to me of those evil *shivaths*," Ari snapped, though she knew that swearing would only upset her kindly old maid even more. "They are the reason Jak is imprisoned in the first place!"

Her brother had been taking their latest crop to market when his ship had been overtaken by pirates just outside the orbit of Yonnie Six, a planet ruled by cruel and heartless women. The pirates—greedy bastards that they were—hadn't been content just to steal Jak's ship and the crop—they had also sold him at the Yonnite slave market where he had been bought by one of the Yonnite mistresses.

She might have been able to save him if she had found out his whereabouts at once, Ari mused grimly. But by the time she was able to locate her older brother, his Yonnite mistress had grown angry with him and had sent him to BleakHall.

BleakHall Penitentiary was a Triple Max security prison located on one of Yonnie Six's small moons. It took up almost the entire moon and was a males only facility where the wealthy Yonnite mistresses sent their most dangerous, murderous, and deadly slaves—the ones so intractable even they could not tame them. And that was saying something since the Yonnites prided themselves on taking on even the largest and most homicidal males and breaking them down to make them the perfect body slaves.

*Apparently Jak couldn't be broken.*

Ari didn't know if she ought to feel proud or regretful about that. It would have been *so* much easier to rescue him from the clutches of the Yonnite mistress. She could simply have posed as a mistress herself and bought him. Instead, she was going to risk her life to save him from the prison.

*But what else can I do? I can't just leave him there,* Ari thought as she positioned the shears under a thick hank of her long, straight black hair and began to cut.

*Hair as dark as a rook's wing...you're my little rook, Ari,* she heard her big brother whisper in her memory. *And your hair is so long—take care that you don't just fly away one day.*

Jak had always liked to tease her when their parents were alive—when the four of them were still a family. That had been when the crumbling estate on Phobos, the tiny planetoid that orbited between Yonnite Six and Zetta Prime, had felt most like a home.

But after their parents were gone—taken in a shuttle explosion when Ari was only fourteen—Jak had become more than a big brother. In the ten cycles that had passed since their parents' death, he had become almost a father, caring for her and making certain she was provided for. He even let Ari spend her time tinkering in her lab while he oversaw the hydroponic garden where their crops of rare, heirloom *tulsa* fruit grew. *Tulsa* was a luxury item—the plump, juicy bright orange berries were their claim to fame and the basis of their wealth but Jak never forced the family business on her.

"*You please yourself, little rook,*" he would tell her. "*Who knows—maybe someday you'll invent something amazing.*"

Well, his words had come true, Ari reflected as she cut away more of her long, blue-black tresses. She had invented a way to get him out of prison—but she had to get to him first. And in order to get to him, she had to infiltrate the prison.

*And in order to do that, I must look like a man,* Ari told herself, remorselessly shearing away more of her long, silky hair. She was making a ragged job of it—her hair was short and choppy on one side now, looking like a haircut someone had done in the dark.

*I look like a beggar boy,* Ari thought. Well, so much the better if she looked poor and ragged—who ever heard of a prisoner from one of the Great Houses?

Not that the Great Houses of Phobos amounted to much. Phobos was a quiet, unassuming little planetoid but its people were happy. They were a true democracy where men and women were equal, unlike Yonnie Six where males were enslaved and Zetta Prime where they were outlawed. The citizens of Phobos were happy to live differently from their neighbors—happy to live in peace.

*I doubt I'll have peace for some time, once I get where I'm going,* Ari thought grimly. Aloud she said, "There, finished," as she made the final cut and the last long strands fluttered to the flagstones at her feet.

"Your hair," Hanna mourned, her wrinkled face creased with regret. "Oh my Lady, all your lovely hair..."

"It'll grow back when Jak and I come home," Ari said firmly.

Putting down the shears, she rubbed a hand over her shorn head, rumpling her hair which wanted to stand up in cowlicks and corkscrews now that the weight of its length was no longer holding it down.

*I look very boyish,* she decided, watching herself in the viewer. *Well...boyish enough.*

She had dark eyes to match her hair, a sharp nose and a wide, mobile mouth that didn't look in the least ladylike. Her skin was a little pale and soft perhaps, since she spent so much time in her lab, but without her long hair, there were no other clues that definitely marked her as female. Well, other than her height. She was barely five foot four—a definite disadvantage. But that would only add to the illusion that she was a ragged boy who hadn't gotten his full growth—or his beard—in yet.

*I'll pass,* Ari told herself firmly. *Especially with the look/touch field in place.*

The look/touch was her own invention—well partly anyway. She had modified a holo projection field so that it produced tangible effects as well as visual ones. It was hidden in the fake prison ID she'd paid to have implanted in her skin so the metal of the ID would mask it completely. Her other failsafe—the one she was counting on to get both herself and Jak out of BleakHall once she found him—was hidden there as well.

Of course she had to get to him first, before she could use it.

"My Lady," Hanna begged again. "Please, *please* reconsider! BleakHall is full of big, violent males and you are *female.* What will they do to you when they find out what you are?"

"They're not going to find out," Ari said firmly. "Believe me, Hanna—I have a foolproof disguise."

"My Lady, just cutting your hair isn't enough to hide your beauty!" her maid protested.

Ari laughed. "Oh Hanna—you always did look at me with a fond eye. I'm nothing special and believe me, right now I'm glad I'm not. But I'm not just talking about cutting my hair. Look..."

Reaching up to the hollow of her throat, she tapped lightly at the top of the triangular prison ID tag. The ID was coded to respond only to her DNA and inside it was the tiny bead which housed the look/touch projector. Ari felt rather than heard the hum and a prickling sensation ran down her body from her clavicles to her crotch.

"I don't understand, My Lady." Hanna looked at her blankly. "What do you mean? What should I be looking at?"

Ari looked at herself in the mirror but she was still wearing her dressing gown—dark blue silk, belted at the waist. It had been a present from Jak last Winter Solstice when the *tulsa* crop had been especially good.

"Oh, well of course you can't tell with this on," she said. Taking a deep breath, she unbelted the gown and shrugged it down around her waist. "Now look," she told her old maid.

"My Lady?" Hanna stared at her blankly, her seamed and wrinkled face bewildered. Then her watery blue eyes widened and she gave a little gasp. "My Lady what have you done to yourself? Where are your *breasts?*"

Ari stared down at the flat, male chest the look/touch projected. Her breasts were nothing remarkable—they were teacup-sized with dark pink nipples that tended to be more puffy than Ari liked. But now they were completely invisible—hidden by the illusion of a scrawny male chest with nipples that were small copper disks, flat enough to make the walls jealous.

"They're still there," she assured her maid. "You just can't see them." Of course, if someone was to grab at her chest, they would be able to *feel* the soft, pillowy mounds of her breasts. Ari wished it wasn't so but she hadn't had time to perfect the top part of the projection as much as she'd wanted to—she'd been working too hard on the bottom half which was arguably the most important part.

She parted the robe further and looked into the viewer. There, plainly visible, was a male shaft. It was small and soft, curled like a sleeping worm against her thigh but it was there—and in more than just sight. The look/touch manifested an actual fleshy organ between her thighs which fit over her own pubic mound and hid her vagina from sight completely.

The organ wasn't completely functional—it was mostly

hollow for one thing and so was unable to become erect. That was fine with Ari, though—she didn't need to get a hard-on—she just wanted to look like a male and she needed her disguise to be utterly believable. Which it was—she was certain. Since the fake shaft fit over her cleft so tightly, she could even urinate standing up if she had to—the shaft acted like a kind of funnel.

She had shaved her mound to make the fit perfect and tried it out only that morning—it definitely worked. The texture of the skin felt a little strange—too slick to be real since it was, after all, only a solid holo projection. But the look of it was perfect and that was all she needed.

"Oh, My Lady!" Hanna's eyes grew so wide they looked likely to swallow her wrinkled face and she took a staggering step backward. "What...what have you done?" she gasped, her hands fluttering weakly. "You...you...this isn't right! I used to change your nappies as a baby and I know you don't...you can't have a...a..."

"It's all right, Hanna!" Seeing how upset the old maid was getting, Ari quickly tapped the prison ID and turned the look/touch off. At once her breasts and mound came into view, though she quickly covered them with her blue silk gown. "See? I'm fine," she assured her maid who still looked like she didn't know whether to scream or faint.

"How...what...?" Hanna shook her head, clearly bewildered. "How did you do that? Is it something you cooked up in that lab of yours?"

"It is." Ari didn't even try to keep the pride from her voice. "I call it a look/touch—it's a solid holo projector. See, when you bend the light beam just the right way and treat it with a cadmium stream—"

"Please, My Lady, none of your science talk." Hanna waved as though shooing a fly. "You know it only makes me confused. Well...so *that's* how you plan to sneak into BleakHall. I must say, it's awfully convincing." She shuddered.

"Thank you—I thought so too." Ari grinned. "So you see, Hanna, I'll be perfectly safe."

"How, My Lady?" the maid protested. "Just because you look like a male doesn't mean you won't be attacked. You're so small and those awful males they keep locked up in that place are so *big*."

"One of those males is Jak, which is why I have to go," Ari reminded her. "And size doesn't matter so much. You know Jak's been teaching me *Ton-kwa* self defense for years. I can take on an opponent twice as large as me and throw him."

"Maybe in the sparring ring, My Lady," Hanna objected. "But never in a desperate, awful place like BleakHall! They won't obey the rules there—there's no referee to stop the match if things get too rough. And what if more than one attacks you at a time? Oh..." She brought her faded apron up to her eyes and began to cry. "Oh Goddess of Mercy, what will you do then?"

Ari felt a sudden cold chill go down her back. What *would* she do if she was attacked by multiple assailants at once? Hanna actually made a very good point.

Resolutely, she pushed the fear away.

"That's not going to happen, Hanna," she said firmly. "In fact, I'll probably barely be in the prison for an hour. All I have to do is get in and find Jak. The moment I can touch him..."

Grabbing the old nurse by her arm, she touched her Prison ID again, rubbing the lower point of the triangular metal plate in a specific rhythm. At once a glowing golden bubble enclosed them both and they began to float upward.

"My Lady!" Hanna gasped, grabbing for Ari's hand. "What—?"

Once more Ari rubbed her ID, turning off the switch hidden beneath it. The bubble popped noiselessly and they fell the inch and a half they'd floated back down to the flagstones.

"Oh!" Hanna stumbled and would have fallen to her knees if Ari hadn't caught her. "What was that?"

"A *tribian* transport bubble," Ari said. "It cost me almost all the profits Jak had saved from his last three harvests but I don't think he'll mind if it works. *When* it works," she corrected herself quickly.

"But how...how does it work? If you can tell me without getting too technical, My Lady," Hanna added quickly.

"I think I can manage." Ari smiled at her. "The transport bubble is a solid lightbeam sphere just big enough for two. It can be deployed at any time and as long as you're out in open air, it will take you straight up into the sky."

"It...it will?" Hanna still looked shaken. "But then how...?"

"Don't you see?" Ari asked. "I've just got to get to Jak when we're both outside—probably in the exercise yard, which I know they have because I've studied the plans of the prison. Then the two of us float up...up...and away to a remote life support craft I've already got orbiting the moon where BleakHall is located. It's not much but it will get us back to Phobos with no problem. So you see, Hanna, I really *do* have everything planned out to the last degree. *Now* do you feel better?"

The old maid nodded thoughtfully.

"You know, I do a bit. Although..." she gestured to Ari's closed robe doubtfully. "I had no idea you were getting up to such things in your lab, My Lady."

Ari coughed, feeling her cheeks get a bit hot. "Well obviously this wasn't the originally intended use for the solid-holo tech I've been working on. I was thinking more along the lines of people being able to hug their loved ones when they made a holo call. I was just getting ready to publish my findings before..." Her throat was suddenly tight. "Before Jak was taken."

"Well I must say—what you've come up with is nothing short of amazing. I do hope it will help keep you safe." She enfolded Ari in a hug, her frail old body trembling with emotion. "I pray the Goddess of Mercy will watch over you, My Lady. No matter how many gadgets and gizmos you have hidden inside that awful metal tag you're wearing, I still worry about you."

"I know you do, Hanna." Ari hugged the old lady back and reflected that Hanna was much more than a servant. She'd been with Ari's family her entire life and though Hanna insisted on calling her "My Lady" and Jak, "My Lord" she was really more of a surrogate grandmother than a domestic.

"Oh, My Lady..." Hanna mourned softly. "I can't believe you're really going to do this."

"I have to—what other choice do we have? You know the Yonnites don't allow their prisoners appeals—Jak has no hope unless I go for him. Besides, I'm going to be all right." Firmly but gently, she disengaged from the embrace and held Hanna at arms length, looking earnestly into her eyes. "I'm going to go get Jak and the two of us will be home before you know it—you'll see."

"From your mouth to the Goddess of Mercy's ear, My Lady," Hanna whispered. But though she tried to smile and put on a brave face for Ari's benefit, her faded blue eyes still filled with tears.

Ari smiled and tried to comfort her but she couldn't help worrying herself. No matter how prepared she was, the fact was, she was a small female walking into a triple max prison filled with violent, dangerous males—many of them murderers, rapists, and homicidal sociopaths.

She couldn't help wondering if she would make it out alive.

# ONE

## Six Months Before

"Commander Lathe, I think you know why I asked you here." Sylvan drummed restlessly on his desk, a frown hovering around his mouth as he waited for the other male to be seated.

"I think so." Lathe nodded, a fierce look coming into his piercing turquoise eyes as he settled in the chair across from Sylvan's desk. "Is it about BleakHall?"

"It is." Sylvan spoke quietly, still studying the other male.

For a Blood Kindred, Lathe had unusual coloring, he thought. Most of his kind had the same pale blond hair and ice blue eyes that Sylvan did himself. Lathe had brown hair though—a deep chocolate brown with auburn highlights and long, thick lashes to match, which fringed his strange turquoise eyes. But then, his coloring probably had something to do with the special *type* of Blood Kindred he was.

More than almost any other branch of the Kindred family tree, the Blood Kindred seemed to have a penchant for mutations and variations. And Lathe was the rarest of them all. In fact, Sylvan hated to risk him on this mission, which was horribly dangerous. Like himself, Lathe was a doctor aboard the Mother Ship and a well-respected scientist as well. Such a mind and such rare talents shouldn't be wasted on such a hazardous assignment. But the other male had a personal stake in this and honor demanded that Sylvan offer the mission to him first before he asked anyone else.

"As you know, the complaints about BleakHall have been piling up—from all corners of the galaxy," Sylvan said, choosing his words carefully. "Ever since the Yonnites outsourced the guard duties to the Horvaths, there have been reports of abuses. Cruelty, torture..."

"And death," Lathe finished for him, his eyes flashing.

"And death," Sylvan agreed heavily. "Yes, I'm sorry for I know how it pains you to speak of this."

Lathe's younger brother, a promising young officer aboard a Kindred freighter, had been captured and sold into slavery on Yonnie Six. When he refused to submit to his mistress, he had been sent to BleakHall. Lathe had learned of his brother's incarceration and had asked the High Council for help in rescuing him. But before a rescue effort could be made, word came that Thonolan had died in the dungeons of the Triple Max penitentiary.

Lathe's eyes were bright, but with fury, not tears, Sylvan saw.

"I don't mind speaking of death as long as we also speak of justice," he said, his voice a low, angry growl. "What can be done to avenge my brother's murder?"

"First and foremost we must prove the problem exists," Sylvan said.

"What?" Lathe demanded. "Of course it exists! You said it yourself—complaints are pouring in from *everywhere*. Clearly this prison is corrupt—the *Horvaths* are torturing the prisoners, killing them! They—"

"No one cares," Sylvan cut in harshly. Seeing the shocked look on Lathe's face, he made his tone softer. "Forgive me, Brother. I should have said, no one in *Yonnite society* cares. More specifically, no one on the Yonnite Council of Mistresses—the Sacred Seven—cares. And until we can bring the matter to them with corroborating evidence to prove that there is wanton cruelty and abuse being committed by the guards, they aren't going to listen to us."

"Why can't we just attack the damn prison?" Lathe growled. "It's full of males who shouldn't be there."

"It's also full of males who *should*," Sylvan said gently. "BleakHall is the only penitentiary in the galaxy that accepts many of the felons housed there. If we attack the prison, not only do the Kindred declare war on Yonnie Six, we also release more rapists, murderers, and sociopaths on the galaxy than have been free since the Scourge were at full strength."

"What about the honest males? The ones who were captured as slaves and refused to bow their heads to Yonnite mistresses?" Lathe demanded. "What about them? Do we just forget them because they happen to be in BleakHall and the Council doesn't want to risk war with Yonnie Six?"

"Nobody is forgetting them," Sylvan said evenly. "In fact, we're in the process of arranging a back-channel to get them out."

"Too bad no one could arrange such a thing for Thonolan." Lathe's deep voice was bitter.

"It's because of your brother's death that we are doing so now," Sylvan said, speaking as gently as he could. "We're going to try to make certain that no more innocent lives are lost to Bleak-Hall. But we need a male on the inside to help facilitate the channel *and* to gather evidence to present to the Yonnite Council of Mistresses about what is really going on in their prison."

"You mean..." Lathe's turquoise eyes went wide. "You want someone to go into the prison under cover? Pretending to be a prisoner?"

"Exactly." Sylvan nodded. "If we can prove the abuse, we can make them see that the current ownership of the prison is corrupt and force them to do something about it. If they don't, other planets will stop sending them prisoners and their bottom line will suffer." He shook his head grimly. "That's about the only thing that Yonnites understand. The Goddess knows most of them don't have much in the way of compassion or pity."

"You speak as though you had personal experience of them," Lathe remarked, keeping his tone neutral.

"Only in passing but that was enough." Sylvan told him of his recent encounter with a Yonnite Mistress—Mistress Hellenix and her Kindred slave, Malik.

"And you say he was a Volt Kindred?" Lathe's eyes widened. "I didn't know there were any left. How did she keep such a powerful male contained?"

Sylvan shook his head. "It was my impression that she didn't—he stayed with her for a reason. Though what that reason was, I never found out. In fact..." He steepled his fingers and leaned forward. "We have reason to believe that Mistress

Hellenix is one of the Yonnites responsible for outsourcing BleakHall's guard positions to the Horvaths. She sits on the prison's board of directors and plays a most active roll in its administration."

"I wonder if she ever bothers to come to the prison itself to see how its being run?" Lathe muttered. "I wonder if I'll see her while I'm there."

"While you're there?" Sylvan frowned.

"Isn't that why you called me here? To offer me the mission?" Lathe asked. "You don't have to ask, Commander Sylvan—my answer is yes. I'll do everything I can to avenge my brother's death and make certain no other innocent males are trapped at BleakHall."

"It's very dangerous," Sylvan pointed out. Though honor demanded that he offer the assignment to Lathe, he couldn't help wishing that the other male would turn it down. But one look at the fury in those turquoise eyes let him know his wish was in vain.

"I don't give a damn," Lathe growled. "I'll do whatever's necessary—danger or not."

"You'll need to wear a vid-corder. We have one implanted in a prison ID you'll be wearing—it's only five microns wide by eight microns across," Sylvan told him. "With it you can record everything that happens all around you—especially the evidence of abuse. We've got a few other tools we can send with you too. We've arranged to get you in as a prisoner and your backstory is that you're a medic. With any luck the Horvaths will allow you into the BleakHall infirmary. You can record first-hand accounts of every injury that occurs there."

"Sounds perfect." Lathe nodded. "I'm in."

"You won't be able to take any weapons with you. It's going to be insanely dangerous," Sylvan couldn't help saying again. "Some might even call it suicide to take this mission."

"I can take care of myself," Lathe said shortly.

Sylvan nodded reluctantly.

"You *are* uniquely suited to defend yourself in such a situation, I suppose."

"Because of my mutation, you mean?" Lathe barked a short, unhappy laugh and the motion showed his extra-long fangs. Though a Blood Kindred's fangs were only supposed to grow and sharpen when he found a female he wanted to bond to him, Lathe's were always razor-sharp.

"I've thought of that, you know," he continued. "If only it had been me that was taken instead of Thonolan. He was just a regular Blood Kindred. If only he'd had my abilities..."

"You can't do that to yourself," Sylvan said gently. "You can't trade souls like cards in a pack or let yourself feel responsible for what happened to your brother. He was a grown male, Lathe—it wasn't your fault."

"That's easy for you to say." Lathe looked away. "It should have been me. I should have been with him."

"Lathe—"

"How soon can I go?" the other male cut him off, turning his eyes back to Sylvan. They glowed with intensity. "I'm ready now."

"Then we can have you there by as early as tomorrow if you like," Sylvan said. "But let me urge you to take some time to think about this. To go to the Sacred Grove and pray about if it's the right decision for you—"

"I don't need to think or pray—I *know*," Lathe growled. "Put me into BleakHall and leave the rest to me."

"Very well." Sylvan sighed. "Tomorrow it is then. I hate to say this, Commander Lathe, but maybe you should take this evening to get your affairs in order."

"I've got nothing to get in order." Lathe shrugged. "My brother is dead—my parents too. And I don't have a mate."

"Are you currently dream-sharing with anyone, though?" Sylvan asked. "If you are, you might want to reconsider taking this assignment."

Lathe frowned and for a moment a puzzled expression came over his face. Then he shook his head, like a male pushing away some ridiculous thought.

"No, I'm not dreaming of any female—I doubt I ever will. Once I thought I might have found my true mate but..."

"But what?" Sylvan prompted gently.

Lathe shook his head. "But I was mistaken." He sighed. "I believe I'm one of those males the Goddess created to be single."

"I used to think that about myself, you know," Sylvan said quietly. "It turned out not to be true. I think the Goddess has someone for everyone."

"Not me." Lathe shook his head firmly. "I've got no one and I don't *want* anyone." His eyes gleamed. "I only want to bring down the fucking evil mistresses responsible for my brother's death and make sure no one else shares his fate."

"Well..." Sylvan sighed. "Maybe this is the Goddess's purpose for you—I pray her grace and protection will go with you into BleakHall."

"Thank you but the time for prayers is over. It's time for action." Lathe stood and nodded respectfully. "I'll get my affairs in order and see you tomorrow morning."

Then he turned and strode from Sylvan's office, back straight and broad shoulders set.

"Goddess," Sylvan muttered as he watched the other male go. "What have I done?" He looked to the ceiling, his words turning into a prayer. "Please protect him and lend him your strength and guidance, Mother of All Life. Though he thinks he needs no prayers, he will need them now more than ever as he walks willingly into danger and death."

# TWO

## Present Day

"What do you mean this is as far as you go? You told me you could take me all the way to the exercise yard to find my brother!"

Ari glared up at the huge, scaly Horvath who had claimed to be one of the guards when she hired him to smuggle her into BleakHall.

Horvaths were lizard-like humanoids covered in greenish scales with slitted, shifty yellow eyes, forked tongues, and thick tails that could knock a man off his feet with one powerful swing.

They were also lying, cheating scum, apparently.

"Zzorry. Thizz is azz far azz I can take you." The Horvath shrugged his scaly shoulders.

"But this is just a holding area for new prisoners," Ari hissed, looking around. "It's not even all the way inside the prison!"

They were standing in the doorway of BleakHall—already past the first checkpoint so there was no turning back. All around her loomed tall black walls, sweating with moisture. They rose up higher than the eye could see, lined with lighted cells—glass cubes in a metal box. Ahead of them was a disorganized hoard of prisoners, all waiting to be processed. Most wore heavy shackles or spiked pain collars but a few were wandering around freely, making notations on battered electronic tablets.

"Zzorry," the Horvath said again, clearly not sorry a bit.

"How am I supposed to get to my brother?" Ari demanded. "You were supposed to take me right to him!"

"Get prosezzed like all the other prizzoners," the Horvath said. "Then you can zzee him inzide."

*"This is not what I paid you for!"* Ari whispered in a low, furious voice. "You promised me—"

But the Horvath didn't even stay to hear the rest of her complaint. He turned and ambled off towards the guard station where several others of his kind were lounging on a bench sipping clear plasti-glass bottles full of what appeared to be green slime.

"Hey!" Ari started to go after him, but a man stepped in front of her and she ran directly into his protruding gut. "Oof!" She was knocked off her feet by the sudden impact and fell on her back, losing her breath.

"What's this? Trying to get away already before you're even processed?" a mocking male voice asked. "I thought you were that guard's pet but it seems like he's gone and left you all alone, sweet thing."

Shading her eyes against the harsh overhead glows, Ari looked up...and up and up. The speaker was one of the prisoners she'd seen wandering around without restraints but he wasn't alone and he wasn't holding a tablet himself. He was flanked by two other males, both almost as big and beefy as he was, and one of *them* was holding the tablet.

"Who...who are you?" Ari had a sinking feeling in her stomach that she didn't want to know the answer. The male towering over her was at least a foot and a half taller than her and probably triple her body weight. He was wearing a prison jumpsuit but it wasn't orange and blue striped like the ones the men flanking him wore—distinctive green stripes ran parallel to the blue instead.

He had stripped down the top part of the jumpsuit, letting the arms dangle free behind him to reveal broad, beefy shoulders where all the hair that had apparently migrated from his bald head now grew. Coarse black tufts stuck out of his ears and nostrils too. A heavy gold ring with a red stone decorated the middle finger of his right hand.

But it wasn't his jewelry or his body hair, repulsive though it was, that worried Ari. She was much more concerned about the sneer on his face. There was cruelty in his small, mud-colored eyes and in the set of his rubbery lips. He had slabs for cheeks and his monstrous, hairy gut overhung the unfastened jumpsuit obscenely as he looked down at her appraisingly.

"Who are you?" Ari asked again, trying to make her voice low and at least semi-masculine, since he seemed to be content to just stare.

"Get that, Tapper—he don't even know who you are! Dumb shit," sneered the man on his left.

"Course he don't know Tapper. He's new, 'ent he?" the one on the right, holding the tablet said, elbowing the other one.

"Help him up, boys." Tapper nodded at Ari, who was still

sprawled on the floor in front of him, feeling as vulnerable as a bug pinned to a card.

At once, the two henchmen (because could they really be anything else?) each took one of her arms and hauled her upright so that she was facing Tapper.

She still had to look up to see him, not that it was a very pleasant view.

"Th-thank you, er...Mr. Tapper," she said, hoping that maybe if she was polite and unassuming they would leave her alone. But her response only seemed to make Tapper more interested in her.

"Hmm, polite one, 'ent he boys?" He looked at Ari speculatively. "Face as pretty as a girl's—soft skin, too. He's kinder skinny a'course but I think I like him." He nodded decisively. "Yap, I like him. Put 'im on the list."

"What list?" Ari blurted as the male with the tablet looked at her, one dirty finger poised over the glowing surface.

"List of fresh meat Tapper wants to taste. Now what's your name, pretty boy?" he asked casually, as though he was a waiter putting her name on a waiting list at a busy restaurant.

"What?" Ari took a step back. "I...I'm not telling you my name for *that*."

"He won't tell his name." The man with the tablet looked upset. The whites of his eyes and his protruding teeth were both yellow, Ari noticed distractedly.

"Never mind." Tapper shrugged his hairy shoulders. "Just put him down as 'pretty boy.' It's his ass I'm interested in—not his name."

"Tapper wants his ass, not his name! His ass not his name!" the other man chortled with glee. His long, crooked nose looked like it had been broken and badly set several times and his teeth were nothing but blackened stumps.

Ari stared at them in disbelief. Was this man actually saying what she *thought* he was saying? Was Tapper casually telling her he was planning to rape her as soon as she was processed into the prison?

"You heard him, pretty boy," chortled the one on the left. "Tapper's gonna taste you. And when he's finished, maybe Gorn 'n me will have a taste too."

"Shut up, Fenrus—you're scaring the lad," growled the one with the tablet. "Don't worry, laddie," he said to her. "Tapper don't share with the likes of us. You give 'im a taste and he'll most likely let you go."

"Unless you get to be one of his favorites," the one called Fenrus said. His lumpish face was filled with stupid, brutal glee. "Then maybe you'll get to share his cell. He's got a real nice cell, does Tapper."

"He's got a carpet," Gorn added thoughtfully. "Nice and thick —nice as the one my old mistress had in her sitting room back on Yonnie Six."

"A...a carpet?" This detail seemed apropos of nothing. Ari licked her dry lips, wondering what the two henchmen were talking about.

"You'll get to see it soon enough," Fenrus predicted. "You'll be getting' rug burns from it when Tapper kneels you down on it and takes your pretty little ass."

"That's enough, boys. You know I don't share my cell."

Tapper had been standing there with his slab-like arms crossed over his hairy, bare chest. Honestly, he had so much body hair he looked more like an animal than a man, Ari thought, feeling sick.

"Although I might make an exception for a pretty little boy whore like you." He licked his thick lips and grinned knowingly at Ari.

"I'm not a whore!" She could scarcely force the words out. "I've never...I don't *do* things like that!"

"Oh, a virgin, eh?" Unfortunately, this seemed to make Tapper more interested in her than ever. "I 'ent had a true virgin in *ages*. Nothing I like better than ramming my shaft in a virgin hole." His small eyes grew greedy and his voice was eager, like a man talking about eating his favorite dish. "So nice and tight...not all stretched out like the rest of the narrow-assed patsies around here."

"He won't be tight for long after you get after him, Tapper," Fenrus chortled. "You'll ream him proper!"

"The Horvaths'll stretch him out for you a bit too," Gorn added. "I hear Mukluk's on search duty today. You know what them claws of his does to the newbies' arses. Worse luck for them."

"He'll be tight enough to suit me—a virgin's a virgin." Tapper nodded decisively and pointed at Ari with one pudgy finger. "I'll find you, boy—you're on my list."

"You can't do that," Ari protested, finding her voice at last. "You can't just...do whatever you want to people." Part of her brain knew it was stupid and dangerous to argue with the thuggish felon but she couldn't help herself—she'd been raised in a society where people respected each other—where males and females were equal. She couldn't just stand there and listen to

Tapper talking about raping her as causally as he'd speak of sampling a new dish he wanted to try.

"Tapper can do what he likes, pretty boy," Fenrus told her. "See these here green stripes on his suit?" He pointed to the stripes running through the big inmate's jumpsuit. "That says 'trustee' that does. Means he can do what he likes."

"Not with me he can't!" Ari lifted her chin. She might be small but she was *not* helpless, she told herself. If Tapper tried something with her, she would use his massive weight against him to throw him to the dirty metal floor.

*Or I'll **try** anyway,* she thought feeling a twinge of doubt as she looked at the huge man. She had thrown Jak many times when they were sparring, and even bigger opponents during competition, but that was while observing the strict *Ton-kwa* code of conduct. She very much doubted if Tapper would agree to abide by any such rules if they got into a fight.

She expected her defiance to make the huge inmate mad but Tapper only looked at her and clucked his tongue.

"You just made it to the top of the list, my pretty little virgin," he said. "I'll have a taste of that sweet ass of yours the minute you're processed, I will."

"You heard him Gorn—the top of the list! The top of the list!" Fenrus chortled.

"Got it." Gorn nodded and tapped at the tablet, apparently moving Ari up to the top slot.

"Come on, boys—there's plenty more fresh meat to see to," Tapper told them. "Let's see if any of the rest of the newbies is worth puttin' on the list."

Then he swaggered off with the other two in tow, looking over the crowd of new prisoners like a man at a butcher's shop looking for prime cuts of meat.

Ari watched them go, speechless with dread.

*What am I going to do? Goddess of Mercy, what am I going to **do**?* she thought, feeling sick to her stomach.

She wished for the hundredth time that she could have brought some kind of a weapon but she knew that all prisoners were carefully searched during processing—in fact, she was fully expecting she would have to strip which was one reason she'd worked so hard to make the tactile holo-field the look/touch projected accurate. It was also the main reason she'd hidden both the look/touch's projection bead and the controls to the transport bubble in the metal of the prison ID tag she wore at her throat. Only there, surrounded by the metal of the tag, were the tiny devices hidden from the prying eyes of the X-ray scanner and the mobile Magnetic Resonance Imager.

Since there was no way to hide weapons of any kind on her body, she had been relying on her *Ton-kwa* skills to protect herself. Actually, she'd been hoping to avoid this kind of situation altogether, she thought unhappily. If the guard she'd hired had done his job and taken her straight to Jak, they would already be floating upwards towards the waiting life support craft which was orbiting over the prison.

*Well, it can't be helped now,* she told herself, straightening her shoulders. *I'll just have to be sure I find Jak right away, the minute I get through processing. Then we'll—*

Just then a fight broke out in the ranks of men closest to the processing counter. There was a lot of shouting and shoving and Ari heard someone yell,

"Watch out! He's got a knife!"

*What? How did someone get a knife in here?* she wondered. There was a pretty thorough search procedure at the first check point—where could the prisoner who had it have hidden it?

Keeping to the sidelines to avoid being drawn into the conflict, she sidled closer to the front of the immense holding area, watching to see what might happen. Two men were rolling on the scuffed metal floor and Ari saw the flash of silver in one of their hands. So someone *did* have a knife or something like one —interesting.

Suddenly a door opened in the high, black metal wall that housed the glassed-in processing counter and a male even bigger than Tapper came out. Ari watched him in awe as he stalked over to where the two men were rolling on the ground.

He was positively the biggest male she had ever seen, she thought. He had dark brown hair that glinted red in the harsh overhead glows and his jewel-toned eyes flashed fury.

Those eyes bothered Ari for some reason—she almost felt like she'd seen them before? But where? In a dream? Because if she'd met this huge man in real life, she was certain she would have remembered him.

Like Tapper, he was wearing a blue and green striped jump-suit rather than a blue and orange striped one but that was where the resemblance ended. The giant was tall and broad but he didn't have a gut like Tapper—his stomach was flat beneath the prison jumpsuit and he moved with the fluid grace of a big cat.

"Stop it!" he roared, his deep voice rolling and echoing in the vast metal chamber. "Gods damn you, stop it, I said! The guards don't care if you kill each other but I do—so stop now or I'll stop you."

Sure enough, Ari saw, the Horvath guards weren't doing

anything to break up the conflict. They sat on their bench and guzzled their green slime, swiping at their slitted yellow eyeballs from time to time with their forked tongues. Apparently breaking up fights among the prisoners they were supposed to be guarding held no interest for them.

The fight went on but then the big male did something completely unexpected. He bared his teeth and Ari saw two double sets of long, curving fangs protruding from under his upper lip.

The sight was so surprising that she gasped and put a hand to her own mouth wondering what in the galaxy was going on.

Then, even more surprising, a murmur ran through the crowd and the fight abruptly ceased.

"Kill-All," she heard some of the men around her muttering. "Watch out—he's a Kill-All—the Kill-All's here."

Whatever it meant, the men who had been fighting apparently feared the tall male. They broke apart and the one with the knife dropped it obediently into the tall male's hands. Ari couldn't understand it—what could make hardened criminals become so suddenly docile?

"Aye, that's right, he'd better give up the knife," said a cracked, wheezy voice in her ear.

Ari turned, startled, and saw an ancient man—not much taller than she was—standing to her right. He was also wearing the trustee uniform of blue and green stripes and he was bald except for a few wispy gray tufts of hair over his large, pink ears. A pair of oculars that looked almost as old as he was were perched on his nose. One of their lenses was cracked but it didn't appear to bother their wearer.

"What?" Ari asked, frowning. "Why should he give the knife

up to him?" She nodded at the tall male with the fangs who now had the knife in one large hand.

"That's Medic, that is," the old man said, nodding sagely. "He's a Kill-All."

"A Kill-All? What does that mean?" Ari shook her head.

"T'aint you never heard of a Kill-All, girl? They're marvelous rare—Kindred they are. One bite of them fangs contains enough poison to kill every last male in this room." He nodded again and repeated, "Kill-All."

"Oh..." Ari bit her own lip, looking at those impossibly long, sharp fangs. "No, I...I've never heard of that."

"Best you know now afore you go in for processing," the little old man said. "You don't want to give no trouble to Medic. He'll treat you straight and patch you up if the Horvaths get too rough, but he won't stand no trouble—that he won't."

"I...I'll remember that," Ari said faintly, her eyes still fixed on the tall male's mouth. His sensuous lips were closed now, hiding his fangs but the sight of them was burned into her memory and she knew she would dream of them later that night. Or maybe she had already dreamed of them—of the big Kindred? The thought was confusing and she pushed it away.

"Yes, you remember that. Remember, remember," the old man crooned in a sing-song voice. "Anyway, enough of that." He produced a tablet like the one Gorn had been carrying and poised one gnarled finger over it. "All right now, what's your name, boy? Tell me true so I can put you in for processing. Need your clothes and shoe size too. Not that you can call these here things they give us to wear shoes."

He held up one foot, covered in a thin rubber slipper and cackled with laughter.

"Oh, uh..." After her experience with Tapper, Ari wasn't sure if she should give her name to anyone, even a seemingly harmless old man. But the old prisoner seemed to understand her concern.

"Come now, you can trust old Wheezer, that you can," he said coaxingly. "I saw Tapper talkin' to you afore and I heard you wouldn't give Gorn your name. That's all fine and well but I don't have nothin' to do with it—no I don't. I'm just trying to do my job and get you processed like the rest of this lot."

"All right," Ari answered reluctantly. Honestly, she hadn't been planning on being processed at all when she first came to BleakHall. She'd prepared for the worst—making certain the image her look/see produced was accurate in case she was strip-searched—but she'd been hoping to go straight to her brother and then float the two of them away to safety. Now it looked like she would be staying a while—at least long enough to be processed.

"Well then?" The old man frowned at her impatiently. "Tell me, boy—what's your name?"

"Ari," she said before she considered it. But then, why not give her real name? Her nickname, anyway. It would never do to call herself Lady Arianna but Ari worked well as a boy's name, she thought.

"Good, good—now we're getting somewhere," Wheezer cackled, tapping out her name onto the ancient tablet he held.

"Do you need my last name too?" Ari asked, wondering if she ought to give her real last name as well or make one up. But Wheezer shook his head.

"No—just a peep at your ID tag should do."

He leaned forward, squinting to see the number—which was a long string of numerals ending in 117. He tapped something into his tablet and frowned.

"Hmm...now that's odd, so it is."

"What's odd?" Ari's heart was suddenly beating in her throat. The prison ID tag had cost her a pretty penny, but mostly because she'd had to have the controls to her look/see and the transport bubble installed in it. She'd never given a thought as to whether the information on it would pass a test of authenticity. After all, actually getting processed into BleakHall's system hadn't been part of her plan.

"Well, seems to say here that we already *have* a prisoner with your same number, lad," Wheezer said, confirming her fear that her ID tag wouldn't withstand scrutiny. But then he shrugged his scrawny shoulders. "Oh well—must be he died this morning and they fed the number back into the system." He tapped at the tablet some more and nodded. "There—you're entered."

"Oh..." Ari cleared her throat, feeling a cautious wave of relief that he had passed her through the system. "Does...does that happen much? People dying, I mean?"

"All the time since the damn Horvaths took over." Wheezer gave the lizard guards a dark look. "They're quick with the pain-prod, they are. And they like to poke most everyone, even us trustees which 'ent fair, nohow."

"I'll try to keep away from them," Ari said. "Thanks for the warning."

"Oh, it 'ent a warning, lad—you'll not be able to keep clear of them, no matter what you do. No more than you can keep clear of Tapper once he's got a taste for you."

"What...what do you mean?" Ari's mouth was suddenly dry. For a moment, she'd almost forgotten the hairy convict and his promise to put her on his "list" but Wheezer's words brought her situation home again in a visceral way.

"I mean if Tapper's got you on his list, there's nowhere to run and nowhere to hide, laddie. He's at the top of the heap here—does what he likes." Wheezer shook his head regretfully. "Sorry about that. You seem so nice and young too. But then..." He sighed. "That's the way Tapper likes 'em."

"I can't just let him *rape* me!" Ari protested.

"Now, now—it's no fun but just between you and me Tapper don't last forever—especially in the tight ones." Wheezer winked conspiratorially. "Just squeeze him a bit once he's all the way in you and he'll blow his load before you know it. Your arsehole will be sore for a bit, so it will, but you'll get over it."

"I don't want to 'get over' being raped!" Ari protested. "I can't—"

But just then Wheezer's tablet made a soft *ding*.

"Oh, lookit that—your number already came up." He nodded at the tablet. "Come along with me, boy. We'll get you to the processing desk and into BleakHall before you know it."

That was exactly what Ari was afraid of.

# THREE

The day was going like every other day in the past six months, Lathe thought morosely as he straightened the medical supplies in the small infirmary. The guttural grunts of the Horvath guards, the shouts of the prisoners which sometimes escalated into screams of fury until he went out and broke up whatever fight had started about who was next in line or who had stepped on whose foot or some other inconsequential disagreement. The endless stream of small injustices and cruelties that wore a male down to the bone because there was nothing light or good—no vestige of kindness or decency—anywhere in the echoing black metal halls of BleakHall.

It was always the same—it would never end. He would never see daylight outside these walls or breathe clean air, uncontaminated by screams of pain or the rough, trollish laughter of the Horvaths again...

*Easy, Lathe,* he told himself, running a hand through his hair and sighing. *You have all the evidence you need for the Yonnite Council of Mistresses and you'll be out of here soon. The tunneler nanites are almost finished with their job.*

Yes, the nanites. He sighed again. They were supposed to be plan B—something that he would only use if there were no other options. But the same day he'd gotten into BleakHall himself, the inmate who was supposed to be his inside contact had been fatally shanked in the exercise yard. There went plan A and so Lathe was forced to employ plan B—the tunneler nanites he'd brought in his Prison ID tag. Even now they were digging a passageway, starting in the small supply room closet of the Infirmary, right under the prison to the far edge of the perimeter fence outside.

Sitting outside the fence and camouflaged by light-bending see-me-not tech was a Kindred shuttle outfitted and fueled up—just waiting for Lathe to take charge of it. The minute the nanites informed him the tunnel was done, via uplink to the controls in his ID badge, Lathe would be out of here. He would take any Kindred who might be imprisoned with him too—though there weren't any right now.

Which meant he was all alone in this hell hole of misery and cruelty. And since the nanites could only dig a certain amount a day to avoid tripping the prison's sensors, he seemed likely to remain here alone for at least another week.

*You can hang in there for a week,* Lathe told himself. *You can do anything for a week. Soon you'll be out. Soon you can bring the evidence of what the Horvaths are doing in this place to light and bring the people who own BleakHall to justice. Thonolan will be avenged...*

Speaking of the Horvaths and their cruelty, he could hear

evidence of it now, right outside the infirmary room door. Grunts and screams were coming from the cavity search line where Mukluk, the sadistic head of the guards, was currently doing searches.

Most of the Horvaths were simple creatures—stupid and slow-witted, Lathe had found. But there were some, like Mukluk, who were brighter than the rest. And unfortunately what they turned their superior intelligence to was finding new ways to be cruel to the prisoners. Or simply twisting routine prison procedures to suit their sadistic needs. As Mukluk apparently was now, just outside the infirmary room door.

"Please," Lathe heard a high, almost feminine voice pleading. "Please don't! I swear I don't...don't have anything up there. Didn't the X-ray and the mobile Magnetic device tell you that?"

There was a burst of rough laughter from Mukluk and the other Horvath guards and then a hissing, growling voice answered the new inmate.

"Thoze scanz only zzhow metal. Have to do a manual cavity zzearch for everything elzz. Now bend over and zzpread your legzz."

Lathe tried not to listen. As a medical doctor, the kinds of atrocities that went on here turned his stomach. Yet even *he* had been forced to kill twice since coming to BleakHall. He had been fighting for his life and the kills had cemented his reputation as someone not to be messed with, since he'd been using the poison attribute of his fangs. But still—he had killed. And not guards either but other prisoners. Though the Goddess knew there were some here that deserved to stay behind BleakHall's walls forever. He hadn't understood that when Commander Sylvan had first tried to tell him but—

"Please! Please, *no!*" The pleading voice outside his door sounded so young—so innocent somehow. Lathe tried in vain to ignore it. There was nothing he could do—he'd tried to institute a new, more humane way of cavity searches when he first gained access to the infirmary but the Horvaths wouldn't allow it. They *liked* inflicting pain.

"Please!" the voice moaned again and this time Lathe broke. He couldn't stand it somehow—couldn't stand to hear the pain of this unseen prisoner. Though he doubted the Horvaths would let him interfere, he had to at least try.

He slammed open the infirmary door and saw a youngish man —really no more than a boy—bent naked over the searching table. The boy had tousled black hair and big, dark eyes that were filled with fright. Two of the Horvath guards had him by the arms, forcing his flat chest down to the cold metal of the table and the third—Mukluk—was standing behind him, one thick clawed finger ready to probe.

The Horvaths had digits about twice as thick as a normal humanoid's and their scaly skin was as rough as sandpaper. Even worse, each thick finger was tipped with a blunt, curving claw.

The combination meant that Mukluk almost always drew blood when he was doing the cavity searches for new prisoners. Not that the other Horvath guards were particularly gentle but Mukluk was especially rough—he took sadistic delight in the pain and humiliation he caused when he shoved a sandpaper-rough digit into each new prisoner's arse and dug around, looking for contraband.

And now he was about to do it to the dark-haired boy the other Horvaths had spread out over the table.

Though Lathe had witnessed this particular cruelty more

times than he cared to count, he suddenly couldn't anymore. As the lizard guard prepared to shove one scaly, clawed finger into the helpless, trembling body before him, Lathe held up a hand and shouted, "Stop!"

"Zztop?" The two Horvaths holding the boy's arms looked confused. Mukluk only looked irritated.

"Why zzhould I zztop?" he demanded, flickering out his forked tongue to swipe at one slitted yellow eyeball. "Thiz zzearch muzt be done."

Lathe had to think quickly.

"Of course it has to be done, but you don't want to be the one to do it. Not on this prisoner," he said quickly. "Not if he has what I think he has."

"What he hazz?" Mukluk peered at the prisoner suspiciously. "What do you mean?"

"Hang on—let me examine him. I need to verify my suspicions," Lathe said brusquely.

Walking over to the table, he yanked the boy's chin up and stared into his eyes.

*Those eyes. Dark eyes—a blue so deep they're nearly black. I've seen them before...where?*

He pushed the strange thought away. It wasn't important right now. Saving the boy at least this one indignity and pain—that was what mattered.

"Uh-huh...mm-hmm," he muttered to himself as he lifted the boy's lids and made a great show of examining his eyes. The boy trembled under his touch, the great, dark eyes pleading with Lathe. The expression of hope and fear tore at his heart but knowing the guards were watching, he forced himself to keep a blank face. He made the boy open his mouth and stick out his tongue before he nodded and stepped back.

"Just what I thought—he's got Zamwer's syndrome."

"Zzzzwhat?" Mukluk demanded suspiciously.

"Zamwer's syndrome," Lathe repeated patiently. "An inflammation of the mucus membranes that causes the patient to produce acidic secretions harmful to saurian life forms."

The two Horvath guards who were holding the boy's arms looked at each other in apparent confusion but Mukluk was still staring at Lathe suspiciously.

"And thizz meanzz what?" he inquired, his forked tongue lashing in irritation.

"Well, it's completely harmless to non-saurian life forms—those not evolved from reptiles," he clarified, hoping Mukluk was following him. "Me, for instance—I can touch him with no problem. But if you or any of the other Horvaths come in contact with any mucus producing membranes, well..." He shook his head.

"Well what?" one of the other guards insisted, his yellow eyes wide.

"Well, any number of things. Depending on how strong the acid produced, it could do anything from giving you a simple third degree burn, to causing your scales to drop off." Lathe shrugged, trying to appear unconcerned. "I guess it's a chance you'll have to take to search him properly."

"Zzcales drop off?" The guards looked horrified and even Mukluk looked non-plussed. Lathe could see the Horvath weighing his words. He was trying to decide if he believed Lathe or if he thought he was lying and trying to save this particular prisoner.

Suddenly it seemed incredibly important to Lathe that he did save the boy. He didn't know why—maybe because of his youth or apparent innocence but he didn't want to watch the boy violated...didn't want to hear his screams of agony as Mukluk dug around inside him with a cruel claw.

But he couldn't let Mukluk know that.

"Well, I just thought I'd warn you," he remarked. With studied indifference, he turned away from the table, as though he was going back into the infirmary.

*Please, Goddess,* he prayed as he walked. *Please, help me save him—please!*

One step...two...the infirmary room door was almost within his grasp. Were they really going to continue with the cavity search and ignore everything he'd just said? Was he not going to be able to save the boy? Three steps...he was reaching for the door handle...

"Zztop!" Mukluk's voice hissed at him.

Slowly, Lathe turned his head.

"Yes? What do you want?"

"You—*you* zzearch him." Mukluk stabbed a clawed finger at the boy, still spread trembling over the table. "You do it, Medic."

"All right, fine." Lathe nodded. "Let him up. I'll do it in the infirmary."

"No!" Mukluk's forked tongue whipped out, lashing the air angrily. "You do it here! Now! Zzearch him while we watch."

Inwardly Lathe cursed. He had wanted to spare the boy violation—not violate him himself! But there was no choice now and at least he knew he would be gentler than the cruel Horvath guard.

"Fine," he said again, shortly. "I'll do it."

Coming up behind the boy, still pressed to the cold black metal of the table, he reached for a box of plasti-shield gloves.

They were sized for him of course—they wouldn't fit the scaly claws of the Horvaths.

But when Lathe picked up the box, Mukluk knocked it out of his hand.

"None of that, Medic. You zzaid the dizeaze wouldn't affect you. No glovezz."

*Fucking great.* Lathe resisted the urge to growl and bare his fangs at the head guard. It would do no good and would probably only provoke Mukluk to use his pain-prod on both Lathe and the boy.

"Fine," he said yet again. "No gloves. But I have to at least use some lubricant. Otherwise the membranes will be irritated and will produce even more acid which might become toxic."

Mukluk looked like he wanted to protest again but in the end, he only lashed his tail and licked his yellow slitted eyeballs with his tongue as Lathe reached for the seldom-used tube and spread a liberal dollop of the pale blue jelly over the pad of his middle finger.

Very conscious of the Horvaths watching him, he put one hand on the small of the boy's back, trying to soothe him. He wished he could say some words of comfort—wished he could let the boy know he'd be gentle. But he could do nothing with Mukluk and his crew watching—nothing but get on with the business.

Reaching between the boy's thighs, he probed gently but firmly, feeling for the tender opening to the lad's body.

The boy tensed at once, his buttocks going rock-hard as he tried to keep the invader out. Lathe didn't blame him but he couldn't stop. With the Horvath's watching, he knew he had to do this.

"Easy, little one," he murmured, the words rising to his lips though he had told himself he shouldn't say anything. He rubbed gently at the small of the boy's back, trying to soothe the trembling...wishing he could ease the boy's fear.

"Please..." came the whispered reply, so soft that Lathe could barely hear it. There were tears in the boy's voice—they tugged at Lathe's heart. But there was nothing he could do but continue.

"I'm sorry, little one," he murmured, rubbing between the shoulder blades. "But I must do this. It's either me or one of the Horvaths—you understand?"

For a moment the soft buttocks tensed even more. Then the boy seemed to go limp beneath his hands and the small body relaxed.

"All...all right," came the whisper Lathe could barely hear. "I...understand."

"Good lad," Lathe murmured comfortingly. "I'll make it quick. In and out—just have to be certain you're not hiding anything you shouldn't."

"Hiding...anything I shouldn't," the boy repeated in that same, soft whisper and gave a broken little laugh. "Goddess of Mercy..."

"If she's anything like my Goddess, she'll watch over you," Lathe said comfortingly. "Here it comes...just open up and let me in."

As he spoke, he breached the boy's tight rosebud with his middle finger, sliding smoothly and slowly into the hot, tight depths to be certain there was no contraband. These searches were actually necessary, he knew. The most amazing and alarming things had been found secreted in this most private area of some of the prisoner's bodies. He needed to be thorough but he tried to be gentle too, mindful of the fact that the boy had probably never been touched in this way before.

Or maybe he had, if he was a slave sent from Yonnie Six. But somehow Lathe didn't think so. The tension in the small body under his spoke of a sheltered life—an existence before this one where the boy had not been touched against his will. What had he done to be sent to this hell hole, Lathe wondered as he continued the exam. How could anyone send such a defenseless looking lad to BleakHall?

As he slipped his finger in to the hilt the boy stiffened again and then gave a soft little sob before relaxing once more. It was a hopeless, broken sound—a sound of surrender and it seemed to squeeze Lathe's heart.

*All right,* the boy seemed to be saying, *Do what you want to me. I can't stop you—I give up.*

Lathe finished the search as quickly as he could and then withdrew, wiping his hands on a sani-towel to clean them and kill any germs.

"There—nothing," he said roughly. "And now I'll finish the exam in the infirmary."

But at this, Mukluk balked.

"No! The cavity zzearch is done. He will be moved to zentral prozzezing like all the rest."

Lathe wanted to protest but the big Horvath guard had taken out his pain-prod and was tapping it against one scaly palm. The message was clear—if Lathe tried to interfere any more, both he and the boy would taste the prod.

"Fine—then I'll take him to central processing and get him dressed," he said.

"Glukgag—go with them," Mukluk ordered one of the other

Horvath guards who had held the boy down. "Make zzure they are not plotting anything."

The other Horvath saluted and motioned with his own pain-prod at Lathe.

"Come on, little one." Lathe helped the boy off the table and led him, naked and shivering, through the door and into Central Processing, followed closely by the Horvath guard.

# FOUR

Ari tried not to cry but she hadn't been expecting the cavity search—hadn't been expecting any of this, although she supposed she should have. Oh, she'd been prepared to strip and to be scanned with both X-rays and the Magnetic Imager every which way. But she had *not* been prepared to have anyone probing inside her body. And though it could have been much worse if the tall Kindred called Medic hadn't interfered, it was still more than she felt she could handle at the moment.

*You have to handle it,* she told herself angrily. *And you're going to have to handle a hell of a lot more if you can't find Jak and get the hell out of here quick! So suck it up and stop moaning. After all, it's not like you're a virgin.*

Of course it wasn't like she had much experience either. There had been a few sweaty fumblings with other contestants when she and Jak went to overnight *Ton-kwa* tournaments but those had been few and far between and never very satisfactory.

The few (okay, *two*) males she'd been with never seemed to know how to please her or what to do with their hands.

*Unlike Medic who apparently knows **exactly** what to do with his hands,* whispered a sarcastic little voice in her head.

Ari shivered and tried to push the thought away as they moved from one room into another, this one filled with stacks of prison uniforms and rubber slippers. She could still feel the big Kindred's hands on her...*in* her. And she still didn't understand why he had done what he did.

Was he just being kind and trying to spare her the pain of having a Horvath digit shoved roughly up her back channel? Or was he trying to claim her in some way, as Tapper had been doing when he added her name to his "list?"

Ari considered this second possibility much more likely. Why else would the big Kindred have been so eager to get her into the infirmary alone? Had he been planning to use the cold, slimy stuff she could still feel running down her inner thighs as lubricant to ease another part of himself inside her? Was there anyone here she could trust besides Jak, when she found him? Anyone who *wouldn't* want to rape her?

And what would she do if the big Kindred *did* try something? The Horvath guard was right behind them but Ari got the distinct impression he wouldn't give a damn if she got assaulted right in front of his eyes. He was only watching them to make sure they weren't plotting—whatever that meant. The Kindred was almost seven feet tall and outweighed her by at least a hundred and fifty pounds, all of it pure muscle—plus he had poison fangs. If he wanted to do something to her, Ari doubted she could defend herself. All her years of *Ton-kwa* training wouldn't help her if she was poisoned. He—

"Here—these look about your size. Put them on."

Looking up, she saw that the big Kindred was holding out an orange and blue striped prison uniform and a small pair of rubber slippers.

"Thank you," Ari said, clutching the bundle to her chest, and was appalled at how weak and girly her voice sounded. She needed to butch up quickly or she was going to be dead meat in here. "I mean, thanks a lot," she said, making an effort to deepen her voice and look the big Kindred directly in the eyes.

But she shouldn't have done that because the moment she looked, she was lost. His eyes were jewel-toned—the most mesmerizing shade of clear, bluish-green that she'd ever seen. They reminded her of clear tropical waters...of gem stones...of...

*Of someone I've seen before. But who? Where? My dreams?*

The big Kindred was staring just as intently at her, a worried frown on his face.

"Are you well, little one?" he rumbled softly.

"I..." Suddenly Ari remembered the feeling of his big warm hand on her bare back while the other probed inside her and she had to look away. "I'm fine," she whispered in a choked voice.

"No plotting!" the Horvath guard hissed at them. "Get drezzed."

Quickly, Ari scrambled into the blue and orange striped jumpsuit. It was clearly the smallest one available but it still hung on her petite frame. She didn't care—she was grateful to be covered at all. Being naked in front of so many strangers—even wearing her solid-holo body disguise—had been humiliating and extremely uncomfortable.

"Now what?" she made herself ask as she slipped the too-big plastic slippers on her feet where they flapped at her heels.

"Now you go into a holding area until all the rest of the new prisoners are processed," Medic said. "After that, Last Meal—or 'supper' as they call it here. After that, you'll get your permanent cell assignment and you sleep."

"But..." Ari felt panic building up inside her and fought to keep it down. "But what about the exercise yard? When...when do I get to go there?"

"Already missing the zzky?" the Horvath guard asked. He chortled guttural laughter. "Get uzed to it."

"We get recreation hour every day after Mid Meal as long as there's not a lockdown going on," the big Kindred told her.

"So...I can't go out until *tomorrow?*" Ari tried to keep the dread out of her voice and couldn't. So much could happen between now and the exercise period the next day. Tapper could catch her or she could get hurt in whatever cell she was assigned to or any of a hundred other awful, lethal, disgusting things that sprang readily to mind.

The big Kindred shrugged, his broad shoulders rolling under the green and blue striped uniform.

"Sorry. That's the way it is."

"But...will I...do I get my own cell at least?" Ari was aware that she sounded weak and frightened but just at that moment she couldn't help it—she *felt* weak and frightened.

"Only trusteezz have their own zellz," the Horvath guard hissed. "Now come—to the holding area."

He shoved Ari hard between the shoulder blades with the butt of his pain-prod and she stumbled and nearly fell. Only the big Kindred's hand under her arm kept her from face-planting on the scuffed metal floor.

"Watch it," the Kindred growled at the guard, his fangs plainly visible. "Can't you see how small this little one is?"

Ari shook off the big male's hand, feeling vulnerable and not liking it.

"I'm fine." She lifted her chin. "I can take care of myself."

He didn't answer, just put himself between her and the guard as the three of them proceeded into the next room which was divided up into several large, clear plasti-glass boxes with air holes cut into them near the top.

The holding areas were lined with metal benches and had a dull silver commode in the corner. They were big enough to hold ten or twelve inmates in relative comfort—or eighteen to twenty if they were really packed in. Most were already filled past capacity with newly minted prisoners, all wearing the same blue and orange striped jumpsuits Ari had on herself. None of them looked happy, probably because of the way they were jammed into the overflowing holding areas.

There was shouting coming from almost all of them and several large males were fighting in the closest one, which was apparently where they were headed. There were smears of blood on the clear walls of the holding area and Ari saw something sticking out of one of the ventilation holes near the top.

When they got closer, she saw it was a severed finger.

*Goddess of Mercy.*

"Here." The Horvath guard motioned for her. "In here until zzupper time."

"He won't be alive come supper time if you put him in there." The big Kindred's deep voice was an angry growl.

The Horvath shrugged. "Not my problem. Mukluk zzaid to put him in a holding area."

"Put him in a cage," Medic said.

"A what?" Ari looked up at him but he didn't even spare her a glance. His brilliant turquoise eyes were locked with the Horvath's in what appeared to be a silent battle of wills.

Finally, the guard shrugged.

"Fine. A cage it izz."

He shoved Ari again but this time she was prepared for the brutal action and leaped nimbly forward almost before the butt of his weapon could touch her.

"Where are we going? Where are you taking me?" she asked, looking up at both the guard and the Kindred.

Neither one answered her. She was marched to the back of the big room where a lot of identical black metal structures made of heavy-duty chain-link stood. There were fifteen of them, all in a row, all about six feet tall and three feet wide like coffins stood up on either ends.

Ari looked at the closest one—it really *was* a cage.

"In here," the Horvath hissed, unlocking the mechanism on the front with a wave of his scaly hand.

Claustrophobia clawed at Ari's throat. For a moment she felt almost faint.

"But I can't...I don't need to be in there," she protested, feeling sick. "Please, I—"

"Shut up," Medic said harshly, glaring down at her. "Get in—it's the safest place for a little one like you."

"I'm a grown wo—uh, man," Ari protested, so upset she almost forgot her disguise. She *hated* small spaces. She'd gotten trapped in a tiny closet once playing hide and find with Jak when they were kids and it had been hours before anyone found her. She couldn't go in the tiny, cramped metal box—she just *couldn't*.

"Get in or should I *put* you in?" the big Kindred demanded, showing her his fangs.

At the sight of those four sharp points—he had a double set on either side where a normal humanoid's canine teeth would be— Ari shrank back. She didn't need to be poisoned before she could get to Jak. Still, she couldn't help appealing to him one more time.

"Honestly, I can take care of myself. I...I'm claustrophobic," she confessed in a low voice.

"I'm sorry about that." His tone softened a little but there was still firm conviction in his eyes. "But better claustrophobic than dead, little one. Now get in the cage or I'll put you in myself."

Ari saw that nothing she did or said would change his mind or make any difference. She could either get into the cage quietly or make a scene and *that* would only make her look girly and weak, which she didn't need.

Taking a deep breath, she did her best to swallow her fear.

*At least there are holes in it—it's made of chain link,* she told herself. *It's not like the closet—I'll be able to see out. It'll be okay. It's not forever. Just until supper time.*

"Go on," the big Kindred rumbled. "Hurry up—we have other new prisoners to see to." He cast a glance at the Horvath who was idly twirling his pain-prod. Clearly he was afraid the lizard-guard would get tired of this drama and put Ari into one of the crowded, clear plasti-glass holding areas after all.

*And if he did that, I might not be fresh meat anymore by the time I got out,* she thought bitterly. It was becoming clearer and clearer to her that the big Kindred just wanted to keep her intact for his own private use later—just like Tapper. But there didn't seem to be anything she could do about it. Not now, anyway.

"All right, fine." She put up her hands, backing into the black cage. When the door banged shut, she had to bite back a cry as panic wrapped a clammy hand around her throat and squeezed tight.

"There. Back to cavity zzearch," the Horvath guard announced as he locked the cage door. But the big Kindred lingered, looking down through the black chain link at Ari. There was an unreadable look in his jewel-toned eyes. It might have been pity or possessiveness—Ari couldn't tell but either way she didn't like it.

"You'll be all right, little one. I'll come back later to check on you," he rumbled.

"Don't bother." Ari lifted her chin, glaring up at him. "I told you, I'm *fine*."

His eyes went hard.

"Don't fool yourself. Nobody in BleakHall is 'fine.' Everyone here is just marking time until they die and if you're not damn careful that'll happen sooner rather than later."

Then he turned, and Ari watched the angry set of his broad shoulders as he walked swiftly away.

# FIVE

Damn it, *why* did he feel so protective of the boy?
Lathe wished he knew...wished he could fight it somehow. But the emotion rose up in him like a wave when he was near the new prisoner—so compelling and overpowering he couldn't control it.

Even now the thought of the boy trapped in the cage, quietly fighting his panic and claustrophobia, tore at his heart deeply. Lathe had to restrain himself because all he wanted to do was go back and open the cage and take the new prisoner someplace safe where none of the animals in this hell hole could hurt him.

*Stop it,* he told himself fiercely. *This feeling isn't logical. You don't know this boy—you've never even seen him before.*

But that didn't feel true or right. Somehow he felt that he knew the boy. Those eyes—those huge, dark eyes, vulnerable even when the lad was trying to be tough—seemed burned into Lathe's brain somehow. He felt as though he had seen them before—not just once but many times.

*But that's ridiculous. How could you have seen him? You don't know him—you don't even know his name!* he argued with himself.

Well, that last part was easily fixed. Going back to the infirmary and trying to block out the cries of the poor bastard Mukluk was currently probing, Lathe shut the door firmly behind him. He picked up the battered tablet he'd been assigned when he'd become a trustee—about a day after coming here since BleakHall needed medics—and did a quick search.

There was surprisingly little information about the boy. Most of the prisoners brought in had rap sheets as long as his arm but there was almost nothing besides the first name, (Ari,) his age (24 cycles, which Lathe found hard to believe since the lad didn't have even the hint of a beard yet) and the serial number which someone had noted was an accidental duplicate. No reason was given for Ari's incarceration, no planet of origin, no family or gang affiliations—nothing. So what was he doing here? What had he done that warranted such a severe punishment as life in BleakHall?

Lathe didn't know but he wanted to. Rather than quenching his thirst for knowledge, the tablet search had done nothing but fan the flames of his curiosity. He found he wanted to know all about the boy—where was he from? What were his likes and dislikes? Why was he here?

Abruptly he stopped his speculation.

*Wait—why would I need to know so much about a fellow prisoner? What's wrong with me? I've never reacted this way to a new inmate before. What is this strange compulsion I feel to protect him and know all about him?*

Lathe had no answers but he didn't like it—didn't like feeling manipulated this way by his own feelings. He was a doctor and a scientist—he lived by logic, not emotion.

*I have to fight it,* he told himself. *I'm almost out of here. Growing some kind of strange attachment to a new prisoner is nothing but a liability. I have to get over this right now. Just get back to work and put him from my mind.*

With that idea firmly in place, he began straightening the infirmary's medical supplies once more...only to find himself staring at the page on the tablet with the boy's information again.

*Ari,* he thought, tracing the letters with his eyes. *Why do I feel like I've seen you before? And how can I make myself forget you?*

# SIX

"Zzupper now," remarked the Horvath guard who came to unlock Ari's cage, two hours and several eternities after she had been locked in.

She was leaning against the front door of the cage, so eager to get out that she stumbled and fell to her knees when it finally swung open and she was granted her very nominal freedom.

"Here, get up. Did you hurt yourself?" The deep voice was familiar—as was the hand under her arm, hauling her up.

It was the Kindred again—Medic. He was looking at her with an unreadable expression in those gorgeous eyes of his.

*A look like he wants to own me,* Ari thought. Only she didn't intend to be owned by anyone.

She had made up her mind while she was stuck in the cage, fighting panic and claustrophobia, that she was *not* going to let anyone stop her from what she had come to do. Somehow she would survive this first (and hopefully last) night in BleakHall and then tomorrow, the minute she saw Jak, she would grab him, activate the transport bubble, and float out of here, as free as a bird.

With that plan in mind, she didn't intend to let anyone—even a seven-foot tall Kindred with poison fangs—stand in her way.

"Let me go." She yanked away from him—or tried to anyway. But she couldn't break his grip on her wrist which was gentle but extremely firm.

"Listen to me, Ari," he said urgently. "BleakHall isn't like other prisons—every sentence here is a life sentence and the only way out is death. The guards aren't here to protect you or keep the prisoners from fighting each other—their only concern is to keep us contained. Which means they don't give a damn if you get killed on your first day."

"And *you* do?" Ari spat. "You're not telling me anything I don't already know. And how do you know my name?"

"I looked it up." He spoke unwillingly, as though reluctant to admit that he'd researched her. Well, he wouldn't have found much—only the few pieces of information she'd given to Wheezer before processing. It wasn't like she actually had any kind of a criminal past.

"Why would you look me up?" Ari demanded. "You're just like that disgusting Tapper, aren't you? Well, I'm not interested!"

His eyes narrowed.

"You've already met Tapper? What happened? Did he hurt you?"

"None of your business. Let me go!" She tugged at her wrist again and this time he reluctantly released her.

As she pushed into the crowd of prisoners heading through the vast double doors of the holding area into what presumably was the dining room, she heard the big Kindred shout one last thing.

"Sit at table thirteen, Ari! Be sure you sit at *table thirteen.*"

"Yeah, right," Ari muttered to herself. "Like I'll sit at your table just because you tell me to. I don't think so."

She joined the rush and dove through the double doors, leaving him behind.

Lathe watched the boy go with a deep sense of disquiet. Every instinct he had said that he needed to follow Ari and make certain he was all right. The Mess Hall could be a difficult and dangerous place to navigate, especially for a new prisoner.

But he had duties that had to be finished before he could eat his own Last Meal and if he didn't finish them, he could be punished with confinement to his cell. If he had to spend a day on lockdown, he wouldn't be able to look out for the boy at all tomorrow.

Reluctantly, he turned back towards the infirmary. He just prayed to the Goddess that Ari listened to him and sat at the correct table.

Otherwise he was going to be in a lot of trouble.

# SEVEN

The dining room—what Ari heard some inmates calling the Mess Hall—was already half filled with prisoners when the bunch of new inmates from the holding area arrived. She surveyed the scene in front of her, careful to stay to the far edge of the seething group of males who were heading for the cafeteria style line as though they hadn't eaten in cycles.

Though she scanned the crowd for her brother, Jak was nowhere in sight. He must have eaten on a different shift. As BleakHall was so big, there must be at least two or maybe even three separate seatings for each meal, she reasoned.

Ari sighed. Well, they couldn't have gotten away together tonight anyway—her plan required a clear, open sky above to work. But still, it would have been nice to see her older brother. It had been over six solar months since he'd hugged her goodbye on his way to sell the *tulsa* crop and had gotten captured by pirates and sold to the Yonnite mistress who eventually sent him here.

Putting the memory aside, she scanned the Mess Hall.

There were about thirty long tables arranged in five rows of six which ran the length of the large, echoing room. The walls were made of black metal, just like the holding area and all the rest of the prison, at least as far as Ari could see. Near the front of the room was a long countertop with a plasti-glass shield running the length of it.

Inmates took a battered metal tray and cup from piles near the front of the counter and walked through the line, shoving the tray in front of them. As they went, long, silver mechanical arms protruded from under the plasti-glass shield and deposited lumps of food on the trays. At the very end was a cooler filled with cloudy liquid—presumably water—where each man could fill his cup.

None of it looked very appetizing from where Ari was standing but she was well aware that she hadn't had anything to eat or drink since that morning before arriving at the BleakHall gates. Even now she was beginning to feel a little faint. If she didn't get some nourishment, she was going to have a hard time staying alive and unmolested until she could get to Jak tomorrow.

Reluctantly, she went to the back of the line and grabbed a tray and a cup from the stacks and began pushing it along the counter. She kept her face bowed and her head low, hoping not to attract any attention along the way. Though she snuck glances from side to side, no one seemed to be noticing her and no one bothered her—apparently her strategy of keeping a low profile was working. Ari breathed a sigh of relief and kept going.

She soon found that she couldn't spend too much time looking around her, though, because the rusted mechanical arms coming out from under the plasti-glass shield were creaky and none-too accurate. Ari had to be fast to catch the globs of food they scooped out, maneuvering her tray around quickly as the arms delivered it with herky-jerky motions.

*Wow, these really need some maintenance work!* she thought as she caught the last scoop. *I wonder how long it's been since they had a tune-up?*

A little while in her lab back home and she bet she could have come up with a fix for them, but of course, home was too far away to even think about right now. In the meantime, she just tried to keep her tray out of the mess—there were sticky smears and slimy trails all up and down the long counter, proving that not all the prisoners were as quick as she was at catching the food.

Of course "food" was a relative term, she thought as she reached the end of the counter and looked down at what her tray contained. There was some pinkish, spongy cubes swimming in thin black gravy that might have been meat and a scattering of dirty orange things that might once have been some kind of vegetable. For dessert, there was a smear of bright green pudding with purple specs in it that looked suspiciously like insect parts.

*Ugh!* Ari thought as she filled her cup from the vast, burbling cooler of cloudy water. *This looks horrible! I'm really glad this is my only supper here.*

But no matter how bad the stuff looked and smelled, she could feel her stomach growling and she knew she needed to choke at least some of it down for energy. Grabbing a bundle of plasti-utensils, she scanned the vast, echoing Mess Hall, looking for a place to sit.

The tables were numbered from 1 to 30 but most of them looked occupied. Still, Ari saw inmates crowding into them and the prisoners sitting at the tables were surprisingly accommodating about making room for the newcomers. Well, that was nice but she still didn't want to try squeezing into any of the mostly full tables.

She couldn't help looking at table 13—the one the big Kindred had ordered her to sit at. It wasn't nearly as full as the rest of the tables—however the people who were sitting there looked extremely odd.

Not all the prisoners at BleakHall were humanoid apparently and it seemed that most of the ones who weren't had chosen lucky number 13 as their preferred seating. Ari saw a purple creature with eight tentacles sitting there—it was using four of them to shove food into its beak-like mouth and the other four were exploring the length of the table, including its immediate neighbors.

One of those neighbors was a male so vast he took up most of one side of the bench himself. He had bright green skin and he was wearing some kind of harness that fit over his shoulders and ran down his back. Poking out of the harness were vials of green fluid that ran in a ridge along his spine. Was it some kind of fluid delivery system, Ari wondered. Or was there some other reason for the strange vials?

Sitting across from the green-skinned male was one with orange skin. Aside from the strange skin color, this one looked vaguely humanoid. He even had a tuft of straw-like blond hair on his head and he was holding a small communications device in one tiny hand and tapping at it with his thumbs. In between bites of food he appeared to be yelling at the other males at the table, none of which were listening to him.

Ari couldn't hear what he was saying but she decided she didn't want to. Why had the big Kindred ordered her to sit at the one table in the Mess Hall which appeared to have the strangest occupants?

*Probably so he can isolate me and get me to himself,* she thought with a shiver. Well, no thank you—she was going to sit where she wanted, Ari decided. And what she most wanted right now was to be alone.

With that in mind, she turned and spotted exactly what she was looking for—a completely deserted table. It was the far one in the right corner of the Mess Hall—table number 30—and she was glad to see it. Surely there she could eat her dinner in peace—or as much of it as she could stomach anyway. Then maybe she could find a good hiding place and try to stay away from Tapper until it was time for lights out.

What exactly she was going to do once she was assigned to a cell for the night, Ari had no idea. She had a vague hope that maybe she could hide and skip being assigned at all. If she could just hang around the edges of the prison until it was time to go out in the exercise yard, she could find Jak and get them out of here.

Seating herself in the middle of the empty table, she began picking at her food with a blunt plasti-utensil. She had almost gotten up the nerve to try one of the orange vegetable blobs when a tray was plunked down to her right with a loud clatter. Then one was deposited to her left and, as Ari looked up, the entire formerly-empty table began to fill with hard-faced felons, all wearing the same ominous looking serpent tattoo in purple ink across their foreheads.

Suddenly Ari became aware that someone was standing right behind her. She didn't know how she knew—she just knew. Maybe it was the crawling sensation between her shoulder blades or the expression on the face of the man across from her. Whichever it was, she put down her plasti-utensil and turned to see a tall, impossibly thin male standing there. He was looking down at her with a blank expression on his long, thin face but Ari heard the man to her left mutter, "Holy shit!" as he scooted a little farther away from her.

"I believe," said the stone-faced man who was as thin as a skeleton and twice as frightening, "That you are sitting in my seat."

# EIGHT

The crawling sensation between Ari's shoulder blades got worse, spreading up along her body to make her scalp prickle with fear. Clearly this "empty" table she had sat down at wasn't empty at all. In fact, if the purple serpent tattoo she saw on all these inmates' foreheads was any indication, she might have sat herself directly in the territory of some kind of cult or gang.

"I...I'm sorry," she said, picking up her tray and starting to stand up. "I didn't mean to sit here. I mean, I didn't know this was your seat."

One thin but incredibly strong hand landed on her shoulder and pushed her back down into the plasti-steel chair.

"Are you a Serpent?" The thin man spoke so quietly she could barely hear him but his eyes flashed with anger.

"Am I a *what?*" Ari could scarcely get the words out.

"Are you a Port-side Serpent from Yonnie Six—from the Opulex warehouse district?" the man asked her. "And more specifically, are you the Grand *Jiho* of the Port-side Serpents of the warehouse district?"

"No." Ari's mouth was dry and her stomach was tied in knots. "No, of...of course not."

"Well then, *why are you sitting in the seat reserved for the Grand Jiho of the Port-side Serpents when you are not he?*" the man screamed suddenly in her face, flecks of spittle flying from his thin lips. *"Can you tell me that? CAN YOU?"*

"I...I'm new here," Ari gasped, feeling nearly faint with fear. The skeletal man had spoken so softly before that his sudden screaming fit came as a terrible shock. She thought of trying to use a *Ton-kwa* throw on him but there was no room—she was stuck at the table and surrounded by the gang of inmates.

*My self defense skills aren't nearly as useful as I thought they would be in here,* she thought numbly and wondered what the gang members were going to do to her.

"Please," she said, daring to speak again. "I didn't mean to offend you. I just wanted to eat alone so I didn't have to be surrounded by—"

She broke off abruptly, aware that she'd been about to say "murderers and thugs" and that those words might be taken very badly. "Surrounded by other people," she finished at last, lamely. "I, uh, like to be by myself."

"Ah, solitude. Yes, I enjoy it as well." The thin man was suddenly quiet again, almost cordial as he spoke. "Do you know where it is said one can find a great deal of solitude and peace?" he asked Ari conversationally.

"Um...no." She cleared her throat nervously. "Where...where might that be?"

*"Death!"* screamed the man again. *"There is solitude in*

*DEATH!"* Turning to the man at Ari's right, who happened to be a hugely muscular inmate with arms as big around as her thighs, he made an expressive gesture with one finger, slicing across his throat as he pointed at her.

The man nodded once and grabbed Ari by the shoulders, lifting her bodily from her chair and holding her in the air in front of him like a rag doll.

Ari began to fight and struggle, trying to get away. Clearly this was a life and death situation and she most certainly didn't want to die. But through she aimed several well-placed kicks at the huge man holding her, he simply held her further away so that she couldn't reach him.

"Well, well—so I see you found my new cell mate, so you did."

The new voice was horribly familiar and when Ari looked to her left, she saw Tapper with his two henchman, Fenrus and Gorn, standing behind him. He also had one of the Horvath guards with him—the big one that had been doing the body cavity searches before—the one Medic had convinced to let him search her instead.

Medic—where was the big Kindred? Maybe he would save her if for no other reason than to keep her for himself? But a quick glance around the Mess Hall showed that he was nowhere in sight.

Ari was on her own.

"What do you mean, your new cell mate?" The thin man, who was surely the Grand *Jiho* of the Serpents, frowned. "This newbie came and sat at our table in *my* seat—his life is *mine.*"

"And you can have it, so you can," Tapper said amiably. "But not before I claim his ass. See, he's a virgin—a *true* virgin—and you know how I've been wanting to have one of those. Haven't had one in ages. Besides, he's on my list."

"Your list, eh?" The Grand *Jiho* frowned. "And you say I can have him tomorrow, after you are finished claiming his ass?"

"Sure can." Tapper's small, piggy eyes lit up greedily. "In fact, you might even have him later on this evening—depending on how many times I want to taste him before lights out. I don't like to share my cell at night, as you know."

"Yes, I know. Neither do I." The Grand *Jiho* nodded. "Very well, as a gesture of friendship from my squad to yours, I cede this little *chirro-putango* to you for the night. I will claim his life for the insolence he committed against me tomorrow." He turned to his henchman, who was still dangling Ari from his meat hook hands. "Let him down. For tonight he is Tapper's."

"Mighty fine of you, *Jiho*." Tapper nodded agreeably.

Ari had watched this whole exchange with a growing feeling of unreality. Surely this was some kind of a dream, wasn't it? She couldn't really be listening to these two men discussing her rape and murder in the same tones they might discuss last night's *bibble-ball* match, could she? Yes, it must surely be a dream.

*That's the kind of thinking that's going to get you killed,* whispered an urgent little voice in her head. *This is no dream, Ari and if you don't get away now, you won't get away at all. You'll be raped and murdered and probably served up in the prison commissary for breakfast tomorrow. You have to get out of here—now!*

The thought seemed to bring her back to herself and she blinked her eyes and shook her head, just as the huge Serpent gang member was lowering her to the scuffed metal floor.

"Git him, Fenrus," Tapper said, nodding at one of his own henchman. "You and Gorn bring pretty boy here up to my cell.

Strip him down and put him in the middle of my carpet so I can admire him, like, before I take that virgin ass."

"So we will, Tapper! So we will," chortled Fenrus through the blackened stumps of what were left of his teeth. He reached for Ari as the Serpent released her but she was ready for him. With a swift jab of her elbow to the felon's solar plexus, she was off and running, making her way through the crowded tables as fleet as a small woodland creature with a predator at her back.

"Git him, boys!" she heard Tapper howl. "He's at the top of my list and he's getting away, he is!"

Ari ran like the devil himself was after her and for all she knew he might be. If being raped and killed wasn't reason enough to run away, she didn't know what was.

She leaped nimbly through the crowd of prisoners, dodging around the ones that were in the aisle, her eyes fixed on the exit to the Mess Hall. Surely if she got through it she could find some-place to hide. In a building as huge as BleakHall, there had to be numerous cracks and crannies a person of her small stature could squeeze herself into.

*Almost there!* Ari cast a glance over her shoulder...and promptly tripped over an outstretched leg.

Amid loud guffaws and coarse catcalls, she tried to scramble to her feet. But a pincer-like grip suddenly latched onto her elbow.

"Sorry boy." A hard-faced con—the same one who had tripped her—dragged her to her feet. "But it's always good to have Tapper in your debt. Nothin' personal-like. Just business—you understand." He raised his voice. "Tapper! Over here—I've got 'im!"

"Let me go! Let me *go!*" Ari yanked and pulled in vain but the con had a grip like iron—there was no way she was getting away from him.

As Ari's panic grew, Tapper came strolling up in a leisurely manner, the top and sleeves of his trustee jumpsuit dragging through the spilled puddles of water and smears of food, his hairy belly protruding like an obscene pregnancy.

"Now, now, pretty boy," he said to Ari, who was yanking desperately to get away from the convict who held her. "Looks to me like Yoder there has caught you proper, 'ent he?"

"Caught 'im just for you, Tapper," the big con said, nodding his head respectfully.

"Just so, just so. You'll be remembered next time you're needing privileges, Yoder, so you will," the hairy gang boss said.

"Let me go! I'm not a piece of property to be traded away!" Ari shouted. She aimed a kick at Yoder's hard midsection but though it connected solidly, the man never lost his grip on her, though he did cough and double over.

"He's a wild one, he is," he said in a low, choked voice to Tapper.

"That he is. Hold him a minute longer for me, won't you, Yoder?"

Taking a step forward, Tapper drew back and punched Ari full in the face.

Ari saw the blow coming and managed to turn her head at the last second so that his fist fell on her cheek instead of her nose, where he had aimed it. But though she might have saved herself a broken nose, the pain was still intense—like a bomb bursting under her skin.

She'd never been struck like this before—not even during *Tonkwa* combat—and she heard something crunch as the heavy gold ring scraped ruthlessly across her skin and plowed into her face. It hurt so much that for a moment she could barely breathe.

"Ahh!" she gasped, tears of pain and rage springing to her eyes. "You *asshole!*"

The minute the words were out she knew she probably shouldn't have said them—they would only make Tapper angrier. Then again, what worse could he do to her than what he already had planned?

Her answer wasn't long in coming.

Tapper's face darkened, his bushy brows drawing together low on his bald head.

"Did you hear that boys? Did you hear what this pretty boy just called me?" he demanded, looking at Fenrus and Gorn.

"Sure did, Tapper. He called you an arsehole, so he did." Fenrus, who had apparently recovered nicely from the elbow Ari had thrown to his midsection earlier, spoke eagerly.

"Shame-shame..." Gorn clucked his tongue and shook his head disapprovingly. "Terrible to hear such language from such a pretty mouth as that."

"It most certainly is, Gorn." Tapper nodded, wiping Ari's blood off his ring with one trailing sleeve of his prison jumpsuit. "And can I just tell you now how disappointed I am in this pretty boy? Saying such nasty, nasty things..."

Leaning down, he grabbed Ari by the face. His fingers tightened, squeezing until she gasped in pain as his rough actions displaced the thing that had broken in her cheek, causing jagged pain to knife through the left side of her face.

"Well let me tell you what I'm going to do about those nasty words, boys," he said, glaring into Ari's defiant, tear-filled eyes, his hot, fetid breath blowing in her face. "I'm going to wash that pretty mouth out with my *cock*. Right before I take his pretty virgin ass," he snarled, squeezing Ari's face until she cried out in agony. It felt like he was breaking her face all over again! "And then I'll turn you over to the Serpents and let them get their revenge," Tapper finished. "Now what do you think of *that*, pretty boy?"

Ari couldn't even answer. She was in too much pain, tears leaking from her eyes to sting her torn cheek. How had things gone so wrong so quickly, she wondered dimly. She'd had what she thought was a fool-proof plan and now she was about to be raped and killed without even seeing Jak again. How had this happened?

*Hanna was right—I never should have come here. I underestimated this place and overestimated my own skills.*

Well now she was going to pay for her hubris—pay with her life.

*Goddess of Mercy,* she prayed as Fenrus and Gorn grabbed her firmly by the arms. *Please, I know I was stupid coming here but I wanted so badly to save Jak. I know I haven't prayed to you since I was a little girl but could you please help me now? I'm in so much trouble...oh please...**please...***

There was no answer and no way out. Amid the cheers and mocking shouts of the other inmates, she was dragged away towards the direction of the cell blocks as the indifferent Horvath guards watched and did nothing to save her.

Ari was sure she was going to die.

# NINE

Lathe heard the shouting as he neared the Mess Hall and wondered uneasily what in the Seven Hells was going on. He scanned the hall quickly as he came to the wide double doors leading into it, but he couldn't immediately see the cause of the ruckus. Inmates were talking animatedly and gesturing but for once there was no fight going on, which was surprising.

He made his way to table 13—the one designated for neutral parties who refused to affiliate themselves with any of the many gangs—and looked for Ari.

The boy wasn't there.

Lathe swore under his breath as he looked around and registered the fact that Ari wasn't *anywhere* in the Mess Hall. Where could he have gone? If he was thinking he could get out by the large exit located perpendicular to the entrance from the holding area, he was wrong. You needed trustee status added to your ID tag or the presence of one of the Horvath guards to get through the huge double doors which shut once all the inmates were accounted for each mealtime and only opened when the designated hour was up.

So where could Ari be?

"Greetings, Medic," burbled Xolox, waving one of his eight tentacles at Lathe. He was a Sporran from Gibbous Seven who had been imprisoned for the offense of killing one of his Yonnite Mistress's favorite slaves. But it had been a crime of passion and he was usually genial enough and more worth talking to than most of the humanoid inmates, at least in Lathe's opinion.

"Greetings, Xolox," he returned. "Excuse me, but have any of you seen a new prisoner—a boy with black hair and dark blue eyes here today? I told him to come to table 13 to eat but I don't see him anywhere around."

"A boy? Apologies, Medic, but almost all of you humanoids look the same to me." Xolox shrugged his tentacles apologetically.

Drumph, the orange-skinned exopod sitting across from him simply gibbered and typed something into his toy com-link. He was clinically insane and never said anything that made sense, though Lathe had heard he had once been a charismatic though extremely dishonest, leader among his people.

But Gumper, who was sitting beside Xolox raised his heavy head.

"He might be talking...about the boy...Tapper took," he said in his slow, ponderous voice. He was chemically dependent on *sloth*, a drug which caused his skin to turn green and his bulk to balloon to enormous size.

"What?" Lathe demanded, turning to him. "What did you say? You saw the boy and Tapper took him? Took him where?"

"Took him...to his...cell...I think." The drug, which was

constantly delivered to his spinal canal via permanent injection sites in his spine, also made Gumper's thinking and speech agonizingly slow.

"Why? Why did he take him?" Lathe demanded, then shook his head. "Never mind." He didn't have time for Gumper's labored explanation and anyway, he didn't need it. There was only one reason Tapper ever took a newbie prisoner up to his cell and it *wasn't* to play a friendly game of cards.

"Damn it!" he swore as he left table 13 and ran for the exit doors. He'd been afraid something like this would happen—afraid the boy's unique beauty would draw Tapper's attention. And once the crime boss had someone in his sights, it was over for them. As the ranking gang leader with syndicate connections, Tapper's word was law in BleakHall. There was no way to get Ari back from him now.

Still, Lathe had to try.

Swearing again, he ran faster, hitting the exit doors so fast they whined in protest as their ancient mechanisms slid open to let him out. Then he was pounding up the stairs towards the cell block where Tapper and the rest of the trustees—himself included —had their cells.

*Goddess,* he prayed as he ran. *Goddess, please—help me save him! I don't know why it's so important, I only know it is. I have to save Ari—please!*

# TEN

Ari knelt nude on the rug in the middle of the well-appointed cell. It was so nicely decorated it could almost have passed for a high-priced single unit domicile on Phobos, where she came from. Except for the clear plasti-glass walls on either side, of course.

It actually *was* a very nice rug, she noticed dully, as she looked down. A deep red pile worked with golden threads that formed all kinds of marvelous patterns. She ought to know—she'd been studying it ever since Fenrus and Gorn had brought her in here and stripped her. It probably wouldn't even show any blood.

Her new prison jumpsuit was lying in a crumpled heap near the foot of Tapper's bunk and her hands were bound behind her back with some kind of sticky tape. Her look/touch device was still working well, projecting the male chest and genitalia which appeared to be dangling between her thighs—but that was a small comfort at this point.

She'd been afraid of what the inmates at BleakHall would do to her if they found out she was female instead of male—now she knew they would rape and kill her either way.

*Please, Goddess—don't let it hurt too much,* she prayed dully. *And don't let Jak find out what happened to me. He'll feel so bad if he knows I got myself killed trying to save him.*

"Well, well—look what we have here. Supper's over and it appears to be dessert time, lads!" a voice over her head said.

Ari felt a chill go through her naked body. Tapper was here. Which meant her brief respite was over.

The hairy gang boss swaggered over, his rubber slippers whispering across the deep nap of the lush carpet. He came to a stop, looming over Ari with his hairy belly almost right over her head. It looked like a practiced pose.

*How many others has he done this to?* she wondered, looking up with a wince, since the motion made her swollen left cheek throb with pain. *How many innocent victims has he raped and killed just because he felt like it?*

The thought made her angry and she glared defiance at Tapper, who was still looking down at her like she was a prime cut of meat and he was wondering where to take the first bite.

"Now, now, pretty boy—none of that scowling," he said, giving her a deceptively gentle smile. "It's time for your punishment, so it is. And as I recall, I promised to wash your filthy mouth out with my cock, so I did."

Reaching under his pendulous belly, he unfastened more of his green and blue striped jumpsuit, revealing what appeared to be a short, stubby root vegetable growing out of a huge patch of thick black hair.

The smell of sour, unwashed male flesh hit her nose, making

Ari want to gag and the sight of his member, growing and twitching like an overeager worm, turned her stomach too.

"I swear by the Goddess of Mercy," she said thickly. "If you put that thing anywhere near my face I'm going to bite it off and then puke all over you. When's the last time you had a bath?"

The reckless words poured out of her mouth before she could stop them—she'd never been good at holding her tongue. Jak used to laugh at her about it but it was no laughing matter now.

Tapper's face grew dark with rage.

"Bite it off, will you, pretty boy?" he snarled. "I don't think so. Fenrus, Gorn—one of you fetch me some pliers. Let's pull those pretty white teeth out and then we'll see how bitey our little friend feels."

"I'll get them, Tapper—so I will!" Fenrus hopped from one foot to the other eagerly. "Can I have a pull? Can I? Can I?"

"So you can, Fenrus my lad. And Gorn too. And you'll both have a taste of his ass and mouth once I'm finished with him, so you will," Tapper promised. "We're going to make this pretty boy wish the Serpents had finished him off before I got to him, so we will."

So *that's* what's worse than being raped and murdered, Ari thought dully. *Having all your teeth pulled first and then being passed around—*

"Stop!" The new voice came from the open door of Tapper's cell and Ari looked up to see Medic standing there. Beside him was Mukluk, idly twirling his pain-prod in one scaly hand.

"Stop? What's that you say, *stop?*" His hairy member still clutched in one pudgy hand, Tapper looked up to the door of the cell. "And why should you be telling me what to do with *my* property, Medic?"

"Because he's not your property—he's mine. I claimed him in the infirmary," the big Kindred said.

"Well, *I* claimed him before he was even processed—out in the waiting hall," Tapper retorted. "I put him on my list—top of the list. Gorn, show 'im."

"Right you are, Tapper." Gorn pulled out his tablet and tapped on it before showing the results to Medic and Mukluk.

The Horvath guard took a look and shrugged.

"It zzeemz correct."

"It's not," the big Kindred growled. "He's mine—Ari is mine and I won't allow anyone else to touch him."

"Oh, and how are you gonna *stop* me from 'touching' 'im, ay, Medic?" Leering at the big Kindred, Tapper shoved his crotch in Ari's face.

At the overpowering sweaty stench of him, her gorge rose. Though she hadn't had much to eat in the past twenty-four hours, a wave of nausea gripped her and she threw up what little she had all over his short, stubby member.

"Gods of Crime and Lords of Damnation!" he swore, jumping back and swiping at his now-wilting shaft. "You'll pay for that, pretty boy!"

But the moment he jumped back and Fenrus and Gorn were distracted, Medic seized the opportunity to rush into the cell and pull Ari back outside.

It happened so fast her head was spinning as he shoved her behind him, keeping his muscular bulk between her and Tapper.

"And just what do you think you're doing, Medic?" the gang boss snarled, stepping forward as he finished wiping his member with the dirty sleeve of his jumpsuit. "How dare you take what's mine?"

"I told you, the boy is *mine*." The big Kindred bared his double set of fangs and seemed to grow twice as large, somehow.

Tapper shrank back somewhat but the look on his face remained mulish and defiant.

"He insulted me—he's mine to punish, so he is. And after that, the Serpents have dibs on him."

"The Serpents?" Ari could hear the disbelief in the big Kindred's voice. "What do *they* want with him?"

"He sat at their table—in the Grand *Jiho's* chair—so he did!" Gorn exclaimed. "They're going to kill him just as soon as Tapper here finishes with tasting his mouth and ass, so they are."

"Goddess, Mother of All Life, give me strength," Ari heard the big Kindred mutter to himself. Aloud he said, "No one is 'tasting' Ari or touching him or doing anything else to him. He's mine —under *my* protection from now on. Anyone who even gets near him will answer to *me*."

The menace in his deep, rumbling voice made Ari shiver even though she knew it wasn't directed at her. Tapper looked cowed as well—but not enough to give up.

"This 'ent fair, so it 'ent," he said, turning to Mukluk. "I had 'im first. Medic can't just take another man's property and get away with it!"

Mukluk flickered out his black forked tongue and swiped one slitted yellow eyeball thoughtfully.

"Izz true—Tapper hazz a point," he remarked.

"And I have plenty of credit too," Tapper said temptingly. "I can pay you handsome-like, Mukluk, old son—you know I can."

"You can't do that," Medic said quickly. "You own me a debt, Mukluk. If I hadn't told you about the boy's condition, you would have gotten injured—all your scales would have fallen out by now."

The Horvath licked his other eyeball.

"Alzo true," he admitted.

"What condition?" Tapper demanded. "What is he talking about?"

"Zamwer's syndrome," the big Kindred said. "Very destructive."

"To zzaurian life formzz only," Mukluk added.

"And I saved you from getting it—you owe me a debt," Medic repeated. *"A debt of honor,"* he emphasized.

Apparently this was important in Horvath culture because the lizard-guard nodded regretfully.

"Izz true. The boy stayz with Medic."

Tapper swore angrily but no matter how much pull he had with the other inmates, it appeared that the Hovarths reigned supreme here at BleakHall.

Ari felt a surge of relief and then wondered if she was being premature. Yes, the big Kindred had saved her from a fate worse than death—and death itself for that matter—but she still didn't know why. If he just wanted her for the same reason Tapper did, she could be going out of the frying pan and into the fire.

"Spread the word." Medic pointed at Tapper and his two henchmen. "Tell everyone—the boy is mine. Anyone who touches him—including you, Tapper—will get a taste of my fangs. And you know how well Harner and Tulk the Bullroar did after I finished with them."

"They shriveled up and died," Fenrus said in an awed whisper. "I saw Tulk the Bullroar myself—he died all black in the face and foamin' at the mouth after you bit him, Medic, so he did."

"Shut up, Fenrus," Tapper snarled. He glared at Medic. "We've never had a problem before, Medic, no we 'ent, but now we've got one all right. You've tooken what's rightfully mine, so you have. Which means you'll need to watch your back from now on."

"Do your worst." The big Kindred's voice was a soft growl. "Anyone you send against me dies. Also, I will no longer treat your men in the clinic if you declare war on me."

"Hey, that's not fair-like!" Gorn protested. "What if one of us gets shivved in the Rec Yard?"

Medic shrugged. "Too bad. I took an oath to preserve life but I won't do it at the expense of my own." He gazed at Tapper and his men steadily. "Anyone who comes against me or mine will no longer have access to medical care."

"You'll be sorry for this, so you will, old son," Tapper promised. "And you—I'll not forget you," he said, pointing at Ari, who was still mostly concealed behind the big Kindred's back. "Medic might be protecting you right now but the minute he gets tired of you, you're mine, pretty boy. Do you hear?"

"That's not going to happen," Medic growled. "As of tonight, Ari is moving into my cell as my *permanent* bunkmate."

There were murmurs from Fenrus and Gorn at this announcement.

"Well, well, a trustee sharing his cell—he must really fancy the lad!"

"'Ent he got it bad, then! I thought Medic didn't go for males but I guess I was wrong."

The big Kindred bore this quietly but Ari, looking up at him, thought his face was redder than it had been before. What exactly was the significance of Medic moving her into his cell? Was it like announcing some kind of prison engagement? Was he going to carry her off to his cell and finish what Tapper had started? Oh Goddess of Mercy, would this nightmare *never* end?

Suddenly the overhead lights flickered and a harsh chime sounded over the com-link system.

"Lightzz out zzoon," Mukluk commented. "Go to your celzz now."

"Let's go." Taking Ari by the arm, the big Kindred propelled her down the long balcony-hallway which ran the length of the trustee cell block.

But he had one last word for Tapper, who was glaring after them malevolently.

"He's mine," he growled and then he pushed Ari into a cell, just a few doors down, and the plasti-glass shield door slammed shut behind them. *"Mine."*

# ELEVEN

"Goddess, that was close." After stripping the hold-tight tape from the boy's wrists, Lathe sank onto his bunk and put his head in his hands.

What he had seen when he came to Tapper's cell had shaken him more than he wanted to admit. The sight of Ari kneeling naked and helpless at the gang lord's feet about to be raped and abused had twisted something inside him—something Lathe had thought couldn't be twisted anymore.

He'd seen so many atrocities—so much casual violence and even torture—since he'd first come to BleakHall, that he'd thought himself completely desensitized to it.

Well, he'd been wrong.

The thought of something happening to Ari made him feel angry and sick—the threat of violence against the boy felt like a threat against his own flesh and blood.

*Is that why he affects me so much? Does he remind me of*

*Thonolan?* Lathe asked himself. But no—his brother had been almost as tall as he was himself with the pale blond hair and ice blue eyes of a regular Blood Kindred. Ari, with his slender build and dark, delicate looks was nothing like Lathe's younger brother.

*So why did I put myself on the line to save him?* Lathe asked himself. He still had no answer but he knew what he had done was risky. Before he had held a neutral place in the prison—respected and feared for his fangs and his willingness to use them and his status as the prison's only medical personnel. Now he would have both Tapper and his gang and the Grand *Jiho* and his Serpents after him. He would have to watch his back—and Ari's—constantly.

What had been a difficult life was now going to become almost impossible.

"Ari, Goddess damn it," he muttered, rubbing a hand over his face and hearing the rough, sandpapery sound of his whiskers. "How in the Seven Hells did you manage to make so many enemies in such a short amount of time?"

"I...I d-don't know." The answer, accompanied by the chattering of teeth, made Lathe look up and realize that the boy was standing in the corner, still nude and shivering. Strangely, he was covering both his shaft and his chest with his arms, though why he should bother to try and hide his skinny chest, Lathe had no idea. Still, he could see the lad was cold.

*Gods, what's wrong with you, Lathe? Did you rescue him from Tapper just to let him freeze to death?*

Lathe looked around for the boy's clothes, then remembered that they'd left Ari's prison-issued jumpsuit in Tapper's cell. Well, that was too bad because there was no getting another one tonight—it was too close to lights out to risk going down to the laundry.

Being out after the lights went off in BleakHall was as good as suicide.

Grabbing the blanket from his bunk, Lathe stood up and went to where the boy was standing. He started to drape it around the thin, shivering shoulders but Ari shied away.

"Leave me alone!"

"Leave you alone?" Lathe growled, feeling tired and frustrated and irritated all at once. He'd saved the boy's life—why was he still acting like Lathe was trying to eat him up like a hungry beast?

"You heard me." The boy lifted his chin defiantly. "I know why you took me from Tapper—you're thinking you'll get me to depend on you so you can stick something besides your finger up my ass next time. Well, it won't happen!"

A sharp retort rose to Lathe's lips...then he saw the fear in those large, dark eyes. A fear so great it was eating the boy up inside. And no wonder he was afraid after what he'd just been through. His lip was split, one side of his face was swollen, and he'd nearly been raped and killed all on his first day at BleakHall. Of *course* he was afraid.

*Have to see to those injuries tomorrow, he might have a zygomatic fracture,* Lathe thought. He could tell by the boy's eyes he wouldn't let Lathe anywhere near him tonight.

"I'm sorry," he said quietly. He dropped the blanket at the boy's feet and retreated to his bunk. "I didn't mean to frighten you."

"I'm not frightened of you," Ari said at once, but the look in his large, dark eyes spoke differently.

"No, of course you're not." Lathe sighed deeply, suddenly exhausted. He'd just put his life on the line for this new prisoner who wanted nothing to do with him. And he still had *no idea* why he had done it.

What a fucking day.

Leaning down, Ari snatched the blanket and wrapped it around himself, knotting it at the top, under his armpits so that he was covered from chest to shins. Then he looked at Lathe with big, uncertain eyes.

"Well? What now?" he asked, in a voice that came out sounding more uncertain than defiant.

"What now, what?" Lathe stretched out on the narrow bunk, feeling the weariness of the day sinking him like a stone in a pond. He closed his eyes and sighed heavily.

"What..." Ari cleared his throat. "What are you planning to do with me?"

Lathe opened one eye and looked at the boy.

"You mean do I plan to wait until you're off your guard and come rape you?"

"I...I..." Ari swallowed convulsively and Lathe realized all over again how frightened the boy was.

"Sorry," he muttered. "Didn't mean to scare you again. For the last time, I'm not going to hurt you. Right now I just want to get a good night's sleep."

"What should I do?" Ari asked. "While you sleep, I mean?"

"If you're smart, you'll sleep too. Long day tomorrow—you'll be assigned your job."

"Job?" The boy spoke like it was a foreign word.

"Sure. Everybody has to have a job. How else could they keep this place running? I'll try to keep you with me but I can't promise I'll be able to."

"What...what if you can't?" Ari asked in a small voice.

"Then you'll have to be on your toes," Lathe said grimly. "At least I'll try to keep you out of areas where Tapper and his men are. I'm hopeful the Serpents will forgive their vendetta against you when they're faced with the threat of not being treated at the infirmary anymore."

"Why..." Ari cleared his throat. "Why are you doing this? Protecting me?"

Lathe was too tired to dissemble. He sighed, feeling like his bones were made of lead. Sleep—he needed sleep.

"I don't honestly know," he growled. "It's certainly not for the pure fucking pleasure of your company. Now come on—it's time to get some rest."

"Where am I supposed to sleep, though?" Ari asked. "There's only one bunk."

Lathe shrugged tiredly.

"True—this is supposed to be a single cell. You can share my bunk—not that you will, I can tell by your eyes," he added, seeing the skeptical look on Ari's face. "But it gets pretty Goddess damned cold here after lights out—they drop the temperature twenty degrees to keep the lashers happy."

"The lashers?" Ari looked puzzled.

Lathe was too tired to explain.

"You'll see. Just be glad the cell door is closed."

"Is it locked?" the boy asked, examining the clear plasti-glass door. "I don't see any locking mechanisms."

"Don't need any locks to keep the prisoners in at night." Lathe yawned. "Going out is..." He yawned again. "Suicide."

"I don't understand."

"Too bad. I'm too damn tired to explain."

He closed his eyes and was about to drift off when Ari spoke again.

"Can...can I have a drink of water?"

The boy's voice was a dry rasp and Lathe remembered he'd thrown up on Tapper when the bastard had shoved his shaft in Ari's face. Had that been on purpose—the puking? Or was it just because Tapper smelled like a fucking latrine that hadn't been cleaned in about ten cycles? Lathe's sensitive Kindred nose had been assaulted by the stench when Tapper opened his jumpsuit too—he didn't blame the boy for getting sick.

"In there." He nodded at the tiny cubical enclosing a toilet and sink in the corner of the cell. Having a private fresher was a luxury accorded only to trustees—much coveted by the regular inmates, who only had a row of public holes to use as toilets in their communal bathing areas.

He heard the door open but his eyes had already drifted closed before he heard it latch.

"Just don't stay in there all night," he tried to say but he was too damn tired. With a muttered prayer of thanks to the Goddess that he'd been able to save the boy, Lathe drifted off into an exhausted sleep.

# TWELVE

A ri pulled the folding door of the tiny room shut behind her. Even claustrophobia couldn't stop her from snatching a moment of privacy to pull herself together.

Looking down, she saw a dull silver toilet and mounted above it, a tiny metal sink. She looked at herself in the flat, scratched square of silver that served for a mirror. Her face was a mess—the left side of it, where Tapper had punched her—was bloody and swollen and it looked like she had the beginnings of a pretty good black eye.

*Not such a pretty boy now, are you?* she thought and had to look away as tears welled up in her eyes. Why, oh why hadn't she listened to Hanna and stayed the hell away from this awful place?

*But I couldn't stay away,* she reminded herself. *I had to at least **try** to get Jak—I couldn't let him rot in here! Oh Jak, where are you? Will I live to see you and get out of here tomorrow?*

More tears came, the sobs surprising her with their forcefulness. Quickly she turned on the cold water tap to cover her tears, not that she thought the big Kindred would hear them. He was passed out cold on the only bunk, his muscular bulk taking up most of it.

*Not like I would share it with him,* she told herself, trying to get control of the misery that wracked her. *He says he doesn't know why he saved me from Tapper but that has to be a lie. He wants what Tapper wants, doesn't he? What everyone wants in here!*

The memory of his hands on her in the infirmary—the big, warm hand on her back and the other probing deep in her body came back all over again and with it, a rush of humiliation. She'd never been touched against her will before this—never been punched or kicked or brutalized or threatened with rape or death. These seemed to be everyday occurrences at BleakHall but they were new and horrible and shocking to Ari.

*I'm not tough enough for this place,* she admitted to herself, as she splashed water over her aching face and rinsed out her mouth. *I don't see how anyone could be—it's horrible.*

The stuff coming out of the tap was cloudy and tasted metallic but she was so thirsty from puking and crying that she drank until her belly was full. Then she turned off the tap and blotted her face carefully on the blanket she was wearing, since she didn't see any towels. Then she looked in the mirror again.

"Just until after lunch tomorrow," she told herself in a low voice. "You only have to make it until then, Ari. You can do that—you can survive long enough to save yourself and Jak. You *have* to. You—"

A low, menacing growl interrupted her mini pep-talk.

Ari frowned, her heart beginning to hammer. What in the

galaxy was that? Was the big Kindred growling in his sleep? But the deep, rumbling growl sounded like an animal, not a humanoid. A *big* animal.

Opening the accordion door of the tiny bathroom unit, Ari peeked out into the darkened cell. The lights were mostly doused now, except for a single glow in the far corner which appeared to be permanently on—probably so the guards could keep an eye on the prisoners.

The first thing that hit her was a blast of frigid air. She clutched her arms around herself and shivered. Why was it suddenly freezing? Then she remembered Medic saying something about the temperatures dropping because of something... lashers? Was that what he had said? But what was a lasher?

The low, rumbling growl came again, louder this time. It was coming from just outside the clear cell door, Ari realized. Peering into the darkness she saw a pair of yellow eyes glaring hungrily back at her. *Big* yellow eyes.

"Goddess of Mercy!" she blurted, shrinking back towards the tiny bathroom. "What the hell is *that?*"

"What? What is it?" The big Kindred was suddenly alert. He sat up in the bed, his muscular body tensed and ready for action. He looked at Ari, who was still trembling by the bathroom. "What's wrong? What happened?"

"Th-that *thing.*" Her teeth were chattering and not just from cold as she pointed to the hungry eyes glaring in from just behind the clear plasti-glass door.

"You woke me up for that?" He sounded annoyed. "It's just a lasher. They're probably excited because they smell fresh meat."

"Fresh *meat?*" Ari wrapped her arms around herself. How

could he talk so calmly when there was a hungry wild beast outside the door waiting to eat them?

"It's fine." He sat back down on the bunk. "It'll leave in a minute. Go back to sleep. Or go to sleep in the first place. It's late."

Ari wasn't budging.

"It's right *out there*," she protested. "And you said the cells don't lock. How do you know it can't get in?"

"Because the damn thing doesn't have opposable thumbs to open the door with," Medic growled, clearly completely out of patience. "Look, if you're that bothered..."

Getting wearily out of the bunk, he went right up to the plasti-glass where the huge animal was prowling and pounded on the door.

"Hey, get out of here, you big son-of-a-bitch!" Ari heard him growl. "There's nothing for you here so get the fuck out!"

Ari's heart was in her mouth, watching this display. She was certain the shouting and pounding would only make the big creature angry. But to her surprise, the growl turned into a whine and then the yellow eyes disappeared as the animal padded off into the darkness.

"Oh..." Ari couldn't keep the shock from her voice. "How... how did you do that? How did you make it go away?"

"Lashers don't like me." He came back and sank down on the side of the bunk, rubbing his eyes tiredly. "They sense I'm a predator—like they are. That makes them nervous so the mostly avoid me. That one probably smelled your scent or it wouldn't have come around here in the first place."

"So...you're a predator?" Ari bit her lip.

He sighed. "I just meant they know I'm capable of killing

them. Not that I have other...predatory inclinations." His fangs flashed in the dim light from the single glow as he spoke and Ari shivered.

"Oh," she whispered.

"Look, just go to sleep. They can't get in, all right? We may be fighting for our lives tomorrow—we need to be sharp."

*Sharp like the points of his fangs,* whispered a little voice in her head.

"I'm going back to bed. Don't wake me again." There was a warning note in the big Kindred's voice as he rolled over on his side, facing the wall.

Ari didn't answer. She just sank down in the far corner of the room and wrapped her arms around herself, shivering. Her face ached and throbbed, she was frightened and miserable, and she had only the thin blanket between herself and the freezing night air, which really did feel about twenty degrees cooler than it had earlier.

She had never felt so cold or so alone in her life.

*But it doesn't matter,* she told herself. *It's only for one night. Just one night and then tomorrow Jak and I are out of here. I can make it on my own just one night. Can't I?*

Repeating that to herself over and over she sank into a kind of daze that wasn't quite sleep and wasn't quite wakefulness. At first she was so cold she shivered and shook under the thin blanket. But then, after a while she began to feel numb and calm.

*See this isn't so bad,* she told herself sleepily. *I'm even beginning to feel kind of warm. Everything is going to be fine. Just fine...*

Lathe didn't know what got him out of bed—it wasn't the blaring of the general wake call or a rough hand on his shoulder. It felt more like a whisper in his ear.

***Wake warrior. Wake to save that which is precious…***

The whisper and the feeling that something was wrong brought him up out of the depths of slumber and he sat up on the side of the bunk feeling groggy and confused.

Looking around, he realized it was still night. What in the Seven Hells? Why couldn't he get a good night's sleep when he was so damn tired? What had woken him? Was it Ari, upset about the damn lashers again?

Then he blinked. Where *was* Ari, anyway? Lathe wasn't used to having someone else in his cell—it was pretty much an unwritten policy that trustees kept to themselves and didn't allow anyone else in their precious personal space. So it was strange to be wondering where his new cellmate was.

Still, where *was* he? Had he gone back into the fresher to keep warm? Not that it got very warm anywhere in here at night—at least not until the lights came up. The lashers were fierce predators but they came from a glacier planet and needed cold temperatures to keep active and prowling. Too much heat put the big beasts to sleep.

He got up, rubbing a hand over his face, and checked the bathroom. Nope—no one there. His heart started to beat faster. Surely the boy wouldn't have gone out of the cell while Lathe was asleep, would he? He'd seemed frightened to death by the lashers so there was no way he would have done such a stupid thing. He—

Lathe stumbled over something on the floor—something slumped in the shadows of the corner.

*What the hell?*

Stooping down, he saw Ari lying crumpled in a heap. His hand, when Lathe touched it, was ice cold, and he appeared to be barely breathing.

*Goddess damn it, he's going into hypothermia!* Many people thought that you could only die of cold if you fell into an icy lake or stream but Lathe knew that wasn't true. All you needed for a really good case of hypothermia to set in was for your core body temperature to go below 95 degrees and Ari felt much colder than that.

Swearing to himself, Lathe gathered the boy in his arms and stumbled over to the bed. He should have known that giving Ari the one thin blanket wouldn't keep him warm enough, but the boy had seemed so frightened of him Lathe didn't want to force him to share his bed.

*Well now he has no choice. It's share my bed and my body heat or he won't wake up the next morning,* Lathe thought grimly as he wrapped himself around the much smaller, slighter body and pulled Ari close to his chest. The boy felt so fragile in his arms—so breakable. He felt that strange wave of protective possessiveness come over him again and thought, *Mine,* before he could stop himself.

Grimly, he pushed the possessive thought away and concentrated on getting Ari warm. He himself had no problems with the cold. Blood Kindred came from an extremely cold environment— Tranq Prime was much like the planet the lashers came from—so Lathe had self-regulating body temperature. Which was to say, when it got cold, his body put out heat like a furnace—lucky for the boy. Being close to Lathe would heat him up faster than if he'd piled a bunch of *vranna* skin blankets on himself.

But despite the heat Lathe's body was putting out, the boy was so still at first that Lathe was worried he hadn't gotten to him in time. Then Ari stirred and moaned softly, burrowing closer to Lathe's chest as if he was seeking the heat of the Kindred's much larger body by instinct.

Lathe breathed a sigh of relief. So the boy would be all right. Ari moaned again and then began to talk in his sleep.

"Jak...Jak where are you?" he mumbled. "I can't...can't find you. Jak, please don't leave me..."

Lathe felt a strange emotion he couldn't immediately identify. Then it came to him—the feeling was envy. Who was this Jak that Ari called out for? What relationship did he have with the boy?

*What's wrong with you?* he scolded himself fiercely. *What does it matter who the boy cries for? Why should you care if he cares for another?*

But the fact was, he did. Why?

Pressing the boy closer to him, Lathe buried his face in the riot of thick, black, almost-curly hair and breathed deeply. That scent...the boy's scent smelled so strange...so good but so *wrong* somehow. Why?

*He smells like a female,* Lathe realized at last. But that was impossible—he'd seen the lad naked not once but twice. He was definitely male.

And yet he smelled female. *Female.*

A burst of understanding washed over Lathe. No *wonder* he'd felt compelled to save Ari even at the risk of his own life! The boy's scent had been working on him, manipulating him the same way a Kindred's bonding scent worked on a female he wanted to bond to him.

Of course, Lathe didn't want to bond with a male. He had nothing against males who loved other males but the fact was, he wasn't one of them. He'd never felt attracted to another male in his life.

*Until now,* whispered a little voice in his head.

No. No, it wasn't real—it was the boy's scent working on him —that was all. A Kindred's first instinct was to protect any helpless female—no wonder he hadn't been able to stop himself from coming to Ari's rescue. The boy's feminine scent had compelled him.

Lathe wondered for a moment if the boy was putting out the scent deliberately and then decided he couldn't possibly be. He seemed so upset when Lathe came anywhere near him and his fear was genuine—such terror couldn't be faked. So he certainly wasn't drawing Lathe to him on purpose. No, the boy must not even know he smelled so good...so *feminine.*

*Maybe it's a trait of his people,* Lathe thought. He'd have to ask Ari more about where he came from...if he ever got over his fear of Lathe enough to talk, that was.

*Well, he's certainly not going to get over it if he wakes up and finds himself cradled in your arms,* whispered a practical little voice in his head. *Better let him go before you go back to sleep.*

Lathe knew the voice was right. Ari seemed warm enough now—as long as he kept the boy beside him in bed, near the heat of his own much larger body, he should get through the night well enough.

But it was surprisingly hard to let the boy go and turn his back when all he wanted to do was gather Ari to his chest and keep him close for the rest of the night.

*It's his scent—just his scent working on me,* he told himself. But breathing in that warm, feminine scent made it very difficult to be still. Even with his back to the boy, it was a long, long time before Lathe at last drifted off to sleep.

# THIRTEEN

Something smelled really good. *Amazingly* good. *Warm...spicy... clean...masculine* were the words that drifted through her half-asleep mind. Ari inhaled deeply and found that the source of the good smell was close—close and deliciously warm. Had Hanna put a new warmer-pillow in her bed while she slept last night?

But when she pressed her face to the warm thing, it didn't feel soft like a pillow at all. It was firm and hard like a wall and it moved in slow, deep waves almost like someone breathing.

*Someone breathing? Who's in my bed?* she wondered sleepily. *And why does the left side of my face ache?*

Putting her fingers up, she gingerly explored the area of pain and winced at her own touch. Ow, that *really* hurt. What had happened to her? Had she gotten kicked in a *Ton-kwa* combat? But she hadn't been to any combats lately. Not since Jak had gone missing...

*Jak! BleakHall! I'm at BleakHall! And I'm in bed with someone—with Medic!*

Suddenly everything came rushing back: her horrible first day, the run-in with the Serpents gang, nearly getting raped and killed by Tapper and his crew, and then getting dragged away to the big Kindred's cell.

*And now I'm in bed with him. How did I get here? What's going on?*

She distinctly remembered falling asleep in the corner, wrapped in the blanket. But now she was in the bunk with the big Kindred—and worse, on the *inside* of the bunk in the part facing the wall.

*Trapped,* she thought wildly. *I'm trapped between him and the wall. How can I get out? What am I going to do?*

She lay stiff and frightened for a moment, her breath coming in short, terrified gasps. Part of her wanted to shove against his broad back and try to get away but she was afraid of what he might do to her if she did that. After all, he had those fangs...

*Kill-All,* whispered the voice in her head. Ari's imagination wouldn't stop. She could imagine the big Kindred pinning her to the bed...leaning over her, his fangs bared...

Would he bite her if she tried to run? Would he threaten her with his fangs and take what Tapper had wanted? Would he—

Abruptly a loud, blaring alarm came over the exterior com-link system. At the same time, a blinding light flashed on, flooding the cell with dirty gold brilliance.

*Goddess!* Ari's heart jumped into her mouth and she could barely breathe. What was happening now? Was it some kind of drill? An attack?

To her surprise the big Kindred didn't jump out of bed as he had the night before when she'd been frightened of the lasher. Instead he yawned and stretched hugely, his big body seeming to take up even more space for a moment.

Ari squeezed herself flat against the wall, trying to avoid him but his broad shoulder brushed against her bare breasts anyway and she jumped, realizing that the blanket she'd wrapped herself in the night before had fallen down around her waist.

"Oh, good morning." He turned his head, frowning sleepily at her. "Why do you look like you just saw a ghost?"

"What...what am I doing in here? In...in your bed?" she managed to make herself ask. She also somehow kept herself from covering her bare breasts with her arm though it felt incredibly wrong to sit there in front of him completely exposed.

Of course, her look/touch showed only a flat, boyish chest but what if Medic realized that what he'd accidentally touched didn't match up with what he saw? She held her breath when he frowned at her and shook his head.

"What you're doing in bed with me is *not* freezing to death," he growled. "And it's where you're going to sleep every night from now on. You're too little to sleep on your own when the temperature drops—nearly lost you to hypothermia last night."

"What? I don't believe that," Ari exclaimed. "It's just an excuse to get me into your bed."

"Look, Ari, let me make this very, *very* clear to you..." The big Kindred sat up and glared at her. "I am *not* interested in you in...in the way Tapper is. Sexually, I mean. I don't...don't desire you." He cleared his throat, his face going ever so slightly red and Ari wondered who he was trying to convince—her or himself.

"Yesterday, in the Infirmary—" she began but he held up a hand to stop her.

"You had to be searched and it was either me or Mukluk doing the searching," he said firmly. "I've seen the damage he can do with those claws of his—I didn't want that to happen to you. But believe me I took no pleasure in..." He cleared his throat again. "In searching you."

Ari glared at him uncertainly, wondering if she ought to believe him. The memory of his hands on her was hard to shake. The gentle way he had touched her...entered her...

*No, I won't think about it,* she told herself fiercely. *I won't!*

"I *don't like* other males," the big Kindred emphasized firmly, as though cementing the fact in his own mind. "I swear that to you, Ari."

"I don't think you have to like other males to want to do horrible things to them here," Ari said, but she was beginning to feel cautiously optimistic that maybe she wouldn't start her morning by being raped after all.

"That's true," Medic acknowledged. "Nevertheless, I'm not interested in doing all the horrible things that were almost done to you yesterday." His deep voice, still gruff from sleep, got softer. "I know how frightened you must have been."

"I'm fine." Ari looked away, pulling the blanket up over her chest. "I guess if you really don't want *that* then I should thank you...Medic," she added, using his name for the first time.

"Call me Lathe," he said unexpectedly. "That's my name. Medic is only my title."

Ari thought of his other title. *Kill-All*...Did his fangs ever retract or were they always that long and sharp? She realized she was staring at his mouth and quickly looked away.

"All right, Lathe. Thank you for everything you did for me

yesterday," she said. "Though I still don't understand why you did it."

"That makes two of us, little one." He sighed and ran a hand through his thick, dark brown hair, rumpling it into a sleepy halo around his head. "Well, time to get up."

"All right—so what do we do now? Go straight to the Mess Hall?" Ari asked.

Lathe shook his head.

"Shower first. But I think we'd better skip that this morning." He grimaced. "It's a shame—I hate to start the day without a shower. But I don't think it would be very wise of us to show up in the communal showers until the first strike is over."

"The first strike?" Ari frowned. "What do you mean?"

"Someone's going to try to kill me." Medic—no, Lathe, she reminded herself—spoke matter-of-factly, as though he was discussing the weather. "Probably one of Tapper's crew, but maybe one of the Serpents. Once I get that out of the way, it'll remind the rest of them that I know how to defend myself and what's mine." He looked at her speculatively. "Need to put a little fear into them—then it'll be safe for us to use the shower again."

Ari felt sick.

"You really think someone's going to try to assassinate you today?"

"Oh, I know it. The question is, will Tapper make it a private affair and try to hide it—or will he make a production of it and try to make an 'example' of me."

"But that's *awful*," Ari exclaimed.

"No, that's Tapper," Lathe said grimly. "In his mind I disrespected him and now he has to retaliate." He gave her a level look. "You've seen what he's capable of."

"Yes," she admitted biting her lip. "I...I have." Looking down at her hands, she tried to think of something else to talk about —*anything* else. The memory of kneeling on Tapper's nice carpet waiting to be raped and killed made panic crawl up her throat like bile. "What...what can I wear?" she asked desperately. "I, uh, lost my jumpsuit."

"Yeah, we'll have to take care of that."

Lathe was still wearing his own jumpsuit—the one he'd had on the night before. Ari wondered if he'd kept it on for warmth. He certainly didn't seem to need it—his big body put out heat like a furnace. Heat which had presumably kept her from freezing to death the night before.

*How close did I come to not waking up?* she wondered. And how closely had she been pressed to the big Kindred before she *had* woken up and remembered where she was? She found the thought didn't bear thinking.

"Let's get you a new uniform." Lathe got out of bed and went to a high shelf in the corner of the room. He took down a wooden box and opened it, shaking out two long, thin cylindrical objects which appeared to be made of dirty white paper, twisted at the ends.

"What are those?" Ari asked as he held them carefully in one hand and put back the box with the other.

"Nico-sticks," Lathe said shortly. "Terrible for your health but they're excellent barter here in BleakHall."

Opening the front door of their cell, he went to the railing which surrounded the high balcony which ran the length of this upper floor block of cells.

From studying the blueprints of the prison as she made her plans, Ari knew that BleakHall was mostly vertical, with three sides of clear plasti-glass cube cells overlooking the Mess Hall and processing area for new prisoners. Other areas like the prison laundry, the kitchens, the factory work-halls, and the Infirmary were located on the bottom floor of the sprawling complex.

Looking out, Ari saw was a metal mesh net that extended from the waist-high top of the rail all the way up to the next floor above. She supposed it was to prevent suicides…or more probably murders from occurring.

When she took a tentative step towards the open front door and looked down, she saw that they were many floors above the Mess Hall, which Lathe's cell overlooked. Vaguely she remembered being dragged up a seemingly never-ending flight of stairs but she hadn't realized how high they were going. Of course, she thought with a shiver, she'd had other things on her mind at the time, like her impending rape and murder.

Other inmates were moving around on various levels now. Clearly the ravenous lashers had been locked up for the night and now it was safe to be out and about. Many inmates were swathed in towels or blankets, obviously going to the showers. Ari wished she could have one herself but then she thought of all the dangers involved—not to mention seeing so many strange men naked and up close—and decided she could do with a sponge bath in the sink instead.

Lathe was scanning the crowd and when he saw the person he was looking for, he gave a piercing whistle and shouted, "Wheezer! Hey, Wheezer—up here!"

The ancient little man with the cracked oculars was down a level across from them. He looked up and waved when he saw Lathe and then he rapidly disappeared from sight.

A few minutes later he appeared in front of Lathe's cell,

puffing and blowing but with a look of bright-eyed expectancy on his wrinkled face.

"Yes, Medic? What can I do for you?" he asked eagerly.

"I need two fresh jumpsuits from the laundry," Lathe told him, giving him the nico-sticks. "One sized extra-extra small and one extra-extra-extra large. Oh, and some more small slippers for Ari here—he lost his."

"Yes, yes—I heard about that, so I did." The little old man turned his attention on Ari who shifted uncomfortably under his bright, bird-like stare. "Word is that Tapper's out for blood after you stole the lad right out from under his nose," he told Lathe.

"Yes, I'm aware," Lathe said grimly. "And the Serpents will probably want a piece too. Do me a favor, Wheezer, put the word out that any male who comes against me forfeits all medical care for himself and his entire gang. All right?"

"Oh my—yes, yes—so I see." The old man nodded thoughtfully. "Yes, that might make a few who'd take the job from Tapper reconsider."

"It won't make Tapper reconsider, though," Lathe said matter-of-factly. "But I'll be ready for him when he comes."

His fangs flashed as he spoke and Wheezer took a step back and made a sign to avert the evil eye.

"Kill-All," he whispered hoarsely.

"That's right," Lathe rumbled. "I will kill any and all who try to hurt me or mine. Spread the word, Wheezer."

"That I will! And I'll be right back with them suits and slippers."

The little old man scrambled off and Lathe came back inside the cell.

"Well, that should get the word out that we're prepared, at

least. Wheezer's like the town crier around here—he'll let everyone know."

It occurred to Ari that the big Kindred was basically preparing to go to war for her and she still didn't know why. But there didn't seem to be any point in asking him since he didn't appear to know why himself.

"I'm going to wash up as well as I can in the bathroom," she said. "If...that's okay?"

Lathe shrugged and smiled wryly.

"My cell is your cell, Ari. Help yourself."

That unreadable expression was back in his turquoise eyes as he looked at her. It made Ari feel hot and cold all over when the big Kindred stared at her like that. With a shiver, she disappeared into the bathroom to take the best bath she could in the limited facilities.

When she came out again, Wheezer had come back with the new prison uniforms—orange and blue for her and green and blue for Lathe—and the big Kindred was in the act of changing.

He already had the bottom half of the jumpsuit on but the top was dangling down his legs, much like Tapper wore his. But that was where the similarity ended.

Lathe's broad, bare back was muscular and smooth, the heavy biceps bunching and flexing as he moved. When he half turned towards her, Ari could see that his chest was just as muscular, though he did have a little brown, curly hair around his well-developed pecs and the flat copper disks of his nipples. With his height and those intense jewel-toned eyes, there was no denying the big Kindred was a striking male specimen.

*He looks like a god!* The thought popped into Ari's head before she could stop it. Then she scolded herself and made herself look away. After all, this "god" had fangs like a devil and she still wasn't completely certain of his intentions towards her.

Lathe must have heard her behind him because he turned more fully.

"Oh, there you are. Here, Wheezer brought your new uniform—catch."

He tossed the prison jumpsuit to Ari who nearly fumbled it. She returned modestly into the cramped bathroom to put it on and when she came out, Lathe was completely dressed too and sitting on the side of the bunk.

"What now?" Ari asked, coming out of the bathroom and laying the neatly folded blanket over the foot of the bunk. "Breakfast?" She wasn't looking forward to stepping foot in the Mess Hall again, but the fact was, she hadn't had anything to eat for over twenty-four solar hours now and she was feeling faint with hunger.

"In a minute." Lathe rose, a frown on his face, and came towards her. He put out a big hand but Ari dodged away.

"What are you doing?" she demanded, heart pounding. Had he changed his mind about liking other males and now he wanted to make her pay for his protection?

The big Kindred sighed and dropped his hand.

"Never mind for now, but eventually you'll have to let me see to that cheek of yours. I'm afraid you have a zygomatic fracture."

"A zygo—what?" So he had just been trying to examine her? Was that really all?

"Your zygomatic arch—your cheekbone—may be fractured," he explained and frowned. "How did that happen anyway? I didn't see it."

"Tapper punched me." Ari kept her voice low. "I...I've never been punched in the face before," she admitted. "Not even during a combat match. We, uh, used to compete in *Ton-kwa*—my brother and I."

"I see." Lathe nodded gravely. "I'm afraid being punched in the face is the least of your worries at BleakHall. You'll have to be careful if you want to get along here and follow the code of conduct."

"Code of conduct?" Ari frowned. "What do you mean? No one has mentioned any kind of code to me."

"And they won't either—it's something you're expected to learn quickly or already know." Lathe shrugged. "Some of it is easy—you have to be polite and deferential to the other prisoners. If you bump or brush someone or step on their foot, apologize immediately to avoid a conflict."

"Got it." Ari nodded. "What else?"

"Well..." Lathe counted them off on his fingers. "Don't piss in the communal shower—that's disrespectful to everyone. Keep your cell clean and your bunk made up. No unopened food containers in your personal area—that draws insects and the Goddess knows this place is hellish enough as it is without an infestation."

"I agree." Ari nodded. "Okay, I can do all that. Anything else?"

"The most important thing is to stay out of gang territories unless you have permission to be there. For instance, the Serpents —whom you've already met—" Lathe spoke dryly, "Claim Cell-block S, table 30, and run the hovercar parts work-hall. The OhNos run the library, sit at table 8 and claim Cellblock N. The Spice Lords claim Cellblock D, sit at table 11 and run the pornography ring."

"Wow, that's a lot to remember," Ari murmured. "Uh, pornography ring? The prison officials allow that? I thought BleakHall was owned by Mistresses from Yonnie Six. Doesn't porn objectify women?"

"They have to allow it—they'd have a riot on their hands if they tried to take away the porn," Lathe said grimly. "You can't lock over a thousand hardened felons away for life with no access of any kind to females and not give them some outlet. Males have urges—hungers—that have to be met somehow. That's why they don't allow any female staff at BleakHall at all—not even female Horvaths as guards and you can imagine what *their* females look like."

"Pretty much like the males?" Ari guessed.

Lathe nodded. "But even *that* would be too much temptation for some of these desperate bastards. If a female—any female—somehow got into BleakHall she'd probably be raped to death in the first fifteen minutes."

His words, spoken in that matter-of-fact tone, sent a chill like ice down Ari's spine.

"That's a horrible thought," she whispered, putting a hand to her throat, unconsciously checking the projection bead of her look/touch, imbedded in her ID. She was glad she was getting out of here today. The power supply for the little bead wasn't infinite—in fact, she estimated she had less than a week before it ran out. But of course, she didn't need that long since she planned to be floating off in her transport bubble with Jak just after lunch.

"It *is* horrible," Lathe admitted soberly. "But you have to remember, most of the prisoners in here are misogynistic bastards —they *hate* females."

"Because they come from Yonnie Six where women rule?" Ari said.

Lathe nodded. "And most were sent here by their Mistresses for one reason or another. Mostly rape and murder," he added darkly.

"And you..." Ari cleared her throat. "Do *you* feel that way about women? Do you hate them?"

Lathe looked shocked.

"No, of course not—I'm a Kindred," he said, as though that explained everything.

Ari shook her head. "Wheezer told me that was the name of your race when he was helping me get processed yesterday but I'd never heard of them before. What does being a 'Kindred' mean?"

"We protect and revere females," Lathe explained. "We are a race of genetic traders—our DNA makes our people 95% male, so we are always looking for new females of different races to bond with."

"That's fascinating." Ari couldn't help being interested despite herself. "So you can mate with any other race you find?"

"We're compatible with many races," Lathe admitted in a low voice. "What people are *you* from, Ari?" he asked.

"Me? Oh, I...my people come from Phobos. It's not a very big planet but we believe in the equality of males and females—we believe they're two sides of the same coin," she said, wondering why she was telling him all this.

"Two sides of the same coin," he murmured speculatively and the way he was looking at her made Ari nervous.

"So, if the Kindred love females so much then why are you in here? I mean, what did you do to be sent to BleakHall?" she asked, trying to change the subject.

Lathe frowned. "That's another unwritten rule here—you never ask another male his crime."

"Oh..." She looked down, feeling suddenly abashed. "I'm sorry."

"It's all right." He sighed. "The charge on my official documents says 'murder' but it wasn't true until I got here. I swore an oath as a physician to protect life but BleakHall has made a killer out of me."

He sounded so desolate when he said it that Ari almost wanted to go to him and comfort him. But she checked the impulse hastily. Firstly because she didn't need to get any closer to the big Kindred than she already was. And secondly because her wish to put and arm around him and hug him was a female impulse.

Males didn't comfort each other that way, she knew. She had seen Jak with his friends before—they punched each other on the arm or slapped each other on the back. But they never embraced and held each other the way she suddenly wished she could do with Lathe.

"I'm sorry," she said instead, truly meaning it.

He shook his head.

"Killing...torture...pain—they're all part of life here. Before you came through processing yesterday, I thought I'd become inured to it—desensitized. But I was wrong."

"You...you were?" Ari wondered why her heart was suddenly beating harder and her face felt hot and flushed.

Slowly, the big Kindred nodded.

"When I heard your voice pleading with that bastard Mukluk yesterday, something seemed to...to break inside me." He sighed and clenched one big hand into a fist, studying it intently. "I just wish I knew why I...why I feel what I feel."

"I thought you didn't like other males," Ari said quickly, her heart hammering faster. "You said—"

"I know what I said and I *don't* like other males," he interrupted. "I just..." He ran a hand through his hair in a gesture of frustration. "This is just really bad timing, that's all," he said roughly. "Look, are you hungry? It's time to go down for First Meal."

"I *am* hungry," Ari admitted. "But..." She bit her lip. "But I'm scared too. I feel like it's safe in here—in your cell. Outside...well, anything can happen."

"You can't live your life in fear, little one," Lathe murmured, taking a step closer to her.

Ari had the feeling that he wanted to put an arm around her—to touch her in some way and comfort her—the same way she'd had the impulse to comfort him earlier. But he didn't come any nearer.

"You have to be brave," he told Ari. "And believe me when I say that I'll protect you—with my life, if necessary."

"You will?" She could hear her pulse rushing in her ears and her whole body felt warm and flushed and tingly. Why was that? "Even..." She cleared her throat. "Even though you don't know *why* you're protecting me?"

"Even though," he agreed, his deep voice a soft, sincere growl. "Now come on, little one—we need to eat. Have to keep our strength up."

"All right." Ari followed him out of the cell, keeping her eyes on his broad back and hoping he could do what he had promised and keep her safe.

# FOURTEEN

Lathe had much to consider as they walked down the innumerable flights of stairs to get to the Mess Hall. The trustees were in Cellblock X—almost at the top of the towering living area of BleakHall—so he had plenty of time to think.

He had told Ari he had no interest in other males and that was true, he assured himself. Yet that didn't stop him from wanting to be near the boy—to comfort and protect him and ease his pain.

He wanted desperately to treat Ari's swollen cheek but it was clear the boy was still shy of him—still as skittish as a kitten. Which was actually the Earth animal that Ari most reminded him of. With his big, bright eyes and soft black hair and lithe, deft movements the boy was very like a stray kitten who had somehow wandered up onto Lathe's doorstep.

*And you took him in like a stray kitten too. Only what are you going to do with him once you leave this place?* he asked himself as they walked. *The nanites are almost finished digging the passage out of here. Will you take him with you when you go?*

Lathe supposed he would have to. He couldn't leave Ari here on his own now—it would be a death sentence with Tapper out to get him. But would Ari come with him? Would he come to trust Lathe at some point in the future? Right now the boy shied away every time Lathe so much as took a step in his direction.

*Except last night,* whispered a voice in his head. *Last night he cuddled close to you, pressing against your chest as you held him in your arms...*

But that was because he was asleep, Lathe reminded himself roughly. And anyway, he didn't *want* to cuddle with another male —not even one as pretty as Ari. It was just the boy's damn female scent working on him.

*The scent...* That was something to think about too. He remembered Ari saying that his people believed males and females were two sides of the same coin. Could that mean that Ari and his kind had characteristics of both sexes? That they were somehow...both?

As a medical doctor who flew among the stars and was part of a people who looked for genetic trades as a way of life, Lathe had seen stranger things. There were the Piloth people from Genry Eight for instance—they were male one sex cycle and then they switched to female the next. Or the Vargans of Choth Prime—a subset of their people had sexual characteristics of all three of their sexes—male, female, and okoi. They were called "the blended" and were revered in all levels of the Vargan society where they could breed with anyone they chose.

Was it possible that Ari came from a society like that—that he had a mixed biology that caused his feminine facial features and scent to be wedded to a male body?

Lathe had no idea but he told himself it didn't matter. He had taken the boy under his wing and now it was his duty to protect him. Clearly Ari wouldn't last a day in BleakHall on his own so until the nanites sent the signal telling Lathe the exit tunnel was finished, he had to be vigilant to keep both himself and the boy alive.

He just prayed to the Goddess he could do it.

# FIFTEEN

Wen the attack Lathe had predicted happened, it came from behind and it was so fast that Ari almost missed it.

One minute they were walking through the chow line, pushing their trays and doing their best to catch the globs of food the jerky mechanical arms doled out, and the next thing she knew, Lathe was in a fight for his life.

Ari was ahead of the big Kindred in line because he insisted on staying at her back, the better to protect her, she supposed. Right behind him in line was a bandy-legged little prisoner with shifty, weasely eyes, hardly taller than Ari was herself.

As though to make up for his lack of stature, the short prisoner's upper body was massively muscular. The sleeves of his prison jumpsuit had been torn off revealing arms bulging with muscle, roped with veins, and covered in colorful tattoos.

It was his arms that had caught Ari's attention as she was scanning the Mess Hall, trying to be alert for any sign of danger.

Although she hoped Lathe was wrong about an impending attack, she had to admit he'd been right about almost everything else to do with BleakHall so far, so she felt she couldn't afford to ignore his warning.

*Look at those arms,* she was thinking as she pushed her tray along. *I wonder how much he can lift? He must be massively strong but it makes him look so strange...*

And at that moment the little inmate dropped his tray and jumped for Lathe's broad back.

"Lathe! Behind you!" Ari barely had time to scream before the murderous felon whipped a slim black cord around the big Kindred's neck and pulled it tight.

Her warning gave Lathe just enough time to get his hands up and his fingers between the black cord and the sides of his neck. But the assassin still got the lethal string around the front part of his throat, yanking hard in an apparent attempted to either strangle the big Kindred or possibly just cut his head off.

Ari screamed and grabbed her half-full tray, rushing around to beat the would-be killer over the head and shoulders with it as Lathe struggled to free himself. The battered metal tray didn't serve as much of a weapon but the slippery yellow glop that was on it rolled down into the attacker's eyes and face, making him gasp and sputter as he tried with all his might to kill the big Kindred.

"Let go—let him go!" Ari shouted, hearing the panic in her own voice. The inmates all around them were roaring and chanting, but Lathe fought in deadly silence. Slowly, grimly he worked his fingers closer to the front of his neck, where the black cord had made a bloody indentation. Then, with a sudden yank, he jerked the cord forward.

The motion brought the attackers massively muscular fore-arms forward too, as though he was throwing his arms around Lathe to try and hug him from behind.

That one moment of vulnerability was all the big Kindred needed.

Quick as a striking snake, he turned his head and sank his fangs deep into the muscular, tattooed arm. His attacker howled—a sound of pure agony—and Ari saw his spine bow out and his entire body go rigid with pain.

Then he began to jerk and seize, his body flopping like a newly landed fish. Lathe flipped him off his back and threw him to the floor where he went on thrashing while thin black foam bubbled up from between his lips.

"Goddess," Ari whispered and heard the inmates all around her murmuring in awe.

"Kill-All...Kill-All..."

"Medic said he would do it and so he did. Old Hexer's a gonner, he is."

"He's a Kill-All...anyone he bites, *dies.*"

"I wouldn't want to get cross-wise of those fangs, no I wouldn't."

And through it all, Lathe just stood there, breathing heavily but not distressed. He had a blank look in his turquoise eyes and Ari wondered what he was thinking. How hard was it really for him to take a life? And to take a life in such an *awful* way, too.

The would-be assassin had finally stopped moving and was dead now—his blank eyes bulging. His mouth was curled into a rictus of agony and filled with black foam that drooled out onto the dirty metal floor. His body seemed to have wasted away, shriv-eled from the inside out into a dried stick.

It was a horrible sight and it occurred to Ari that aside from watching action vids with Jak, she had never seen anyone die before. Much less die in such a violent way.

*Kill-All,* she thought, looking up at Lathe, and wondered how close those fangs had been to her throat last night as she slept in his bunk. The very thought made her shiver.

The first words Lathe spoke after the attack were to her.

"You all right, little one?" he asked, looking down at Ari anxiously. His voice was slightly hoarse, probably from the slim black cord the attacker had used. "You fought bravely."

"I...I'm fine." Ari tried not to focus on his fangs, so long and sharp and gleaming in the glaring Mess Hall lights. "You...you did to. Fought bravely, I mean," she whispered, trying not to look at the dead man at their feet again, though her eyes kept wanting to be drawn back to the gruesome sight.

"I did what I had to do," Lathe said grimly. He raised his voice then, and addressed the whole Mess Hall.

"Hear me now, inmates of BleakHall," he roared, his deep voice echoing and reverberating against the high metal ceiling. "This male, Hexer, attacked me and he has paid the ultimate price—death."

There were murmurs from all sides again and chants of "Kill-All...Kill-All" until Lathe raised his hands for silence.

"Hexer is dead," he continued. "And I refuse to treat anyone from his gang, The Rabs, at the Infirmary until the leader comes to me and gives his word not to try and harm me or mine again."

He put an arm around Ari and though she wanted to shrink away from the big Kindred, she knew it would be a very bad visual for the rest of the prison. She had just been getting somewhat comfortable with Lathe, she thought, until she saw him kill.

Now she was scared of him all over again but she held herself rigidly still and didn't move as he publicly claimed her and placed her under his protection.

"Any male who comes after me or Ari, here, will get exactly what Hexer got," Lathe growled. "To die at the fangs of a Kill-All like myself is not an easy death—every nerve is on fire at the end. Think about that before any of you accepts an offer to kill me."

From the wide-eyed looks on the prisoner's faces, Lathe's words were hitting home. There was silence for a long moment after he finished speaking. Then he nodded at Ari and spoke in a normal tone of voice.

"Come on—we still have fifteen minutes. Enough time to eat First Meal if we hurry."

Stepping casually over the body of the man he'd killed, the big Kindred picked up his tray and kept moving down the line.

After a moment, Ari realized she had no choice but to do the same. But she could feel the eyes of every prisoner in the Mess Hall on her and Lathe as they moved.

Though she felt safer from the rest of the inmates, she felt more uncertain than ever about the big Kindred.

---

"That was quite a display you put on up there, Medic," Xolox burbled, waving his tentacles as Lathe and Ari seated themselves at table 13.

"It wasn't by choice," Lathe growled. The front of his neck was bleeding and his throat hurt from the sawing of the cut-cord—Hexer had been a strong little son-of-a-bitch, he would give the male that.

But it wasn't just his throat that hurt—his heart ached too. He had killed again. And worse, Hexer had been one of his patients—one that Lathe had worked closely with in the past.

*Fuck, how could he? I saved his arm after that accident with the link-saw in the work-house. And then he used the arm I saved to try to kill me.*

The huge muscular appendage had been nearly severed and Lathe had managed to reattach it—a feat he was well aware that not many physicians could have pulled off, especially considering the limited facilities BleakHall offered. He had monitored Hexer every day—even going to his cell to check on the little male and change his dressings. The day the bandages had come off, Hexer had given Lathe a hug and thanked him with tears in his eyes.

And now this.

*I wonder what Tapper paid him to try it,* Lathe wondered sourly. *A full pack of nico-sticks? A 3-D porn mag—what? What is my life worth in this fucking hellhole?*

Whatever it was, it had been enough to overcome any feelings of friendship or gratitude the little man had towards Lathe. Enough to make him try to kill him.

*It was a damn good thing Ari shouted when he did,* Lathe thought, stirring his blunt plasti-utensil idly through the re-structured protein mush which was what BleakHall served most mornings for First Meal. *If he hadn't warned me, I never would have gotten my hands up in time.*

But he hadn't thought he needed to worry about having Hexer in line behind him. He'd even felt a measure of safety knowing that his old patient was at his back as they moved through the chow line.

*How stupid I was,* Lathe thought angrily. *Tapper probably picked Hexer on purpose, knowing I would trust him—knowing I would be off my guard.*

But the truth was, he couldn't trust anybody anymore. This hellhole of a prison was filled with nothing but murderers and thugs—rapists and thieves and traitors. And liars, all of them liars.

"I hate liars," he muttered savagely, stirring his mush again.

"What's that you say, Medic?" Xolox burbled. Beside him, Gumper's green face showed a slow kind of sympathy.

"Hexer. You saved...his arm," he said simply.

"Yes." Lathe looked away. "I did."

"And he betrayed you," Xolox remarked mournfully. "Ah, there is no honor among thieves. Everywhere liars... betrayers...colluders..."

Drumph, his orange skin sagging in the overhead lights, his straw-like hair pasted to his head, tapped on his toy com-link and shouted, "Liars! Sad! No Collusion—Sad!"

"Oh!" Ari jumped, apparently startled by the sudden exclamation.

"Don't pay any attention to Drumph," Lathe told the boy, making an effort to get over the black mood the assassination attempt had brought on. "He's clinically insane—doesn't know what he's saying."

"I see." Ari edged a little further from Drumph's hunched figure and picked at his protein mush. "Do...do you feel all right?" he asked Lathe.

"Except for a sore throat, I'll be fine." He tried to keep his tone light but it wasn't easy. "Hurry and eat. After First Meal all new prisoners get their job assignments—we don't want to be late to the assignment line or who knows what you'll get."

"All right." But though the boy continued to pick at the yellow protein mush, he still seemed deeply troubled.

"Hey, it's all right," Lathe told him, seeing the look of fear in those big dark eyes again. "No one else will try anything for a while. You'll be safe now that everyone knows you're under my protection."

"Thank you," Ari murmured but his eyes darted away and wouldn't meet Lathe's. Was he really still so frightened?

*Suppose I'll have to give him some time,* Lathe told himself. Nearly getting murdered might be almost commonplace in Bleak-Hall but it was still a traumatic experience—especially for someone as innocent as Ari. Sighing, he went back to his own mush.

There was nothing else he could do.

# SIXTEEN

"Number 117—prizon laundry," the Horvath guard announced in his buzzing, guttural voice.

"Laundry?" Lathe protested, from his spot behind Ari, who was standing in a long row of new prisoners, most of whom had already gotten their work assignments. "I specifically requested him in the Infirmary. There are over a thousand prisoners at BleakHall and only one of me—I need an assistant."

"Mukluk sayzz you'll get an azziztant when you zztart treating *all* the prizonerz again," the guard told him. "He heard your announzement that you would no longer treat The Rabzz."

"That's a matter of self-defense," Lathe protested. "I have to have something to hold over the other inmates' heads or I'll be dead by sundown."

"Neverthelezz, Mukluk's word izz law. Take it up with him. Number 117—laundry," the guard remarked imperturbably.

Lathe gave a frustrated growl under his breath that made

the short hairs at the back of Ari's neck prickle. She kept thinking about those fangs right behind her—long and curving and filled with deadly poison. She didn't think the big Kindred would bite her but she hadn't even known him twenty-four solar hours yet. And any atrocity seemed horribly possible at BleakHall.

"Fine, but I need to see Ari—number 117—in the Infirmary before he starts his shift. I need to X-ray that cheek of his," Lathe said.

The guard appeared to think about it for a moment, then nodded.

"But not too long. A zzhort examinazion," he said.

"Fine. Come on, Ari," Lathe growled, jerking his head.

"Report to the Laundry when finizhed," the guard said to her and then she had no choice but to follow Lathe out of the Mess Hall and through the double doors that led towards the Infirmary.

---

"It's worse than I thought—you have an orbital fracture." Lathe couldn't keep the grimness out of his voice as he studied the digital picture generated by the X-ray scanner. The machine was supposed to be used only for making certain new prisoners weren't bringing in knives or blasters or any other metal weapons. But Lathe had learned to collimate its beam and adjust the intensity in order to take much smaller and more detailed radiographs for diagnostic purposes.

And he wasn't liking what he saw on the one he had taken of Ari one bit.

"What does that mean?" Ari was sitting on the battered exam

table, looking at him with that frightened uncertainty he'd had since the altercation in the Mess Hall.

*Right—altercation,* sneered a little voice in Lathe's head. *Call it what it is, why don't you, Lathe—an assassination attempt and a killing. A killing in self-defense but a killing nonetheless. The boy saw you kill Hexer and if you'd died, he would have been next. Of course he's still a little spooked.*

Lathe hated to give Ari such bad news after what he'd so recently endured but as a doctor, there was nothing else he could do.

"The bones in your eye socked are cracked," he said, as gently as he could. "What's more, it's the bones at the floor of your orbit that are most affected. You have what we call a trapdoor fracture."

"Meaning what? That the bones could give way and my eye will fall down into my cheek?" the boy scoffed, apparently trying to make light of the situation. Using sarcasm to deflect fear was a normal reaction that Lathe had seen often as a physician. Unfortunately, a trapdoor orbital fracture was nothing to make light of.

"It could fall down into your maxillary sinus, yes," he said seriously. "I'm afraid that's a real possibility."

"What?" Ari clutched at his bruised and swelling eye, his voice going high with fear. "But that's...that sounds really bad."

"I'm afraid it's not good." Lathe sighed and folded his arms across his chest. He wanted to take the boy in his arms and comfort him—which was a completely unprofessional impulse. Lathe restrained it—he sensed that Ari wouldn't be receptive to such comfort even if it had been proper.

"But what...what can you do? Some kind of surgery? Here?" Ari gestured expressively around the sparse confines of the prison infirmary. He had a point—BleakHall didn't even have things like tongue depressors or gauze—let alone expensive surgical instruments for delicate orbital surgery. Lathe considered himself lucky to have access to disinfectant and a rough suture kit.

"No, I couldn't do that kind of surgery here," he admitted. "But..." He hesitated, wondering how much to say. "But there *is* a way to heal you—to knit your bones together and make certain no further injury occurs," he said at last.

"How?" Ari demanded. "I don't want my eye to fall down inside my skull—what can you do?"

This was the tricky part. Lathe took a deep breath, trying to think how to explain.

"The inmates here call me 'Kill-All'," he told Ari. "But my own people have a different name for me. The call me 'Cure-All.'"

The boy shook his head.

"I don't understand."

"I have the power to cure as well as to kill within my fangs," Lathe told him. "Most Blood Kindred—which is the type of warrior I am—have only the ability to heal their mates with their bite. I am able to heal anyone, male or female, of almost any illness or injury. In this way I am unique."

But it was clear Ari hadn't heard a thing past the word, 'fangs.' His eyes were wide with fear and his entire slender body was tensed for flight.

"You...you want to bite me? The same way you bit that man in the Mess Hall?" His voice was so tight and high he almost sounded female.

"No, not like that at all," Lathe tried to reassure him. "I can control which kind of essence comes from my fangs—that which heals or that which kills. In the Mess Hall I had no choice—I *had* to kill."

"I...I can't..." Fear seemed to choke the boy to silence and Ari only shook his head, his hands fisted at his sides on the cracked and dirty plasti-cover of the exam table.

"Ari..." Lathe did his best to make his voice gentle and soothing. "Little one, I would never hurt you," he murmured, taking a step closer and putting one hand on the boy's thin, trembling shoulder.

"No!" At his touch, Ari was off the table and across the room like a shot. "No biting," he gasped, his back pressed against the wall, his eyes wide and wild with fear. "I don't want that—I don't want you to bite me!"

"All right...all right..." Lathe held up his hands in a gesture of peace. He wished he could go to the boy and reassure him but it was clear that Ari didn't trust him. Goddess damn it—he'd put his own life on the line to protect the lad—what else could he do to earn his trust?

*Maybe nothing,* whispered the little voice in his head. *After everything he went through yesterday, he may be beyond trust, at least for a little while. You have to be patient, Lathe.*

"I won't bite you," he said again, staying where he was though he wanted badly to go to the boy. "But you have to promise you'll tell me if you start having headaches or nausea or double vision. Also, if you notice any enophthalmos—meaning your eye sinking down into your socket," he said, seeing the look of incomprehension on the boy's face. "If you notice any of those symptoms come and tell me *immediately.*"

"Why, so you can bite me?" Ari demanded.

Lathe finally lost his patience.

"Would you rather lose your eye?" he growled.

"But that man—when you bit him...he...he..." Ari shook his head, apparently unable to continue. "You said that every nerve was on fire before the end," he whispered at last. "And the look of *agony* on his face..."

"It's true that I cannot give you pleasure with my healing bite since you're not a female," Lathe said roughly. "But I *can* heal your fracture. Think about it, Ari—have I offered you any harm since the moment you came to BleakHall?"

"No," the boy whispered but his gaze was on Lathe's fangs, not his eyes, and the look of fear on his face twisted Lathe's heart.

"Never mind," he said, turning away. "I've taken you into my cell and defended you with my life. I don't know what else I can do to earn your trust. If you want to lose your eye, be my guest."

"I'm sorry..." Ari's voice was paper-thin. "I just...I've never... your fangs look so...so *sharp*."

"Of course they're sharp—what would be the point of blunt fangs?" Lathe snapped. "Just know this, Ari—I can cure you now or even if your symptoms get worse. But if the floor of your orbit gives way entirely and you experience complete enophthalmos, then it's too late—there's not a damn thing I can do at that point."

Which was what made him so angry, he tried to tell himself. Ari was just another patient refusing treatment that would do him good—that would save him permanent injury and pain. It would frustrate any physician in Lathe's place to have a patient willfully refuse healing that could save them. That was why he was being so harsh—so abrupt.

But the fearful look on the boy's face was like a slap to his own and he knew it wasn't true.

As he and Ari stood staring at each other across the room,

there was a knock at the Infirmary door and a cracked and cheery voice cried, "Well now, Medic, it's old Wheezer—may I come in?"

"Come," Lathe said brusquely. He didn't know why he was allowing Ari's fear to get to him this way. *The boy has a right to be frightened of my fangs after seeing Hexer die of my bite,* he told himself. *And anyway, I only met him yesterday—why should I care what he thinks of me?*

But he couldn't deny that the lad's distrust wounded him to the core. Which made him angry and terse. When Wheezer stepped through the door, he didn't even try to muster a smile for the old inmate.

"Well, well, seems the two of you must be finished with the exam?" Wheezer asked uncertainty, looking from one to the other of them. "If you are, old Wheezer is here to show the lad to the laundry. For it's my work assignment too, so it is," he said to Ari, who was still pressed against the far wall looking white and shaken. "And I thought you might like me to keep an eye on the lad," he added to Lathe.

"Do as you like," Lathe growled. "Ari is finished with his exam. He can go to work."

"Very well, Medic." Wheezer coughed. "And I thought you might like to know, the word is spreading about Hexer, yes it is. Already the Grand *Jiho* of the Serpents has renounced his claim on Ari's life and the rest of the gang leaders are said to be telling their members they'll be risking their own lives if they try to take yours or the lad's. Nobody wants to lose their access to the Infirmary, no they don't."

"That's good to hear." Despite his irritation at the lad, Lathe felt a loosening around his heart. At least he could be fairly certain that Ari was safe when he was away from his side. Well, except for... "What about Tapper and his gang?" he asked Wheezer.

"Ah, well...there's the rub, so it is." Wheezer took off his cracked oculars and polished them on the sleeve of his neatly pressed prison uniform. "Tapper's still out for blood. But I think as long as you and the lad stay clear of his territory, you should be all right—for a time."

Lathe knew what he meant—doubtless Tapper would try again. But probably not for a while. He would want Lathe to be off his guard.

*Which isn't going to happen,* Lathe told himself.

"For a time," he echoed, agreeing with Wheezer. "Well, the two of you had better go before the Horvaths come looking."

"As you say, Medic." Wheezer bobbed his gray head and nodded at Ari. "Come lad—it's none so bad a job. Course, 'twould be better if the main clothes-press wasn't broken but we make do...we make do."

Ari nodded but didn't move. Instead he stood there staring at Lathe. His large, dark eyes seemed full of some emotion he couldn't communicate. Maybe something he wanted to say?

"Well, what are you waiting for?" Lathe asked irritably. "Go. You don't want to get on the wrong end of a Horvath's pain-prod."

"Yes, Lathe. I...I'll see you later." With one last, white-faced look, Ari slipped past him and followed Wheezer out of the Infirmary.

# SEVENTEEN

"No, the Laundry isn't nearly the worst place to work in BleakHall," Wheezer said as he took Ari down the long metal hallway that led deeper into the bowels of the prison.

"It's not?" Ari asked, though to be honest she was just talking to get her mind off what had happened with Lathe.

*He wants to bite me—to **bite** me,* whispered a panicked little voice in her brain. She couldn't get the image of the inmate who had jumped Lathe in the Mess Hall out of her mind—the bowed back... the face a rictus of agony...the thin black foam seeping from between his clenched teeth as his body shriveled to a dry stick...

*But he said his bite doesn't always kill—he claims to heal with it too. Could that be true? Well, why would he lie? It's not like he **enjoys** killing.*

Ari was fairly certain that was true. She'd seen the look on the big Kindred's face as they sat at the table, eating breakfast, after that scary, blank expression had passed. Though he'd been doing his best to look stoic and calm, she'd been able to read the emotion in those vivid turquoise eyes—killing the other inmate had bothered him—bothered him a lot.

So if he didn't want to kill her, did it mean he really *did* want to heal her? But even if that was true, could she stand to have those long, shining fangs driven into her face, right by her eye?

Ari assumed that would be where he'd have to bite—the place where she was hurt. She'd never been a big fan of injections or needles and the idea of allowing the big Kindred to sink his deadly fangs into her flesh was frightening.

Still...if the alternative was having her eye fall out...

She reached up gingerly and patted around the base of her swollen left eye. Could he have been reading the X-ray wrong? Was she really in that much danger? She wasn't having any of the symptoms he'd warned about but what if she started having double vision or getting blinding headaches or—the Goddess of Mercy forbid—what if her eye started sinking into its socket? What if—

"No indeed, Laundry's not nearly the worse job in the joint," Wheezer said cheerfully, interrupting her frantic thoughts.

"Oh?" Ari said, trying to drag her mind away from the morbid topic of possibly losing her eye. "What...what is the worst job then?"

"Oh shower cleaner's no fun. Lots of dirtiness and filth because so many of the inmates use the shower as their pleasure center-like," the old man said matter-of-factly. He made a fist with one hand and jerked it back and forth near his groin to illustrate his point. "And pot cleaner's no fun either," he continued as Ari felt her face get red. "Nor is latrine cleaner—that's for those as

have to use the communal toilets because they aren't trustees." He
flicked a speck of imaginary dust off the sleeve of his green and
blue striped trustee uniform with elaborate care. "But the very
worst job has got to be muck-raker—so it has."

"Muck-raker?" Ari shook her head. "Do I even want to know
what that is?"

"It's a punishment assignment, so it is and no mistake."
Wheezer nodded knowingly. "It's for when one of the toilets gets
clogged up. You have to go down into the overflow yard where the
pipes pour out their filth and get it unclogged. Like being in a big
metal cage full of shit, so it is. No fun, that!"

"No, it...doesn't sound like it," Ari said faintly. "So what do
we do in the Laundry?"

"Oh, I'll show you, my lad. You'll see...you'll learn..."

Laundry duty might not be the worst prison job but it certainly
wasn't the easiest either, Ari reflected after several back-breaking
hours of labor. The huge industrial laundry room was in the bowls
of the prison. It had seven huge washers but only three dryers.
The constant heat the machinery generated meant that the metal
walls were always sweating with condensation and the humidity
had Ari's prison jumpsuit sticking between her shoulder blades
inside of fifteen minutes.

The most laborious step in the process came between taking
the clothes from the washers and feeding them into one of the
huge industrial dryers. Since the material was soaking wet, it had
to be wrung out or pressed before it could safely go into a dryer.

"Or it could cause a short and fry us all! So it could, so it
could," Wheezer told her, cackling merrily at the thought.

In order to get the excess moisture out, the sodden jumpsuits were fed into several small clothes presses—none of which could do more than a single jumpsuit at a time. The suits had to be fed in, one by one, and then hand-cracked through the press in a process that wrung out the water before they were thrown into a rolling bin of uniforms ready for the dryer.

It was a backbreaking process that had Ari's arms aching in no time since, as a newbie inmate, she was of course assigned the most difficult job. The inmates with more seniority loaded the washers and dryers or took turns on folding duty while Wheezer, as a trustee, only had to supervise.

"Why don't they have a bigger clothes press?" Ari asked after what felt like hours of cranking wet, sodden garments through one of the hand-operated presses. "Something that can do more than one uniform at a time?"

"Oh, we do—we do." He nodded vigorously, the dim overhead lights winking off his cracked oculars. "It's just over there."

He pointed to a huge drum-like machine in the corner of the laundry, to one side of the row of washers.

"But it's broken, so it is. Stopped working more than a cycle ago and none of the lads who tried have had any luck fixing it. And of course the Yonnite Mistresses who own BleakHall ain't going to buy us a new one—no they 'ent! Why, what do they care if our arms break off cranking those presses?"

Ari wanted to point out that it was *her* arms about to break off—Wheezer did nothing but go around the room gossiping as far as she could see. His tongue was the only part of him that got any exercise.

But she was wise enough to hold her own tongue this time, remembering how her remarks to Tapper the day before had only made her situation worse. Maybe BleakHall was teaching her something about discretion—if so, it was certainly a hard way to learn that particular lesson.

"Can I have a look at the big press?" she asked Wheezer. "Maybe I can fix it."

"Oh, handy with a tool-belt, are you, lad?" He gave her an interested look. "Sure, you can try, I suppose. But I'm afraid I mislike your chances, so I do. As I said, lots of lads had a crack at it back when it first broke and none could get it going again."

"Let me just try," Ari said. She'd always been handy with mechanical things and even if she couldn't fix the beast of a machine sitting in the corner gathering dust, at least poking around in its works was better than this eternal cranking.

"Just as you please." Wheezer nodded at her genially. "But if you need some tools, I'll have to sign them out for you. Can't have wrenches and hammers and the like just lying around in a Triple Max pen, don't you know."

"I guess not," Ari said. "Well, let me see what I can see."

She found the latch to open the side of the machine and began poking around inside. Wheezer helpfully held a glowstick over her head so she could see what she was doing. It took a little digging, but before long Ari found the problem.

*They must not have very mechanically-minded inmates here,* she thought. *It's nothing but a slipped belt!*

Possibly none of the men who had tried to fix the machine had even seen the problem, though. It was far back in a corner behind the engine cover and Ari doubted any of their big hands would fit in such a tiny area.

She got her own hands black to the elbows with grease getting the belt back in place but it was worth it the moment she flipped the switch and watched the machine begin to chug.

"Well, I'm a nunky's uncle, so I am!" Wheezer cried. "That's a good job you did, lad. You're a fix-it, so you are! A fix-it! I'll be sure to tell Mukluk."

"Um, all right. Thank you, I guess," Ari said uncertainly. The other inmates gathered around to pat her on the back and the second load of jumpsuits they'd put in the washers was done in no time.

After her achievement, Ari was allowed to stand by Wheezer and talk instead of feeding the wet clothes into the machine she'd fixed. Since the old man seemed to know all about the prison and its inmates, she decided it was a good time to pick his brains.

"Wheezer," she said as he watched the industrial-sized press at work. "Do you know of an inmate called Jak? Jak Blackthorn?"

"Heh?" Wheezer frowned at her. "Blackthorn?"

"He's about a head taller than me," Ari said. "Black hair and blue eyes—a shade lighter than mine. He's in his twenties."

"Oh, young fella with a little scar on the bridge of his nose just here?" Wheezer pointed to his own face to demonstrate and Ari nodded eagerly. Jak had gotten that scar playing tuk-ball with their father when he was just a kid and it had never really faded.

"Yes, that's him! Do you know where he is? I've been looking for him in the Mess Hall but I haven't seen him."

"Were you in lock-up with him somewhere else?" Wheezer asked.

"Yes, exactly. Do you know where he is?"

"Well, now—I haven't seen him in some time but we *are* on different floors. Last I heard he was assigned to the prison garden and that's clear across the complex, so it is."

"So you *did* see him? He *is* here?" Ari pressed, feeling her heart swell. The fact that she had yet to see her older brother had been gnawing at her mind. What if the information she'd been given was inaccurate? What if Jak was somewhere in another prison or even with another Mistress or something awful like that? But Wheezer's words gave her hope.

"Yes, lad, of course. I don't know exactly where he is but mayhap I can find out for you. Yes, mayhap I can." The little old man nodded and smiled genially.

"Oh thank you, Wheezer!" For a moment, Ari almost threw her arms around him and hugged him. But she realized at the last minute this would be a girlish thing to do. And what if Wheezer felt her breasts when she pressed against him? Ugh—that would be too awkward and would cause all kinds of questions! She contented herself with grinning broadly at the old man and thanking him again.

"You're more than welcome, so you are," Wheezer said, smiling at her enthusiasm. "And mayhap you'll find 'im yourself in the yard after lunch. Meal times are staggered but we all go out for yard time at the same time here at BleakHall." He lowered his voice, though there were no guards around. "The Gods-damned Horvaths don't like the outside air so they refuse to go out more than once a day."

Ari's heart soared even higher. Today after lunch, she would be certain to find Jak in the exercise yard. They would escape in her bubble and go directly home to Phobos.

*We'll be safe,* she told herself. *And we'll never come back here and I won't have to worry about whether I should let Lathe bite me or not because I can go see an eye surgeon on Phobos and get my orbital fracture fixed there.*

The thought of leaving the big Kindred gave her pause and she found herself wondering what would happen to him when she was gone. Would he be upset to see her leave? Would he miss her?

Ari tried to put the thought out of her mind. Lathe could take care of himself, couldn't he? And after all, the transport bubble was only good for two moderately sized people. It could never carry three-especially if one of them was as huge and muscular as Lathe.

Still, the thought of abandoning the big Kindred bothered her and wouldn't leave her mind. The look on his face when she'd refused to let him bite her kept returning to her mind's eye and Ari felt a little of her joy at her impending escape leak away, like air let out of a pinhole in a balloon.

# EIGHTEEN

L unch, or Mid-Meal, as Lathe called it, was a silent affair.
Silent between Ari and Lathe, that was. Xolox the
Sporran kept up a constant stream of burbling conversation with
Gumper who answered back in slow monosyllables while
Drumph punctuated the meal with shouts of, "Sad!" and tapped
on his toy device as they all ate the dreadful slop the mechanical
arms had glopped on their trays. But the big Kindred scarcely said
a word to her.

Ari wondered if he was mad at her for not letting him bite
her. But he wasn't glaring or acting cold to her in any way. He just
seemed withdrawn—inside himself somehow. As though he had
some secret sorrow he couldn't share.

It made her wish she could bring him out...could find out
what was wrong and why he was so quiet. Then she realized what
she was thinking.

*What's wrong with you, Ari? Are you starting to have some*

*kind of feelings for him?* she asked herself angrily. *When you're about to leave this place and you still don't even know his true intentions? Not to mention the fact that everyone—including Lathe—thinks you're a guy which is the way it **has** to stay. Stop being an idiot and forget about him.*

But somehow she couldn't.

When lunch was over, Mukluk blew a shrill note on a whistle he wore on a silk cord around his scaly neck and the prisoners all trooped out into the Rec Yard.

Ari looked eagerly for Jak, but she didn't see her older brother. Several of the prison gangs had formed into teams and were playing some kind of simple game that appeared to involve two hoops and a ball and some other inmates appeared to be gambling in one of the corners. At the far end of the yard she saw a large collection of what appeared to be homemade weights—long metal poles with iron-brick blocks loaded on the ends of them. Inmates of all gang affiliations were working out here—it must be a kind of neutral zone.

Among the prisoners working out was Lathe.

Ari tried not to look but she couldn't help herself—somehow her eyes were drawn to the big Kindred. He was lying on his back on a rough wooden bench and he was stripped to the waist, the top part of his prison jumpsuit pulled down and the arms tied around his narrow hips. This left his muscular chest and arms bare and she could see his pecs and biceps flex with each smooth lift as he pressed a bar full of heavy weights over his head.

*Goddess, how strong is he, anyway? Those bricks have to weigh five times as much as me,* Ari thought. Then she reminded herself she was supposed to be looking for her brother and forced herself to glance away.

The best way to find Jak, she decided, was to wander slowly around the perimeter of the Rec Yard, being careful to avoid obvious gang territories and steer clear of Tapper and his men. When she saw her brother, she would rush over to him and grab his arm with one hand while she activated her transport bubble with the other. They would be floating free of this horrible place before she knew it.

Trying to appear casual, Ari started wandering around the yard, keeping a sharp lookout for both her brother and trouble. She knew what to expect out here from her previous study of BleakHall's blueprints, having called up every plan and layout possible on the big prison as she made her own plans for rescuing Jak. She knew the exact dimensions of the yard and more importantly, she knew what it lacked.

Unlike most maximum security prisons, there were no watchtowers in the corners of this yard. The Horvaths who ran Bleak-Hall were indoor creatures with a dread of wide open, outdoor spaces. Being outside affected all but the hardiest of them the same way being in a tight, locked space affected Ari. They hated it.

So instead of watchtowers where armed guards could watch for escape attempts and shoot the would-be escapees, the entire vast, fifty-foot wall of the Rec Yard was covered in electrified and barbed razor wire. To attempt to climb it was death by electrification or at the very least, the loss of your fingers and toes and any other body parts that came in contact with the micro-thin edged wire.

But Ari didn't need to climb the wall or even get anywhere near it. All she needed was a clear blue sky and her brother within touching distance so she could activate the transport bubble. As long as there were no guard towers with guards using projectile weapons that could burst the fragile bubble, there was nothing to stop her.

*Well, the sky is good, anyway,* she thought, looking up at the steely gray cloud cover overhead. It might not be blue but it was certainly wide open. Freedom was so close she could almost *taste* it.

As she was looking up, she saw a bird overhead diving towards the Rec Yard. Glancing to see what it was aiming for, she saw that a massive prisoner was holding up a crust of bread he'd apparently saved from his meal.

"Here, boy," he called coaxingly and whistled. "Here boy, come on down, why don't you?"

*That's nice, I guess,* Ari thought uncertainly. She wondered if the prisoner was trying to make friends with the bird out of loneliness. Or maybe he had tamed it to carry messages for him? Either way it was kind of heartwarming to think that even the hardened felons that populated BleakHall could have tender feelings for an animal.

But just as the thought entered her mind, the bird dived down into the Rec Yard...or tried to anyway. The moment it got level with the top of the wall—which was about fifty feet above their heads—there was a flash like lightning and the bird made a horrible, strangled squawking sound. It seemed to catch on fire for an instant, then it fell, smoking to the feet of the huge prisoner who had a big smile on his lumpish face.

Ari was shocked but the inmate who had called to the bird didn't seem upset or surprised at all.

"Ah, fresh meat," he growled hungrily. Stuffing the crust he'd used as a lure into his pocket, he began ripping charred feathers out of the dead bird before taking a huge bite out of its still-smoking flesh.

"He got another one, so he did. That's Wayboid for you—allus hungry," came Wheezer's familiar voice in her ear.

Ari still didn't understand what was going on.

"What happened?" she asked, trying not to watch how the huge convict Wheezer had called "Wayboid" was tearing into the charred bird flesh. "How did he know the bird was going to be hit by lightning?"

A small part of her brain tried to tell her she was missing something here—some vital information—but she didn't want to hear it.

"Hit by lightning?" Wheezer broke out into a gasping laugh. "Why bless me, lad—that warn't no lightning—no it twarn't!"

"What was it then?" Ari demanded. "I saw what happened to that poor bird—it looked like it was electrified and then it caught on fire. What else could cause that but lightning?"

"Why, the invisi-laser ceiling the Yonnite Mistresses had installed last solar month, that's what," Wheezer exclaimed.

"What? Why?" Ari looked up into the seemingly-clear sky, her mind churning in panic as she tried to process this new development.

"Oh, there was some concern over a high-risk prisoner—a real animal he is—that was comin' in from Priux Prime. The more dangerous the prisoner, the more the Yonnites get paid for keepin' 'im, you understand. But the Priux Prime Minister refused to send 'im unless there was absolutely no likelihood of him ever escaping." He snorted laughter. "As if anything—man or beast—could go up fifty feet of electrified razor wire. Still, to keep the

Priuxs happy, the Mistresses installed the laser ceiling. And Wayboid's been getting a bit of extra protein ever since."

"Do..." Ari's lips were so dry she had to lick them twice before she could go on. "Do the lasers extend over the entire Rec Yard? Or is it just a...a few beams here and there?"

"Well, I don't know the exact measurements of the damn thing but I do know it's called a 'ceiling' for a reason, so I do," Wheezer remarked. "I heard the Yonnite Mistresses talking when they met here for council right before it was put in place. It's meant to cover the entire rec-yard, as I understand it, and run a few meters out on the sides for good measure."

"Oh..." Ari whispered. The panic inside her had turned to dread—dread as cold and heavy as a lead weight in her stomach. The transport balloon she'd paid so much for was structurally strong but vulnerable to projectile weapons and beams. In other words, if she and Jak tried to escape in it, they'd be fried and burned exactly like the hapless bird she'd seen lured down by the huge inmate.

*Goddess of Mercy—how are we ever going to get out of here now?* she thought, feeling sick. *And where is Jak anyway? I have to see him...have to tell him...*

"But watchin' Wayboid eat birds isn't why I came to find you," Wheezer said, breaking her desperate train of thought. "I told old Mukluk that you're a fixit and he was real pleased, so he was. We've been needing another fixit around here for some time."

"Oh, thank you," Ari said vaguely, hardly knowing what she was saying.

"And I found that Blackthorn fella that you were looking for," Wheezer went on.

"What?" Ari rounded on him, her heart in her throat. "Where is he? I don't see him out here in the yard anywhere."

"That's because he ain't in the yard." Wheezer looked suddenly grave. "I'm afraid he's in the hole, Ari-lad. And according to what I heard, that's where he's bound to stay for a time yet."

"The hole?" Ari asked. "What's that?"

Wheezer shook his head and chuckled.

"You really *are* green, aren't you lad? The hole is solitary—way down in the dungeons-like. They stick you down there on nothin' but protein paste and water and you don't never seen sunlight. Cramped up in a tiny cell—smaller than ours even—in the dark with no light or companionship. It ain't much fun, I can tell you that!"

Ari was horrified.

"So he's locked up in the dark with hardly anything to eat and nobody to talk to?" she exclaimed. "How can anyone survive like that—it would drive you crazy!"

"Most often it does," Wheezer said seriously. "The good news is, though, that this friend of yours has only been in the hole five or six solar months." He frowned. "I *knew* there was a reason I hadn't seen him around lately."

"Five or six months!" Ari cried. "That would feel like an eternity with no light or anyone to talk to! That's...that's cruel and unusual punishment!"

Wheezer shrugged. "That's Yonnite Mistresses for you. Sorry, lad."

"But...when can I go see him?" Ari asked. She looked around wildly, wondering if she could go right now. She would probably get into trouble if she snuck out of the yard early but—

"Oh, you can't see him, I'm afraid." Wheezer shook his head, his cracked glasses winking in the weak sunlight. "Nobody's allowed down in the hole but the prisoners stuck down there and the guards. You get caught down there without having some official business or a damn good reason to be there and you'll likely be thrown in the hole yourself. Worse luck for you."

"So...Jak's *stuck* down there and I can't even *see* him?" Ari demanded.

"I'm sorry, lad." Wheezer patted her shoulder awkwardly. "You were that close, were you?"

"I..." Ari shook her head. She couldn't answer, couldn't even begin to form words. The pain and disappointment and panic were still too raw—too fresh and new to process. Shaking her head again, she wandered away from Wheezer in a daze.

*Jak's down there—down in the hole and I can't get him out—can't even see him. And even if he was out in the general population again, there's no way I can save him or myself. I'm trapped—stuck here in BleakHall and there's no getting out.*

The thoughts ran over and over in her mind—an endless loop of fear and pain and despair as she wandered aimlessly in the vast Rec Yard. She didn't even realize that tears were dripping down her cheeks until a deep, familiar voice said,

"Ari? What are you doing? Don't you know it's dangerous to be out here?"

---

Though Lathe told himself he didn't care what Ari did or where he went, he couldn't stop himself from keeping an eye on the boy, even when he was supposed to be working out. The yard could be a dangerous place if you wandered into the wrong territory and Ari had already proven he was good at that.

In the meantime, Lathe had a lot of frustration to work out and exercise was a damn good way to do that. He pumped the heavy steel-bricks with a single-minded purpose, trying to purge himself of the unwanted emotions that rose inside him like dark currents in the waters of his psyche.

It didn't matter what Ari thought of him or his fangs, he told himself as he pumped, lifting the heavy weights over his head as the wooden bench strained beneath him. It didn't matter if the boy refused to be healed. There was always the chance that the orbital fracture would heal on its own once the swelling went down. But he didn't have a lot of hope for that—a trapdoor fracture was nothing to fool around with and—

Lathe became suddenly aware that Ari was out of his line of sight—the boy must have wandered off while he was preoccupied with pumping.

With a grunt of effort, he came up, still holding the bar full of heavy weights, and deposited them carefully on the ground in front of the bench. He never used a spotter because no one else at BleakHall could lift as much as he could. Like every other aspect of his prison life, Lathe was alone when it came to working out.

*Alone until Ari came along,* whispered a little voice in his head. But where was the boy? If Tapper was anywhere near him...

Then he saw Ari, wandering out in the middle of the yard where he wasn't supposed to go. The prisoners were supposed to keep to the perimeter for the most part, leaving the interior of the vast rectangular yard free for the guards to keep an eye on them.

Of course, that was how it worked in a regular prison staffed with humanoid guards. Since the Horvaths hated the outside so much, it would probably take them some time to come out into the middle of the yard. But once they did, Ari would be in for a world of hurt. Any of the lizard-guard forced to come out under the open sky to retrieve a prisoner was going to be short on patience and generous with his pain-prod.

"Ari?" Lathe jogged over to the boy, whose back was to him. "What are you doing?" Lathe demanded. "Don't you know it's dangerous to be out here?"

Still the boy didn't answer.

"Ari!" Fed up with the silent treatment, Lathe took him roughly by the shoulder and spun him around.

What he saw shocked and worried him.

Ari was crying. Not outright sobbing, thank the Goddess, but his large, dark eyes were filled with tears that were rolling silently down his flushed cheeks. He looked utterly miserable...and utterly vulnerable.

"Gods," Lathe muttered harshly, looking around to see if anyone had noticed the boy's state. Tears were dangerous at BleakHall—they were an obvious, outward sign of weakness. Crying anywhere—especially in the yard where everyone in the whole damn prison could see—was like hanging a "fuck me up and rape me" sign around your neck.

"Ari, you have to stop," he told the boy urgently. "I don't know what started you off but you can't cry in the fucking yard. It's *dangerous.*"

The boy looked up at him, his face full of so much sorrow and misery that Lathe's heart ached for him. He understood suddenly that the boy *couldn't* stop. He was in the middle of an emotional upheaval as unstoppable as any physical urge. In fact, it might only be a matter of time before things got worse—a whole hell of a lot worse.

"Here..." Lathe put an arm around the boy's shoulders and for once Ari didn't pull away. "Come on," Lathe muttered, leading him away from the middle of the rectangular field, overgrown with stubby gray vegetation. "Come on—over here."

He led the boy to the far corner of the yard which was currently unoccupied, hiding Ari's face with his arm as much as possible. He took a look behind him and saw that Wheezer was watching with a sharp eye but no one else seemed to have noticed. Making a sign to the old trustee, he raised his eyebrows.

Wheezer nodded back and hooked a thumb towards his cracked oculars.

"*I'll watch your back,*" the gesture said. Good.

Lathe nodded and then turned back to Ari. When he was certain the boy's slender frame was completely sheltered by his own broad back and that no one could see Ari's face, he tilted the boy's chin up and looked into his tear-filled eyes.

"What is it?" he asked softly. "What happened, Ari? Can you talk about it?"

The large eyes overflowed and the boy shook his head mutely. Clearly whatever the pain was, it went too deep for words.

Lathe felt his heart twist at the boy's mute misery. What was it about Ari that affected him so deeply? Why couldn't he stop feeling for the boy?

"All right then," he said roughly. "If you can't talk, that's all right. Just let it out but try to keep quiet if you can. It really isn't safe to cry in the yard."

Then he did what he'd been wanting to do from the first

moment he saw the boy. Putting his arms around the slender shoulders, he drew Ari close and held him.

At first Ari felt stiff in his arms—a block of wood. But then he seemed to melt against Lathe. Burying his face in Lathe's chest, he began to sob—a low, heartbroken sound that seemed to tear at Lathe's own heart.

"All right, little one," he murmured soothingly. "I don't know what it is but it's going to be all right. I swear it." Gently he rubbed Ari's back and trembling shoulders, noticing that the boy felt a lot softer in his arms than he looked on the outside. But maybe it was just the material of his jumpsuit bunching against his chest—it really *was* too big for him.

*This whole place is too big for him,* Lathe thought ruefully. *He shouldn't be here. I don't know what crime he committed but whatever it was, there was no call to send such an innocent to BleakHall.*

Ari's face was hot and wet against his chest but the boy managed to keep his crying to low, choked sobs that hopefully weren't audible to anyone wandering by to see what they were doing in the corner.

Of course, Lathe knew what he *hoped* the other prisoners thought they were doing. This far corner of the Rec Yard was usually reserved for casual sexual encounters between inmates who couldn't see each other anyplace else. If the other inmates saw him and Ari locked together in an embrace, they would hopefully think they were doing what was usually done in this corner —the "fuck and suck corner"—as it was called.

Lathe thought dryly that if, at any other time in his life, he'd had the idea that people thought he was having a romantic encounter with another male, he would have been concerned that he was giving the wrong impression. Now he *hoped* he was giving the wrong impression. It would be much safer for Ari if he was.

At last the boy's sobs trailed off into sniffles and he looked up at Lathe.

"I'm sorry," he said thickly. "I didn't...didn't mean to cry all over you."

"Crying all over me isn't the problem," Lathe told him. "It's crying where anyone can see you that makes you look weak and could get you killed. Hopefully nobody noticed before I got to you. Here..."

Seeing that Ari's eyes were still wet, he unknotted the sleeves of his jumpsuit, which he'd tied around his waist so he wouldn't sweat through the striped material when he worked out, and used one sleeve to dab gently at the boy's swollen eyes.

"Thank you," Ari whispered, his voice still rough with tears. "Why are you so good to me?" he asked. "Even after I refused to let you bite me?"

"I didn't want to bite you for my own pleasure," Lathe said, though to be honest, his fangs were throbbing at the thought—throbbing in the way they only did when a Blood Kindred wanted to bite and bond a female to him. Telling himself his body was simply reacting to Ari's sweet female scent, he added, "I wanted to bite you to heal you. That's all, little one."

"It doesn't matter anymore—nothing matters." There was a calm despair in Ari's dark eyes as he spoke. "Anyway, I *want* you to bite me, now."

"You do?" Lathe frowned, confused by the boy's sudden change of heart. "Now you've decided you trust me and you want to be healed?"

"No." Ari shook his head. "I don't want you to heal me—I

want you to bite me like you bit that man, Hexer, in the Mess Hall this morning. I want you to bite me so I can *die.*"

"What are you talking about?" This sudden suicidal bent worried Lathe even more than the boy's tears. "You *can't* be serious," he exclaimed, searching the boy's eyes with his own.

"I want you to bite me," Ari repeated stubbornly and his eyes filled again. "I'll never see Jak again and it's the only way...the only way I'll ever be free of this place," he choked. "The only way."

Lathe didn't know who Jak was—it was the same name Ari had called out the night before in his sleep—but he knew despair when he saw it.

"Come here, little one," he rumbled, pulling the boy to him again. "Whatever is going on, I swear it's not as bad as that. We'll get through it together, you'll see."

Ari made no answer but his shoulders shook miserably and it was a long time before he could regain control of himself again.

Lathe held him close and found himself sending up a silent prayer.

*Goddess, I don't know his pain but let me help Ari. Let me ease this misery and despair and bring him new hope. And help me to keep him and myself safe in this pit of vipers. Please...*

He heard no answer, though it was not unheard of for the Goddess to speak to her people. But he felt a sense of peace stealing over him and he stroked Ari's tangled black almost-curls and rubbed the shaking shoulders until the boy's sobs at last quieted again and he pressed silently against Lathe's chest and was still.

# NINETEEN

A ri really wanted to die.

She knew it might sound to an outsider like her death wish was giving up but really, what choice did she have? It was either die now or a week from now, when the power source on her look/touch holo projector ran out. She remembered Lathe's words to her that morning:

*"If a female walked into BleakHall she'd be raped to death inside of fifteen minutes...most of the inmates here are misogynists who hate females."*

Ari felt a shiver run through her. *I'd rather die quickly than wait for that kind of fate,* she told herself. And if letting Lathe bite her was the only way to kill herself, well, then she would do it.

*I'll ask him again tonight, when it's lights out,* she told herself as she went through the rest of her day—more work in the prison laundry and then a hideous, barely-edible supper in the Mess Hall. She couldn't imagine living like this, day after day, anyway.

The sheer monotony of it would kill her. And if there was no way to see Jak and no way to get out, it was better to die now with her secret still intact.

She waited until she'd taken a cat-bath in the sink and gotten into a fresh jumpsuit for sleeping, (one benefit of working in the laundry was access to plenty of fresh clothes), before she approached the big Kindred again.

Lathe had also washed up in the small sink and he was sitting on the edge of the bunk wearing a pair of dark blue sleep trousers —as a trustee he had access to pajamas which the other prisoners were not allowed to wear. His reddish-brown hair was slicked back from his high forehead with water and his turquoise eyes were thoughtful as Ari approached him.

"Why aren't you dressed for bed?" he asked, motioning to her jumpsuit. "You work in the laundry—didn't you get yourself sleep clothes?"

"I, uh, thought they were only for trustees," Ari faltered.

He shrugged, his broad, bare shoulders rolling.

"Mostly they are but I'm sure Wheezer would turn a blind eye if you took a pair for yourself. Be a hell of a lot more comfortable than sleeping in one of those damn jumpsuits."

"You slept in one last night," Ari pointed out.

He nodded. "Because I didn't want to scare you by taking off my clothes. You were already jumpy enough as it was without me adding to your fear." He raised an eyebrow. "But seeing that we know each other a little better now, I'd rather be comfortable—if you don't mind."

"No, it...it's fine with me." Ari bit her lip, her eyes roving over his broad bare chest, thinking of how it had felt against her face when he held her close that afternoon in the Rec Yard. The hard muscle of his pecs... the heat of his big body...the rough scratch of his chest hair against her cheek...the warm, masculine scent of him...God, he smelled so *good*—why was that?

*Stop it*, she told herself angrily. *Why are you thinking about that now? You're about to ask him to kill you! You can't seriously be getting turned on right now. That's ridiculous!*

"Here—you can wear the top to my sleep set," Lathe said, breaking her train of thought. Picking up a dark blue shirt so big Ari could probably wear it for a dress, he tossed it to her.

She caught it reflexively. "No really—I'll be fine in my jump-suit," she protested.

"But I won't," Lathe said firmly. "The fabric they make those things out of is damn rough. If you're going to be rubbing against me every time one of us turns over at night I'd just as soon not feel like I'm getting scratched by sandpaper."

Ari started to protest and then thought, *what does it matter? I'm going to die tonight anyway. It would be nice to be wearing something slightly more comfortable when I do.*

"All right," she said and took the top back into the tiny bathroom to change. It felt funny not to have anything covering her legs but, as she had guessed, the garment was so big it fell to her mid thighs. She'd worn skirts shorter than this when she dressed up back home on Phobos, so it ought to be okay she told herself.

*Of course when you dressed like that back home you weren't planning on getting into bed with a huge, muscular man,* whispered a little voice in her head.

*Shut up,* Ari told it. *I'm getting into bed to **die.** It doesn't matter that he's big and warm and muscular—I'm going to ask him to kill me. So it really doesn't matter how I'm dressed, now does it?*

"You know, your modesty is commendable but you don't

always have to change in the fresher," Lathe remarked when she finally came out, her neatly folded jumpsuit in her arms. "I won't watch you change if you promise not to watch me."

*Don't know if you can make that promise, Ari,* whispered the teasing little voice in her head. Ari did her best to ignore it.

"Oh, I...we're very modest on Phobos," she said weakly. Looking down at herself she motioned to her bare legs. "Won't I be cold? Didn't you say they drop the temperature every night for the lashers?"

"They do." He nodded. "But you'll be in the bunk with me, remember? And I put out enough heat for both of us—as a Blood Kindred, I have a self-regulating body temperature."

"Oh, right... Okay, then. Do..." She cleared her throat. "Do you mind if I take the outside of the bunk this time? I'm claustrophobic and when I woke up this morning I felt kind of...trapped."

"Oh of course—I'm sorry." Lathe looked remorseful. "I didn't think about that last night when I brought you to bed. I just wanted to get you warm."

"That's very kind of you." Ari took another hesitant step towards the bed. "So should we—" Just then the lights flickered in warning and then the entire cell went dark except for the soft, barely-there glow in the corner. There was a shushing sound through the overhead vents and suddenly a gust of freezing air swept through the room.

"Oh my G-goddess that's c-cold!" Ari exclaimed through chattering teeth.

"Time for bed." Lathe's deep voice rumbled in the darkness. She could hear a rustling sound as he got under the thin blanket. "Come on, little one. Another long day tomorrow."

*Not for me,* Ari thought.

Feeling a strange mixture of desire, fear, and fatalism, she climbed into the clear space beside his big body.

*I can't believe I'm doing this on purpose of my own free will when I was so scared of him earlier,* she thought as she snuggled under the cover. But now that she had decided to die, she no longer feared his fangs. In fact, she needed to get the big Kindred to use them on her soon, before she lost her nerve.

Lathe was already lying on his side, turned considerately away from her so that his back was to her. Ari supposed he was doing his best not to crowd her and also trying to be comfortable sleeping with what he thought was another male in his bed by putting a little space between them.

*Although he didn't seem to have trouble getting close when he held you out in the Rec Yard,* whispered a voice in her head.

Ari pushed it away and reached up hesitantly to tap Lathe on his broad, bare shoulder.

"Yes, little one?" His deep voice seemed to shake the entire bed as he turned his head in her direction.

"Lathe..." She took a deep breath. "Lathe, I still want you to bite me."

"You do, do you?"

He turned over completely so that he was lying on his other side and facing her. In the semi-gloom of the one lonely glow he seemed to loom over her and for a moment Ari felt her heart quail. Then she took a deep breath and told herself to be brave.

*This is the only way out other than being horribly raped to death so I'm taking it,* she reminded herself. She made her voice firm when she answered.

"Yes—I do."

She expected him to protest as he had in the Rec Yard but to her surprise he rumbled, "All right then."

"What...just like that?" Ari blurted.

"Yes, just like that. If you want my fangs in you, who am I to say no?" His voice was a soft, sensual growl that seemed to do strange things to her insides. But Ari tried to ignore the butterflies taking off in her stomach and hold firm to her purpose.

"All right." She thrust out an arm. "Do it."

"Not like that." He lowered her arm gently, his large, warm hand lingering on her elbow and sending a shiver through her. "For it to be quick and effective, I need to bite closer to an artery."

Ari felt her breath catch in her throat but she forced herself to ignore the way her heart was pounding. If this was how it had to be, then she could deal with it, she thought.

"All right," she said, and her voice only wavered a little bit. "Then where?"

"Your throat would be best." Lathe's voice was deceptively mild. "My essence would travel through your carotid artery straight to your heart."

"And..." Ari swallowed hard. "And it'll be...faster that way? Maybe...maybe less painful?" Her voice felt squeezed and tight in her throat but she forced the words out anyway.

"Unfortunately, I can't make it pleasurable for you," Lathe murmured. "I told you, I can only do that for a female. But yes, it will be faster this way. And hopefully less painful."

"All right, then do it." Ari sat up in bed and tilted her head to one side. "Go ahead—I want you to," she added defiantly.

"Not like that, little one." Lathe urged her back down and she found herself suddenly cradled in one of his large, muscular arms. "Here," he murmured, getting her into position. "Like this."

Ari found herself held against him with her head pillowed on his muscular bicep and her back to his front. The new position made her feel completely surrounded by the big Kindred...his breath...his warmth...his big body cupping and cradling hers...

*Ought to feel claustrophobic,* she thought, but somehow she didn't, even though she could feel the hard wall of his chest radiating heat against her entire back.

"What...what now?" she asked, wishing her voice wouldn't come out sounding so breathless.

"Now, this..." Lathe leaned over her, his breath warm against the left side of her throat, which was exposed for him. It tickled and Ari had to bite back a nervous giggle.

*You're about to die,* she reminded herself, *there's nothing funny about this.* But her nerves were suddenly so on edge it was all she could do to hold still in the big Kindred's arms.

"Hey, it's all right, little one," he murmured, one big, warm hand running lightly over her shivering arm and side. "Just try to relax, okay?"

"T-trying," Ari stammered.

"Good. Now I need to prepare the place I'm going to bite," he told her. Without any further warning, Ari felt his warm, wet tongue caressing the side of her neck from her collar bone all the way up to the sensitive place right behind her ear.

"*Oh...*" she moaned, unable to help herself. The side of her neck had always been an especially sensitive place for her. During her second sexual encounter—the one she'd enjoyed the most of the two she'd had—her lover had spent a long time licking and kissing the side of her throat. Ari had enjoyed that part much more than the actual sex, which had been a big letdown, to be honest.

"Oh..." she sighed again as the big Kindred's hot, wet tongue continued to caress her vulnerable flesh. For some reason her nipples felt like hard little points at the tips of her breasts and her pussy was throbbing between her thighs—which was hardly the proper response to what was about to happen. But she couldn't seem to help it.

"All right, little one?" Lathe murmured softly, his breath hot against her ear. "Think you're ready?"

"Y...yes," Ari somehow managed to get out. God, why was her heart pounding so hard? Was it because she was about to die? But that didn't seem like the reason why her whole body felt flushed and she could scarcely get a deep enough breath. It felt like... something else. Something Ari couldn't name, even to herself.

"Gently now. I'll try not to hurt you." Lathe's deep voice was soothing and seductive at the same time. His right arm came up, cradling her close to him and he bent his mouth to her throat once more. His breath smelled like some exotic, delicious spice Ari couldn't name.

*Goddess, what a strange idea to have as my last thought,* she said to herself as she felt the sharp edges of his fangs skate gently along her vulnerable throat.

"Gods, little one—you taste so sweet," she heard him say hoarsely and then the sharp prick of his fangs sinking into the side of her neck stole her breath away.

Ari tensed herself, waiting for the terrible pain which was now surely coming. She had seen the way Hexer reacted when Lathe had bit him—she well remembered the grimace of agony on his ugly face and the way his back had bowed outward as though his body could scarcely contain the awful anguish of the big Kindred's fatal bite.

Instead, she felt a completely different sensation flooding through her—pleasure. Pleasure so intense she could scarcely hold still.

"Ah!" she gasped, arching her back as warm tendrils of sensation rushed through her body, teasing her nipples to even greater tightness and making her pussy so hot and wet she clamped her thighs together, trying to control it.

But there was no controlling this pleasure—not with the big Kindred's fangs in her throat, presumably still injecting her with his essence.

Before she could even think of trying to stop herself, Ari found she was coming—coming so hard and fast that she saw stars flashing in the darkness before her eyes. Her pussy throbbed, suddenly so wet and could feel her juices sliding down between her thighs and her body ached to be filled.

"Oh," she moaned, her body writhing against the big male form that was holding it. "Oh, Lathe...what...what are you doing to me?"

For a long moment he crushed her to him, his big body surrounding and enveloping hers and Ari felt something hot and hard throbbing through the thin material of his sleep trousers against her bare ass.

Then, finally, he withdrew.

"Healing you," he said, answering her question in a low, growling voice. "I'm sorry—did it hurt too much?"

"I'm not...you didn't hur—" Ari started to say, then clamped her lips shut. She remembered the big Kindred saying he could only bring pleasure with his bite to a female. Therefore admitting what had just happened—how she had come when he bit her—would be tantamount to telling her secret. She couldn't do that.

"No, it...it didn't hurt too much," she answered breathlessly. Now that he was no longer biting her, the incredible pleasure had stopped. But she could sense it out there, just beyond the horizon, hovering like a wave of warm water ready to rush forward and crash over her again at the least provocation.

Then his words finally registered with her.

"Wait a minute—did you say you were *healing* me? What are you doing healing me when I asked you to kill me?" she demanded, turning in his arms to face him.

"You didn't say that—you just said you wanted me to bite you," he pointed out. There was a lazy amusement in his deep voice that both irritated Ari and somehow drew her to him.

"I told you out on the Rec Yard," she pointed out.

"You were upset in the Rec Yard," he said softly. Reaching down, he brushed the back of his hand gently over her left cheek and Ari realized it didn't hurt at all now—it didn't even feel swollen. "I didn't want you to do anything you couldn't take back until you talked it out some."

"Talked what out?" Ari demanded, being deliberately obtuse, mostly to cover the way her heart was still pounding and her knees felt so weak.

"The reason you were upset enough to ask me to kill you," Lathe said patiently. "What happened on the yard that made you so hopeless you wanted to die?" In the darkness his turquoise eyes seemed to glow as he looked down at her.

"I..." Ari bit her lip. "I can't talk about it," she murmured in a low voice.

"How about this then—who's Jak?" he asked.

Ari felt a surge of fear and twisted in his arms.

"I told you, I can't talk about it!"

"Is he someone dear to you?" Lathe murmured. "Someone you care for greatly? A lover?"

"He's my brother—all right? My older brother," Ari exclaimed, finally goaded into telling at least part of the truth. "And I...I'll never see him again."

"I lost my brother too." His voice was unexpectedly sympathetic. "Thonolan. He was sent to this hellhole and he died here. I still mourn for him every day."

"Oh, Lathe..." Ari didn't know what to say. At least her brother wasn't dead, although he might as well be, stuck in the hole as he was.

"I understand your pain, Ari." His warm hand brushed her newly healed cheek again. "I know how difficult it is to be separated from those you love. But death isn't the answer." Leaning down, he placed a feather-light kiss on her forehead. "Never give up," he murmured.

The press of his warm lips against her skin and the feeling of his big body surrounding hers seemed to short-circuit Ari's brain somehow.

"I...I..." She couldn't make any intelligent words come out, no matter how hard she tried.

"You're too young to die," Lathe continued still in that low, sensual voice that seemed to shake her entire body. "Too inexperienced."

"I've had experience," Ari protested breathlessly.

"Oh? Have you bedded a female, then?" His deep voice rumbled with amusement.

"Well...no," Ari admitted. She started to add—"I've been with two men though"—but decided that would definitely send the wrong message. "No," she said again, lamely. "And I suppose you have?"

"I've never had bonding sex with a female—never found one I cared to tie to me for life," Lathe said. "But we Kindred are great lovers of females. Holding a beautiful female in my arms...pleasuring her...hearing her call my name—there's nothing better in the entire universe."

"Really?" Ari breathed. For some reason she wanted to hear more. "So...you have a special technique you use to, uh, pleasure her?"

"In a way, I suppose. Why—do you want some pointers?" Lathe's deep voice sounded half amused, half aroused. "Maybe I should tell you so you have something to live for in the future?"

"Maybe," Ari breathed. Her body was still throbbing from the intense orgasm he'd given her when he bit her and being cradled in the big Kindred's arms made her feel hot and shaky and needy all over. "Tell me," she whispered.

"Well first of all, contrary to what you'd hear in a place like this, you must never force her." Lathe's tone was unexpectedly serious. "Her mood must be as yours—seduce her. And be patient —females take a little warming up sometimes. If you build the fire slowly and put her needs first, she'll reward you by giving herself completely. There's no greater pleasure than that."

"But I want *details*," Ari insisted. She knew she was pushing into dangerous territory but she didn't want to stop. "What's the first thing you do when you're with a woman?" she asked.

"Talk to her," Lathe said promptly. "There can be no passion without communication."

"Really, you *talk* to her?" Ari scoffed. "That's your big sexy secret?"

"Talking can be very sensual," Lathe argued softly. "Especially in an intimate situation. Say...if you're lying together, skin-to-skin in the dark."

Ari bit her lip. *Just like we are now,* she thought but didn't say aloud.

"And...and what do you say to her?" she asked feeling breathless again.

"I might ask her what she likes...where she likes to be touched...tasted," Lathe murmured. "Or if she's shy, I might ask her to show me. I might tell her to take my hand and guide it to where she wants to be caressed and stroked. Her neck...her breasts...her soft little pussy..."

Ari felt her breath catch in her throat. She could imagine taking the big hand she felt on her arm right now...taking it and guiding it over the sensitive tips of her breasts...and then lower, pushing his hand between her thighs and feeling his long fingers slip deep into her pussy... Goddess of Mercy, she had to stop thinking like this!

"Really?" she managed to get out at last. "That's...that's how you talk to her?"

"Yes, really," Lathe rumbled. "Or I might tell her exactly what I want to do to her."

"Tell me...give me an example of what you might say," Ari said, her heart pounding. She could feel the pleasure hovering again, like a wave waiting to rush back in with the tide. Just lying here half naked in the darkness, hearing the big Kindred growl in such a soft, sensual voice in her ear was doing all kinds of things to her body. Things she didn't want to admit but certainly didn't want to stop either.

"I might tell her, 'I want to kiss your neck,'" Lathe murmured. "Or, 'I want to suck your nipples and hear you moan for me.'"

"Tell me more," Ari breathed.

"Or I might tell her," Lathe continued in a low voice, "'Spread your legs for me, baby—I want to lick your soft little pussy and taste how wet you are.'"

"Oh..." Ari half moaned. Without quite knowing how it was happening, one of her hands somehow found its way down between her legs. The fake holo projection of male genitalia was absent, since Ari had turned down the projection bead's power to try and conserve energy. As she listened to the big Kindred speak, it was easy to let her fingertips part the swollen lips of her pussy and begin to stroke her slippery inner folds.

"Do you want me to go on?" Lathe breathed in her ear.

"Yes...yes, please," Ari managed to get out. "Once you're done, uh, talking...then what do you do?"

"Mmm," Lathe hummed thoughtfully. "Suit actions to words, I suppose. The first thing I like to kiss is her mouth...and then her neck. Blood Kindred love to lick and kiss and suck a female's neck because that leads to biting and biting is part of bonding sex for us."

"Oh...r-right," Ari stammered. She couldn't help thinking of the long, slow, leisurely licks Lathe had given her throat as he had been preparing to bite her. God, she wished he would bite her again! But she didn't have any excuse to ask him to do it since she was healed now. "And then what?" she asked, her fingers still stroking slowly inside her slippery folds.

"Then after I'd gotten her all warmed up, I would move down to her nipples," Lathe murmured. "Some females like it when you just lap and tease around the nipples with your tongue. Others like it when you suck them hard—deep in your mouth. You have to experiment—see what makes her moan. What makes her wet."

"Wet?" Ari asked nervously. She couldn't help feeling guilty —she herself was wetter than she'd ever been before, with her juices coating her inner thighs. Listening to him talk in the dark about how to make love to a woman while she touched herself was sending her closer and closer to the edge.

*Have to be careful,* she thought. *What if he figures out what I'm doing?*

But somehow she couldn't seem to stop.

"Yes, wet," Lathe growled. "I love a female whose soft little pussy gets extra wet for me. We Blood Kindred even have a name for a female like that—we call her a *numalla.*"

"*Numalla?*" Ari repeated breathlessly.

"Mm-hmm. It means, 'liquid pussy'," Lathe told her. "There's nothing better than getting between a female's thighs and finding her all wet and slippery."

*Just like I am now.* Ari's fingers moved faster in her pussy and her hips jerked slightly—it was so hard to hold still as her pleasure was building. But somehow she knew she had to try.

"I love lapping up all the sweet honey on the outside of her pussy...cleaning her with my tongue and marking her with my scent," Lathe went on in a soft, growling voice. "Then spreading her soft little pussy lips wide and licking her inner folds...putting my tongue deep inside her and tasting her honey straight from the source."

"Oh!" Ari gasped and her hips jerked again. Goddess she was so close...

"Are you touching yourself?" Lathe murmured in her ear.

Ari's hand froze between her thighs and her entire body seemed to throb—hot and guilty.

"I...I..." She bit her lip, not knowing what to say. Would he be disgusted by her? Kick her out of the bunk to freeze? Get angry because he thought she was another male who was pleasuring himself so close to him?

"Sorry, I didn't mean to frighten you," Lathe murmured, clearly guessing at her consternation. "It's all right, little one—you can stroke yourself as I talk to you. Just be certain to catch your seed in your hand when you come so you don't make a mess on the blanket."

"Oh...I..." Ari wasn't sure what to do. Her heart was pounding so loudly she was certain the big Kindred could hear it. Goddess, it was so embarrassing to be caught like this!

"You don't have to be embarrassed," he murmured. Could he read her mind? "It's all right to feel aroused...to bring yourself pleasure. I'm not upset with you, Ari."

"I want...want to hear more about how you, uh, pleasure a woman," Ari managed at last, trying to get off the subject of the way she was touching herself. "You said you like to...to taste her?"

"As a Kindred, I have a biological need to taste my lover—to lap and suck her pussy and give her pleasure," Lathe told her, his voice rough with desire. "There's nothing better than being on your knees, your face buried between your female's thighs while you tease her sweet clit with your tongue and lap up her juices."

"Oh..." Slowly, Ari's fingers began moving again, tracing the throbbing button of her own clit as the big Kindred spoke. "And... and after that?" she asked softly.

"After I've brought her to pleasure and made her come with my mouth several times, only then is it time to fill her with my shaft," Lathe murmured.

"And how...what position would you take?" Ari whispered.

"That depends, little one. On if we're making love...or having bonding sex."

"B-bonding sex?" Ari asked. It seemed like he had said something about that before but she didn't understand what he meant.

"Bonding sex is the way a Kindred male bonds a female to him for life," Lathe explained. "It's deeper than regular sex—a step beyond making love."

"And how do you do this, uh, bonding sex?" Ari asked breathlessly. "Say if...if *I* was a female. How would you bond me to you?" She knew it was dangerous to ask but she couldn't help it—the words came out of her mouth before she could stop them.

"Hmm...I would need to be on top of you," Lathe growled. "Face-to-face and inside you—deep inside you, little one."

"You...you would?" Ari managed to say. Her fingers flew, stroking her throbbing clit. "Why...why would we have to be face-to-face?" she breathed.

"Because I'd need to look into your eyes as I thrust my cock deep inside you," Lathe growled.

He was bending over her, looking into her eyes now. Ari's heart was pounding so hard it felt like it might break out of her body and race away.

"More," she managed to whisper. "Then what?"

"I'd take my time with you," Lathe promised, his eyes and fangs gleaming in the dim light of the single glow. "I'd spread you wide with my cock and fill you over and over until I knew you were right on the edge, little one."

"And then?" Ari panted. Goddess she was close...so close...

"And then I'd sink my fangs into your neck, biting you and filling you with my essence at the same time I filled your pussy with my cum," Lathe growled. "And that's how I'd bond you to me. *If* you were female," he added.

It was on the tip of Ari's tongue to say, "I *am* female," but something held her back. Her secret wasn't just her sex—it was her life. She was beginning to feel very close to the big Kindred but she'd still known him less than forty-eight hours. If he reacted badly to her deception or if the wrong person found out she was female...well, that would be the end for her here in BleakHall.

Instead what came out of her mouth was, "Bite me again!"

Earlier, she'd thought that she couldn't ask this of the big Kindred because she had no excuse to ask him to bite her. She *still* didn't have an excuse but Lathe didn't seem to mind.

His big hand stroked up to caress her throat and he turned her head gently to one side, baring her neck for him. He leaned close, his hot breath stirring her hair.

"Come for me, little one," he growled softly in Ari's ear. "Come while I sink my fangs deep in your flesh."

Ari felt the four sharp points against her vulnerable skin and then pleasure flooded her again and she was coming...coming so hard all she could do was gasp and moan as the big Kindred shot his essence inside her, invading her and owning her in the most intimate way she'd ever known...

"Ah!" she gasped as the pleasure seized her and shook her like a rag doll. "Oh, Lathe...oh Goddess, yes...*yes!*"

It was the most intense orgasm Ari had ever had and it seemed to go on and on. But at last Lathe withdrew his fangs from her neck and the pleasure ebbed a little, leaving her panting for breath.

Slowly, she became aware of herself again. Her pussy was still throbbing and she was so wet and sticky between her thighs she felt as though she'd spilled a bottle of warm lotion over herself. What a mess!

"Goddess," she whispered. "I...I need to go clean up."

"No—don't leave the bed. You'll freeze," Lathe objected.

"But..." she bit her lip. "You said about...not making a...a mess on the blanket..."

"Here—give me your hand. The one you used to touch yourself."

He held out his own large hand and Ari felt she had no choice. Slowly, she pulled her hand from beneath the thin blanket. Goddess it was embarrassing how wet and sticky her fingers were!

"See?" she said. "I really need to go wash up. I—"

But before she could finish, Lathe had taken her hand in his and brought her fingers to his mouth.

"Gods, little one...your scent is so sweet," he groaned softly.

Then, with long, slow, deliberate strokes of his hot, wet tongue, he cleaned Ari's fingers and hand, lapping away all of her juices as though he enjoyed the flavor.

Watching him, Ari felt her heart pound even harder. What was he thinking? Did he know she was a female now? Or did he still think she was a male? If so, could he really be so willing to lap away another male's seed?

"Lathe," she whispered when he was finished. "I...I don't understand."

He was silent for a long time before he spoke.

"I don't either, little one," he said at last. Then he sat up and climbed over her, leaving Ari alone in the bunk as he shut himself into the bathroom.

# TWENTY

*What's wrong with me? Why did I act like that? How could I do that with anther male?*

Lathe stared at himself in the scratched metal mirror, as though looking to see if the encounter had somehow changed him. He looked the same though—same eyes and nose and hair.

*The same fangs except now you apparently like sinking them into other males,* whispered a voice in the back of his head.

But damn it, Ari didn't *feel* male! The boy was warm and soft in his arms—his flesh as yielding as a female's. And the flavor of his seed which Lathe had surprised himself by licking off the boy's hand...

*It tastes like honey—a female's honey,* he thought.

Ari's cries of passion were likewise feminine—soft and high instead of low and rough like Lathe's own tended to be.

And speaking of passion, he had yet to spend his. Looking

down at his sleep trousers, Lathe saw that his shaft was still rock hard, despite his confusion about the boy.

*I need to come—need a release to clear my head,* he thought. But when he took himself in hand, the images in his head were all of Ari—the sound of the boy's cries and moans...the way he bucked his hips...his sweet feminine scent and the delicious flavor of his seed...

Lathe stopped in mid stroke.

*I tasted anther male's seed,* he thought. *It should have disgusted me but I licked it off his fingers as eagerly as I would have licked the honey from a female's. What's wrong with me?*

Was BleakHall getting to him...making him do things he wouldn't normally desire to do? Turning him into an entirely different person—a male who loved other males?

Lathe tried to imagine himself sucking another male's shaft and couldn't do it. Even when he put Ari's face on the figure in his imagination, the idea did nothing for him. In fact, just thinking about it made his own shaft start to wilt in his hand.

*This is wrong—what I'm doing with Ari is wrong,* he thought grimly. Not because he thought two males together was wrong— the idea didn't do anything for him but he didn't abhor it either. But it was wrong to start a relationship with the boy in which Lathe couldn't reciprocate fully.

*I won't be able to give him what he needs...what he wants,* he thought. Giving up on pleasuring himself, he tucked his shaft back into his sleep trousers and then splashed some water on his face. Goddess, he couldn't believe he was thinking about this. When he'd been considering all the dangers that might be involved in infiltrating BleakHall prison, falling in love had never made the list.

*Wait a minute—falling in love? What are you talking about? You barely know the boy!*

Right—he barely knew him and yet he'd bitten Ari and injected the boy with his essence twice. For a Blood Kindred, that was an extremely sexual and possessive act. Not to mention he'd held Ari and spoken words of sensuality and desire...had encouraged the boy to come as he spoke to him and had cleaned him up afterwards with his tongue...

*This isn't me—what am I doing?* Lathe asked himself again. *What's wrong with me? Goddess, I'm so fucking **confused**...*

Just then he heard a muffled thud and a cry of fright from the cell outside.

Confusion was swept away and he felt an instant surge of possessive protectiveness rush over him.

Bursting out of the fresher, he came out into the cell.

"What is it? What's wrong?" he asked, looking for whatever danger had threatened the boy.

"Th-there..." Ari pointed with a trembling finger to the clear door-wall of the cell.

Prowling hungrily outside was a lasher—a huge one—with lantern-yellow eyes and fangs twice as long as Lathe's.

Lathe frowned. Was this the same lasher that had frightened Ari last night? The beast must smell the boy's scent, but he'd never seen a lasher that interested in an inmate before. Usually they were just content to prowl around the prison complex without bothering anyone unless a cell door was opened. Then the hapless prisoner who was trying to escape was usually run down and torn to pieces. But Lathe had never seen a lasher single out any one person and stalk them like this.

"Go! Get away from here!" he rushed at the cell door, waving his arms and shouting to scare the beast away.

The lasher growled and hissed, spitting angrily. But when it caught a whiff of Lathe's scent, it retreated immediately.

"It's all right, little one," he went to Ari who was huddled under the blanket, breathing in short, terrified pants. "It's gone."

"Is it?" Ari peered over the edge of the blanket. His eyes were huge and fearful in the dim lighting. "It...it threw itself against the door, Lathe! As though it was trying to come in after me!"

"Really?" Lathe frowned. "I've never heard of a lasher acting so aggressively before." He shook his head. "It must *really* like your scent."

*Just like I do,* he thought and then pushed the confusing idea away. He would have to deal with his own inner turmoil later. Right now he needed to comfort the boy.

"It was growling and pawing at the plasti-glass." Ari's voice was still tight with fear. "I thought...I was sure it was going to get in."

"I told you, little one—the lashers can't get into the cells." Lathe slid into bed beside the boy. He started to climb over to the wall side of the bunk but Ari stopped him with a hand on his arm.

"Would you...could you stay on the outside this time? I'd feel so much safer if you did. The lasher's afraid of you—I don't think it would bother me if you were on the outside."

Lathe raised an eyebrow at him.

"I thought you were claustrophobic."

"I am...I was. But I don't feel..." Ari took a deep breath. "I don't feel so anxious—so scared around you anymore. That... makes it easier. Unless..." His voice wavered a bit. "Unless you left so suddenly because you're mad at me?"

Lathe sighed. He *had* made an extremely abrupt departure, and right after Ari had finished coming too. No wonder the boy thought he might be upset.

"Of course I'm not angry at you," he said, stroking the boy's cheek tenderly. "It's just...I've never done...anything like what we did with another male before. I didn't know I could *want* to..." He shook his head. "Never mind."

"Oh," Ari said in a small voice. "I...I'm really sorry, Lathe. I didn't mean to...to cause you any trouble."

"The trouble is all of my own making and all in my own head," Lathe assured him. "Now come on, let's get some sleep."

He started to roll on his side but Ari tapped his shoulder.

"Lathe," he asked timidly. "Would you...could you put your arm around me for a minute? Just until I get warm again? It was so cold in the bunk without you."

Lathe felt a surge of affection wash over him.

"Of course I'll hold you, Ari," he murmured.

He tucked the boy neatly into his arm and waited while Ari sighed and nestled against him, fitting his small frame to Lathe's much larger, more muscular one.

"Better, little one?" Lathe asked with a grin of amusement as the boy got comfortable. Ari reminded him more than ever of a kitten when he snuggled against Lathe's side this way.

"So much better," Ari murmured and yawned. "Mmm, you're so *warm.*"

"You will be too, soon," Lathe promised him. But he had no intention of letting the boy go, even after Ari had warmed up. Confusing and wrong it might be, but he wanted to sleep with the boy in his arms all night. And that was exactly what he intended to do.

# TWENTY-ONE

The wake-up alarm blaring and harsh lights flashing woke Ari with a start.

Lathe was already sitting on the side of the bunk, a towel wrapped around his muscular hips.

"Morning, sleepy head. Come on and get up—I think it will be safe to get a shower this morning."

He threw another towel at Ari—a thin one made of some gray, rough material—and stood.

"Well—come on."

Carefully, Ari reached up to her prison ID and adjusted the power flow of her look/touch projector to maximum. The already limited life-span of her power supply would be strained but if she was going to be naked in a room full of naked men, she needed all the realism her solid-holo projector could give her.

*But what happens in a week or so when the power runs out?*

whispered a little voice in her head. *What are you going to do then? Especially since you've apparently decided to live.*

Yes, she *had* decided to live, Ari thought as she turned modestly and slipped off Lathe's sleep top to wrap the thin gray towel around her and knot it under her arm. And no, she hadn't decided what she would do when her power supply ran out. Maybe she could risk telling Lathe about her secret? After all, the big Kindred didn't hate females the way all the other men in BleakHall did. So maybe...

"Are you ready to go? We have to make the bunk first," Lathe said, breaking her train of thought.

"Oh yes—let me do it."

"There's a certain way it needs to be done. I'll show you." Lathe showed her the correct folding and tucking technique and then straightened up and frowned. "Is there a reason you're wearing your towel so high?"

"Huh?" Ari looked down at herself. Since she was naked, she had automatically placed the towel so it would cover from her breasts down to her upper thighs. But now she realized that she was wearing the towel like a female would—not like Lathe, who had his own towel knotted around his hips.

Plus, though the material was baggy, it was still clinging closer to her breasts than it should. The shape of them was almost visible through the thin gray material, which was causing Lathe to look at her chest strangely.

"Oh, uh...sorry." Ari hastened to change her towel so that it hung around her hips. It felt incredibly uncomfortable to be walking around bare-breasted but since her look/touch projected the image of a flat, boyish chest, it greatly enhanced her disguise as a male.

"Is everything all right?" she asked Lathe, who was still staring fixedly at her chest.

"Everything's fine. Before you moved your towel, I thought I saw..." He shook his head. "Never mind."

Ari's heart caught in her throat. So he *had* seen the shape of her breasts under the towel before she moved it! How stupid and careless could she be? Feeling comfortable with the big Kindred was making her sloppy—she had to get back on track.

Twitching the towel to one side as though straightening it, she made sure to flash the big Kindred with the sight of her projected phallus. She saw his eyes widen and then he looked away. Good—that was certain to throw him off the scent—at least until she could decide if she ought to trust him with her secret.

"So...you're sure we won't have a repeat of yesterday like what happened with...with Hexer?" she asked, to change the subject... and also to reassure herself.

Lathe shook his head.

"Shouldn't be a problem." He frowned. "Hexer, Gods...I hated like the Seven Hells to kill him."

"You did?" Ari was surprised. "Why? After the way he came after you I would think you'd have no compunction at all about taking him down."

"He was my patient." Lathe sighed and ran a hand though his hair. "Well, they're *all* my patients, really. But Hexer was special. When I first came here, he nearly lost an arm in an industrial accident. I managed to reattach it—the Goddess alone knows how it didn't become infected. I used every skill and tool I had—I even milked my fangs and gave him a little of my essence to help with the healing. I didn't tell him that, of course..." He shook his head.

"But he acted so grateful when he made a complete recovery. I just never thought…"

"That he would be the one to try to kill you?" Ari finished for him in a low voice.

Lathe nodded. "Exactly." His face went suddenly hard. "I hate people who don't tell the truth about who they are. If Hexer had showed himself to be an ungrateful bastard from the first, it wouldn't have hurt so much when he came after me."

"Oh," Ari whispered. Suddenly she remembered his muttered words as he sat at the table after killing Hexer. *"I hate liars,"* he'd said and now he had just told her the same thing again.

*He hates people who don't tell the truth…who lie about what they are,* she thought, her heart sinking down to her toes. So much for telling the big Kindred her secret. He would hate her for fooling him—for making him feel confusion and doubt over his own sexuality. Because that was surely what he had been feeling last night when he left the bunk so suddenly—Ari was certain of it.

*I'll have to find another way to keep my identity as a female a secret,* she thought, despair creeping over her. *I can't tell Lathe— he'll feel betrayed and be angry at me. I'll have to find another way…*

But what way that was, she had no idea.

"Well, come on." Lathe sighed. "It's time for a quick shower before First Meal. Let's go."

"Right behind you," Ari said. She followed the big Kindred out of the cell but under the thin gray towel, her stomach was tied in knots.

# TWENTY-TWO

"So there are some rules you need to remember in the shower," Lathe told her as they walked down the corridor leading to the trustee shower facilities. They were dressed only in their towels and holding two identical bars of gritty brown soap. Ari was still having trouble with the feeling of parading around bare-breasted. But her holo-projection was holding up well and as long as no one grabbed for her chest, she ought to be all right. Safer than if someone happened to see the curves of her breasts under her towel, for instance.

*I'll just have to deal with it,* she told herself sternly. But how would she manage once the limited power source for her holo-projector ran dry?

Since she had no answers, she tried to put the question from her head and concentrate on what the big Kindred was saying.

"What rules?" she asked, looking up at him. She had been having trouble keeping up with his long stride, taking two or three steps to every one of his. Seeing this, Lathe shortened his gait a little so that they could walk together without Ari having to run.

"First and foremost, keep your eyes up," he instructed. "You don't need to be looking around—you don't want to be perceived as a shaft-gazer."

"A shaft-gazer?" Ari didn't know whether to laugh or be offended. "I wouldn't want to look at men's—uh, *other* men's shafts," she protested.

"Of course not. I'm just telling you to keep your eyes up so no one thinks you are," Lathe said mildly. "Also, if you drop anything in the shower, let it go—it's gone."

"So...don't bend over for any reason?" Ari asked.

"Exactly." He nodded. "That kind of behavior is seen as...an invitation. And unfortunately we share this shower room with Tapper, as well as the other prison trustees, most of whom are gang leaders. You don't want to give any of them any ideas."

"Tapper showers?" Ari couldn't keep the skepticism out of her voice. "He certainly doesn't *smell* like he does."

"I agree with you about his stench." Lathe wrinkled his nose in apparent disgust. "He mostly just wets his face and hands—that's his idea of a morning wash. But he likes to make a showing in the shower—strut around and let the rest of the trustees see that he's in top form. Just stay away from him."

"Won't I be safe if I stick with you?" Ari asked. "I mean, after what you said yesterday in the Mess Hall—"

"You should be," Lathe said grimly. "I swear I'll do everything in my power to keep you safe, little one. But it's best not to invite trouble."

"Got it." Ari nodded. "Keep my eyes up and don't drop the soap. Anything else I should know?"

"Don't ignore a barrier if there's one up," Lathe said.

"A barrier? What do you mean?" Ari asked, confused.

"A trashcan standing in the doorway...a towel hung across the entrance—basically anything that might serve to block the showers is a message."

"A message? What kind of message?" Ari frowned.

"A message that there's something private going on in the showers—something you're probably not going to want to see," Lathe said darkly. "Also, never go to the showers alone. It's not a safe place to be unless there's a crowd."

"Okay," Ari said neutrally. She was fairly certain she could promise not to wander into any dark corners of the prison on her own but she couldn't help wondering how she would get a shower once her look/touch stopped working.

*Worry about it later,* she told herself. *Right now concentrate on the matter at hand.*

There was a lot to concentrate on because just then they came to the end of the hallway and found themselves at the entrance of a large, echoing room rapidly filling with men.

The slap of bare feet and the deep, masculine voices that echoed from the tiled space filled the air. Tattooed flesh was on display everywhere but Ari resolutely didn't look below the waist. As she and Lathe walked in with some of the other prison trustees, she scanned her surroundings—careful to keep her eyes up as she did so.

What she saw made her heart sink. The walls were dirty yellow tile that might once have been white and there were no stalls for separate showers. Instead, rusted showerheads were placed every few feet around the long wall—about fifteen in all. Great—so she couldn't even wear a towel into the shower stall and hope to get some privacy that way. She was really going to be in trouble once her look/touch power supply ran out.

"Come on," Lathe said and jerked his head at the far corner which was, as yet, unoccupied. As he walked, he casually removed his towel, just as all the other men around them were doing.

Biting her lip, Ari removed hers as well. She thought she had never felt so vulnerable in her life as she did standing naked in a room full of nude male convicts, any one of which wouldn't hesitate to rape and kill her if they got the chance.

*But I'm here with Lathe,* she reminded herself. *He'll keep me safe. Well, as long as he doesn't know who I really am, anyway.*

Speaking of Lathe, he was right in front of her. And though she had been told to keep her eyes up, Ari couldn't help staring at the big Kindred's firm, muscular ass. She had absolutely no urge to look at any of the other naked men filling the shower room—in fact, she would really rather not be anywhere near them. But she couldn't help wanting to see Lathe naked.

*You're not supposed to be looking,* she reminded herself as the big Kindred turned on a shower and adjusted the temperature until steaming water rushed out. But as he stood under the stream of water and lathered himself with the bar of coarse brown soap, she found that her eyes were drawn inevitably downward.

What she saw nearly took her breath away.

*Goddess of Mercy is that thing real?*

His shaft was *huge.* It hung down to his mid-thigh like a sleepy snake, so thick that, even flaccid, Ari seriously doubted she'd be able to wrap her fingers all the way around it.

*Why are you thinking about wrapping your fingers around his shaft?* whispered a sharp little voice in her head. *What's wrong* *with you, Ari? You know you can't do anything like that! You're not even supposed to be **looking** at it.*

"Well, well—looks like the newbie here is a peter-peeker, 'ent he?" a horribly familiar voice said quite close to her ear.

"What?" Ari jumped away instinctively and looked up to see a naked, hairy Tapper standing there—his massive belly protruding pregnantly over a low-slung towel.

"A peter-peeker...a shaft-gazer...a cock-looker." Tapper leered at her. "And here I thought you didn't like cock, pretty boy. But maybe you were just saving your virgin ass for Medic over there."

"What's the problem?" Lathe came over and stood by Ari protectively, his big hands balled into fists at his sides. "You looking for trouble already, so early in the morning Tapper?" His voice came out in a low, menacing growl.

"Oh no, not now anyway." Tapper smiled benignly, showing his crooked yellow teeth. "I was just sayin' as how it seems like pretty boy here can't get enough of your cock—seeing as how you gave it to him all night long and now he can't stop looking at it."

"That's not true," Ari blurted, feeling hot all over with embarrassment. "Lathe—I mean Medic—never did *that* to me. And I wasn't looking at his, uh, his equipment either," she finished lamely.

"Oh, so you're *still* a virgin, are you?" Tapper looked at her with renewed interest and Ari felt her heart sink. Somehow she always managed to say the wrong thing!

"I—" she began but Tapper cut her off.

"I thought sure Medic here would sheathe his cock in your sweet ass last night—especially after seeing how you swallowed his snake on the Rec Yard yesterday. Looked like a pretty good warm up to me, so it did."

"How I *what?*" Ari demanded. "What are you talking about? I didn't...we weren't..." But then Lathe caught her eye and gave a swift, short shake of his head. Abruptly, she shut her mouth.

"Don't try to deny it, pretty boy." Tapper leered at her again. "The two of you were in the fuck and suck corner long enough for you to swallow his load at least twice. We couldn't see much cause Medic was blocking the view but there were plenty of us who noticed what the two of you were up to."

"What Ari and I do in the privacy of our bunk or anywhere else is none of your business," Lathe growled. "Are we going to have trouble, Tapper? Because I can give you some of the same medicine I gave Hexer after you sent him for me." He bared his teeth, his fangs long and white and glistening. "They don't call me Kill-All for nothing."

Tapper paled ever so slightly but since the entire shower was watching now, it was clearly a matter of honor for him not to back down.

"You kill me and my whole gang will be out for your blood and you know it," he said. "You might be big but you can't bite 'em all before one of 'em gets you. That you know, old son."

"That may be so but I'd take at least ten of them with me before I went." Lathe's voice was still a menacing growl, his big body tensed and ready for action.

"Easy now—easy," Tapper put up both hands. "There's no need to speak of such...*unpleasantness.* You'll find no trouble here, Medic. Just agree to start treating my boys at the Infirmary again and we'll call it even."

Lathe barked a laugh.

"As though we could be even after you tried to have me killed! But fine, I'll take your deal—as long as you agree to leave Ari alone." He put a hand on Ari's shoulder and drew her close to him. "The boy is mine—swear not to touch him and I'll treat your gang again."

Tapper gave him a regretful little smile.

"Ah now, old son—I'm afraid I 'ent able to do that. You see, pretty boy here is still on my list. Especially after hearing that he's still a virgin. Tell you what—" He leaned forward and pointed at Ari. "Let me ride his ass once and take his cherry for you, and then I'll never touch him again."

"No!" Ari took a step back involuntarily. She found herself pressed back against Lathe's front with his crotch against the small of her back since he was so tall. But no matter how embarrassing the intimate contact was, she couldn't bring herself to step away from the shelter of his muscular form.

"Absolutely not," Lathe rumbled angrily. "I told you, Ari is *mine*. You touch him and you die, Tapper. Just like Hexer did. Am I understood?"

Tapper still didn't look upset.

"Understood, old son. At least for now." And giving Ari one last lascivious look, he took off his towel and turned away whistling to stand under a nearby showerhead, although it appeared he was only washing his hands and face while the rest of his hairy body remained dry.

The exchange left Ari feeling shaken and disgusted and twice as vulnerable as before. She looked up at Lathe, who was still glaring daggers at Tapper, a possessive growl rising in his throat.

"Lathe," she said, her voice tight and dry. "Can...can we go now?"

He leaned down to her.

"I'm afraid not—that would be showing weakness," he

murmured in her ear. "If you look weak at BleakHall, you're dead."

"Oh...okay." Ari certainly *felt* weak but she understood why she couldn't show it.

"Have to get you a shower, little one," Lathe said in a louder voice. "Come on—we'll make it quick."

Ari didn't want a shower anymore—she didn't want to do anything but get out of the shower room and get far away from Tapper. But she followed Lathe to the still-steaming showerhead and washed herself quickly anyway. It felt funny to be naked and wet and soapy so near to the big Kindred. She might actually have enjoyed it if they hadn't had such an ugly scene with the hairy gang boss.

When she finished, Ari blotted herself dry and wrapped herself in her towel again to follow Lathe from the showers. But she could feel Tapper's greedy little eyes on her as she walked away and it was as though she'd taken a shower in slime.

# TWENTY-THREE

"No more laundry duty for you—you're a fix-it now—so you are, my lad!" Wheezer beamed at Ari as though he'd just given her a beautiful birthday present.

"I'm sorry—what?" She stared at him, uncomprehending.

"A fix-it. You're to go around the place fixing things that need fixing," the old inmate explained patiently. "After you did such a bang-up job on the main clothes press, I went to Mukluk and told him you was wasted in the Laundry—so I did! And since things is allus getting busted around here and we're short handed of inmates who can be trusted not to kill someone the minute they get their hands on a wrench or hammer, you're the new fix-it!"

"So...I'm supposed to go all around fixing whatever mechanical things are broken?" Ari asked, finally understanding what he meant. "I'm a kind of handyman?"

"Exactly! You're BleakHall's new fix-it and it's lucky to have you this place is," Wheezer exclaimed, nodding. "Only thing is, now you report to Stubbins of the Spice Lords."

"The Spice Lords?" Ari frowned, trying to remember what Lathe had said about that particular gang. "Don't they run the, uh, pornography ring?"

"Aye, lad and that they do." Wheezer nodded enthusiastically. "And you'll have access to some mighty-fine pussy vids and holo-mags as long as you stay on Stubbins' good side, so you will!"

"I'll be sure to take advantage of that," Ari said dryly. "But why do the same people who do pornography also head up the maintenance department?"

"Since the Spice Lords don't claim a specific area in Bleak-Hall, they get the honor of keeping track of the fix-its," Wheezer explained. "Stubbins is a good boss if you stay on the right side of him. Just don't try stealing any of the porno—ask nice and he'll like as not loan it to you. Try and take it and he'll chop off your hand."

"All right, all right—I can safely promise I won't try to steal any of the porn," Ari assured him.

"See that you don't!" Wheezer's eyes were wide behind his cracked glasses. "That's what happened to the last fix-it. Couldn't keep his hands to himself, don't you know. Now he's wipin' his arse with a stump. And seein' as how it's damn hard to fix things one-handed, well, that's how the position came open."

Ari swallowed. Well, it sounded like her new boss had a very literal hands-off policy. It was a good thing she wasn't even remotely tempted by porn.

"Thanks for the warning," she told Wheezer. "But honestly, I promise I'll just do my job and leave all of Mr. Stubbins', uh *products* alone."

"Ah, I know you will. You're a good lad—a good lad." And Wheezer clapped her on the back again. He sighed regretfully. "Of course, I'll be sorry to see you go but being a fix-it is a big step up, so it is. Hopefully you'll get more status and you won't have to hide in Medic's shadow so much."

"I'm not hiding in his shadow," Ari protested, feeling irritated.

"Yes, you are lad and it's good he's willing to let you," Wheezer said seriously. "I heard about what happened in the trustee showers today. If Medic hadn't stood by you, you'd be Tapper's bum-boy by now and that you would."

Ari had to admit he was right. She might have been able to get in a few *Ton-kwa* kicks or moves against Tapper but in the end she was pretty certain the rest of the prisoners would have taken her down. Tapper held a lot of sway here at BleakHall—the other trustees wouldn't have tolerated her disrespecting him.

"That's true, I guess," she said in a low voice. "I just wish Tapper would leave me alone! Why can't he just move on down his list and bother somebody else?" Not that she wished Tapper's attentions on anyone else but still, it seemed he had been focused on her since she had gotten to BleakHall and she wished the sweaty, hairy gang boss would just move on.

"I think what draws him is the idea that you're a virgin-like," Wheezer said thoughtfully. "You really shouldn't have told him Medic didn't take you. The whole of the prison was sure he would after what they thought they saw in the Rec Yard yesterday."

"What do you mean what they *thought* they saw?" Ari demanded, remembering what Tapper had said. "Lathe—I mean Medic—and I weren't doing anything. I was upset and he was, um, comforting me."

"Well you know that and Medic knows that and *I* know that because I was watching Medic's back, so I was," Wheezer said, nodding. "But all the rest of the prison knows is that you and Medic were in the fuck-and-suck corner for a goodish amount of time. Nobody could see much because Medic's such a big, tall fellow, so he is. But being as where you were and how close you were, everybody just kind of *assumed*."

"Well, they shouldn't," Ari protested. "I never...I didn't..." She broke off, feeling her cheeks get hot with a guilty blush. No, she hadn't done what the rest of the BleakHall inmates assumed she had with Lathe, but she *had* done more than she should have the night before. Especially if she wanted to keep her secret from the big Kindred.

*I didn't mean to, though!* she protested to herself. *How could I know that letting him bite me would make me come?*

It was such a mess. She'd been trying to end it all and instead she'd started something she wasn't sure she could stop or control with Lathe.

"Doesn't matter whether you did what Tapper said or no," Wheezer told her, breaking her guilty chain of thought. "The fact is, 'tis better to let the other inmates *think* so. If they believe that Medic is protecting you out of love rather than just pity, they're much more likely to steer clear of you and let you be."

"Do you really think so?" Ari frowned. "Why would that be?"

"Because a man in love will fight to his last breath to protect what's precious to him. Whereas a man who's just playing the big brother to a newbie because he feels sorry for the little guy getting picked on, well... He's much more likely to get tired of the job and eventually turn a blind eye if the newbie gets roughed-up a bit-like," Wheezer explained. "Does that make sense to you, boy?"

Actually, it did. And it made Ari wonder how Lathe really felt about her. Why was he actually protecting her in the first place? Did he just feel sorry for her and would he eventually get tired of running interference to keep Tapper off her?

"You'd better stay as close to Medic as you can," Wheezer went on, apparently in lecture mode. "Yes, you should! And it wouldn't hurt to let the rest of the inmates in the prison see the two of you together in the way they *thought* you was together on the yard yesterday, if you take my meaning."

"I do," Ari whispered numbly. "Thank you, Wheezer. You've...certainly given me a lot to think about."

"Well, I like you, Ari-lad." The old inmate clapped her on the back with one hard, wrinkled claw and grinned. "Now, I'm supposed to send you off to Stubbins now. So just you be a good lad and run over to the main stairwell by the entrance to the Mess Hall—that's where the Spice Lords set up shop."

"But...how can I get there?" Ari asked. "I don't have trustee status to let me open doors between the different parts of the prison the way you and Medic do."

"True enough. Though Mukluk promised to put you in the system soon." Wheezer nodded. "Well, I'll walk you over myself, then, so I will. Come on." And with a nod at his second-in-command—an inmate with loose, hanging, rubbery lips and drooping eyelids—he led Ari out of the Laundry and down the metal hallway towards her new work assignment.

# TWENTY-FOUR

Lathe waited until he was safely alone in the Infirmary to check on the nanites' progress. Going into the supply closet, he moved the cleaning equipment—a broom and a mop with light, non-lethal aluminum handles, some weak cleaning solution that couldn't be used to poison anyone because it was so diluted, and a bucket of rags and soft sponges—also non-lethal. Under the bucket was a ragged bit of carpeting that had been there since before Lathe got to BleakHall.

Under it, was something which *hadn't* been there until he arrived. A hole just big enough to admit a male with his dimensions—he had programmed the nanites exactly—led down into the darkness. Reaching for the prison ID tag imbedded in his flesh, just between his clavicles, Lathe tapped a special sequence with the tip of his index finger.

At once, the nanites responded. A pattern of silent vibrations played through the ID, informing Lathe that the nanites were working at eighty percent capacity at the moment, digging and flattening exactly two cubic feet of soil a day and lengthening the tunnel by a commensurate amount. At this cautious rate of speed, they avoided tripping the sensors that were all around BleakHall and were attuned to such escape attempts. Which meant the tunnel would be ready for use in five or six days.

Lathe hesitated, then tapped a code on his ID, increasing the nanites' speed to ninety percent. It was pushing things a little but should still be within the safe limits—just under the level of digging that would trip the prison's sensors. He was taking a bit of a chance but he wanted to be out of here sooner rather than later. The scene today between Ari and Tapper convinced him that he needed to get the lad away from BleakHall as soon as possible.

For a moment he wondered when he should tell Ari they were going. Should he wait until the night of the escape? Or should he warn the boy ahead of time? Let him know they would soon be running for their lives? Should he—

"Medic? Medic where are you? Zzhould be here," a gravelly alien voice called from the front of the Infirmary.

Quickly, Lathe replaced the ragged bit of carpet and the rest of the paraphernalia that camouflaged the hole. Grabbing a bottle of disinfectant and a rag as cover, he exited the supply closet, trying to look cool and collected though his heart was slamming against his ribs.

Mukluk was standing there waiting for him, an impatient look on his reptilian face. As always when he saw the head guard, Lathe felt the skin at the back of his neck prickle. He couldn't be sure but he had a feeling that Mukluk must have had a hand in his brother Thonolan's death.

*It's probably a good thing I'm not sure,* he told himself grimly.

*If I knew he was the one who had killed Thonolan, I wouldn't be able to stop myself from wringing his scaly neck!*

"Yes?" he said shortly, keeping his murderous thoughts to himself as he uncapped the disinfectant and began swabbing the cracked plasti-cover of his exam table with the rag. "What do you want, Mukluk?"

"Izz not what I want, Medic," the big Horvath growled. "Izz what the Mizztrezzez want."

"What?" Lathe frowned. "What do you mean? What Mistresses?"

"Mizztrezzez on BleakHall Board of Directorzz," Mukluk said. "They are vizziting tomorrow night—having a meeting. But zzeveral of them are not bringing their body zzlaves."

"Oh?" Lathe frowned. He knew, of course, that the Yonnite Mistresses on the BleakHall Board—most of whom had monetary stakes in the prison—met at least once a cycle, sometimes more, but he had never been present at one of their meetings before. "So why are you telling me this?" he asked Mukluk.

The lizard guard's forked tongue shot out and swiped in a leisurely way over one yellow, slitted eyeball.

"We need zzerving zzlaves," he told Lathe. "You and your new little friend will zzerve."

Lathe felt his heart leap in his chest. Here was a chance not only to record the brutality that went on at BleakHall, but the actual words of the Mistresses who ran it! He couldn't have asked for better evidence of corruption to show to the Yonnite Sacred Seven. And now Mukluk was offering it to him for free. Still, he kept his face neutral as he answered.

"And why are Ari and I being given this honor? Are you

afraid Tapper would try to cut someone's throat if you let him out among the Mistresses?"

Mukluk made a gravelly buzzing-humming sound of dissatisfaction deep in his scaly throat.

"You are one of the only prizzoners we have that doezzn't hate femalezz," he admitted at last. "And the boy izz too young to hate azz the older malezz do."

"We'll serve," Lathe said shortly. "Tomorrow night is it? What time? And where?"

"The upper confernze room in the private wing after lightzz out," Mukluk informed him.

"After lights out?" Lathe frowned. "And how the hell are we supposed to get up there without being devoured by lashers?" The lashers wouldn't bother him, of course but Ari was a different story.

Mukluk made an impatient noise at the back of his throat.

"I will zzet the climate control zzyztem not to blow the cold air until fifteen minutezz after the lazzst zzhip hazz left. That zzhould give you plenty of time to get from the private wing back down to your zzell."

"Thirty minutes," Lathe said firmly. "We might have to clean up afterwards." As a matter of fact, he had hacked into the prison's control system and written a small override to the climate system himself, when he'd first come to BleakHall. He'd thought it might be necessary if he had to bring other prisoners out with him when he left. But he had never tested it and he preferred not to have to now.

Mukluk lashed his heavy tail in annoyance.

"Very well. Thirty minutezz but not a zzecond more."

"Fine—that should be sufficient." Lathe nodded. "We'll be there."

"Zzee that you are." With a flicker of his forked tongue, Mukluk turned and left the Infirmary.

Lathe watched him go, trying to control his excitement. Finally he would get incontrovertible proof that the Yonnites running BleakHall were corrupt! When he finally got out of this hellhole, he would have enough evidence to prosecute every last one of them.

Which was exactly what he planned to do.

*Thonolan, my brother—you shall be avenged!*

# TWENTY-FIVE

"So you're the new fix-it, are you? Wheezer says you're good. He'd better be right."

Stubbins, Ari's new boss, was a short, squat troll of a man with bristly black hair and bushy caterpillar-like eyebrows drawn low over narrow, suspicious blue eyes. He was sitting in the stairwell leaning on a folding table placed in the stairwell with the stump of a thick nico-stick smoldering in an ashtray at his side. He ignored it, however, in favor of cleaning his fingernails with a long, sharp piece of metal which looked suspiciously like a knife to Ari. She'd been under the impression that the inmates weren't allowed to have weapons but she wasn't exactly surprised to see the rules being broken. Stubbins was surrounded by other members of his gang—all of them heavily tattooed and ferocious looking.

"Yes, Mr. Stubbins," she said, nodding her head respectfully. "I'll do my very best for you."

"The way I hear it, the one you're doing your best for is

Medic—down on your knees in the Rec Yard sucking his shaft, were you?" Stubbins looked up, fixing her with a bright blue gaze, his fingers still busy with the knife.

Words of denial rose hotly to her lips but Ari remembered Wheezer's advice about letting the other inmates believe what they wanted about herself and Lathe. Taking a deep breath, she swallowed her anger down with difficulty.

"I promise my private life won't affect my work, Sir," she said stiffly. "I'm a hard worker."

"A *hard worker*. Yes, that's what I heard." Stubbins roared with laughter and the other members of the Spice Lords gang laughed with him, their shouts echoing in the stairwell.

"A hard worker—that's him! Workin' his mouth and ass on Medic's pole, that is!" one of the men chortled.

"Well, at least you don't have to worry about this one stealin' the pussy mags and vids like the last fix-it did," another one of the gang members told Stubbins. "He won't care about pussy when he's too busy handling Medic's cock."

"All right now, boys—cut the lad a break." Stubbins wiped tears of mirth from the corner of one sharp blue eye and took a puff on his nico-stick. "We shouldn't tease 'im so on his first day." His face went suddenly serious as he stared at Ari. "Fix'it's have a lot of responsibility, lad. You're on your own and you have tools that can be lethal." The silver knife in his hands flickered as he flipped it into the air and caught it—all without looking since his gaze never left Ari's face. "Plus you have the same access as a trustee. Wheezer says you can be trusted even though you're new. I say he'd better be right or you'll be sorry. Am I making myself clear?"

Ari swallowed hard, remembering Wheezer's tale of how the last fix-it had lost his hand.

"Absolutely, Mr. Stubbins, Sir," she said respectfully, trying to keep her voice from wavering. "I can handle the responsibility—I promise."

"You'd better, lad." He frowned at her. "You go and do the job I tell you to do and you come right back and report—got it? You don't go anywhere else in the prison and you bring back the tools I give you in perfect working order—tools which you will use *only* on the machinery you're supposed to fix and *not* on other inmates."

"But...what if someone *takes* the tools?" Ari blurted. "I mean, I would never do anything wrong but—"

"Of course you wouldn't do nothin' wrong—*none* of us would," Stubbins said dryly. "That's why we're all locked up here in fuckin' BleakHall."

There was a roar of laugher again which he cut off with an abrupt movement of his knife-hand.

"But you don't have to worry about someone taking your tools, lad," he told Ari. "Every time you check them out, they're coded only to you. Anyone else who tries to touch them...well, they'd better not for reasons that will be clear in a minute. Want to see?"

"Oh, no! I...I'd really rather not," Ari protested quickly. "I'll take your word for it, Sir."

"Pretty words, lad, but you need to know first-hand why nobody can take your tools." There was a grim practicality in Stubbins's grizzled face as he spoke. He jerked his head at one of his gang. "Hey Tubby—bring out the tool chest."

"You got it, boss." A large inmate with a round belly that distended the front of his orange and blue striped jumpsuit, hauled out a heavy looking dull red box with padded handles. Placing it carefully on the folding table in front of Stubbins, he backed respectfully away.

"Here we go." The Spice Lords boss rose and flipped open the red metal lid. Inside were rows of dull silver metal tools, all with red handles.

Hammers and wrenches, screw-drivers and spanners all stared back at Ari when she looked down into the box. They would have seemed innocent enough to her back on Phobos but here they gleamed with a grim lethality. Any one of them could be used as a murder weapon and she was certain they *would* be if one of the other inmates got them away from her. Stubbins seemed certain that couldn't happen but how could he be for sure? How—?

"Catch." Stubbins picked up a small wrench and tossed it in Ari's direction. She caught it reflexively and then gasped as a painful electric shock went through her fingertips and up her arm, numbing her from fingers to elbow.

"Oh!" She dropped the wrench with a clatter amid the trollish roaring laughter of the Spice Lords members.

"See there—what did I tell you?" Stubbins bent to retrieve the wrench himself. "A shock like that'll will pop your balls like corn in a hot pan, lad! And don't think any would-be thieves can defend against it either. Wearin' rubber gloves or any other kind of protection doesn't work. The shock's insulation proof—it travels through anything if someone who isn't meant to touch a tool grabs one."

"I see." Ari shook her shocked hand, trying to coax some life back into it.

"No you don't lad, but you will...you will. The minute some

idiot newbie who don't know the rules tries to grab your hammer, you'll see."

"If the new fix-it's not too busy grabbing Medic's hammer to notice, that is," roared one of the gang members. Laugher erupted, predictably, Ari thought.

She was getting tired of the insinuations and not-very-subtle double entendres but she knew it was best to bear them in silence, though she itched to shoot back a sharp reply.

"Now then," Stubbins continued when the laughter died down. "Here's the way the system works: I get a work order—we call them 'kites' around here—from one of the other trustees. I determine what tools you'll need and I send you down with them to fix what's broken." He glared at Ari. "You go fix whatever it is and then come *directly* back and *return my tools.* No going all around in between jobs, stirring the shit with the other inmates. Just do your job right and come directly back here. Understand?"

Ari swallowed hard.

"Yes. Yes, of course, Sir."

Stubbins nodded approvingly.

"All right then, good. Then here's your first kite." He held up a slip of grubby white paper. "Says there's a glow out in the cell-block E bathrooms. You'll need a new glow and a screwdriver."

As he spoke, he drew the items out of the toolbox, spat on his thumb, and then pressed his wet thumb to the base of each where there was a small, black button Ari hadn't noticed before.

"Now you," he said, motioning for her.

"Now me what?" Ari asked uncertainly.

"Now you spit on your thumb and put it over where I had mine." Stubbins sounded impatient. "Haven't you ever used restricted tools before?"

"Um, no." What he was asking her to do sounded gross and unsanitary to Ari but she didn't dare say so. Instead, she licked her thumb and pressed it tentatively to the red button on the base of the screwdriver.

She was half expecting to get a horrendous shock again but to her surprise, she felt nothing but a slight, humming vibration and then the red handle of the tool turned blue for a moment. The same thing happened when she pressed her thumb to the base of the new glow.

"This is amazing," she remarked, examining her new tools. "Is it DNA activated?"

"You got it, lad." Stubbins nodded. "Any kind of body fluid works, really. Piss, spit, or blood. But I ain't about to bleed just to get a damn glow changed in a cellblock shithole." The other Spice Lords roared dutifully at his joke as he cocked an eye at Ari. "I might piss on the tools though, if you get me mad enough. Let you lick them to activate them afterwards—how'd you like that?"

Ari felt her gorge rise. Why was everyone here at BleakHall so willing to threaten and humiliate others? *Probably because it's a freaking prison, Ari,* whispered a little voice in her head. *Get over it and get on with your new job.*

"I wouldn't like it at all, Sir," she said in a low voice. "And I promise you, it won't be necessary. I'll do a good job and come right back as soon as I finish."

"All right." He nodded. "Prove it. Go change that glow. And mind you don't take too long about it."

"Yes, Sir." Tucking the fragile glow globe in one pocket of her jumpsuit and the screwdriver in the other, Ari ran up the stairs heading for cellblock E. Behind her, she could hear the deep, raucous masculine laughter as the Spice Lords enjoyed yet another joke at her expense.

Assholes.

But she was stuck with them—and with this new job. There was nothing she could do but complete her tasks and get back down to Stubbins before her new boss got impatient.

Ari just hoped she could be fast enough.

# TWENTY-SIX

Cellblock E was up five flights of stairs but Ari was getting used to climbing steps everywhere she went. BleakHall's vertical construction insured that all the inmates got plenty of exercise in their daily routine, though it was hell on the knees of the older prisoners.

As she found the communal restroom and rounded the corner, Ari was confronted by a long row of open stalls, each housing a small rounded fixture with a black gaping mouth-like hole in the center. There was no toilet paper in sight—not even the brown scratchy stuff that felt like sandpaper against her sensitive parts that Lathe had in his small bathroom.

Ari began to understand why the trustees with their tiny private restrooms were so envied by the other prisoners. The idea of having to eliminate in front of everyone, squatting over one of those awful, stained and splattered fixtures and not having anything to clean up with afterwards made her shiver with disgust.

Luckily, there was no one using the Cellblock E bathroom at the moment so she was able to change the burnt out glow by standing on the dull silver sink and reaching over her head. It was a precarious position but Ari was light on her toes and had good balance—she managed easily enough and was about to go when she heard a strange noise coming from deeper in the bathroom.

Leaping lightly and soundlessly to the floor, she took an uncertain step towards the strange sound. There was a rounded archway that led from the toilets into what she assumed was the communal shower room. It sounded like choking and gasping—was someone being sick?

*It doesn't matter if someone's sick, you should just leave them alone, Ari,* whispered the voice of caution in her brain. *Get out of here now—it's not safe to be someplace like this by yourself! Remember what Lathe said—never go in the showers alone!*

But the choking got louder. What if someone was really in trouble? What if they died just because she was too afraid to put her head in the door and see if there was a problem? At the very least she could run and fetch Lathe to help them. Couldn't she?

A broom had fallen across the entrance to the showers, its long handle positioned as though to bar access but somehow Ari found herself stepping over it and making her way down the short, tiled hallway that led to the communal showers.

The choking and gasping sounds were louder in here, echoes bouncing off the dirty tiles, magnifying the noise which made the short hairs at the back of Ari's neck stand up for some reason.

At last she reached the end of the hallway and peeked carefully around the corner, trying to keep her breathing as quiet as possible so as not to disturb whoever or whatever was making the awful sound.

What she saw made her stomach churn.

Tapper was standing there with his dirty jumpsuit unbuttoned past the crotch, exposing his short, stubby root of a cock. Kneeling on the floor in front of him was a young man Ari vaguely recognized from the large hall where she'd waited to be processed into the prison.

He was a tall, good-looking guy with short brown hair, brown eyes, and intimidating-looking tattoos. Ari remembered thinking that she'd better steer clear of him—he looked tough.

But he wasn't so tough now. His hands were balled into fists at his sides and he was gagging and choking as Tapper shoved his dirty member down the tattooed man's throat.

"That's right, lad," he was growling, as he pumped his hips steadily. "That's right—suck it good, there's a good boy."

Ari felt faint and weak with disgust. Tapper's vile body odor wafted towards her and she had to fight not to puke, just as she had when he'd shoved that dirty, malodorous root in her face. She felt sorry for the tattooed man but she didn't know what she could do for him. Rape and abuse seemed to be the order of the day at BleakHall and there was no one she could think of who would even care if she told them what was going on.

The guards turned a blind eye to everything and none of the other gang lords would bother to lift a finger. Wheezer would probably just shrug and tell her that was life in BleakHall and as for Lathe—well, the big Kindred might care but he and Tapper were already in a kind of war. Would it really be wise to involve him in something like this?

As she stood weighing her options, her rubber slipper slipped in a puddle of water on the floor and made a sound. Not a very big sound, but the tiled walls magnified everything.

Tapper's head jerked up, quick as a wink, and before Ari could pull her own head back behind the corner the crime lord had seen her.

His small, piggy eyes widened, then narrowed as he took her in but to Ari's horrified fascination, he never left off thrusting into the other prisoner's mouth.

"Well, now—if it 'ent pretty boy come to see me. Didn't you see the barrier I put up, pretty boy? This here's a private moment you're interrupting, so you are," he snarled, smiling at her in a shark-like way that made Ari's heart pound so fast she felt dizzy.

"B-barrier," she managed to get out. "What...?"

"The barrier—the broom I laid over the threshold of the showers." Tapper was still speaking casually, as though he wasn't currently in the act of raping the hapless prisoner's mouth. "Didn't you see it, pretty boy? Or did you come to watch the show? Maybe you wanted to see what's in store for you the minute Medic gets tired of you? Turn around!"

This last command was directed at the tattooed prisoner who was still gagging and choking on Tapper's cock. With a jerk of the other man's hair, Tapper yanked the man off his shaft and turned him roughly so that he was kneeling with his back to the crime boss.

"That's good. Now drop trou and put your ass in the air," Tapper commanded.

The other prisoner whimpered but did as he was told, tears running down his tattooed cheeks as he slowly unbuttoned his orange and blue striped jumpsuit and shucked it down, baring a pair of pale white buttocks.

Tapper examined the other man's backside for a moment and then nodded approvingly.

"Good—that's good. Not too hairy. I likes 'em smooth, I do. Yes indeed, lad—I was right to put you on my list. Although you're not at the top of it. *That* honor is reserved for someone else."

As he spoke, he spread the other man's ass cheeks roughly apart and thrust deep and hard into his anus.

An agonized cry was forced from the tattooed prisoner's throat as Tapper began sawing back and forth, forcing himself deeper and deeper into the recesses of the other man's body as his victim shivered and cried in pain.

"See, now *this* is what I'm going to do to you, pretty boy," he told Ari, who was still staring in mute horror at the spectacle playing out in front of her. "I'll use your mouth and your ass right proper and then I'll pass you on to Gorn and Fenrus and let them have my sloppy seconds. Just as soon as Medic gets tired of playing big brother to the newbie and kicks you out of his cell."

"He...he's not going to...Medic would never do that," Ari protested, unable to think of a more coherent response. She'd never seen anyone raped before—nor had she ever wanted to. It was a horrible sight and yet she felt frozen to the spot, unable to look away.

"Oh yes he *will* kick you out pretty boy," Tapper huffed, apparently warming to his task. "You keep claiming you're still a virgin. If he hasn't taken you yet, he's not going to. Which means that sooner rather than later, he's going to get tired of sharing his personal cell with you and boot you out on your delectable little rear, so he will."

"You...you don't know anything about it," Ari exclaimed.

"You're sick—all you think of is...is *this*." She pointed at the spectacle before her—the tattooed prisoner bent over, his jaw clenched, tears running down his stubbled cheeks as Tapper rode his ass.

"I know enough to know that a man's not going to keep a pretty boy like you around unless he's putting out," Tapper grunted, shoving hard into the trembling body kneeling before him. "You can't expect to get Medic's protection for free forever. Eventually he's going to get tired of you stringing him along, 'ent he? And then...there I'll be. *Waiting...for...you.*"

He thrust forward forcefully on the last three words, forcing the tattooed prisoner from his hands and knees, down to his elbows. He went with an anguished cry and tried to get away from Tapper but the crime lord held him fast by the hips, a look of twisted concentration on his ugly face. It was clear he was finishing inside the other man, Ari thought sickly. Goddess, of Mercy, how could anyone treat another person so horribly?

At last Tapper withdrew, grinning at her.

"There we go—all nice and broken in, lad," he said and slapped the tattooed inmate on his quivering ass. There were trickles of blood running down the insides of the man's thighs, Ari saw, feeling sick all over again. Clearly Tapper didn't give a damn who he hurt in order to get his own pleasure. In fact, she had an idea that the pain he caused was part of the pleasure for the crime lord.

"You can get up now." Tapper prodded the other man with the toe of one rubber-slippered foot. "Unless you want to wait for me to go again."

His words seemed to galvanize his shivering, crying victim

into action. Wincing in pain, he pulled up his prison-issued jump-suit and got to his feet as quickly as he could.

"You'll bleed for a bit," Tapper told him matter-of-factly. "But you're off my list, lad. For now, anyway." Then he looked at Ari. "Just remember, pretty boy—you're next."

His menacing words seemed to break the paralysis that had gripped her. Turning on her heel, Ari ran as fast as she could, her rubber slippers flapping and squeaking down the tiled hallway as she rushed away from the awful scene.

*Never,* she thought frantically, her heart pounding, her throat filled with bile and her eyes stinging with tears of pity and disgust. *He'll never do that to me! Lathe won't let him!*

But even as she tried to reassure herself, Tapper's words echoed in her head.

*"I know enough to know that a man's not going to keep a pretty boy like you around unless he's putting out."*

Did Lathe really feel that way about her? Was he getting disgusted with waiting for her to "put out" as Tapper had said?

*Of course not,* Ari told herself uneasily. *He thinks I'm a male and he doesn't like other males—he said so himself.*

Yes, but he had also held her in his arms and urged her to come and then licked her fingers clean afterwards. Even in Ari's limited experience those weren't the actions of an uninterested male. Maybe Tapper was right. Maybe Lathe *was* waiting for her to give him some compensation in return for his protection. Maybe—

"No, stop it. It's not true—*it's not true,*" Ari hissed to herself angrily as she took the stairs two at a time back down and away from the awful sight she'd witnessed in E-block.

But if it wasn't true, then why did Tapper's words weigh so

heavily on her? And why couldn't she get the big Kindred and his possible motives for protecting her out of her mind?

*Maybe it would be better to hedge your bets,* whispered a little voice in her mind. *Do something about the situation before it gets out of control.*

But what could she do?

Slowly an idea formed in Ari's mind. At first she pushed it away, unwilling to even consider it. But it kept nudging at her, wiggling under the corners of her consciousness until she had to acknowledge it.

*Surely not,* she told herself. *I couldn't do that—could I?*

But it would certainly solve her problems—both of them. It would show everyone in BleakHall that she most certainly belonged to Lathe in every way. And it would prove to the big Kindred that she was worth keeping around...worth protecting.

It was also humiliating and something she would never, *ever* have considered doing for any man during her life out in the free world away from BleakHall.

But the prison seemed to make things that might once have seemed like impossibilities into necessities.

*I'll do it,* Ari thought, squeezing her hands into fists at her sides. *Maybe...*

# TWENTY-SEVEN

Ari was quiet during Mid Meal, answering only in monosyllables when Lathe asked how his first day at his new prison job had gone. But his large dark eyes kept darting to Lathe's face when he thought Lathe wasn't looking and then darting away again when Lathe locked gazes with him.

What in the Seven Hells was going on with the boy? Lathe wished he knew. All this jumpiness and uncertainty made him worried. Had something happened to Ari? Had someone threatened or hurt him?

Just the thought made a fierce, protective anger rise in his chest which Lathe subdued only with some difficulty. He was getting used to this strange, insistent urge to keep the boy safe but it wouldn't do him any good to go into Rage, like a Kindred male trying to protect his female, when he didn't even know what was going on.

*Maybe I can get him to talk on the Rec Yard,* he thought

hopefully as Mukluk blew a blast on his incongruously dainty silver whistle, sending all the inmates scrambling for the outside door.

He went to the weight station as he usually did and noticed that Ari was following close on his heels. That was a good sign—at least the boy was staying near. But of course he couldn't talk to Ari while he was pumping iron. There were too many listening ears on this end of the yard and besides, it was damn hard to talk when you were lifting a thousand-weight of iron-bricks over your head.

Ari broke the silence at last as Lathe loaded the heavy bar with weights, testing as he went to make certain they were balanced.

"Need a spotter?" he asked as Lathe lay back against the bench and gripped the thick metal bar.

"A spotter?" Lathe suppressed the laugh that tried to rise in his throat because he recognized that no matter how ridiculous Ari's offer was, it had been made in good faith. The boy was genuinely trying to be useful here. "All right, sure—you can spot me," he said seriously. "Ready?"

"Um...sure." Ari grasped the metal bar in the middle and helped—a very little bit—lower it down for Lathe. "Merciful Goddess that's *heavy*," he breathed when he at last relinquished his hold on it and watched as Lathe began to pump the weighty load slowly but steadily.

"Have to... stay in shape... at BleakHall," Lathe informed him, grunting a little as he started another set.

"Yes, I...I guess so," Ari muttered. He still seemed distracted, his eyes darting everywhere but lingering, Lathe saw, on the corner where Tapper was holding court with his cronies.

At last he couldn't stand it anymore. Putting the heavy bar back on the stand with a bang, he sat up and frowned at the boy.

"Is something bothering you, Ari? Has Tapper been at you again?"

"At me?" Ari gave a jagged little laugh. "I guess you could say that. Tapper's been 'at me.' But not nearly as much as he wants."

Lathe wiped the sweat from his forehead with one sleeve of his trustee jumpsuit. He had the top part of it tied around his waist to keep him from sweating through it as he pumped.

"What's this all about, Ari?" he asked in a low voice. "Come on—you can tell me. You can tell me *anything*."

"Anything?" For some reason, his words drew another jagged laugh from the boy and then Ari shook his head and walked away, towards the less populated end of the Rec Yard.

Lathe followed him, feeling more worried than ever.

"Ari please... Ari..." He waited until they were at a deserted corner of the yard—the fuck-and-suck corner as a matter of fact he saw distractedly—and then took Ari by one bird-like shoulder and turned him around. "Ari," he said as gently as he could. "What is it? Did something happen to you this morning before Mid Meal?"

"You could say that," Ari looked away and abruptly changed the subject. "You know, Wheezer told me that what Tapper said in the showers this morning was pretty much what everyone is thinking. About...you know—you and me? And what we, uh, were supposedly doing here yesterday?"

"It doesn't matter what anyone thinks when we know the truth," Lathe said firmly. "Don't give it another thought, Ari."

"I can't *help* thinking about it," the boy protested. "Especially when...when Wheezer told me it would be better to let them think it. Think that we're... together. You know?"

"Oh?" Lathe raised an eyebrow at him. "And why is that?"

"Because..." Ari looked down, scuffing the toe of one small slipper in the sparse, dry grass of the Rec Yard. "Because Wheezer said that a man who's protecting someone he loves—uh, cares about—is much more likely to fight for them and stay protective. Whereas a man who's only looking out for a weaker inmate out of the goodness of his heart is probably going to get tired of playing that role and get rid of the person he's protecting."

"Is that what you think?" Lathe demanded, feeling blindsided by the boy's words. "That I want to get *rid* of you?"

"No... not exactly."

Ari bit his full lower lip, a distractingly erotic gesture, Lathe couldn't help thinking. Gods damn it, if only the boy didn't have such a pretty face!

"What are you saying then?" he asked, trying not to be distracted by Ari's beauty.

"I'm just saying...maybe it would be a good idea to let the other inmates—some of them in particular—believe we really are together. It might...help. You know?"

His dark eyes darted to Tapper who was lounging idly in the far corner of the Rec Yard, laughing at something that Fenrus had said. Something stupid no doubt, knowing the dim-witted henchman.

"Oh?" Lathe frowned at him. "And how do you propose we do that?"

"Like this." And Ari dropped suddenly to his knees before him. Reaching up, he had Lathe's trustee jumpsuit open in a moment and was pulling out his shaft before Lathe could protest.

"Wait! Ari, you don't—" Lathe started but Ari was already licking the head of his cock, swirling his soft, pink tongue around the wide crown in a way that made Lathe—who hadn't been erect at all before—instantly hard.

For a moment he let it continue. Ari's mouth was so hot and wet and the sight of the boy on his knees before him, looking up with those big, dark eyes as he licked and sucked Lathe's aching member was unbearably erotic.

*But he's not doing this because he wants to,* Lathe reminded himself. *He's doing it because he's afraid I'll get rid of him—stop protecting him—if he doesn't give me sexual favors.*

"Ari, no," he said gently, pulling the boy away although his shaft ached in protest at the loss of the hot, wet mouth. "You don't have to do that for me," he told the boy, trying to raise him to his feet. "There is no price for my protection and I'm not going to get tired of you and throw you out of my cell just because the two of us aren't...uh, intimate."

But Ari stayed stubbornly on his knees.

"They're all watching us now," he pointed out, jerking his head at the rest of the Rec Yard. "If you make me stop before... before you finish, they'll assume you're angry with me. That you don't want me anymore. At least...Tapper will think that."

Looking up at the interested eyes of the rest of the inmates, Lathe realized the boy was right. The last time they'd been in the fuck-and-suck corner of the Rec Yard, he had carefully hidden Ari with his own, much larger body. This time, however, the boy was in plain view, down on his knees before Lathe. It was almost as though Ari had positioned them for maximum visibility on purpose.

*Which is probably exactly what he did,* Lathe thought grimly. Was Ari trying to manipulate him for some reason?

Angry words rose to his lips but when he looked down again, he saw the fear and uncertainly in the large, dark eyes.

*He's scared to death,* Lathe realized, his heart aching for the boy's fear. *He's got it into his head that I'll leave him to Tapper's tender mercies if he doesn't please me.*

"Ari..." he said gently, leaning down to cup the boy's soft cheek. "This isn't right or necessary. I'll protect you no matter what. Tapper won't lay a hand on you, I swear. And," he added, straightening up. "I don't want you to do things for me you don't want to do. I don't want unwilling sexual favors."

Still Ari wouldn't budge.

"I'm not unwilling," he protested, looking up at Lathe. "Please, Lathe, I admit I didn't think I'd, uh, like this before I started. I've never...never done this before and all I could think of was Tapper and the way he shoved..." He shook his head, clearly pushing away the bad memory.

"Little one—" Lathe began.

"But it's not like that with you," Ari interrupted. "I like the way you feel in my hands...in my mouth. And you smell so *good.*"

"I...do?" Lathe frowned, a suspicion forming in his mind. "What do you mean?"

"I mean your scent. It's like...warmth and safety and protection and it's clean and masculine and it just makes me want to *be* with you." He looked up at Lathe, frowning. "I don't understand it. At first I thought it must be some kind of soap or cologne. But I've never seen you put anything on and you just use that same awful coarse brown soap that I do. Why do you smell so good, Lathe?"

"I...I'm not sure," Lathe muttered but inside his suspicion was becoming a reality.

*My bonding scent...he must be smelling my bonding scent.*

But that *couldn't* be right. Why would his body make his bonding scent for another male? Lathe had never heard of such a thing. It must be that his body was unconsciously reacting to Ari's female scent and making the same pheromones it would if the boy had really been a woman.

Gods, this was confusing! Lathe shook his head, wishing for a moment that he'd never seen Ari in the first place...never rescued the boy from Mukluk and Tapper and every other Goddess-damned person who seemed out to get the lad in the evil depths of BleakHall.

But then he looked into Ari's eyes again. Large and beautiful and beseeching. The boy's soft rosebud mouth was slightly open as though to plead...or to suck.

*Gods...* Lathe groaned internally. This was so *wrong. I can't give him what he wants...what he needs. I can't be with another male sexually...can I?*

He would have been certain of that fact only a week ago. And the sight of another male on his knees before him, begging to suck his cock would have turned his stomach. Now the thought of letting Ari wrap those soft, sweet lips around his shaft had him achingly hard. Was he changing? Becoming the kind of male who loved other males? Could someone change their sexual orientation so abruptly and completely?

*But I don't desire all other males...just Ari. Only him,* Lathe told himself. But just because he desired the boy didn't mean he ought to let Ari—

His thoughts were cut off abruptly when Ari leaned forward and placed a soft, sucking open-mouthed kiss against the head of his cock, making his shaft pulse back to aching hardness.

"Please," the boy whispered. "Please let me do this, Lathe. Please let me suck you."

He kissed Lathe again and then ran his small, pink tongue from the base of Lathe's shaft all the way to the crown.

Lathe groaned with conflicted pleasure.

"I shouldn't," he muttered harshly but one more glance at the boy's pleading eyes broke his resolve. "All right," he said at last. "All right but only...only this once. Do you understand?"

"Yes, Lathe," Ari murmured softly. And then he bent to his task, using his soft hands and hot, wet mouth to pleasure Lathe as he had never been pleasured before.

***

Ari hadn't expected to enjoy it.

When she'd first formed the plan of sucking the big Kindred in full view of the rest of the inmates in the Rec Yard, she'd expected that it would be a demeaning, disgusting experience. Maybe not as bad as if it was Tapper forcing himself on her, but still—it was something she'd never done before and had no urge to do either.

But from the minute she'd knelt at Lathe's feet and pulled out the big Kindred's shaft, the warm, masculine scent had enveloped her, filling her with desire and erotic need.

Having Lathe's shaft in her face was nothing like having Tapper's twisted, dirty root shoved at her. There was his amazing warm, delicious scent for one thing. And the hard, silky feel of the big Kindred's flesh in her hands—so solid and hot, like a bar of iron warm from the forge—also called to her. She loved the texture of his big shaft—the skin soft as flower petals even while the shaft itself was hard as iron and pulsed like a live thing in her grasp.

Ari thought she could feel his heartbeat as she held him—and it was beating just for her.

Blocking out the rest of the curious eyes on her, she leaned forward and kissed him again...then took the entire broad head in her mouth and swirled her tongue around it. There was a tiny slit at the top of the tender nugget of flesh and Ari took a moment to explore it with the tip of her tongue. She tasted a drop of wetness there—salty and slightly bitter and completely delicious. Completely Lathe, somehow.

"Gods, little one..." The low groan made her look up and she saw that the big Kindred was watching her, an unreadable expression in his turquoise eyes. Never breaking eye-contact, Ari licked him again and then sucked as much of his shaft into her mouth as she could at one time.

It wasn't much, actually because he was simply too big. But Ari had seen a few of her brother's porn vids, which he'd always been careful to hide from their parents when they were younger. In several of them, she'd seen a technique for orally pleasuring a male who was extremely large.

Using her hands, she stroked up and down his thick shaft as she continued to work the sensitive crown of his cock with her mouth and tongue. It was her first time trying such a thing—or sucking a male's shaft at all for that matter—so she wasn't exactly an expert. Still, from the way Lathe was groaning low in his throat and stroking her hair, she wasn't doing too badly either.

*He's enjoying it,* Ari thought and felt a rush of wetness between her thighs. *Goddess of Mercy, and I'm enjoying it too! It's turning me on—sucking Lathe is making me so hot I can hardly hold still.*

It was true. She squeezed her thighs together hard, trying to control the surge of pleasure she got from performing the erotic act on the big Kindred but she couldn't help the way her pussy pulsed with need as she sucked and stroked him. Goddess of Mercy, was she turning into some kind of an exhibitionist? Or was it just the fact that this was Lathe, she was pleasuring...Lathe who had protected and defended her from the first...who had sheltered and warmed her with his big body, asking nothing in return. Lathe, who—

*Listen to yourself, Ari,* whispered a little voice in the back of her head. *You're falling in love with him!*

No—surely not! Ari pushed the thought away—or tried to, anyway. She barely knew the big Kindred, she told herself. They'd only been cellmates for two days. And yet...there was no denying that she found his gentle touch and the way he held her at night comforting. His big body curled around hers and his big hands on her skin were so warm...so tender. And just the thought of his sharp fangs sinking into her neck again was enough to make her pussy throb with desire.

Goddess, maybe she *was* falling in love with him. But what would she do when he found out the truth about her? When he found out she'd been lying?

Ari didn't know and she couldn't concentrate on such questions at the moment. All she wanted now was to please the big Kindred...to pleasure him and make him come the way he had made her come the night before when he bit her.

As if in answer to her thoughts, she felt Lathe's big hand tighten in her hair.

"Gods, little one, you'd better pull off," he groaned. "Think I'm close and I don't want...don't want to come in your mouth."

But that was exactly what Ari *did* want. She gripped him harder and bobbed her head, working the broad crown with her mouth and tongue, sucking and lapping the big Kindred for all she was worth. She didn't care what the rest of the inmates would think when they saw her obviously swallowing Lathe's seed—to be honest, she didn't think of them at all. She just wanted to pleasure the big Kindred all the way to the end—to help him reach completion and lap away the evidence of his pleasure just as he had licked up hers when he'd sucked her fingers the night before.

"Little one...Ari...*Gods!*" Lathe groaned. And then he was coming, spurting hot and hard against the back of her throat and filling her mouth with a rich cream like nothing Ari had ever tasted before.

She'd expected his load to taste like the droplets of precum she'd lapped away while she was sucking him—salty and slightly bitter. Instead, it was somehow sweet. Not overpoweringly so, but just enough that it reminded her of melted snow-cream—a frozen dessert they had on her part of Phobos which had always been one of her favorite sweets.

Lathe groaned and stopped trying to pull away when he saw she was serious about swallowing. Instead he held still, his hands buried in her hair as he fed her his cum, allowing it to pump into her mouth as Ari swallowed eagerly, enjoying every creamy drop as he fed it to her.

At last his flow stopped and Ari sucked the last droplet away from his cock and let his shaft slip from her lips, Lathe sighed and stroked her cheek.

"Thank you, little one," he murmured, looking into her eyes. "You didn't have to do that but it felt amazing."

"It was...amazing for me too," Ari admitted in a low voice, licking her lips. "I...I never thought I...I would want to do that but..."

"I never thought I'd want to let another male do that to me either," Lathe told her in a low voice. He pulled away gently and tucked his shaft back into his jumpsuit. Ari couldn't help noticing it was still hard. If it wasn't for the way his creamy cum was currently warming her belly—making her feel much fuller and more satisfied than the awful Mid Meal food—she would have wondered if he had come at all.

"I—" she began but she was interrupted by a catcall from one of the other inmates.

"Look at Medic, gettin' his knob polished! Here I thought he walked the straight and narrow but I guess he was just waitin' for the right pretty mouth to come along."

Ari felt a hot blush creep into her cheeks. Rising hastily, she wiped her mouth on the sleeve of her jumpsuit.

"Ari—" Lathe began but just then the whistle blew again and rec time was over.

Not daring to look the big Kindred in the eyes again, Ari hurried away, keeping her gaze down and not looking at any of the laughing, jeering inmates who had seen her performance.

*I wanted them to see,* she reminded herself impatiently, wishing she could stop blushing. But the fact was, she'd shown a lot more than she intended. When she'd first come up with the idea to go down on Lathe in public, she'd only intended to do it as a distasteful duty that would keep her safe—both by pleasing the big Kindred so much he wouldn't want to get rid of her and by proving to the other inmates—Tapper in particular—that she and Lathe truly were being intimate with each other.

She hadn't expected to enjoy it. Hadn't expected to feel so much for the big Kindred or love the feeling of his hands in her hair or like the warm, creamy taste of his cum which was even now warming her belly.

*Forget about it,* she told herself angrily. *Just go back to work and forget about him. Do your job.*

But somehow the feel of his long, thick shaft in her mouth and hands in her hair wouldn't leave her mind. And the taste of his seed lingered in her mouth, like a bitter-sweet memory of forbidden love.

# TWENTY-EIGHT

"Well, that was quite a show you put on out in the Rec Yard," Stubbins said, arching one bushy eyebrow at her when Ari reported for duty after Mid Meal. For once he was alone—the rest of the Spice Lords gang was conspicuous by their absence. The gang leader was sitting at his folding table as usual, puffing on a nico-stick as he stared at her.

"Yes, Sir," Ari mumbled, looking down at her feet and not knowing what else to say. "Do you have any kites for me?" she added, trying to change the subject.

But her new boss wasn't so easily put off.

"You were making a point, I'd say—you and Medic both," he remarked thoughtfully. "Lettin' everyone know that you belong to each other and nobody'd better try getting between you. 'Ent that right?"

"I...I guess so." Ari looked up at her new boss, her face flaming. "I...I'm sorry if it, uh, offended you."

Stubbins laughed and spat on the floor beside the folding table.

"Offended? We're in BleakHall, lad! I see worse on my way to the shower every morning." He gave her a sharp look. "Speaking of which, it's my understanding you saw something pretty bad in the showers on E-block when I sent you up there this morning. I heard it had to do with Tapper—maybe *that's* why you felt the need to put on a show?"

Ari wondered how in the world the Spice Lords boss had found out about her run-in with Tapper. She shrugged and nodded, not having the words to express what she was feeling.

"Uh-huh. I thought as much." Stubbins nodded and took another puff of his nico-stick. "All right then—I understand. I just want you to know I don't approve of what Tapper does with his Gods-damned list and wearing out the asses of all the littlest and weakest newbies. We was all newbies once—even me, lad." He reached up and chucked Ari gently under the chin with his callused, nico-stained fingers.

"You...you were? I mean, of course you were, Sir," she stumbled the words out haltingly.

Stubbins nodded.

"Uh-huh. So I understand that you're doin' what you have to in order to survive, lad. And I want you to know I don't blame you —nor will I shame you for it."

"Um...thank you, Sir," Ari murmured. This seemed like quite a reversal from the laughter and joking she'd endured this morning when the whole Spice Lords gang was around. But maybe Stubbins had just been putting on an act for his underlings, being tougher on her in order to prove he was the boss.

"You're welcome." He nodded and dropped his hand to take

another puff of his stick. "Now then—as it happens, I *do* have a kite for you but you might not like it."

"Does it matter if I like it or not?" Ari asked, gathering her courage and looking up at the Spice Lords boss boldly.

He laughed and shook his head.

"Actually, no. But it's a kite for the hole and I'm not sure about sending such a fresh fish as yourself down to tend to it."

"The hole? As in...solitary?" Ari's heart began to bang against her ribs. *The hole—that's where Wheezer said they're keeping Jak! I could see him again! I could see my brother!* She didn't know why the possibility hadn't occurred to her earlier, when she'd first been made a fix-it. But she'd had the idea that the solitary confinement area was hidden and locked away somewhere—accessible only to the Horvath guards.

"Yep—that's the hole all right." Stubbins nodded. "Seems like there's a short in the wiring down there and the guards don't like it. Not that I give a good Gods-damn what those lizard-faced fuckers want." He spat on the floor again, a look of anger crossing his rough face. "But that's the job so we're stuck with it. Can you handle it?"

Could she handle it? Ari thought she could have handled rewiring the entire huge prison as long as it meant getting to see her beloved big brother again. Still, she didn't want to seem over-eager.

"Yes, Sir, I can," she said, trying to look calm and cautious. "But, can you tell me how to get to the hole? I've never seen it before."

"That's because the entrance is way down under the Laundry room in the sub-basement," Stubbins said grimly. "It's past where they keep the lasher kennels."

Ari felt like someone had dumped a bucket of ice cubes directly into the pit of her stomach.

"The...the lashers?" she asked, hoping her voice didn't shake too much. She couldn't help thinking of those lantern-yellow eyes in the darkness... the way the huge, hungry lasher had tried to get in to Lathe's cell before the big Kindred had sent it away with a shout.

"Sure, lad. Where'd you think the damn Horvaths keep their scaly little pets?" Stubbins spit again in apparent disgust. "They sleep all day in their kennels down there at the entrance of the hole. Then the minute lights out sounds, the cold air starts blowin'—wakes 'em right up. They come prowling, looking for food. The Horvath's don't feed them until about five minutes before lights up in the morning. Keeps them hungry and lean, don't you know."

"I...guess that makes sense," Ari said faintly.

"So—that being said, you still think you can handle it?" Stubbins raised a bushy black eyebrow at her. "It's a hard way to go, that path to the hole. I've seen men a hell of a lot bigger and stronger than you come back squallin' like scared little girls when I tried to send them down there to fix something."

Ari wondered what her new boss would think if he knew she was a girl herself. Somehow, the thought gave her courage.

*I can handle anything a man can handle and more. I can do this!*

She squared her shoulders and lifted her chin. If the only way to get to see Jak again was to go past the sleeping lashers, well then she would do it. Jak would do it for her if their situations were reversed. And even if she couldn't free her big brother, at least she could offer him some hope and let him know he wasn't alone.

"I can do it," she said in a firm voice. "I know I can, Sir."

"All right, lad—I'll take your word for it. Now, let's see..." Stubbins flipped open the red tool box and lifted out the top section, searching deeper inside for what he wanted.

Ari stood respectfully to one side but she couldn't help staring curiously at the contents of the box. There was every kind of tool imaginable—even a hard-burn torch for welding high-density metals. There was a pair of dark goggles attached to it, clearly for safety. Well, it was good to see that the Spice Lords boss tried to make certain the fix-its under his supervision had the tools and the safety precautions they needed.

All in all, Stubbins was turning out to be a pretty good boss— at least so far. Ari thought that her predecessor—the one who had lost a hand—must have been a real idiot not to just follow the rules and leave the porn alone.

Though speaking of porn, she had yet to see any of the vids or mags Wheezer had talked about. Maybe Stubbins kept them in a different place? There was another box sitting behind the folding table, under the stairwell. This one was bigger than the tool box and it was painted blue instead of faded red. Maybe that was where it was kept? Ari really didn't care. Even the few porn vids Jak had kept hidden from their parents had only been a curiosity to her—not something to actively seek out time and again. She had no use for porn and no interest in it.

*Especially now that you're putting on your own porno shows, huh?* snickered a nasty little voice in her head. Ari pushed it aside. As Stubbins had said, she'd just been doing what she had to in order to survive. She'd been trying to send a message to Tapper, telling him that she belonged to Lathe.

*Oh yeah? And what message were you trying to send to Lathe, then? I love you? I want you?* whispered the voice. Honestly, Ari wished she could get rid of it! She wasn't sure if it was the voice of her conscious or self-shame or both.

*I don't love him—I barely know him,* she tried to argue with herself. But there was no denying that just the thought of the big Kindred made her stomach quiver with longing. She wanted to be close to him again...to smell his warm, masculine scent and feel his strong arms around her...she wanted to feel his fangs in her throat and hear his deep voice in her ear telling her—

"Here you go—these should do to start." Stubbins' voice broke into her illicit fantasy and Ari jumped. When she looked up, she saw her new boss had put a pile of tools on the table, along with a broad leather strap that turned out to be a tool-belt. Licking his thumb, he pressed it to the black button on the bottoms of all the tools and then nodded for Ari to do the same.

She dutifully licked her thumb and copied his motions, watching as the red handles of the designated tools turned briefly blue, letting her know they were attuned to her and safe to touch.

"Good," Stubbins said, watching as she slung the leather belt around her waist and began loading in the tools. "Now be careful down in the hole. And whatever you do, don't get too close to the cells at the end of the tunnel down there."

"Oh no?" Ari felt that cold, ice cubes in her stomach sensation again. "Why is that?"

"Because one of 'em is holding the Beast," Stubbins said darkly. "A fuckin' bad one, he is and 'ent no mistake about that. He's the reason those damn Yonnite Mistresses who own this place had the laser ceiling installed on the Rec Yard that kills all the fuckin' birds." He shook his head. "Not that the Horvaths'll ever let him out of the hole. But they wanted to be sure he couldn't get away if he ever *did* get out." He pointed his still-smoldering nico-stick at Ari. "See that he doesn't get out on your shift, lad. Stay the *fuck* away from his cell. Got it?"

"Yes, Sir. I understand completely." Ari nodded but inside she couldn't help wondering about her brother. How long had he been trapped down in the dark with a monster so vile even the Yonnite Mistresses and the Horvath guards were wary of him?

*Poor Jak! I hope he's okay. I hope that Beast prisoner hasn't been able to hurt him!*

Ari supposed she would find out. She finished loading her tool belt and nodded at Stubbins again. He nodded back.

"Go on, lad and just be careful," he warned her. "Leave the lashers and the Beast alone—just tend to the wiring."

"Yes, Sir," Ari said again and with a final nod, she slipped away to find the hole.

# TWENTY-NINE

The sub-basement under the Laundry room was dank and dark and filled with shadows. Lit by a single glow, which swung from a long cord in the center of the ceiling, it had a musty feel about it, as though it wasn't used for much. A few empty crates in one corner suggested that it might have been a storage area once but the inch or so of dust collected on their lids let Ari know it hadn't been used that way for a long time.

Where were the lasher kennels that Stubbins had talked about? Though she looked all around her, Ari could see no sign of the animals that prowled the corridors of BleakHall each night. Not that she wanted to. She would be much happier if she could avoid the huge predators completely.

She moved further into the room. The echoes of her footsteps seemed to fall flat—killed by the muffling pressure of the entire prison right over her head. It was a claustrophobic space despite the high metal ceiling but Ari strove to keep her fear in check. She hadn't even gotten to the hole yet—she couldn't let the entryway of the haunted house freak her out or she would never get through the house itself!

Then she saw it—at the far end of the room was a large rectangular opening which served as a doorway.

Ari's breath felt thick in her throat. *That must be the entrance to the hole.* She approached it warily, her largest wrench gripped tightly in one hand. If anything came out of that dark opening she would be ready for it—she hoped.

She drew closer and closer but nothing stirred except a sighing gust of dank-smelling air that breathed from the dark mouth of the tunnel. One of the tools Stubbins had checked out to her was a hand glow. Ari pulled it out of her tool belt and turned it on, using it to light her way as she stepped reluctantly into the entrance to the hole.

For the first few yards she saw nothing—just black metal walls and floor which could have been any of the other corridors in BleakHall. Then the hand glow's beam swept across something new—it looked to Ari a little like the cage she'd been locked in while in the holding area on her first day in the prison. But she realized, as she got closer, that the cage was laid on its side and it had no door. It was just a rectangular chain-link box.

Ari frowned. What was the point of that? Was this where the Horvaths stored old cages when they were broken and no longer useful? But these looked fine—other than the fact that they had no doors. Because, there were more of them, she saw now as she shone the beam down the tunnel that led to the hole. The passageway was lined with cages—there were fifteen or twenty of them on either side—and all of them were lying on their sides.

As she looked closer, she saw that most of them seemed to be at least partially filled with something, though she couldn't see what. Dark hummocks of some kind of material or supplies were stacked in each cage.

Then she saw one of the hummocks move.

It shifted to one side with a rustling like dry leaves rubbing against each other and then one huge yellow eye opened and stared sleepily right into the light. A low rumbling growl came from the cage and then the beast—the lasher Ari realized with numb fascination—was staring directly at her—both eyes open in the darkness.

These weren't broken cages or storage boxes—these were the lasher kennels Stubbins had talked about. Ari stared dumbly at the beast looking back at her as the realization washed over her.

*Goddess of Mercy, it's **huge!***

Her mind felt numb but some instinct of self-preservation made her fingers fumble with the controls to the hand glow and turn it off. Then she stood there in the darkness feeling like her heart was beating right between her teeth, waiting to see if the enormous lasher would come after her.

There was another sleepy growling sound and the huge yellow eyes—each one easily as large as Lathe's fist—blinked several more times. Ari could tell because they glowed in the dark, shining brightly even though she had turned her light off.

*Goddess of Mercy, please...please!*

She was so frightened she couldn't even form a coherent prayer. But someone must have heard her because finally the eyes blinked closed and there was another scaly, rustling sound and a heavy sigh, as if the huge creature was returning to sleep. Then...silence.

Ari stayed where she was, frozen in place and afraid to move for what felt like hours but was probably more like five or ten minutes. Her muscles felt tight and her bladder was heavy with the need to pee—as though her body wanted to dump everything and run. Grimly, she squeezed her thighs together and held it. Her mind kept wanting to show her pictures of the huge lasher crouching in the dark, just waiting for her to walk past it so it could pounce. Ari pushed the thought away.

*Jak,* she told herself. *Jak is down there, past the lashers. I have to get to him—I **have** to.*

Only that thought—the knowledge that her older brother was at the end of the tunnel she was traveling through—got her going again. She forced herself to take a single, shuffling step and then another and another. Finally she was moving again but as she went, she was praying every step of the way.

It seemed to take forever to traverse the tunnel since she was walking blindly in the dark and trying to be as quiet as she could. But after what felt like a small eternity her eyes adjusted and she began to see a dim glow some distance ahead of her. It grew gradually brighter and Ari felt that she was walking uphill a little instead of constantly down, into the depths.

At last she could see her hands in front of her—the hand glow clutched in one and the wrench in the other—and realized they were trembling. In between prayers, she'd had some half-baked idea about shining the light in the lasher's eyes and hitting it with the wrench if it pounced on her.

That was stupid of course—completely foolishness to think she could take on one of the huge predators and win with such meager weapons. But it was all she had been able to think of and having a plan of attack was better than just walking blindly into danger.

As she came to the source of the light, Ari saw it was another single glow, hanging from the metal ceiling. It illuminated a semi-circular room with five metal doorways set in the black metal of the walls. There were narrow windows, set high up in the doors—little more than slits with bars in them as far as Ari could see. Three of the cells looked unoccupied but two—the first and the fifth—had clip charts hanging from magnetic hooks on their doors.

Ari went cautiously to the fifth door and examined the chart.

*Slade Payne,* read the words scrolling across the front of the chart. *Arson, homicide, rape, mutilation. Sentence—six consecutive life sentences.* Then, in large red letters the chart proclaimed *—Use EXTREME CAUTION. Hybrid strength and reflexes make this prisoner difficult to contain or control. High risk of mortality!*

This had to be the cell of the Beast that Stubbins had talked about, Ari thought with a shiver. He sounded like a real charmer. A multiple-murderer rapist who would mutilate you and burn your body when he was through with you. Ugh.

Walking softly so as not to disturb the occupant of the cell, she made her way to the first doorway and looked at the chart.

To her joy, she saw her big brother's name scrolling across the top in red letters.

*Jak Blackthorn, aggravated assault on another inmate. Sentence—seven solar months solitary,* it said. Ari was surprised—the Jak she knew wouldn't have attacked anyone—not even another prisoner. Then again, Lathe had told her that BleakHall changed people.

*It certainly changed you. I doubt you would have given anyone a public blowjob before darkening these doors,* sneered a little voice in her head. But Ari refused to think of that now—not when her older brother was finally within reach.

"Jak?" she whispered softly, standing on her tiptoes to get as close to the barred window at the top of the door as she could. "Jak, can you hear me?"

At first there was no sound but then someone stirred inside the narrow, dark cell. A low, familiar voice muttered, as though to itself, "Can't be...must be...hearing things."

"Jak?" Ari dared to raise her voice a little. "Jak, it's me. It's Ari!"

"Ari?" Her brother's voice sounded choked with disbelief. "Is...is that really you?"

There were dragging sounds, as though he was forcing himself to his feet, and then his tired, dirty, unshaven face appeared in the window. Dark blue eyes, much like her own, looked out at her through the bars.

"Jak!" Ari was so happy and relieved she wanted to cry. In fact, she did feel warm drops slipping down her cheeks but she didn't even care. Reaching as far as she could, she managed to get the tips of her fingers up through the bars. Jak grabbed them, holding her hand as best he could and then Ari began to cry in earnest.

"Oh Jak!" she whispered through her tears. "I thought... thought I would never see you again! I wanted to die when I found out where they had taken you! I've missed you *so much!*"

"Ari?" His voice was hoarse and bewildered. "Ari, my little rook, what are you doing here? Did you come to visit me? I thought BleakHall didn't allow any visitors."

"They don't." Ari swiped at her eyes with the sleeve of her prison jumpsuit. "I came undercover, Jak. I...I came to rescue you," she said although she knew there was no chance of that now.

"What?" He frowned. "Ari, you shouldn't be here! BleakHall is no place for a female!"

"Yes, I'm finding that out," Ari said dryly. "But don't worry, Jak—no one here knows I'm a girl." *Not yet, anyway,* she amended to herself, thinking of her look/touch's dying power source.

"How can that be? How could you hide your, uh, female-ness?" he demanded.

"I cooked up something in my lab to take care of that," Ari assured him, although she wasn't about to show him what the look/touch did. She was keeping it powered down as much as possible to conserve the power source and besides, she wasn't about to open her jumpsuit in front of her brother.

"You did, did you? My clever little rook." He grinned at her. "But you still shouldn't have come!"

"I *had* to," Ari protested. "I couldn't leave you here in this awful place! What did you do to get yourself thrown in the hole, though? Your chart says you assaulted another inmate."

"You're Goddess-damned right I assaulted him," Jak growled. "Fucking Tapper tried to put me on his 'list' like he does all the young males who come in here. But I wasn't fucking having it." He frowned at Ari. "Speaking of which, you make a much prettier boy than me, little rook. How have *you* managed to stay off his list? You have—haven't you?"

He looked so anxious and upset that Ari hastened to reassure him.

"I'm perfectly fine, Jak—Tapper can't touch me. I have...protection."

"Protection?" His frown deepened. "What kind of protection, Ari?"

"I...um..." For some reason she was reluctant to tell him. "Lathe—I mean Medic—has, uh, taken me under his wing."

"Medic? You mean the Kill-All?" Her older brother's eyes widened incredulously. "I've been in the hole for over six months but even *I've* heard of him. You're kidding, right? Please tell me you're kidding, Ari!"

"No, I'm not," she said stiffly. "And don't look at me that way, Jak. Lathe is a good guy and his fangs aren't always deadly. He can also cure with his bite—not that he wants anyone else to know that," she added quickly. "In fact, he cured me of an orbital fracture Tapper gave me when he punched me. He—"

"Wait a minute!" her brother interrupted, his face through the bars looking angry and agitated. "Tapper punched you and the Kill-All bit you but you're trying to tell me you're 'perfectly fine?' I've heard what happens to men when Medic bites them!"

"Well it didn't happen to me, all right?" she flared, crossing her arms over her chest protectively and trying to block out the thought of exactly what *had* happened when Lathe bit her. The rush of pleasure...the instant orgasm so overwhelming it was like nothing she'd ever felt before...

"I don't buy that, Ari!" her brother's angry voice cut through her guilty memories. "This is all wrong, having you here at Bleak-Hall. What the hell have you been doing? "

"Whatever I had to in order to survive, all right?" she snapped. "Don't worry about me, Jak—*you're* the one who's locked in the hole! I was so upset when I couldn't find you and when Wheezer told me you were down here—"

"Wheezer?" Jak frowned. "So you know him too?"

"He was my first boss when I came here—I was in the Laundry," Ari told him. "Then I repaired the main clothes press and now I'm a fix-it—look." She stood back and pointed at the broad leather tool belt that circled her hips proudly. "And supposedly I'm here to fix some faulty wiring down here—though I don't see much to fix," she added, looking around at the bare semi-circular room.

"It's probably the wiring that controls the locks to our cells," Jak said. "It broke some time ago—started cycling open and closed without warning so the cells were locked one minute and unlocked the next. They couldn't have that so now the damn Horvath's have us locked in with old-fashioned padlocks. See?"

He nodded down at the metal handle on the door of his cell. Sure enough, Ari could see a thick, heavy-duty, high-density metal lock swinging just under the latching mechanism.

"Oh, right," she murmured, examining it for a moment. For all its durability it was a simple lock. If only she had the key or some other way to open it!

*But what good would that do?* she asked herself. *How would it help to get Jak out of the hole when I don't have any way to get the two of us out of BleakHall?*

She had no answers so she contented herself with examining the electronic locking mechanism just above the hanging padlock.

"That's not where the problem is," Jak said. His own mechanical abilities were almost as good as Ari's own so she listened to him when he spoke.

"All right then—where?" she asked.

"The box on the wall—it controls everything down here." Jak pointed to a flat gray cover which hung on the black metal wall opposite his cell. "The lights in the lasher tunnel, the locks to our cells, the belt that brings and takes out meal trays... That's been broken for a while—I'm getting pretty damn hungry down here, little rook—I don't mind telling you. Wish I had some food." He made a face. "Not that you can call the protein slop they serve here 'food' but anything starts looking good after two days of enforced starvation."

"Oh Jak, that's terrible! I'll get right to work on it," Ari promised. She went over to the gray cover and pried it open with some difficulty since the hinges were rusted—then stared at the nest of wires inside in consternation.

"Gods," Jak muttered—he was also staring at the contents of the long, flat wall-mounted electrical box. "What a rat's nest."

"Yes, it's not pretty," Ari admitted. "Which means I'd better get to work."

It took most of the rest of the afternoon but she managed to isolate which wires controlled which functions and at least fix the meal tray belt. She knew when she did because she heard a grinding sound coming from within the occupied cells and then Jak made a noise of disgust.

"What? What is it?" she called to him since his face had disappeared from the barred window.

"Two days worth of old food coming down the belt system— that's what it is and it smells a hell of a lot worse now than when it was fresh—if that's even possible," her brother called back. "Don't worry though—I can just send it back through the delivery system to the garbage chute." He paused for a moment. "Mid Meal from today still looks salvageable though. Gods, never thought I'd be hungry enough to eat this protein mush cold but it's better than nothing—thanks little rook."

"You're welcome." Ari felt her heart lift and she was twice as glad she'd gotten the courage to come down through the tunnel to get to Jak. No matter what else happened, she had been able to save her big brother from the fate of slow starvation—that alone was worth coming to BleakHall even though she still had no idea how she was going to get the two of them out.

She started to fix the other wiring problems...and then stopped.

"Jak?" she said, turning back to her brother's cell. "Now that the food tray belt is fixed, I think I'm going to leave the other two issues for another time."

"Oh yeah?" He came back to the window, wiping his mouth with the back of his hand. "Why is that?"

"Because this way I can have an excuse to come down and see you again," Ari explained. "Also, I don't want to turn on the lights in the tunnel and wake up all the lashers when I have no place to run," she added dryly.

"Oh, lights don't bother those big bastards," Jak assured her. "They'd sleep through the midday sun—if any sunlight ever reached down here." His voice held a note of bitterness in it. "It's all about temperature with them. Gods, it gets so fucking cold here at night when the air starts to blow from the vents in the tunnels! Then it gets fucking burning up in the morning when they blow in the hot air to make them go back to sleep."

"I'm so sorry, Jak." Ari shut the gray cover and turned back to her brother. "I wish so much that I could get you out of there."

"There's no way out of the hole other than serving your sentence and I've still got a month to go," Jak said grimly. He cocked an eyebrow at her. "But after I get out, did you say you had a plan to get out of BleakHall?"

"I'm still working on that," Ari admitted. "I had a good plan worked out but circumstances...changed. So it's back to the

drawing board but I promise I'll come up with something."
Though what that might be, she couldn't imagine.

"And how long will that take?" Jak demanded. "How long can
you stay here without anyone finding out who you really are, Ari?
If anyone found out you were a female—"

"They won't!" she interrupted him. "I swear they won't, Jak."
Although how she could keep her oath with the power source of
her look/touch running out she didn't know.

"I don't like this." He was frowning at her through the bars of
his cell. "It's too dangerous for you here, little rook. You should get
out of here any way you can as soon as possible."

"Not without you!" Ari insisted. "And don't worry about me—
my disguise as a man—well, I guess I look more like a boy—is
perfect. For all intents and purposes here in BleakHall I'm male,
and nobody here knows any different."

"Now they do," a deep, rumbling voice from behind her
nearly made Ari jump out of her prison-issued rubber sandals.

"Oh, my Goddess!" she gasped, whipping her head around. A
strange face was peering at her from between the bars of the
fifth cell.

The hair was shaggy and unkempt and a full beard framed
the man's mouth. But it was his eyes that drew Ari's gaze. They
were mismatched—two completely different colors—one brilliant
green and the other blazing gold.

Then the man smiled at her and she forgot all about his eyes.

When he parted his lips, a set of fangs was revealed. Not as
long or as sharp as Lathe's but long enough to make the gooseflesh
crawl up her back and send a chilly hand between her shoulder
blades as though it was reaching for her heart.

"What...what are you?" she gasped, looking at the strange and frightening face peering out at her from between the bars.

"A murderer," came the reply. "And an arsonist. But I'm not a fucking rapist—that part's a lie." His face twisted in anger as he nodded down at the chart that hung on his cell door. "Oh, and I'm a hybrid. Nice to meet you, little girl."

"Jak?" Ari turned to her brother, looking for some explanation.

Her big brother's face was grim.

"So help me Goddess, Slade," he growled. "If you tell anyone about my little sister—"

"Relax." The other man made a soothing gesture with his hands behind the bars of his window. "Who am I gonna tell? I'm stuck down here for life, remember? And you don't have to act like it's such a big secret—I could tell she was female from one whiff of her scent."

"Jak?" Ari whispered again, looking from her brother to the strange male again.

Jak's mouth was tight.

"It's all right, little rook—just don't get too close to him and he can't hurt you."

"Wouldn't hurt her anyway, pretty little girl like that," the male with the mismatched eyes looked her over speculatively. "Anyway, aren't you going to introduce us, Jak?"

Jak sighed and shook his head.

"Slade, this is my little sister Ari. And Ari, meet the Beast."

# THIRTY

L athe paced his cell, waiting for Ari to get out of the small fresher. He and the boy had barely spoken at Last Meal— Ari seemed like he had something on his mind. Lathe, for his part, had been thinking hard ever since their encounter in the Rec Yard. Thinking about what should be—about what *must* be.

*This isn't how my time at BleakHall was supposed to go,* he told himself as he paced. *I was only meant to gather evidence and make a way out so I could rescue any other Kindred who might be trapped here.*

*I wasn't supposed to fall in love—especially not with another male.*

He wished he could deny the idea, even as he thought it. Wished he could pass what he felt off as a momentary infatuation. After all, he'd only known the boy for a little over two days. Surely "love" was too strong a word to use after such a short time together.

But there was no denying the harsh reality before him. His body was making his bonding scent for the boy and he had been close on several occasions to going into Rage when Ari was in danger—the protective anger that comes over Kindred only when their intended mates are threatened.

*He's mine,* Lathe thought, feeling another surge of protective possessiveness rush through him. *He was meant for me—to protect and love and cherish.*

*Even though he's male?* whispered a cautious voice in his head.

Lathe clenched his hands into fists at his sides. Yes—even though Ari was male and he had never believed he would or could want another male sexually—he still wanted the boy.

*But can you give him what he needs and deserves? Can you reciprocate the pleasure he has already given you?*

Lathe drew a deep breath and ran both hands through his hair, thinking. This question tormented him. Ever since he'd allowed Ari to suck him and watched as the boy eagerly swallowed his seed, he'd been able to think of nothing else.

He refused to have a one-sided relationship—the kind the other inmates at BleakHall seemed to think was perfectly fine. The idea of him providing protection to the boy while Ari provided all the pleasure was wrong—unequal. And it turned their relationship—if that was what you could call it—into a business deal. Lathe didn't want that.

But he didn't know if he could return what Ari had given to him out on the Rec Yard. Didn't know if he could bring himself to take another male's shaft in his mouth and suck—didn't know if he could swallow another male's seed.

It went against every instinct he had and yet, Lathe knew he had to try. Had to try to give Ari the same pleasure the boy had given him. How else could he show Ari how he felt about him? How else to reassure him that they were in this together and he would never, ever abandon the boy to the likes of Tapper?

*I'll do it,* he promised himself. *I need to show him how I feel— need to let him know he's loved and desired and cherished. That I won't leave him or let anyone harm him.*

Just as he reached his decision, the fresher door accordioned open and Ari came out, dressed in the overlarge top of Lathe's own sleeping clothes. The faded shade of the fabric brought out the color of the boy's large, dark eyes—they looked bluer than blue in the dim room. Ari's face was freshly washed and droplets of water were clinging to his long, curling eyelashes. His full, pink lips were slightly open—so lush and sweet and kissable Lathe had a hard time looking away from them when he remembered what they had looked like wrapped around his cock.

They boy's beauty struck him all over again like a hammer, nearly making him groan aloud. He wondered again why his body had chosen to want to try and bond with another male. He had heard of it happening to other Kindred before but the phenomenon was extremely rare. Because their DNA made them almost 95% male, the Kindred were biologically programmed to seek out females in order to continue their race. Homosexuality— while not viewed as wrong—was simply not part of their physiological makeup.

Yet here he was and he needed to deal with the situation at hand. Another male might have hated the boy for the wrong and frightening emotions Ari engendered in him. Lathe had known some males with hidden same-sex urges to beat or torment the ones who brought their latent tendencies to the surface.

But he would never do such a thing. It would be shameful and cowardly to run away from what he felt—and wrong to blame it on Ari. The boy couldn't help his beauty any more than Lathe could help the bonding scent his body made for him.

No, he would just have to deal with it in the only way he knew how.

"Ari," he said, taking a step towards the boy. "There's something I need to say. No—something I need to do."

"What?" Ari was looking up at him with wide, uncertain eyes.

Lathe tried to speak but no words would come. Unable to express what he was feeling through speech, he had to rely on actions.

Falling to his knees before the boy, he encircled Ari's waist with his arms. He felt Ari stiffen at first and then, one tentative hand crept into his hair.

"Lathe?" Ari whispered. "What...what are you doing?"

"Returning the pleasure you gave me today." Lathe looked up at him, though he didn't have far to look. Even with him kneeling and Ari standing, he was so much taller than the boy they were nearly eye-to-eye.

"Lathe, really..." Ari's other hand, the one not buried in Lathe's hair, crept to his prison ID tag and began to tap nervously. "Really, you don't have to," he said, shaking his head.

"Yes, I do," Lathe insisted. "I have to...have to know if I can do this. With another male, I mean."

"I know what you mean but you really don't—"

But Lathe was already lifting the tails of the long shirt to bare Ari's shaft. It was curled, pink and innocent, against the boy's thigh, he noted. It wasn't hard at all. Well, his own was similarly soft, so he supposed the two of them were even.

But when he made himself lean closer, he caught the boy's sweet feminine scent and his shaft began to rise.

*Never thought I could get hard just from getting near another male's shaft,* Lathe thought and felt a fresh wave of confusion sweep over him. Gods, was he really going to do this? Was he really going to take another male's shaft in his mouth?

*Ari did it for me,* he reminded himself grimly. *Not only that, he sucked me and swallowed my seed—all of it.* Which was saying something since he tended to come a *lot.*

He forced himself to get closer, until his mouth was almost against Ari's small shaft.

"Lathe, please!" Both of the boy's hands were in his hair now, trying to push him away. At any other time, Lathe would have understood that his advances were being rejected. But he had gone through so many mental calisthenics to nerve himself up for this moment and he was so completely focused on the task at hand, he was slow to understand.

It wasn't until he pressed his lips to the soft, warm surface of Ari's shaft and heard the sharp intake of breath above him that he realized the boy wasn't willing for him to continue.

"Ari?" he looked up and saw an expression of pure panic on the boy's face. "What—?"

But just then the lights flickered a warning and then went out for the night.

---

Ari stumbled in the darkness, trying to get away from the big Kindred just as he was rising from his kneeling position. She tripped on his foot in the darkness and fell forward against him, her upper chest pressing against his face. She felt a burning, stabbing pain just above her breasts and gasped, pushing away hard from Lathe.

"Ari?" His voice sounded panicked in the darkness. "Ari, are you all right? I think one of my fangs—"

"Fine, I'm fine." Fumbling desperately, she found the door of the tiny bathroom and shut herself in it as fast as she could. At least it was light in here so she could see. Latching the door, she leaned against the small metal sink and took deep, shaky breaths, trying to calm the frantic pounding of her heart.

She couldn't believe the solid-holo phallus her look/touch projected had stood up to Lathe's kiss. In fact, she still wasn't sure that it had. She had always thought the holo pseudo-skin felt too slick to be real. Had the big Kindred noticed that it felt wrong?

Lifting the long tails of the sleep shirt, she bent to study the part in question, trying to verify what Lathe had seen and felt.

The fake phallus *looked* real enough, she thought. It should— when she'd realized what Lathe was intent on doing, she had turned the power to her look/touch up as far as it would go. She knew it would probably deplete her already diminishing energy supply but—

The solid-hologram between her legs flickered. Then it flickered again and winked completely out of existence.

Ari's breath caught in her throat.

*Oh Goddess of Mercy,* **no!**

Hastily she reached up to her prison ID, registering only briefly that she had a bloody gash above her breasts where Lathe's fang had scored her. She tapped desperately at the controls of the look/touch but with absolutely no results. Upping the energy to make the solid-holo look and feel more realistic must have finally exhausted her already limited power supply.

Slowly, Ari faced the truth—the look/touch was completely dead and there was no getting it back. Her disguise was gone and now anyone who saw her naked would know she was female. Female in a prison full of female-hating murderers and rapists.

Goddess above, what was she going to do?

# THIRTY-ONE

"Ari? Ari, damn it—open up!" she heard Lathe growling from outside. He pounded urgently on the bathroom door. "Ari, you have to come out. I think one of my fangs scratched you. Did it?"

"O...only a little. I'm fine, really." Ari was nearly panting with fear. What would the big Kindred do if he discovered her secret? She had seen how difficult it was for him to bring himself near her, believing as he did that she was male. He had forced himself to kneel before her and had even pressed his lips to the pseudo-phallus, preparing to take it in his mouth. What would he do to her when he learned that she had allowed him to endure what he would surely see as shame and degradation? What would he do to her when he found out she was a liar?

"*I hate liars,*" growled his deep voice in her memory. And yet, how could she keep the truth from him now? Would he toss her out to Tapper or to the lashers when he knew how she had deceived him? Would he—

"Let me see! I need to examine you *now*." His tone was urgent and upset. "I mean it, Ari—a wound from a Kill-All's fangs can be very dangerous. Open up and come out or I'm going to have to break the door down."

The folding door rattled on its hinges and Ari knew he would make good on his threat. It probably wouldn't take more than a minute either—the bathroom door was a poor, flimsy thing, meant more for privacy than security.

"All right," she called, playing for time. "All right, just give me a minute, I'm coming out."

Panic tried to eat her mind, filling her ears with a blank, buzzing static but she fought it grimly.

*Think, Ari—think! What can you do?*

Well, for starters she really *was* going to have to go out. At least it was dark outside in the main cell area, she reasoned to herself. There was a much smaller chance of Lathe seeing her without her holo-disguise in the dark cell than in the lighted bathroom.

*I'll just have to go out and try to only let him look at the part of my chest that got sliced by his fang,* she told herself, taking a deep breath. Looking down at herself, she saw that the small wound was about midway between the hollow of her throat, where the prison ID was implanted, and the curving slopes of her breasts. Well, at least his fang hadn't nicked her directly on one of her breasts—it should be possible to hide her assets if she was careful.

"Ari!" Lathe pounded on the door again. "Ari, I swear by the Goddess—"

Opening the door, Ari slipped past him into the dark and

chilly cell. She made sure to shut the door behind her, leaving the room in darkness other than the weak glow in the corner.

"All right," she said, trying to make her voice calm and even. "I'm here and I'm fine. So if you'd just stop making such a big fuss—"

But he didn't let her finish. Before she knew what was happening, the big Kindred had swung her up into his arms and was laying her on her back on the bed.

"Stop!" Ari tried to push him away but he wouldn't be deterred.

"Where is it? Where did I cut you?" There was panic in his deep voice.

"Here? Here, all right?" Fumbling in the dark for his hand, she put it over the small wound on her chest. "You can examine it if you want. Just don't...don't touch me anywhere else, all right?"

Lathe didn't answer. Swiftly, he pressed his mouth to the small cut. First he sucked hard enough to make Ari cry out and then he lapped carefully and intently as though he was trying to seal the wound with his tongue.

It seemed to take forever. The whole time Ari lay under his muscular bulk, her arms pressed frantically to her breasts, praying that he wouldn't try to open her shirt or touch her anywhere but her upper chest. Her thoughts were a panicked loop in her brain.

*If he finds out...oh Goddess, if he finds out I've been lying to him...*

But when he finished, the big Kindred moved off her and sat on the edge of the bunk.

"All right." He spoke in a low voice filled with some emotion Ari couldn't interpret. "It should be fine now. I just had to be certain you were all right—a wound from the fangs of a Kill-all can be deadly if the wrong kind of essence gets into your system. I didn't...didn't want anything to happen to you."

"I..." Ari didn't know what to say. "Um, thank you," she whispered. Balling herself tight, she scooted to the inner edge of the bunk, putting as much distance between them as she could. Up until now, she'd been keeping the look/touch turned on low to conserve power but she had always known she could turn it up again if she had to. Now that she no longer had that option she felt vulnerable—naked in a way that had nothing to do with clothing.

"I'm sorry." Lathe's voice was low and rough. "Sorry if I frightened you."

"It's okay. You were just...just trying to heal the cut your, uh, fangs made. I understand," Ari said.

"No, that's not what I'm talking about." He sighed and raked a hand through his hair. "I mean...before you went in the fresher. When I...when I kissed your shaft."

"Oh..." Ari's voice was tight and tense. Had he realized somehow that her male "equipment" wasn't right? Was he going to confront her now?

"I shouldn't have done it," Lathe went on in that same, low, ragged voice. "I just wanted...wanted to be able to return the pleasure you gave to me today in the Rec Yard. But I couldn't." He balled his big hands into fists on his thighs. "I tried, Ari—the Goddess knows I tried. But being with another male that way...it just feels *wrong* to me."

"I'm sorry." Her voice was still tight with fear and uncertainty. "I'm sorry you...you feel that way."

"So am I." There was real agony in his voice now. "Because I think...I think I'm falling in love with you."

Ari's breath seemed to catch in her throat. Had he really just said that? Had Lathe confessed to the same feelings she'd been trying to suppress herself?

*I'm not in love with him—I'm not,* she tried to tell herself. *How can I be in love with him when I'm afraid of him? When I barely know him?*

But she couldn't stop the rising tide of emotion that filled her or the longing that swept over her—the desire to flow into his arms and press herself against him...to kiss him and hold him and be held by him. To let him bite her and bond her to him, exactly as he had described bonding a female the night before when he had held her in his arms and made her come so hard...

"Oh, Lathe..." Her voice broke on his name but she didn't dare to go to him. She had no protection—her armor, such as it had been, was gone.

"I'm sorry if that's hard for you to hear," he said. He was still sitting on the edge of the bunk, elbows resting on his knees, his face shadowed. "To tell the truth, it's fucking hard to say. I never thought I'd be telling another male I love him and I realize..." He cleared his throat. "Realize my feelings might be...unwelcome to you."

"I never said that," Ari said quickly. "I just...you surprised me, that's all. When you said you loved me. And when you...when you kissed me *there.*"

"You kissed me 'there' this afternoon," he pointed out roughly. "I was trying to return the favor."

"But you didn't have to do," Ari protested "I never asked you to. I didn't...didn't *want* you to." She felt miserably unhappy. She'd never meant to twist the big Kindred into emotional knots like this. The truth hovered on the tip of her tongue—the urge to tell him everything and throw herself on his mercy. But how angry would he be when he found out how she'd tricked him?

"I'm sorry if my advances were unwelcome." His deep voice was stiff and formal. "I don't know why my body reacts so strongly to yours. But I'll try to keep my distance in the future if that's what you want."

"I never said that," Ari said before she could stop herself. "Lathe, I feel...I think I feel the same way you do. But I can't... can't let..." She ran a hand through her hair in frustration. "Goddess this is hard! I don't know how to say anything right and all I'm doing is hurting you."

"Well, love hurts." He rumbled a mirthless laugh in the darkness. "Haven't you found that out the hard way by now? I certainly have."

"You...were in love before?" Ari felt a strange twisting sensation in her midsection. Could it be jealousy?

"I thought I was," Lathe clarified. "I mean, I never dream shared with her or anything but—"

"Dream-shared?" Ari asked.

"It's a Kindred thing." He shrugged his broad shoulders. "When you're destined to mate with a female you start to dream of her—and she dreams of you too." He looked at her briefly. "I...I think I had a dream of you, once."

"You did?" Ari's breath seemed to catch in her throat. She remembered the strange feeling she'd had when she first came to BleakHall and had seen Lathe for the first time—the fleeting thought that she'd seen his jewel-like turquoise eyes once in a dream.

Lathe nodded. "When I was sent here someone asked me if I was Dream-sharing with a female—letting me know I ought to get my affairs in order before I came to BleakHall, you know? I hadn't been dreaming of any female but I did have a dream of someone with short black hair and big dark eyes. At the time I thought nothing of it but now..." He shook his head.

"I...I think I dreamed of you—of your eyes, anyway," Ari admitted in a small voice. "I remember thinking that when I first saw you. You were so big and scary but your eyes...your eyes looked so familiar for some reason."

Lathe ran both hands through his hair in agitation.

"I just don't *fucking* understand this! Who ever heard of two males Dream-sharing? It just doesn't *happen*."

His frustration worried Ari.

"Tell me about the girl you were in love with," she said quickly. "The one you, uh, weren't dreaming of."

"Talsa—that was her name. I was head over heels in love with her, as they say on Earth—the planet my people protect. And she told me she loved me too."

"So...what happened?" Ari asked.

"She lied." His voice grew hard. "It turned out she already had a male but she wanted to work aboard the Kindred Mother Ship. She thought I would be a good way to get in."

"I'm so sorry," Ari whispered. "You must have felt awful."

"You know what the worst thing is?" Lathe said. "I would have helped her if she'd just asked me. She didn't have to make me believe she loved me. Didn't have to *lie* to me."

Ari felt sick. Lathe hated liars—hated people who misrepresented themselves and their intentions. Which was exactly what she'd been doing this whole time. For just a moment when he'd said that he loved her she had almost blurted out the whole story —how she'd been forced to pretend she was male to try and save

Jak and how she'd never meant to mislead him. But now she realized all over again that she couldn't. Lathe would hate and despise her if he found out the truth now. And she couldn't risk making him angry—not when she was so dependent on his protection.

"I'm sorry," she said again, feeling like she might cry. "So sorry, Lathe."

He shook his head. "It was a long time ago. Shortly after that was when my brother, Thonolan, got taken to BleakHall and was...was killed." His voice grew low and choked. "I vowed then to do everything I could to avenge him and I decided that the Goddess meant for me to be single—that I wasn't meant to have anyone in my life."

"I...wasn't looking for anyone either," Ari said. "I just...I just want to get out of this awful place. But I don't know how."

Lathe seemed on the verge of saying something but then he shook his head.

"It's late, little one." His voice was heavy with weariness. "Would you like me to sleep on the floor tonight? To give you space?"

"What? No!" Ari protested. "Of course not, Lathe! You'll freeze."

"No I won't—I have self-regulating body temperature, remember?"

"Well then, *I'll* freeze because I *don't* have self-regulating body temperature. And I don't want to kick you out of your own bed," Ari said. "I think...as long as you promise not to...not to touch me anywhere under...under my shirt—"

"I told you before I won't take what you don't want to give." His voice was rough and his turquoise eyes blazed for a moment in the darkness. "I don't go where I'm not wanted."

*But I **do** want you,* Ari longed to say. *I want you so much, Lathe!*

But she knew if she gave in to the temptation to tell him her true feelings, more of the truth would follow. And then he would feel angry and betrayed and hurt and who knew what might happen next. No, nothing good could come of returning his love—only more hurt and heartache. Still, though, the idea of sleeping alone made her feel hollow inside.

"Please, Lathe," she whispered. "Couldn't...couldn't we just sleep side by side as we have been and just not...hate each other?"

"I don't hate you little one." He leaned across the bunk and brushed his knuckles lightly over her cheek. "I could never hate you."

*That's what you think now,* Ari thought miserably. *But if you ever found out what I'm hiding...*

But she couldn't let herself finish the thought. She nuzzled against his hand for a moment and then forced herself to pull away.

"Come to bed," she said softly. "I have another long day tomorrow—I have to go back down in the hole."

"Down in the hole?" His eyes widened. "You went down in the *hole*? Why?"

Ari shrugged. "The wiring is all screwed up down there and I'm a fix-it now so Stubbins sent me to well...fix it."

Lathe's hands curled into fists again.

"I don't like that, Ari—not one fucking bit! You have to go through the tunnel where the lashers are kenneled to get down there. And we already know that at least one of them has shown unusual interest in you—it's not safe."

"None of BleakHall is safe," she pointed out. "You can't

protect me from everyone and everything here, Lathe. It's just not possible."

"I know...I know." He sighed deeply, his broad shoulders slumping. "There I go again—nearly going into Rage because I feel like you're being threatened. It just doesn't make sense."

"Going into rage?" Ari shook her head. "What does that mean?"

"It's a Kindred reaction when he feels his female is threatened," Lathe explained. "It's a kind of...altered state of consciousness. A berserker fury that comes over a Kindred warrior when he thinks his female is in danger. He will kill or even die to protect her in that state. He usually ends up killing," he added dryly. "A Kindred in Rage is...not a pretty sight."

"Oh." Ari shivered. "And you...feel that way towards me?"

"I can't seem to help it." His deep voice sounded bewildered. "It's been that way from the first moment I heard your voice, pleading with Mukluk not to search you right outside the infirmary. Do you know how many of those searches I've had to listen to? Fucking *thousands*." He shook his head. "But *your* voice was the one I couldn't ignore—*you* were the one I felt like I *had* to save, Ari. I just...don't understand why."

"I don't either," Ari whispered. "But we have a saying on Phobos. 'The Goddess of Mercy works in extraordinary ways through ordinary people.'" She half laughed. "Not that there's anything ordinary about you. You're so big and strong and your eyes are that gorgeous shade of ocean blue and of course, your fangs..." She shook her head. "I've never met anyone like you, Lathe."

"I feel the same way about you, you know," he murmured. "You're extraordinary, Ari. Beautiful...intelligent...fierce..." He sighed deeply. "And you make me question everything about myself. I don't know if that's a good thing or a bad thing."

"I'm sorry," Ari said again, feeling miserable once more. "So sorry, Lathe. I wish...wish things were different."

"I do too, little one." He sighed. "Well, we should get some sleep. Long day tomorrow—and a long night too. I forgot to tell you but Mukluk came and informed me that the two of us will be serving at the meeting of the Mistresses tomorrow night."

"The meeting of the Mistresses?" Ari asked, scooting over to make some room as he finally got into the bed beside her. "What's that?"

"A meeting of the BleakHall Board of Directors—the Yonnite Mistresses who own this place." Lathe's voice was grim. "A couple of them aren't bringing body servants and the Goddess knows, they can't be neglected for a moment. So you and I will be helping to serve them."

"Why us?" Ari asked curiously. "Is it a trustee thing or what?"

"It's a non-female-hater thing," Lathe told her. "The Horvaths know that Kindred won't hurt a female so Mukluk chose me for that reason. You...well, I'm guessing he thinks you're too young and innocent to be a female-hater yet. So you get the honors too."

"I don't mind, at least it's something different," Ari said, snuggling down beside him, though she was careful not to press her breasts against his muscular arm. God, he was so *warm*. She'd been freezing when she was sitting apart from him. Now, just having him beside her, radiating heat, was already thawing her out.

Lathe snorted. "Have you ever *seen* Yonnite Mistresses? They're different, all right. And *extremely* picky. You'll have to follow my lead and do exactly what you're told."

"I can handle myself in mixed company," Ari said, stung by his tone. "I know how to act around ladies."

"That's well and good but Yonnite Mistresses are no ladies," Lathe said dryly. He yawned and sighed. "Anyway, it's a problem for tomorrow. It's late and I'm tired. Do you mind if I turn towards you or would you rather sleep back to back?"

Ari's heart ached fiercely.

"You can turn towards me," she whispered. "If...if you don't mind if I turn towards you."

"I'd like that, little one." Lathe shifted towards her and Ari turned towards him as well, looking up into his fierce, beautiful eyes. "Good night, Lathe," she whispered, wishing she could get closer. Wishing she could kiss him or cuddle with him or touch him in any way. But she didn't dare. She could only lay there longing for what she couldn't have...for what she could *never* have.

"Good night, Ari," he rumbled.

He looked at her for a long moment and Ari could almost feel the longing in the air between them. His scent—his bonding scent, she realized—intensified until she could barely keep herself from pressing against him. But somehow she resisted. At last his jewel-like eyes closed, leaving her still wanting.

It was a long time before she could go to sleep. And when she did, Ari had troubled dreams that left her restless and desperately sad. Dreams where she was crying for Lathe, who was standing on the other side of a deep chasm. But when she reached for him, trying to bridge the gap that separated them, the big Kindred just turned away.

*He's gone,* she thought in her dream. *Gone and I'll never get him back.*

# THIRTY-TWO

"Stubbins says you're to fix the mechanical slop arms in the kitchen. They're actin' up worse than usual."

Tubby, the inmate with the enormous belly, spoke without looking up from the porno mag he was holding about a foot from his face.

"Yeah—he already left out the tools you need." Another inmate—Ari had heard him called "Ratty" because of his long nose that twitched constantly, nodded at the dull silver tools with their red handles. They were lying on the folding table, where the gang boss usually sat smoking his endless supply of nico-sticks, just where she had left them before lunch.

"Oh." Ari hesitated, not sure if she ought to take orders from anyone but the gang leader himself. "Where is Stubbins, anyway?" she asked.

"Went to review a new shipment of skin-mags and he'll probably be back real soon-like." Tubby sounded irritated that she was bothering him.

"Yeah, so make yourself scarce and go fix stuff, fix-it. Or you're going to be in big trouble when he gets back, 'ent you?" Ratty demanded. He had a portable vid-viewer strapped to his face and from the sizable tent in the bottom half of his jumpsuit, he also was looking at pornographic material.

Ari tried one more time.

"But...I was under the impression that I was supposed to go back to the hole after lunch. I'm still in the middle of re-wiring—"

"I'm telling you, if you don't fix them fucking slop arms you're going to fucking regret it," Tubby growled. "Now *go!*"

Uncertainly, Ari buckled on her belt and licked her thumb, pressing it in turn to the screwdriver and wrench that were laid out on the table. The handles turned blue obediently and she tucked them into the leather belt.

She wished Stubbins was here to tell her exactly what to do or at least show her the kite that had been sent in describing the exact problem. But then, remembering the herky-jerky motion of the arms as they slopped food all over the place at mealtimes, she realized she didn't really need specifications. The arms just needed a tune-up and she could probably get it done in time to go back to the hole and see Jak some more.

As she made her way to the kitchen, she wished she could tell Lathe about her big brother. But that might bring up the reason why she was here herself...and how she had gotten here...and all kinds of other questions she would rather not answer. So for now, at least, Ari was keeping Jak to herself.

In fact, she was keeping most everything to herself today. She and Lathe had barely spoken and he had made no comment when she'd decided to take a sponge bath in the sink rather than going to the trustee showers with him. He had been similarly quiet at breakfast, lunch, and in the Rec Yard.

The silence between them hurt Ari's heart but she recognized that it was necessary. If she started trying to get Lathe to talk to her she might say more than she should. So it was better to let a barrier grow between them even though it made her feel isolated and sad.

Walking through the vast Mess Hall, she noticed how strangely quiet it was when it was empty. At meal times the inmate's voices boomed and bounced off the metal walls, making it almost unbearably loud. Now the silence felt unnatural and stiff...waiting somehow.

*Stop it, Ari,* she told herself, trying to shake off the weird feeling the eerie quiet in the Mess Hall gave her. *Stop letting your imagination run away with you. Just get this job done so you can go back to the hole and see Jak.*

At least she knew her big brother had someone to talk to while he waited for her. Despite the hybrid's frightening rap sheet and scary appearance, Jak was apparently, if not friends with the Beast—or Slade, as he called him—at least willing to talk to him. Ari had talked to the man a bit herself and though she wouldn't have wanted to be alone in a room with him, he was a personable-enough conversationalist. Then again, sociopaths usually were personable, she reminded herself with a shiver. It was part of the way they lured their victims to them.

She wondered again about the Beast's true crimes. He claimed murder and arson readily—"*Fuck yeah—killed my old master and burned down his house and I'd do it again. He wasn't exactly kind to his slaves, if you know what I mean.*"—but he was adamant that he was *not* a rapist. *"The Mistress who bought me after I killed my old master hung that charge on me because I **wouldn't** fuck her. She knew it was a one-way ticket to prison and that's where they sent me."*

Ari wasn't sure if she believed him or not but it was certainly a colorful story.

With a sigh, she went to the chow line at the front of the Mess Hall and examined the front part of the mechanical arms, which was all most of the inmates ever saw as they pushed their trays through the line.

The arms were basically long metal tubes that the food could flow through. They were jointed in two places with an "elbow in the middle and a "wrist" at the end. But instead of ending in a hand, each arm had a dull silver scoop capable of depositing a load of food—if you could call it that—onto a tray.

Ari shivered with disgust when she saw the old food crusting the insides of the scoops and the flow-tubes of the arms. Lathe had told her that the arms were supposed to be cleaned out regularly but it appeared that whichever gang leader was in charge of the kitchen didn't care much about cleanliness.

Who *was* in charge of the kitchen, anyway, Ari wondered as she pushed through the tall black metal door that led from the Mess Hall to the kitchen. Who—she frowned, losing her train of thought as she looked around.

The vast commercial-sized kitchen was deserted.

But shouldn't *someone* be here? There were only a few hours until supper—or Last Meal as Lathe called it. Ari knew a lot of the kitchen was automated but surely *some* human work was needed to feed the thousand prisoners BleakHall had at every feeding?

Walking over to the back of the mechanical arms, she examined the rusted mechanisms, though she kept looking over her shoulder as she went, because the silence was creepy. There was a row of machines set up in a line just under the mechanical arms that were clearly part of the feeding mechanism.

Ari had a look at them—several were vast cooking vats, crusted with congealed protein paste. Further up the line she saw an industrial sized meat grinder that looked like it could have taken on an entire proto-bovine back on Phobos with no problem. Large grinding wheels were lined with many tiny, murderously sharp teeth, dark with dried blood and matted with fur.

Ari frowned. Wait a minute—*fur?* Leaning forward, she took a closer look. Sure enough, there was grayish-brown hair or fur clogging some of the teeth. What the hell was that from?

Then she heard a rustling sound from the large metal bin beside the industrial-sized meat grinder. A foot petal below it held the on-off switch, presumably to make it easier for a worker to run the mechanism while using both hands to feed the meat into the grinder. There was a hatch at the top with a rusted handle. With a feeling of dread, Ari opened it to look inside.

Bright, black oil-spot eyes looked up at her. Sharp, pointed noses with long whiskers twitched in her direction. Hundreds of rats squeaked and squealed and squirmed all over each other in a flow of brown and gray fur, their sharp claws scrabbling uselessly at the slick metal sides of the holding bin as they tried desperately to climb towards the light.

"Ugh!" Ari started back in horror. Goddess of Mercy was *that* what she had been eating every day at meal times? The very idea made her gorge rise and she thought she might be sick. Gagging, she let the hatch fall closed with a clang and backed away...only to feel a pair of hard hands grip her shoulders.

"I know, pretty boy—it's nasty to think about, 'ent it?" whispered a horribly familiar voice in her ear. "But it 'ent like the Mistresses are gonna shell out to feed the lot of us murderers and rapists prime bovine—now are they? So it's rat protein paste for breakfast, lunch, and supper around here—and it looks like you're for *dessert*."

# THIRTY-THREE

"Get away from me!" Ari threw an elbow back hard into Tapper's hairy, protruding belly. He grunted and a gust of breath smelling of unbrushed teeth and rotten food washed over the side of her face—but he didn't let go.

"Now, now my pretty little lad," he cooed in Ari's ear. "Let's have no more of that, shall we? You're on my list and it's time you gave up that sweet little ass to old Tapper here."

As he spoke, he shifted his hold from gripping her upper arms to putting an arm around her neck.

Ari felt panic trying to take her but this was a move she had trained for in *Ton-kwa* many times.

"No! Leave me alone!" she shouted. Taking a firm grip on the hairy forearm encircling her throat, she threw her weight back and then forward, flipping Tapper over her head.

He landed with a gasp, flat on his back on the dirty metal floor.

"Why, you...you little bastard," he panted, his piggy little eyes narrowing as he looked up at her. "You'll pay for that, you will!"

Ari didn't wait to hear more. She turned to run but Tapper was faster to recover than she could have believed. One hard hand shot out and encircled her ankle. With a desperate cry, Ari tripped and fell to the scuffed metal floor, bruising both knees and her ribs and knocking the breath out of herself.

Almost at once she flipped over, flailing and fishtailing, kicking out at Tapper to make him release his grip on her leg. One slippered foot connected squarely with his nose and there was a crunching sound and a howl from the crime lord.

"Gods, he's gone and broke my nose! Get 'im, boys—get 'im good!"

To Ari's horror, before she could even get to her feet, Gorn and Fenrus were on either side of her, gripping her arms.

Held as she was, she couldn't do any Ton-kwa moves effectively but she *did* have another weapon, she suddenly remembered. Slithering her right arm free of Fenrus's grasp, she reached for her belt and pulled out a petite socket wrench, which was the only tool she could reach.

The idiot inmate caught her arm again almost at once, laughing at the tiny wrench, which was meant to reach into small, tight spaces where larger tools couldn't fit.

"Lookit this, Gorn," he howled, pointing to the miniature wrench. "Lookit what pretty boy has." He held up Ari's arm by the wrist, showing the small tool clutched in her hand. "Whatcha gonna do, pretty boy?" he jeered at Ari. "Gonna hit me with your big bad weapon? Gonna knock me out?"

"I don't need to hit you," Ari said through gritted teeth. "I just need to *touch* you."

As she spoke, she tilted her wrist, holding the wrench by the end of its red handle and tapped the dirty ring of exposed skin on Fenrus's own wrist where the sleeve of his jumpsuit had pulled up.

At once she felt the electrical surge of the protective field the tools generated jolting through the other inmate.

Fenus howled and yanked away from her, gripping the spot on his arm where she'd touched him.

"I'm hurt! He got me, he did! Just lookit—my arm's numb," he screamed at Gorn, his thin lips peeled back in agony to expose the blackened stumps of his teeth.

*"A shock like that'll pop your balls like corn in a hot pan,"* Stubbins' voice whispered in Ari's head and it certainly seemed to be true.

Turning, she grabbed the other tool from her belt—a screwdriver with a narrow, sharp point good for working with the tiny screws and wiring inside the electrical box in the hole. Using Gorn's grip on her other wrist for leverage, she swung around and planted the tiny, sharp screwdriver in the inmate's yellowed eye.

If she'd been just a little taller or the screwdriver had been an inch or two longer, she could have driven it home inside Gorn's brain and finished the man completely. As it was, she only succeeded in popping his eye and giving him an electrical jolt that made him scream and stagger backwards.

"My eye! She got my fuckin' eye!" he wailed, flailing with his arms as the gooey mess of his eyeball dripped down his gaunt cheek. *"My eye!"*

For a moment Ari was transfixed by the sight—horrified by what she had done. And yet, she would have done worse if she could, she realized numbly. She would have done anything to get away from this horrible scene.

The momentary paralysis broke and she ran to the huge door she had come in by, meaning to slam through it and get out of the kitchen, away from danger. She hit the door...and bounced off it, nearly falling backwards.

Panic made her desperate and she staggered to catch her balance and tried the door again. But though she pushed and pulled with all her might, the tall metal door didn't budge.

"Don't bother, pretty boy—it's locked. See the bolt?"

Ari looked wildly and saw through the crack in the door that a bar of metal as thick as her wrist was connecting it to the jam beside it. Beside the bolt was a large keyhole but there was no key in it.

How had Tapper managed to lock the door without her hearing? It must have been when she was distracted by the squeaking and scrabbling of the rats in the metal holding pen. However he had done it, the crime lord had locked her in and there was no way out.

"Lookin' for this, pretty boy?"

She turned to see Tapper holding a key—dangling it in front of her face, maddeningly just out of reach.

"Didn't you know it was my crew that runs the kitchens?" he asked, leering at Ari. "I got the keys to everything around here. Including your pretty little ass." He gestured at Fenrus and Gorn, who was still moaning and clutching at his deflated eye. "Hold 'im boys—I'm gonna make him pay."

"But boss, my *eye!*" Gorn began.

"And my *arm*," Fenrus whined.

"Shut it!" Tapper roared at his henchmen. "He broke my

fucking nose but you don't hear me whining! I said hold pretty boy here and if you don't, you'll be fuckin' sorry."

"I'm gonna make *him* sorry for what he did to my eye!" Gorn announced, pulling himself together and rounding on Ari. The jellied remains of his left eye hung in a gory mess from the socket. "I'm mess him up good when you're done with him boss!"

"Yeah!" Fenrus exclaimed, catching the other inmate's enthusiasm. "Mess 'im up!"

Both of them were headed for Ari and she felt desperately for any other tools she could use as weapons. Unfortunately, she'd lost the socket wrench after hitting Fenrus with it and Gorn's motions had jerked the screwdriver out of her hand when he pulled away. Both tools lay on the dirty metal floor but the wrench was closest—only a yard or so from her feet.

Taking a chance, Ari dived for it. But though Fenrus and Gorn missed her, Tapper, who was up on his feet, grabbed the back of her prison jumpsuit and yanked.

Ari gasped as she felt the cheap buttons at the front of the jumpsuit give way, popping off the worn fabric as easily as though they'd been cut by a sharp pair of scissors.

*Goddess of Mercy, no!*

She tried to stop her forward momentum but it was too late, she was falling forward, slipping out of the baggy jumpsuit to land half-naked on the cold, dirty metal floor.

"Lookit here, boys—pretty boy is already half undressed for me," Tapper crowed. Clearly he had only seen Ari's bare back as yet. Ari was desperate to keep it that way.

Scrambling behind her, she tried to get her arms back into the blue and orange striped jumpsuit. But Tapper gave an ugly laugh and yanked on the fabric again, pulling it down past her hips.

Then he stripped it all the way off and threw it in a corner, reminding Ari horribly of how she'd been stripped and forced to kneel in his cell, waiting to be raped the last time he'd gotten to her.

"Mmm, lookit that ass," he told his henchman. "So curvy and round! As pretty as a girl's, 'ent it?"

"That it is, boss," Fenrus crowed. "Can me and Gorn have a go at it when you're done?"

"Of course boys—didn't I promise that? Come on, get 'im up on 'is hands and knees," Tapper commanded.

Ari was still lying face down and she did her best to fold herself into a ball but hard hands were on her, forcing her up on her knees. She kept her arms stubbornly folded over her breasts but though she wiggled and kicked, there was no getting away this time.

"Spread those legs!" Tapper snarled. "I said spread 'em!" He slapped Ari's ass, hard enough to leave a print, she was sure. She kicked back at him but one of them—either Fenrus or Gorn—grabbed her ankle and forced her to bend the way Tapper wanted her to.

Ari felt sick. Slowly, her thighs were forced apart, the cold metal of the floor scraping against her bare knees. She was still trying to hide her breasts but there was nothing she could do to hide what was—or rather *wasn't*—between her legs. Hard hands were forcing her up and prying open her cheeks. A cold breeze caressed her exposed rosebud and outer pussy lips, making Ari gasp and clench in on herself.

"Hey," she heard Tapper say from behind her, confusion thick in his voice. "Hey, where's his shaft?"

"Lookit that—pretty boy 'ent got no dick," Gorn remarked.

"He 'ent got no dick! He 'ent got no dick!" Fenrus chanted in a sing-song tone.

"Shut up, you idiot," Tapper commanded. "It's true he 'ent got a dick but look what he does have—a pussy!" He flipped Ari over and pried her arms away from her chest. "And tits!"

Fenrus and Gorn goggled at her as though they'd never seen a naked female before. Well, likely they hadn't for several years, at least, Ari thought despairingly.

"Let me go!" she shouted as loudly as she could. "Let me *go!*"

"Oh, I don't think so." Tapper shook his head wonderingly, as though still taking in the reality of the situation. "Lookit this, boys," he said to his henchmen. "Pretty boy is a *girl!*"

# THIRTY-FOUR

"I ain't fucked a girl in *years*," Gorn said, grinning around the gory remains of his left eye. "So I haven't."

"I fucked a girl once," Fenrus volunteered. His face fell. "That's why they sent me here to BleakHall. All 'cause I wanted to try some pussy."

"Well you can try this one as much as you want—*after* I get through with her." Tapper was already unbuttoning the bottom of his green and blue striped trustee jumpsuit. "Hold her, boys—I'm gonna have my first taste of gash in fifteen years, so I am."

Just then the black metal door to the kitchen rattled on its hinges.

"Who's that?" Fenrus's head snapped up like a canine on point.

"Doesn't matter—whoever it is they can't get in." Tapper's voice held a greedy quality and his eyes never left Ari's naked body. "Just ignore it boys. Our business is here."

But as he spoke, the kitchen door rattled again and the thick tongue of metal that held the bolt in place snapped like a brittle stick. The door burst open and Ari saw Lathe standing there, his fangs bared and his eyes narrowed in fury.

"Get the fuck away from Ari." His voice was a deep, inhuman growl. "Right...fucking...now. Or you die—*all* of you."

Ari drew in a breath. Lathe had told her about the state of protective berserker fury a Kindred went into when he felt his female was threatened. What had he called it? Oh yes—Rage. She was certain Rage was what she was seeing now. She had never seen Lathe's fangs look so long and sharp before and his eyes...his eyes were *red*. Red and glowing with a fury so deep only violence could express it.

He also seemed to have grown somehow—he looked positively huge looming over the ugly tableau on the dirty kitchen floor. If he was as surprised as Tapper had been by her suddenly female body, he didn't show it—he only seemed to grow larger and more menacing.

"I mean it," he growled again—his voice more of a vibration than a sound. *"Ari...is...mine."*

Gorn and Fenrus drew away from her but Tapper, his dirty root of a shaft already out and in his hand, didn't look likely to be deterred. He barely spared a glance in Lathe's direction, so focused was he on Ari's naked body.

"Take care of 'im, boys," he ordered his henchmen distractedly. "Don't let Medic bother me—I got a cunt to fuck."

Fenrus and Gorn sprang obediently to their feet but Tapper had underestimated the depth of the big Kindred's fury. With a roar, Lathe sprang on them, his fangs flashing as he bit and bit again—too fast to follow.

Ari gasped as she saw both men begin to choke and strangle, their skin turning an ugly, dusky color as black foam seethed from between their lips.

Tapper turned his head and his eyes widened but he still didn't get off her. Instead, a long silver blade suddenly appeared in his hand. He held it up, showing Lathe and then pressed it to her throat, just under her left ear.

"Better step back, Medic," he snarled. "Or this pretty little girl of yours is going to die."

"You son of a bitch!" Lathe's eyes were glowing brighter than ever but despite his state of Rage, he seemed to understand that a false move on his part meant sudden death for Ari. "Let Ari go!" he demanded, his voice still that low, menacing growl.

"Not until I've had my fun with her." Tapper leered at him as he dragged Ari to her feet, the cold metal of the knife never wavering. Ari felt it prick the skin at the side of her neck and a hot drop of blood welled out against her fear-chilled skin. "This here is no ordinary knife, no it isn't," he told Lathe as he pushed Ari in front of him, apparently heading for one of the kitchen counters. "I got it from a poisoner on Chathm Prime, so I did. It's *deadly*."

"So am I." Lathe nodded at Gorn and Fenrus, now both dead on the floor, their faces frozen in a rictus of agony. "Let Ari go now and I won't...won't kill you." It seemed to take all of the big Kindred's willpower to say the words but he ground them out between his teeth, his fangs winking with deadly intent in the harsh kitchen glows as he spoke.

But Tapper was imperturbable.

"I told you, Medic—not until I've had my fun. Do you know how long it's been since I had a taste of pussy? Not since I raped my old Mistress and all her friends at their fancy garden party and then killed the whole lot of them." His piggy eyes glowed with the memory of his crimes. "That was fun but *this* is going to be even better—so it is. Because you're going to *watch* me fuck this sweet little pussy you've been keepin' all to yourself, so you are, old son. I'm going to fuck her 'till she screams and all you can do is watch while I have what's yours—what should have been mine in the first place!"

As he spoke, he started to bend Ari face-first over the dull silver kitchen counter. But Ari had had enough.

"I'd rather die," she said in a low voice. "I'd rather die than have you anywhere near me you *asshole!*"

On the last word she threw an elbow in Tapper's gut and twisted her head away from the knife.

Everything seemed to happen in slow motion. Tapper's arm jerked and Ari watched from the corner of her eye as the long silver blade passed by her cheek in a blur. He shouted with anger but he didn't let go of her. That was all right—Ari hadn't expected him to. She just wanted to give Lathe an opening and she had.

In a flash, the big Kindred had Tapper by the wrist. He squeezed and Ari heard a crunching sound as the bones in the inmate's arm snapped and crackled like a bundle of twigs being broken for the fire. The knife dropped from his suddenly limp fingers and he let go of Ari at the same time. She took a quick step back, wanting to get away but unable to stop watching.

"Let me go!" Tapper screamed at Lathe, spittle and blood from his broken nose flying from his lips. "You don't dare lay a finger on me! You know what my boys'll do to you if you bite me!"

"Oh, I'm not going to *bite* you," Lathe growled. His face was a mask of fury and his eyes were glowing like hot coals. "That's too clean a death for filth like you, Tapper. You don't deserve my venom."

He grabbed Tapper by the throat and squeezed, yanking him up off the ground as though he weighed nothing at all.

Ari watched in amazement, thinking that Lathe would choke the crime boss to death. But it turned out that Lathe had something worse—much worse—in mind.

Holding Tapper up by the throat, he walked over to the industrial sized meat grinder and stepped on the foot pedal that started the machine. Immediately a humming, grinding buzz began to rise as the big blades with all their tiny teeth began to whir.

Tapper—his face red and his eyes bulging—seemed to finally understand what the big Kindred had in mind for him. He shook his head frantically and made choking sounds of negation, his broken wrist flopping limply.

"Nnnn! *Nnnnnn!*" he gurgled but Lathe was already lowering him down towards the blades.

Tapper kicked frantically, his prison-issued rubber sandals falling down into the churning teeth which chewed them up hungrily. Lathe gave him a swift punch to one knee-cap which seemed to break something in the crime lord's leg. The moment it hung limp, his foot was caught in the grinder's teeth and it began sucking him down.

A piercing shriek, like something a little girl might make, came from Tapper's burly, unshaven throat. He flailed wildly but he couldn't get free with Lathe holding his neck and the grinder chewing relentlessly up his leg. Ari watched with horror as his second flailing foot was caught in the endlessly whirring blades and a gout of blood went up, spattering the big Kindred's trustee uniform with dark scarlet drops.

*Oh Goddess, I don't want to see this... I want to stop watching, I don't want to see this,* she thought. But somehow she couldn't look away.

When the grinder reached both thighs, Lathe dropped Tapper, who flopped like a fish, screaming and swearing.

"Let me out—let me out! They'll kill you! My boys will kill you, Gods damn you! It hurts! It hurts! *My boys will kill you!*" he shrieked, scrabbling at the slick metal surface of the metal holding tank full of rats.

*I guess we'll be having rat and Tapper stew for supper,* Ari thought inanely and a hysterical giggle rose in her throat. She swallowed it down with difficulty but then noises started coming out of her anyway. *I'm laughing,* she thought. *I shouldn't be laughing at this—it's horrible—**horrible!***

But when she put her hands to her face to cover her mouth, she felt wetness on her cheeks and realized she was crying instead.

The grinder had reached Tapper's waist by now but the crime boss had stopped swearing and struggling. His upper torso wiggled and jerked as the grinder methodically chewed him up but his eyes were blank and lifeless. Clearly he was dead already but Lathe made no move to remove the top part of the body. Apparently the grinder was going to finish the job of chopping him into protein paste and feed him into one of the vast tub-sized cooking kettles.

*What's the difference?* Ari thought. *Supper will just be a little more ratty than usual. Probably no one will even notice.*

Another one of those hysterical giggle-sobs tried to come up her throat and she shoved a fist in her mouth and bit down hard to stifle it.

Then Lathe turned to her.

The big Kindred was still in Rage, his eyes burning red. When he looked at Ari she felt her blood run cold. There was no more need to stop herself from cry-laughing or laugh-crying or whatever you wanted to call it. Everything inside her seemed to freeze at once.

*He killed Gorn and Fenrus and Tapper and I'm next,* she thought, a surge of pure terror running through her. *I lied to him —I tricked him and now he'll kill me too!*

The big Kindred came towards her and she shrank back against the cold metal of the steel countertop, her stomach a hard, icy knot inside her, her hands trembling as she tried to cover herself.

"What..." he growled in a low, intense voice, "the *fuck* are you?"

"Please..." Ari's voice shook and she could barely stand. As frightened as she'd been of Tapper and his goons, they were nothing compared to a Kindred warrior in Rage. "Please, Lathe..."

"Are you male? Are you female? What in the Seven Hells is going on?" he demanded, his eyes glowing.

"Please," she whispered again. "Please, don't kill me. Or if you do, please bite me. Don't...don't put me in the grinder like Tapper. Please, Lathe!"

"Kill you?" He looked at her blankly and then the red, terrible glow began to fade from his eyes. He took a step back and shook himself. "What are you talking about? Why would I kill you? I just murdered three males to save you—even though I don't know what the hell you are."

"I'm a girl! I know I shouldn't have lied to you," Ari babbled. "But I was afraid! You said that everyone here hated females! You said any female that came into BleakHall would be raped to death inside of fifteen minutes!"

"So you *are* female then?" He took a step towards her and Ari took a step back, trying to cover her breasts and sex with her hands.

"No—let me *see*, Goddess damn you!" Lathe growled. He put a hand on her arm and Ari shrank back from him.

"Don't hurt me," she begged, unable to help herself. He had just killed three men in the space of five minutes—in the most brutal way possible. And now he was looming over her, angry and huge. She couldn't help being afraid of him.

Lathe's blazing eyes softened, going completely turquoise and losing the last of their red fire.

"It's all right," he murmured, his deep voice more gentle than she'd yet heard it. "I just need to see for myself what you are, Ari. Please, I need to *see*."

Ari forced herself to drop her arms to her sides, baring herself completely. Her nipples were tight with fear and she felt his gaze on her like a laser beam.

"Female," Lathe whispered, half to himself. He reached out, fingers lightly brushing the curve of her left breast. "But how? I saw your shaft myself. Hell, I fucking *kissed* it." His eyes blazed again, though at least they didn't turn red.

Ari flinched away from his touch. Goosebumps had broken out all over her bare skin but she didn't quite dare try to hide herself from him again.

"I had a solid-holo projector—I call it a look/touch—implanted in my prison ID," she said. "It projected a male chest and genitalia. But then, last night, the power supply ran out. Right after you, uh...kissed it. My fake shaft, I mean."

"A solid-holo projector?" Lathe frowned. "I've never heard of anything like that."

Ari lifted her chin.

"That's because I invented it."

"You invented a lot of things, didn't you?" His deep voice was bitter. "A male persona...a lie about what you were...your feelings for me. Why are you even here, Ari? And is Ari even your name? No, stop—I don't care," he said when Ari opened her mouth to answer. "I don't give a fuck. Just put on your clothes and get out of here."

He jerked his head at her prison jumpsuit, which lay crumpled in a corner.

Something loosened inside Ari's chest when she realized he wasn't going to kill her—that he was letting her go. But his words —"I don't care...I don't give a fuck," rang in her head and made her feel empty inside. Right now, though, she just wanted to get away from here, wanted to run far away from this horrible scene and never come back.

She hurried over to where her jumpsuit was and put it on, pulling it tight around her body to hide her breasts. The leather tool belt, which she had been wearing loose around her hips so as not to draw attention to her small waist, slid back into place as easily as it had slid off.

Ari had the presence of mind to grab the wrench and the screwdriver off the floor—they were lying between Gorn and Fenrus's bodies—and shove them back into the belt. Then she edged towards the door. Would Lathe really let her leave?

The big Kindred made no move to stop her. When Ari reached the doorway and looked back at him, she saw him watching her with an unreadable expression in his jewel-toned eyes. Somehow she got the nerve to speak.

"Lathe," she whispered and her cheeks were wet again. "I'm so sor—"

"Save it." His voice was flat—as flat as his eyes. "Just go, Ari. I have to clean up in here and you probably don't want to see it."

He grabbed Fenrus's body and headed for the meat grinder, which had digested Tapper completely by now and was ready for more.

Ari couldn't stay to see it—she felt like if she did, she might go crazy. To be honest, she felt like she was already halfway there. Sick and scared and more shaken than she could ever remember, she fled just as the grinding hum began again.

# THIRTY-FIVE

It was dark and bloody work but Lathe didn't care. He was feeling in a dark and bloody mood at the moment.

*Lied to me...she* **lied to me.** The litany went round and round in his head over and over—a broken recording that wouldn't stop playing.

*Just like Talsa—she never really cared. She put me through a fucking emotional grinder, wondering what the hell was wrong with me...asking myself why I wanted another male sexually...how I could fall in love with someone of my own sex. And all the time she was probably laughing at me! 'Look at the big, stupid Kindred—I've got him twisted around my little finger. The idiot loves me even though he thinks I'm male!"*

Deep down, Lathe knew this characterization of Ari wasn't really fair. After all, it wasn't like Ari had seduced him, the way Talsa had. In this case, *he* had approached *Ari*. Had gone running to save the boy—no, the *girl*—the minute he heard her voice begging not to be searched by the Horvath guards.

*That's right I did—I saved him—no, her, damnit,* **her**—*saved her from Mukluk and Tapper and every other damn threat in this whole fucking place. I came running when Wheezer told me she was going to the kitchens and Tapper was planning a little "welcoming committee." I put my life on the line for her and she played me like a fish on a line. Gods, what an idiot I am!*

The angry thoughts—mostly shame and hurt pride—continued to circle his brain relentlessly as he shoved first Fenrus and then Gorn through the meat grinder. There was really no other way to dispose of the bodies since someone was sure to notice if he started digging graves in the Rec Yard, Lathe thought dryly.

And though it was tempting to leave them lying around as a warning to others, he knew it was in his best interest to try and make Tapper and his closest henchmens' deaths a mystery. The rest of his gang were intensely loyal to their leader and if they figured out that Lathe was behind his death, they would start coming for him and wouldn't stop until Lathe was dead or *all* of them were.

Since he had no wish to take on fifty hardened criminals at once, Lathe disposed of the bodies and cleaned up the messy blood spatter around the grinder, making certain there were no shreds of fabric from the prison jumpsuits left in its teeth before he left the kitchen.

It was supper time soon but for obvious reasons he wouldn't be eating. After that was the Mistresses meeting where he and Ari were supposed to serve. And after that, he had to deal with getting Ari safely back to his cell before the lashers came out.

But Lathe couldn't think about any of that now. He was too angry...and too hurt. He went to his cell wondering what he would say if he found Ari there. But he needn't have worried—she wasn't there. His cell was empty—as empty as it had been before she'd come into his life, bringing her lies and deception and her big dark, pleading eyes and pretty face with her.

Lathe felt empty too. Hollowed out and cold as though someone had scooped out his insides and filled his body cavities with ice instead. He collapsed on his bunk with an arm over his eyes and tried not to think.

He would have to see Ari again eventually but for now, he just wanted to be alone.

# THIRTY-SIX

A ri just wanted to be alone.

Her nerves felt shredded and in her mind's eyes, she couldn't stop seeing the gory deaths she'd witnessed in the kitchen. Her head ached and the tiny scratch Tapper had made with his knife, just below her left ear, stung and throbbed.

But it was her heart that hurt the worst.

She huddled in a corner of the sub-basement, just outside the entrance to the tunnel which led to the hole. It was the only place she could think of in all of BleakHall where it might be safe to cry.

*Except in Lathe's arms,* whispered a little voice in her head. That made her remember the way he'd held her in the Rec Yard, shielding her body with his own so that no one would know she was grieving and think she was weak. The warm scent of his skin as he comforted her...his big hands stroking her hair and her trembling shoulders...the soft words he'd murmured in that deep, gentle voice of his as he soothed her...

*No, stop it!* she told herself savagely. *Stop wishing for something you can never have. He* **hates** *you now! And can you blame him? You should have told him the truth when you had the chance. Now there's no chance at all—none—that he'll ever want you again.*

Where was she going to go tonight? Where could she stay? Ari was almost certain she couldn't go back to Lathe's cell—could she? What would he do when he saw her? Probably tell her to take her things and get out. But get out where? Would she be moved in with the general population of the prison? Ari was certain if that happened her secret would be out inside of an hour and she would be dead an hour after that.

When Lathe was in Rage she'd been afraid the big Kindred might kill her himself for lying to him, but then he had expressed surprise that she would even think that. Well, right before telling her to get out of his sight, anyway, Ari thought dryly. But he *had* come running to her rescue—she still had no idea how he'd known about Tapper's attack on her—and he had claimed her over and over again as he fought Tapper and his minions.

*Ari is mine!* She could still hear his deep, growling voice in her head and see the flashing red eyes, so terrifying in their fury. Would he really cast her aside so easily after killing for her and claiming her? Would he be willing to let her die even if he didn't have an active hand in her death himself?

Ari simply didn't know. She had known the big Kindred for less than a solar week—although it felt like much longer. Their relationship, if you could call it that, had moved with break-neck

speed from fear and distrust to love and longing and back to fear
and distrust again.

*I should have told him,* she thought miserably. *I should have
taken a chance and told him the whole truth last night.*

But it was too late for regrets now. Too late to do anything but
try to deal with the situation at hand.

And she had no idea how to do that.

*I should go talk to Jak since I'm down here—I could do that
much at least. Say goodbye and explain why I probably won't
be back.*

But she couldn't bear that—couldn't tell her older brother
whom she had just reunited with that she was probably going to
be dead soon. And besides, she couldn't explain to Jak how she
felt about Lathe—about how she regretted fooling the big Kindred
and lying to him and hurting him.

About how she loved him even though it was far too late to
talk about love.

Ari cried herself out and sat in the dank subbasement through
supper time, her head on her knees. She thought about just
staying there indefinitely and not going back to the main part of
the prison at all. Maybe snatching food at meal times and bringing
it back down to her new lair. Although even the thought of ever
eating anything again that came from the BleakHall kitchens
turned her stomach. Still, she had to live...

It would have been a good plan if not for the lashers. Every
once in a while she could hear them stirring in their sleep, the
deep, rumbling growls that reminded her of Lathe drifting up
through the dark tunnel. If she was still here when the cold air
started blowing and they woke, she was dead meat—literally. And
while she doubted if being torn apart by a lasher could be more

painful than going through the meat grinder like Tapper had, she still didn't relish the idea of such a death.

At last she got up and dragged herself to the long flight of steps leading up to the main part of the prison. She would have to go back—there was no other way. Maybe Lathe would let her sleep in the corner of his cell on the floor if she promised to stay out of his way. Maybe—

Suddenly a large form blocked out the light from the top of the stairway.

"Ari? Are you down here?" a deep, familiar voice called.

"Lathe?" She could scarcely believe it. Looking up, she tried to see his face but since the light was at his back, it was still in shadows.

"Ari, Goddess-damn it!" He came down the stairs three at a time and seized her by the shoulders. "Where in the Seven Hells have you been?" he demanded.

"I...I was here," Ari said in a small voice. "I thought...thought it would be better to stay out of your way."

"I've been looking for you *everywhere*." His voice was hard and angry. "I thought one of Tapper's men had gotten you. Or someone else maybe—the Goddess knows everyone in BleakHall seems to want to rape you or kill you."

Ari pulled away from his hands.

"Including you? Now that you know what I am?"

"What? No!" Lathe ran a hand through his hair. "Of course not, damn it! I was just worried about you when you never came back to the cell."

Ari felt her heart lift, just a little bit.

"You were worried about me? I thought you didn't care what happened to me. You told me to go away."

"I was angry." Lathe blew out a breath. "I'm *still* angry. What you did to me—what you let me believe—" He shook his head again. "Goddess damn it, even now I can't just leave you alone. What in the Seven Hells is *wrong* with me?"

Ari's heart lifted a little more. *He still cares,* she thought. *Even though he doesn't want to. He still cares—at least a little.*

"Does that mean I can still stay in your cell?" she asked in a small voice. "If I promise not to bother you?"

"Your very *existence* bothers me," Lathe growled. "Having you in my cell or not doesn't seem to make a damn bit of difference." He sighed impatiently. "Look, I came to get you so you can change before the meeting of the Mistresses. We have to serve tonight, remember?"

"Oh, right," Ari said blankly. To be honest, she had forgotten all about serving at the meeting. Her mind had been too filled with horror and misery and regret to remember something as mundane as playing the part of temporary body slave to some spoiled Yonnite Mistress.

"Here." He thrust a clean jumpsuit at her. "I got you a change from the Laundry. Hurry and put it on. We're wanted in the upper conference room in a few minutes."

"All right." Ari started to take off the torn jumpsuit and Lathe turned his back to give her privacy.

"Are you finished?" he demanded after a moment, his voice hard. "We have to go."

"I'm ready." Ari smoothed her hair as well as she could. Leaving the ragged, torn jumpsuit behind, she followed him up out of the subbasement.

Lathe led the way without looking back, up the long flights of stairs that took them to the cell blocks. But this time they kept climbing, past the trustee block and every other block holding prisoners until they came at last to a heavy, sealed double door with a security pad on the wall outside it.

The pad was glowing red but when Lathe crouched down and put the prison ID tag at the hollow of his throat on level with the pad, it lit up green after a moment and there was a hissing click as the door swung open.

"Come on," he told Ari and led her into a part of the prison she had never seen before.

---

Lathe was angry with himself. Why couldn't he leave her alone? He'd been determined to do exactly that as he lay in his cell after the killings in the kitchen. He'd stripped off his stained and spattered jumpsuit, washed himself as well as he could in the tiny sink, and told himself he wouldn't think of Ari for even a moment.

But then an hour had passed...and then another and she still didn't appear in the cell. Lathe found himself wondering where she was...if she was safe. Though he tried to block out the image, he couldn't stop seeing her naked and vulnerable, lying on the cold, dirty kitchen floor with Tapper and his goons crouched over her, ready to violate her.

*What if she's in the same situation again?* whispered a little voice in his head. *What if one of the sociopaths in this fucking hellhole found out what she is, like Tapper did? What if she's being raped and killed right now while you lie here on your bunk feeling sorry for yourself?*

At last he hadn't been able to stand it anymore. He had left his own cell and gone down to the main part of the prison, searching for Ari. His fear for her had mounted steadily when he didn't find her in the library or the laundry or under the stairwell where Stubbins and the Spice Lords made their home.

Stubbins had been smoking one of his ubiquitous nico-sticks and he'd pulled Lathe aside, his grizzled face serious.

"Listen, Medic—just want you to know I didn't have anything to do with Ari getting sent to the kitchen. That was Tubby and Ratty and they've been punished proper-like. So I'm hoping the boy isn't much hurt and you'll still be willing to treat the Spice Lords in the Infirmary."

"Have you seen Ari?" Lathe demanded, blunt to the point of rudeness and ignoring everything else the other male said.

"Well, no..." Stubbins looked uncomfortable. "He's probably somewhere licking his wounds—Tapper ain't never easy on the newbies, I'm afraid. Uh...you can tell Ari he can keep the tools he has checked out for now and just give 'em back in the morning." He cleared his throat. "Have you seen Tapper, by the way? Some of his boys was looking for him."

"I'm sure they'll see him at supper," Lathe said with a humorless laugh. "Excuse me—I have to find Ari."

As he left, he had reflected that at least Tapper's gang still had no idea what had happened to their leader. Still, the minute they put two and two together, he and Ari were going to be in some very hot water. Even though he had disposed of the bodies thoroughly, there was no way they wouldn't deduce that Lathe had something to do with Tapper's disappearance since they surely all knew about the crime boss's plan to rape Ari.

*Might have to speed up the nanites some more,* he thought grimly. But if he wasn't careful, he was going to trip the prison's alarms for sure. His original plan had been to go out after lights out, since he knew the lashers wouldn't bother him. Then he could disappear into the hole the nanites had dug, which led to the outer perimeter of the prison, and come out near the shuttle he had hidden there. But if he also had to contend with a bunch of Horvath guards tracking him, the plan was going to get a hell of a lot more complicated.

*Of course you also didn't plan to bring anyone with you when you left since there are no other Kindred here,* whispered a little voice in his head. *But now you're going to bring Ari, aren't you?*

Gods damn it, yes, he realized—he *was* still going to bring her. Even though she had lied to him and put him through hell, questioning his whole sexual identity and everything about himself—even though she had used him and told him she loved him when he knew it wasn't true, he was still going to take her.

If he could find her, that was.

He had been nearly in a panic after he left Stubbins but then he remembered that she'd said she was working on some wiring problems in the hole. And sure enough, as soon as he made his way down to the subbasement he had finally found her. At the sight of her, his heart had fisted in his chest with a mixture of anger and relief. She looked so small and fragile in the darkness, she might almost have been one of the shadows herself.

*She's all right! Oh, thank the Goddess,* part of him thought. *The little liar,* added another part.

*Conflicted much, Lathe?* whispered a sardonic little voice in his head.

*Hell yes, I'm conflicted,* he thought angrily as he strode along, leading her up the endless flights of steps that led to the upper conference room where the BleakHall Board of Directors was going to meet. *I don't **want** to care about Ari anymore.*

And yet somehow he couldn't seem to stop himself.

Trying to turn his mind to other things, Lathe focused on his surroundings. The part of the prison inside the security door—the wing the Yonnite Mistresses who owned BleakHall had built for themselves—bore absolutely no resemblance to the rest of the prison. So there was plenty to focus on.

Instead of blank, black metal, the walls were covered in muted but colorful *Isoldan* wall murals. Instead of dirty bare floors, plush *Tizodeen* moss in shades of blue and green and purple cushioned their footsteps. There was no sound of hoarse male voices cursing each other—just the hushed strains of a relaxing melody played on the many-stringed *zibathorn* floating through com-link system. And the faint, sweet scent of exotic flowers drifted on the air currents, replacing the stench of unwashed male bodies, stale sweat and rotten protein paste that was the prevalent reek in the rest of BleakHall.

It was like walking directly from hell into paradise.

"Wow..." Ari looked around in obvious wonder. "It's like a seven-star hotel in here! How often do these Yonnite Mistresses meet?"

"About once a year—sometimes more—from what I understand," Lathe growled. "But they're unwilling to forego their luxuries even for a single night. Which is where you and I come in. They can't be without their body slaves so we have to fill in. Come on—in here."

He had only been here once before to help with the cleaning—he was one of the few inmates the Horvaths trusted not to tear everything up or try to steal anything. But he remembered his way around. Now he pulled Ari into the food prep area where they would wait until the Mistresses arrived.

Again he was struck with the contrast between this kitchen and the one below. Instead of a holding tank for rats and a meat grinder and cooking vats, he saw sleek, state-of-the-art appliances. A broiling wave, a micro-heater, a convection cooker, and a vast cold storage cabinet that took up most of one wall were all featured.

Large trays filled with exotic foods—heaps of fresh fruit, platters of candied delicacies, even a dish of too-too fish which was served rare with a side of bitter butter—proved that the caterers had already come and gone. The Mistresses who owned and ran BleakHall were jealous of their privacy—allowing no one but body slaves, whom they considered to be beneath their notice—to witness their meetings.

But though they considered males beneath their notice, they were still extremely picky about the state of the males that served them—*that* Lathe knew. He straightened his own jumpsuit and turned to Ari to tell her to straighten hers. It was the first time he had allowed himself to really look at her in the light, since their confrontation in the kitchen and what he saw made his heart squeeze unwillingly in his chest again.

There were cobwebs in her short, almost-curly black hair and her face was dirty too. Cutting through the dust and grime on her pale cheeks were obvious tear-tracks. It looked like she'd gone down into the subbasement and laid on the dirty ground crying for hours. The thought brought back the memory of holding her in the Rec Yard, the feeling of her shoulders shaking as he tried to comfort her and hide her pain from the rest of the inmates. The softness of her small body in his arms...how right it had felt to finally hold her...

Angrily, Lathe shoved the memory away. He refused to think

of that now—refused to let himself be weak around her. Refused to let himself have feelings for the female who had lied to him and strung him along.

"Look at you," he said roughly. "Don't you know the Yonnites expect their slaves to at least look presentable?"

"What?" She looked at him, wide-eyed and Lathe blew out a breath of frustration.

"Come here." Taking one of the soft cloths the Mistresses used to clean their hands between courses, he wet it at the sink and pulled Ari to him. With swift, efficient strokes he cleaned her cheeks, wiping away the evidence of her tears as well as he could.

He half expected her to protest his brusque treatment but Ari stood quietly, allowing him to do as he wished with her. Her red-rimmed eyes cast down, she waited until Lathe finished the small cat-bath.

Somehow her submissive posture made him even angrier. He wanted her to fight him or protest or insult him as she had when she'd first come to the prison. Instead she just stood there, as pale and quiet as a statue. It was as though she thought she deserved whatever he wanted to do to her and she was willing to endure it, no matter what.

She **does** deserve it, whispered a voice in his head. After what she did...what she made **me** do...

He pushed the angry thoughts aside and stepped back, examining his handiwork.

"There. At least now the Yonnites won't throw you into the hole for the offense of being offensive now," he growled.

"Are they that particular?" Ari asked, looking up at him.

Lathe raised an eyebrow at her.

Have you ever served a Mistress before?"

"Um, no." She shook her head. "Although I have *been* served for most of my life so I *think* I know what's expected."

"Been served, huh?" Lathe frowned at her. "Are you one of the Yonnites yourself then?" It wouldn't have surprised him a bit —just another one of her lies. But Ari was quick to contradict that idea.

"What? No! I hate those evil *shivaths!*" She made a face. "But my family are kind of a minor nobility on Phobos. It's not a big deal or anything—I grew up with servants but really they're more like part of the family."

"I see—minor nobility," Lathe said, not sure he believed her at all. "So who do I have the honor of addressing?"

"Lady Arianna Blackthorn, at your service, sir." Ari spread invisible skirts and dropped him a very passable curtsy that made Lathe raise his eyebrows again. Could she really be telling the truth this time? If so, what was a noblewoman from Phobos doing in BleakHall? How had she gotten here and why?

His questions would have to wait because just then a loud blast of shrill, self-important music sounded over the com-link system and a deep male voice called out,

"Behold, Mistress Hellenix of Opulex, Capital of Yonnie Six has arrived!"

"They're here," Lathe murmured to Ari. "Just follow my lead and act like the other body slaves."

Taking a tray of expensive sugar-jeweled *kanjee* fruit, he strode from the food prep area into the lushly-decorated dining hall, which held a long, low table surrounded by six elaborately carved *lappal*-wood chairs upholstered in *tongle* fur. Ari followed him with a dish of spiced *hinja*-frog intestines and the two of them set their trays on the dining table.

Stalking into the room was a diminutive mistress with long, straight black hair and large, dark, almond-shaped eyes. She was wearing a leather harness which left her large, full breasts bare and *almost* covered her pussy mound. A pair of stylish leather thigh-high boots completed her look which Lathe thought was kinky in a minimalist way. As a finishing touch, her nipples were dusted in some kind of colored sugar—reddish gold on one breast and silvery blue on the other.

Standing by the doorway which led to the Mistress's private landing area was a huge Kindred warrior with wheat-blond hair and a neatly clipped beard of the same color. He also had pure silver eyes. It was he who had been announcing his Mistress's entrance and now he stood silent, as though awaiting her orders.

The slave's outfit was scarcely more decent than hers—consisting of a thick pain collar around his neck and a pair of crotchless black leather trousers which showed a silver-wire chastity device that caged his large shaft.

Lathe felt a shock of recognition when he saw the huge male. This must be Malik—the Volt Kindred who was enslaved to Mistress Hellenix, whom Commander Sylvan had told him about! He wished he could get the male alone for a moment to ask him some questions but clearly that was not to be—not with the Mistresses arriving and expecting to be served.

"That was a rather good announcement, Malik," Mistress Hellenix remarked, throwing herself into a plush, fur-lined chair and draping one leg over the padded arm, apparently careless of the fact that this put her scantily-clad crotch on display.

"My Mistress honors me," the Volt Kindred murmured, his face stony, his eyes facing forward.

"Just stand there and announce the others as they come in,"

Mistress Hellenix commanded. "Mistress Poofinpah isn't bringing her slave, who usually does the announcements so you'll have to manage instead."

"I will do as my Mistress wills. In this, as in all things, it is my pleasure to serve her." The big Volt Kindred spoke blandly but Lathe thought he saw a spark of fiery hatred far back in those pure silver eyes.

Mistress Hellenix, however, appeared to notice nothing.

"Pretty words, Malik," she remarked, reaching for one of the chewy spiced frog intestines and popping it into her mouth. "Mmm—lovely! I'll feed myself until you're done announcing since these two prison idiots are too thick to help out."

She glared at Lathe and Ari as she spoke and Lathe was quick to respond.

"Mistress, can I help you in any way?" he asked. "Would you like me to feed you?"

"No, no..." She waved him off airily. "I prefer to wait for my own slave. But see to it that you're quicker in serving the others when they come. In the meantime, I *know* there must be more food than this. I ordered at least a thousand credits worth from the caterers. So bring it out at once!"

"Yes, Mistress." Lathe bowed and Ari echoed his words and bowed as well.

"Bossy *shivath*," she muttered when the two of them were in the kitchen again. "Those freaking Mistresses think they own everyone and everything, don't they?"

Lathe was surprised to see her dark blue eyes were snapping with anger.

"That's not the half of it," he said grimly. "Just be sure you keep them happy and hope they didn't bring any extra pain collars with them. Come on—let's get these dishes out."

"Mistress Chokeapig of Taber Island, Yonnie Six," Malik, the Volt Kindred was announcing when they came back with more platters.

Mistress Burnabush and Mistress Jankypoo as well as two others soon followed and in short order all the Mistresses were assembled in the fur-lined chairs around the low oval table.

"Very good, Malik," Mistress Hellenix clapped her hands approvingly when the Volt Kindred had made the last announcement. "Now that everyone's here, we can begin."

Malik came around to his Mistress's side and began to feed her delicacies from the various trays. The other body slaves were doing the same and Lathe was quick to find one of the Mistresses who was lacking a body slave and point the other without a slave out to Ari. The two of them stood by and put dainties into the Mistresses' mouths so that they didn't have to bother feeding themselves.

For a time the Yonnite Mistresses ate and chatted of this and that, all the time completely ignoring the slaves who were serving them except to scold or complain periodically. But finally when everyone had eaten enough, Mistress Hellenix clapped her hands for silence and spoke.

"Now then, it seems we've all had just about enough so it's time to get down to the business of this meeting—the future of BleakHall."

"But Mistress Hellenix, *ought* we to speak so freely before, *eh-hem,* the prisoners?" Mistress Jankypoo nodded delicately at Ari and Lathe.

"Not to worry." Mistress Hellenix made a shooing gesture.

"They're witless males. The two of them didn't even have the intelligence to set the table until I told them to. We may speak freely, I believe—at least for now."

"Oh, very well then." Mistress Jankypoo, who had a rather ridiculous looking poof of bright pink hair, looked relieved and nodded at Hellenix. "Do go on then, Mistress Hellenix."

"I certainly will. As I said, the future of BleakHall hangs in the balance."

"What are you talking about?" Mistress Poofinpah, whom Ari was feeding, batted away the piece of sugared fruit Ari was trying to put in her mouth and glared at Mistress Hellenix. "We turned a handsome profit last quarter—*despite* that ridiculous laser ceiling we had to have installed over the Rec Yard."

"Yes we did, thanks to switching from humanoids to Horvaths as guards," Mistress Hellenix agreed. "Unfortunately, that is part of the problem—some of our clients have been complaining that the guards are too rough."

"Too rough? Oh please!" Mistress Burnabush—a plump woman with curly purple hair—made an incredulous face. "The prisoners don't *deserve* to be treated gently. BleakHall houses the worst of the *worst*. Rapist...murderers...sociopaths..."

"Not to mention slaves who prove intractable or impractical to keep in our homes on Yonnie Six," Mistress Hellenix interrupted her. "Let's face it, ladies..." She looked around the table at the assembled board members. "BleakHall has become a dumping ground for unwanted slaves—many of whom are really only guilty of being annoying or stubborn."

"Well, one has to send them *someplace*," Mistress Tingleteller, a thin woman with white-blonde ringlets arranged in a halo around her head, protested haughtily. She looked around the table. "Raise your hand anyone who *hasn't* gotten rid of an annoying slave by sending him to BleakHall."

Not a single hand went up and Mistress Tingleteller looked at Mistress Hellenix triumphantly.

"See? *Everyone* does it. Not just us, either—BleakHall is an open secret in Opulex. For a fee—paid very discreetly, I might add—I personally facilitate putting unwanted slaves here."

"I do as well," Mistress Poofinpah remarked. "It's a lucrative side business."

"Of *course* it is," Mistress Hellenix exclaimed. "We *all* do it— I'm not saying we should stop. I'm just saying we need to be more *discrete* about it. Especially when the slave you're getting rid of wasn't born and raised on Yonnie Six. Males who are imported from the slave markets are more likely to come from ignorant male-dominated worlds where they might be missed if they're sent to BleakHall."

"But the ones who are born free are the most fun to break!" Mistress Jankypoo protested.

"And the most *difficult* to break." Mistress Hellenix raised a finger at her. "Which is why they so often wind up in BleakHall and why the complaints are piling up when the Horvaths kill them."

"Well there's not much we can do about that—we knew the Horvath guards were violent when we hired them," another Mistress objected. "It's one of the reasons *why* we hired them—to keep the male scum in this place in line."

Lathe felt sick but he struggled to keep his face calm. They were talking about taking and discarding slaves so casually—as though they weren't even people. As though they meant less than nothing.

*As I'm sure Thonolan meant nothing to the Mistress who bought him on the black market,* he thought angrily. *I wonder if the one who bought him and sent him to BleakHall when he wouldn't bow his head to her is sitting here now? I wonder—*

His thoughts were cut off abruptly when he looked across the table and saw, to his shock, that Ari's face was a mask of white fury. She had stopped even pretending to feed Mistress Poofinpah and was standing there with her hands clenched into fists, looking like she wanted to kill everyone at the table. What could have made her so angry? Whatever it was, she couldn't stand there glaring at the Mistresses or she was going to get in trouble.

Catching her eye, Lathe gave a small shake of his head and made a motion at his own face with one hand. At first Ari glared at him but then she took a deep breath and seemed to make a visible effort to calm down. Lathe hoped no one had noticed her dark looks but a glance around the table let him know they were being ignored since slaves didn't matter. At the head of the table, Mistress Hellenix was still speaking.

"So I'm not saying we *shouldn't* send unwanted slaves here to BleakHall, just that we need to be a bit more discreet. I have it on good authority that the complaints have reached the Sacred Seven and they are considering giving us a fine or even shutting us down."

"What?" Several of the Mistresses nearly choked on the dainty morsels their slaves were feeding them.

"Shut us *down?*" Mistress Jankypoo gasped. "But I have so much credit invested in BleakHall!"

"As do we all," Mistress Hellenix said grimly. "Which is why I have come up with a plan to keep anything from happening."

"What? What?" All the Mistresses were looking at her eagerly.

Rising to stand at the head of the table, she looked around at the others and answered their questions with one of her own.

"What happens if the ones who are making the complaints disappear? Or rather, the *one?* Because there is one male in particular who is bringing BleakHall to the notice of the Sacred Seven —*he* is the troublemaker."

"So what are we going to do about him?" Mistress Burnabush demanded.

"I'll tell you. But we must have a consensus before I put my plan in motion. I refuse to be culpable all by myself," Mistress Hellenix declared.

"Well tell us and we'll vote," one of the other Mistresses suggested.

"I will. But first, I want all of the body slaves to leave the room," Mistress Hellenix said.

"Really? But they're only males," Mistress Jankypoo protested. "I thought you said they were of no consequence."

"They aren't but this decision must be kept from everyone's ears but our own," Mistress Hellenix said decisively. "I'll even send my own slave out. Malik—go," she directed him, pointing towards the door. The big Volt Kindred nodded mutely and left the room, followed by the rest of the body slaves.

Lathe and Ari left too but as soon as he stepped out the door of the dining room, Lathe felt a hand on his arm.

"Come, Brother," Malik growled in his ear. "I have something to say to you. Is there a place for privacy here?"

Wondering what the other Kindred could have to say, Lathe nodded at the conference room across the hall.

"Good. Come on." Malik led the way and they shut themselves into the plush conference room after Lathe gave Ari a sign to stay outside the door and keep watch.

"Can we speak freely in here?" Malik asked in a low voice.

"As freely as you like. This conference room has soundproof walls," Lathe told him.

"Good, I'll be brief—I know my Mistress's plan. She wants to assassinate Commander Sylvan—the head of the Kindred High Council."

"What?" Lathe looked at the other male in shock. "Are you certain Commander Sylvan is her target?"

"Positive," Malik said grimly. "She tells me everything because she thinks I am completely loyal. She thinks I *love* her." He barked a bitter laugh and Lathe didn't have to ask what his true feelings were. The expression of loathing in the other male's silver eyes spoke far more eloquently than words could have.

"So...she believes that if she gets rid of Commander Sylvan the complaints about BleakHall will go away?" Lathe asked.

"She does and she's probably right," Malik said. "It is the Kindred who have been complaining the most vocally to the Yonnite Council of Mistresses—the Sacred Seven who rule Yonnie Six. Commander Sylvan is leading the charge, so to speak. Hellenix is poised to put a price on his head, hoping that once he's disposed of the complaints will be silenced."

"Gods!" Lathe raked a hand through his hair. "I must warn him!"

"You have to because the Goddess knows there's no way I can," Malik said grimly. "Hellenix keeps me with her night and day—I get scarcely a moment's breathing room." As he spoke, a crackle of silvery sparks ran between his fingertips—almost as though the power inside him, held so long in check, was seeping out.

"Why do you stay with her then?" Lathe asked quietly. "It's clear you despise her. Commander Sylvan told me he tried to get you away from her but you refused to go."

"He told you correctly." Malik sighed. "It's a long story I don't have time to tell all of right now. Sufficient to say my Mistress is a collector of...oddities. And there is something in her collection that I hope might help me restore my home world."

"You mean Uriel Two?" Lathe frowned. "But wasn't it completely overrun by the artificial intelligence your elders allowed to run your communications and weapons systems?"

"Unfortunately, yes," Malik growled. "But that doesn't mean it cannot be reclaimed. The AIs that run Uriel Two are sentient—they'll even make deals with the likes of my Mistress because of the artifact she possesses. If I can just get my hands on the—"

A swift knock sounded on the door and Ari poked her head in.

"Sorry but they're calling for the body slaves," she said quietly. "Thought you might want to know."

"Thank you." Malik nodded at her—then his nostrils wrinkled and he inhaled deeply, frowning. He turned to Lathe. "Why is there a female here among the male prisoners? That cannot be safe for her."

Ari's eyes widened.

"He knows? You told him?"

"Of course not—I smelled your scent," Malik told her. "There's no mistaking the scent of a ripe female." He frowned. "You'd better be careful, you know—I'm not the only one here who can sniff out a female. The lashers who roam these halls at night can get very aggressive if they smell a female's musk. My Mistress Hellenix had to sign multiple statements swearing they were going to be used at an all-male facility and no females would be around anywhere."

Lathe sighed. How was it this other Kindred could tell at once that Ari was female while he himself had struggled to come to the realization?

*Maybe because I trusted my eyes instead of my nose,* Lathe told himself. *That damn solid-holo projector of hers had me completely fooled.* In the future, he promised himself to remember which sense was more reliable.

"It's all right," he told the Volt Kindred. "Ari is with me—I'm protecting her."

"See that you do." Malik frowned. "And give my regards to Commander Sylvan. I hope you may be in time to save him."

"Who?" Ari asked, frowning but just then they all heard the strident voice of Mistress Hellenix drifting through the crack in the door.

"Malik, where *are* you? I insist that you come here to me at once!"

The big Volt Kindred made a face.

"Duty calls." He left the room swiftly and Lathe and Ari followed.

"So it's settled then," Mistress Hellenix was saying as they came back into the room. She was lounging in her chair at the head of the dining table, looking like a cat that had gotten entirely too much cream. "There is already an operative in place to carry out our plan. I'll send out the dispatch tonight, giving them the go-ahead. By tomorrow or the next day at the latest, it should be done."

"Here, here! To Mistress Hellenix—our problem-solver." Mistress Jankypoo raised a delicate blood-crystal goblet and the other Mistresses copied her motions, cheering as they did so.

Lathe pretended to go about the business of refilling wine glasses as the Mistresses chattered and talked but inside his mind was racing frantically.

*Tonight? She's putting out the hit on Commander Sylvan* **tonight?** *We have to get* **out** *of here! I'll have to give the nanites the command to finish the tunnel at once! We can't wait any longer.*

Of course that would mean tripping the prison's escape alarms but that couldn't be helped. He would wait until he and Ari started down into the tunnel in the Infirmary before he gave the command for more rapid digging. Hopefully they could time it so they were exiting the tunnel before the Horvath guards were alerted.

Hopefully.

# THIRTY-SEVEN

"Come on—hurry!" Lathe pulled Ari along faster, one big hand yanking her by the arm as he dragged her back down to their cell.

"What's going on? Why are we in such a rush?" Ari demanded. The big Kindred had been agitated ever since his private meeting with the other Kindred warrior—the one with the silver eyes. She wished he would slow down a little. She was so damn tired and the place where Tapper had scratched her with his knife, just below her left ear, itched fiercely.

"I'll tell you when we get to the cell," Lathe ground out. "But for now, can't you hurry?"

"Are you worried about the lashers coming out?" Ari asked. "I thought you said Mukluk set the system so that the cold air wouldn't start blowing until thirty minutes after the last of the Mistress's ships has left. That should give us plenty of time to get to your cell."

"Yes, it's enough time to get to our cell and let the sensors inside check us in for the night," Lathe growled. "But we have a lot further to go than that before our grace period ends."

"What do you mean a lot further to go?" Ari asked but just then they got to Lathe's cell and he pushed her inside.

"All right," he said, pulling her towards the door almost as soon as they'd gotten inside. "Come on—we need to get to the tunnel before the frigid air starts blowing to wake the lashers. Thirty minutes should be enough but I'd rather not push it."

He started to leave the cell but Ari was rooted to the spot.

"Tunnel?" She looked at him, uncomprehending. "What tunnel?"

"Damn it, the *escape* tunnel I've had nanites digging under BleakHall for the past six solar months," Lathe growled. "I'm going out tonight and you're coming with me. But since the lashers would like nothing better than to make you a midnight snack, we have to go before the cold air starts blowing."

Ari took a step back from him, her arms crossed over her chest.

"I'm sorry Lathe, but I... I'm not going." She couldn't believe the words she was saying but she knew they were true. And she prayed she had the conviction to follow through with them.

"What?" Lathe looked shocked. "What are you talking about? If anyone else finds out what you really are you'll be dead or worse inside of five minutes."

Ari lifted her chin. "Don't you think I know that? After Tapper..." But she shook her head, unable to go down that road. She swallowed hard. "I'm sorry, Lathe, but I'll have to take my chances. I can't leave here without Jak—I can't go without my brother."

"Your brother?" His turquoise eyes widened. "You mean your brother is *here* in BleakHall? But you never told me that! Then again, you never told me a lot of things," he added darkly, frowning.

Ari sighed unhappily.

"I know you're still angry with me for deceiving you about who I really was but try to see things my way, Lathe—I didn't come here for you. I infiltrated BleakHall to save my big brother. I even had a plan to get us out..." She grimaced. "You can probably tell that didn't go very well, but I still won't just leave Jak here to rot."

Lathe raked a hand through his hair distractedly.

"Fine, you can bring him with you—where is he?"

Ari bit her lip. "Locked up in the hole," she said in a small voice. "But I can get him out—I know I can," she went on quickly. "I've been working on the wiring that controls the locking mechanisms and it's almost fixed."

"*Almost* fixed?" He shook his head. "Ari, I don't see how this can work. Unless you can get down into the hole, free your brother, and bring him back to the Infirmary in less than half an hour, you're both going to be lasher food."

"Then I'll just have to stay." Ari tried to make her voice calm and was proud when it only trembled a little bit. "Jak will be out of the hole in another month or so. If I can just make it that long..."

"You won't make it another day now that damn disguise of yours has failed," Lathe said roughly. "What are you going to do the next time you go to the shower? Ask all the other males politely not to look?"

"I'll just keep washing myself in the sink." Ari lifted her chin defiantly. "That way no one will see me, uh, without my clothes."

"That might work if you were allowed to stay here in this cell," Lathe pointed out. "But you're not a trustee, Ari. The minute I'm gone, they'll bust you back down to general population. And believe me, there are *no* private bathing or toilet facilities there."

Ari thought of the open stalls with no doors and the round, stained fixtures that served as rudimentary toilets she'd seen in cell block E. Lathe was right, she realized with a sinking heart. Pretending to be male here at BleakHall was going to get a whole lot more difficult once Lathe wasn't here to shelter and protect her and keep her in his private trustee cell.

Still, she didn't want to leave Jak.

"Lathe please," she pleaded. "Try to put yourself in my shoes. If your brother was still alive, would you want to leave him here? You told me he died here in BleakHall. I'm afraid if I leave Jak, he'll die too."

"Goddess damn it," he growled and ran both hands through his hair in deep frustration. He took a deep breath and closed his eyes for a moment as though thinking hard. Finally he looked at her again.

"All right, but we're going to have to take a chance."

"That's fine," Ari said eagerly. Any chance was better than no chance at all, as far as she was concerned.

Lathe frowned. "Wait until you hear how much we're risking before you agree to it. I wrote an override in BleakHall's control system when I first came here—it allows me to run the climate system for a little while."

"Really?" Ari felt a surge of hope.

He nodded. "I thought I might be taking other Kindred prisoners with me when I went and I didn't know if the lashers would bother them or not. I thought it best not to find out."

Ari's heart started pounding. "So does that mean you can keep the lashers from waking up while I rescue Jak? You can keep the cold air from blowing?"

"I *think* so." Lathe looked troubled. "I wrote the override but I've never tested it before. And in order to make it work, I have to stand right by the climate control system and keep my prison ID tag in its scanner the whole time." He gave Ari a level look. "So you'll have to get your brother by yourself. I won't be able to go with you."

For a moment her stomach clenched in fear. She had gone through the tunnel where the lashers were kenneled several times now on her trips to the hole. But every time she'd gone, it had been in the middle of the day and there was slim to no chance the huge beasts would wake. Now she would be going down at the time they usually ended their daily hibernation and trusting that Lathe could keep the cold air from blowing in order to keep them asleep while she freed Jak. Could she really do this?

*I have to,* she told herself sternly. *Jak would do it for me. I can't leave him here—we have a chance to get out and we won't get one again. We have to take it.*

But could she trust the big Kindred to keep his word and not let the cold air flow—especially when he was so angry with her?

"I can do it," she told Lathe. "And I *will* do it. But I have to know something—why do you even want to take me with you in the first place? I would think after what...what happened between us you would just leave me here."

"You really think so little of me?" Lathe's eyes flashed

turquoise fire. "You think I'd leave you here just to die because you lied to me and deceived me?"

"Some men would," Ari said quietly.

"Kindred aren't like other males," Lathe growled. "We honor females...even when they don't honor us."

Ari felt a surge of irritation.

"I won't say I'm sorry again since you seem determined not to accept my apology. What do you want me to do, Lathe—get down and suck your cock again?"

"I would have sucked yours," he said in a low, angry voice. "Do you know how that makes me feel Ari? That I was willing to do that? I thought I was in love with another male—it turned me inside-fucking-*out!*"

"Well being with you turned me inside out too," she flared. "It made me feel awful not being able to tell you the truth. But you kept talking about how you hated liars and people who misrepresented themselves and I thought..." She trailed off. "I was scared, Lathe," she finished in a small voice.

Lathe gave her a steady look.

"You know what bothers me the most?" he asked, his voice low and rough. "The fact that you have the courage to go down through the lasher kennels when it's time for them to wake—hell, the courage to infiltrate BleakHall in the first place—but you didn't have the courage to tell me who you really are."

"I'm sorry," Ari whispered, even though she'd just said she wouldn't apologize again. "So damn sorry, Lathe. I wish I could make it up to you."

He shook his head moodily.

"Forget that now—we have to get going. But...there's one thing I need to do before we go."

"Something you want to bring with you?" Ari looked around the cell but he didn't go to get anything from under his bunk or the small shelf near the top of the ceiling. Instead he was still looking at her.

"I don't want to take a risk on my override failing," he told Ari. "If it does, the cold air will start blowing, the lashers will wake, and you'll probably be gone before I can get to you."

Ari shivered at the thought but squared her shoulders.

"That's awful but it's a chance we'll have to take, right?"

"Wrong," Lathe said, frowning. "There is an extra step I can take to protect you before I let you go wandering down into the mouth of hell." He took a deep breath. "Strip, Ari."

"What?" Ari took a step back. "I hardly think this is the time—"

"Strip," Lathe repeated impatiently. "I need to cover your scent with my own."

"What?" Ari repeated, taking another step back. "I don't understand."

Lathe made a growl of frustration.

"You heard what Malik said—the lashers are especially attuned to female scent. Which is probably why that big one kept coming around when you first moved into my cell."

"Oh...right." Remembering the huge beast with its glowing yellow eyes, Ari shivered. "But I don't understand what you mean when you say you'll 'cover my scent.'"

"Kindred have scent glands in and around their lips and mouths," Lathe explained. "And their groins," he added darkly. "But I don't fucking trust myself to rub my shaft against you bare."

"Rub...rub against me?" Ari's mouth was suddenly dry and her heart was pounding.

Lathe seemed to see the fear and uncertainty on her face because his voice became somewhat gentler.

"Don't worry, little one—I'm not going to hurt you. Just going to rub my mouth against your skin and spread my scent so that if, the Goddess forbid, the lashers wake up, they'll smell me instead of you. Do you understand?"

"I...think so," Ari said slowly. His sweet nickname for her calmed her down some. "But where...where are you going to, uh, rub me?"

"Where your scent is strongest." Lathe gave her a level look. "I need to hide the sweet fragrance of your pussy."

# THIRTY-EIGHT

At last she seemed to understand him and began to take off her jumpsuit. Lathe tried not to watch—tried not to see her lush curves...the swells of her breasts... her tight pink nipples...the soft, hairless mound of her pussy. Gods, how could he have not known she was female before? No matter how good her disguise was, the warm, feminine scent that drifted up from between her thighs spoke louder than any fake holo she could have projected.

Lathe felt his shaft getting hard but he tried to push his desire away.

*I'm angry with her—she lied to me. Lied about who she was and her feelings for me—she used me just like Talsa did. Besides, I'm only doing this to protect her in case my climate control override fails.*

"We don't have much time so I'm going to make this fast," he told Ari. "Sit on the bunk and spread your legs for me."

Blushing and biting her lip, she did as he directed. Lathe couldn't help noticing that when she parted her thighs, her outer pussy lips parted too, revealing just a hint of her sweet pink interior.

For a moment he was overcome with the need to spread her thighs even wider and lap her sweet little pussy—to suck her plump outer lips into his mouth and explore her pink folds with his tongue until she moaned and cried his name.

But no—bringing her pleasure wasn't his purpose here. He just needed to protect her by masking her scent with his own.

Steeling himself against his erotic impulses, Lathe dropped to his knees before her and bent his face to her pelvis.

The warm, sweet, feminine fragrance of her sex was even stronger here. His shaft was throbbing between his thighs and he could feel his fangs getting long and sharp with the need to bite her—claim her—taste her. But he pushed his desire away and began to rub his cheek against her inner thighs instead.

The sooner they got this done, the sooner they could get out of here.

Ari bit her lip and tried not to gasp as she felt the rough scratch of the big Kindred's whiskers against her tender thighs. God, having him so close like this reminded her of the other night when he'd kissed the holo-shaft. Except...except this was different.

Back then he had believed her a male and had been going against all his natural instincts to kiss her. But now he knew she was female and was only trying to protect her from the lashers.

*That's all he's doing—just protecting me. Just putting his scent on me,* Ari tried to tell herself as Lathe rubbed against her inner thighs with his cheeks and mouth like a feline marking its territory. *He's just...*

And then all the thoughts flew out of her head as he rubbed his cheek directly against the mound of her pussy.

*"Oh!"* she gasped when his scratchy cheek came in contact with her tender flesh. It was an intense sensation—almost too much to bear when she already felt incredibly open and sensitive.

"Sorry," Lathe growled, looking up at her. "Too rough for you, little one?"

"A little," Ari confessed. "Your whiskers..."

"Oh yes, of course." He nodded. "I'll use my mouth instead—more scent glands there anyway." He motioned down at her legs. "I just need you to spread a little wider so I can reach you."

"All...all right," Ari breathed. Feeling even more vulnerable, she opened her thighs wider and was embarrassed to note when she did so that her pussy was spreading open too. "Oh..." She started to close her legs but Lathe stopped her with a large, warm hand on her thigh.

"It's all right, sweetheart," he murmured. "I won't hurt you."

Ari bit her lip. "I know you won't. "It's just I feel so...so *open.*"

"You need to be open," Lathe told her. "I need to rub against you there, too."

"You...you do?" Ari whispered.

He nodded.

"That's the source of your sweet scent, after all. But as I said, I'll try to make it quick. Now spread for me, little one and just relax."

Ari tried to do as he said but it was extremely difficult to relax when she felt so naked and so vulnerable. She'd never had a man go down on her before. Both of her previous sexual encounters had been brief, fumbling affairs and neither of her lovers had offered to lick or taste her.

*And it's not like Lathe is offering to lick or taste me now,* she told herself sternly. *He's just covering my scent. He's just...*

"Oh!" The soft little moan was drawn from her lips because Lathe was rubbing his mouth against her mound now, his sensuous lips caressing her outer pussy in a way that made Ari feel weak in the knees.

Then he started on her slit. But his actions were different now —more like kissing than rubbing. He pressed his mouth to the top of her sensitive mound and then began to move down slowly, as though he was trying to be thorough and cover every bit of her slightly open slit. Was it her imagination or was he lingering over the place where the tight little button of her clit peaked from between her outer folds? For a moment, Ari almost thought she felt the brush of his tongue there. But that couldn't be right, could it?

Lathe kissed all the way down her pussy from top to bottom but when he drew back, he was frowning.

"What...what's wrong?" Ari asked breathlessly. "Is there a problem?"

"I'm afraid so. You appear to be a *numalla.*"

"A what?" Then Ari remembered what he meant. *A female who gets really wet. Oh my Goddess—am I wet?*

Looking down at herself she was ashamed to see that her pussy lips were glistening in the dim light of the cell.

"Oh Goddess," she gasped in embarrassment and tried to close her thighs. But Lathe caught her—his big hands on her knees—and held her open.

"Don't Ari." His voice was low and rough. "It's beautiful... *you're* beautiful. Unfortunately all the honey you're making carries your scent very strongly." He looked up at her. "I'll have to lick it away. That way I can erase your scent and leave my own in its place."

"If...if you think you really need to," Ari said, blushing.

He nodded. "I do. But I'm going to have to spread your pussy lips open to get to all of the honey. Do you understand, Ari?" He held her eyes with his. "I'm going to have to spread your pussy open and lick you out completely."

"Goddess..." she whispered. She felt nervous and shy but what else could she do but submit to him? "All right," she told him at last. "I...I trust you, Lathe. If you say that's the way it has to be, then go ahead and do it."

"Open for me then, little one," he growled softly. "Let me spread your pussy and lick away every last drop of your honey."

Trembling and moaning, Ari parted her legs even further, baring herself completely as long, strong fingers spread her pussy lips, exposing her inner folds to the big Kindred.

"Gods, so beautiful," he muttered hoarsely. "So wet, my *numalla.*"

Then he leaned forward and lapped at her pussy—his tongue bathing her inner folds completely as he licked away her juices.

Ari gasped and arched her back as his warm, wet tongue slid over her tender, secret flesh. He covered her in long, rough strokes, apparently attempting to be thorough and get every drop. But every time she felt his tongue drag over the tender bud of her clit, Ari's inner muscles clenched and she felt fresh wetness as her body responded to his intimate caress. Though she tried to stop herself, she could feel her pleasure growing with each rough, thorough swipe of his tongue until she throbbed and ached and her muscles tensed with need.

At last Lathe drew back, frowning.

"This isn't working," he growled. "Every time I lick you, you get wetter."

"I...I can't help it," Ari whispered. "I know you're only doing it to spread your scent on me but...but it feels so *good.*"

"Feels good to me too, little one," he murmured, looking up at her. "Your pussy is so soft and sweet I could lick you all night— but we don't have time for that." He sighed. "I think I'm going to have to make you come."

"You...what?" Ari bit her lip. "But why—?"

"As long as your pleasure is still building, your pussy will keep making honey," Lathe explained. "But if I can satisfy your need, your body should begin to calm down and stop making so much."

"I understand," Ari murmured. "I just...I'm not sure..."

"Just relax," Lathe told her. "I'm going to use my fingers to spread my scent inside you and to help you come at the same time. Then I'll clean you up with my tongue and we'll go."

Ari nodded and tried to let some of the tension ease from her body. But the moment Lathe began to lick her again, she felt her pussy clench and answer the caress of his tongue with a fresh burst of wetness.

"So sweet and wet and juicy, my little *numalla,*" she heard the big Kindred murmur between licks. "Gods, if only I had all night to give you pleasure..."

Then he looked up at her. Holding her eyes, he sucked his index and middle fingers into his mouth, getting them thoroughly wet. When he withdrew them, he nodded at Ari.

"Get ready, little one. I'm going to enter your pussy now—

going to fuck you with my fingers, as deeply as I can to spread my scent and make you come."

"Yes, Lathe..." Biting her lip, Ari arched her back and opened herself for him, ready for his invasion.

"That's good, sweetheart," he growled softly and she felt his long, strong fingers press inside her, filling her deeply until he reached the end of her channel. "That's good, just spread your legs and let me in."

Ari did as he said, fisting her hands in the thin blanket on either side of her as Lathe bent between her thighs and lapped her open pussy while he thrust deeply into her with his fingers.

Her hips twisted and her back arched as she gave in to the overwhelming pleasure. She could feel his fangs, long and sharp, bracketing her throbbing clit but somehow Lathe managed not to bite her—not even to scratch her with their deadly tips.

Ari wished he would lose some of his iron control. She wanted him to bite her again—wanted the exquisite pleasure-pain of his sharp fangs sinking into her flesh and the burst of brilliant sensation as his essence coursed through her veins and made her come again and again...

But Lathe didn't need to sink his fangs into her to make her come, she soon found. As he sucked her tender clit between his lips and lashed it with his tongue, he also thrust deeply into her, filling her pussy with his long fingers until she was nearly sobbing with desire and need.

"Lathe...oh Goddess, yes, Lathe—*yes!*"

Somehow her hands found their way from the blanket to his hair and then she was clutching him to her frantically as she arched upward to meet his tongue and fingers...as she surrendered herself completely to the pleasure he was giving her.

*Coming,* she thought. *Goddess, I'm coming so hard...*

"Lathe," she cried brokenly. "Oh, Lathe...please...*yes!*"

Her lower back arched right off the bunk and her grip tightened in Lathe's hair so hard it must have hurt, but he didn't seem to mind. In fact, Ari heard a muffled growl of approval come from his throat as he held her close and kept lapping and sucking and pumping, guiding her through her orgasm with a firm, sure hand and never letting her go until she'd had enough.

———

Lathe enjoyed her pleasure much more than he should have.

*You're only doing this to cover her scent,* he reminded himself. But when her little fists closed tight in his hair and he heard her calling his name it was all he could do to keep himself from sinking his fangs into her flesh to claim her as his own. Better yet, he wanted to use his cock instead of his fingers on her—to fill her completely and bite at the same time, bonding her to him, making Ari his irrevocably.

*She doesn't want that,* he told himself roughly. *She doesn't feel for you as you feel for her. She was only pretending—just playing a part.*

Somehow that hurt worse than the way she had caused him to question himself. *"I'm falling in love with you,"* he had told her, and he hadn't been lying. Ari had professed to return his feelings but now he was sure she had been faking that, just like she'd been faking everything else.

But just because he was certain Ari had been pretending to care for him, didn't mean his own emotions had been fake. Even as he cleaned her thoroughly and gently with his tongue, lapping up the rest of her honey, Lathe knew he still wanted her—still cared for her.

Not that it mattered.

After they got out of BleakHall, they would go their separate ways. Ari and her brother would go back to Phobos and he would go on to the Mother Ship and present all the evidence he had collected using the tiny recorder hidden in his ID tag. He would probably be so busy helping prepare the case against Mistress Hellenix and the rest of the Mistresses on the Board of BleakHall that he would barely notice Ari's absence.

*You don't really believe that,* whispered a little voice in his head. *When she goes, she'll leave a fucking black hole in your heart and you know it.*

Lathe pushed it away as he straightened up and wiped his chin and mouth on the sleeve of his trustee jumpsuit.

"There. Finished," he said, trying to make his voice brusque and impersonal.

"Oh..." Ari blinked, her large, dark eyes dazed. "I..." She looked up at him. "I thought you were going to bite me again."

"No," Lathe said shortly. "Biting is for healing or claiming. This was neither of those things."

"Oh," she whispered again and began fumbling for her jump-suit. "Okay. Well, is my scent covered now?"

"As much as possible," Lathe told her. "I did my best—the fact that you're a *numalla* didn't make it easy."

"I'm sorry," Ari murmured. "I didn't...don't mean to be."

"Don't apologize," Lathe murmured. "You can't help how wet your soft little pussy gets, Ari."

"I...I guess not." She looked down, her cheeks coloring in a blush.

Gods, he could still taste her salty-sweet flavor on his tongue—she was so damn delicious. He had the sudden urge to take her in his arms and kiss her—to share her own secret taste with her. But he squashed the impulse immediately and forced himself to turn away from her.

"It's time to go," he told her. "Past time. Hurry up—put on your jumpsuit. We have to get down to the climate controls on the first floor of the prison."

"All right." Ari got up, still looking slightly dazed, and scrambled back into her baggy, prison-issue jumpsuit.

Seeing the hint of her curves under the coarse orange and blue fabric, Lathe wondered again how he could have ever thought she was male. He remembered the way he'd thought he saw her breasts under her bath towel...and how a glimpse of the fake holo-shaft had made him change his mind and think he was seeing things.

*I'll never take anything or anyone at face value again,* he vowed to himself. *And I'll never forget that females are seldom what they seem.*

"Come on," he said as soon as she was dressed. "Let's go."

Ari jumped off the bunk and followed him, out into the darkness of BleakHall.

# THIRTY-NINE

The corridors and stairs were dark but they weren't cold—not yet anyway. As they hurried silently along, Ari estimated they were still within their thirty minute grace period. She wondered how much of it was left—how long had the big Kindred spent between her thighs, licking and kissing her and covering her with his scent?

*Stop thinking about it,* she ordered herself. *It didn't mean anything. Lathe doesn't care for you anymore now that he knows what a liar you are!*

But despite his anger at her, he hadn't been rough with her. In fact, he had been gentle and sweet, bringing her to orgasm and lapping up her honey with a warm tongue she could still somehow feel between her thighs.

*Forget about it,* she told herself angrily. *What you ought to be planning is how to get Jak out of the hole.*

She hadn't been entirely truthful with Lathe when she'd told him it was a simple matter of finishing the wiring to get her brother's cell door open. There was also the matter of the thick, high-density padlock still clasped around the door's latch.

*But I know how to get the lock off, if only—*

"Here we are." Lathe's deep voice broke her train of thought and she realized they were down the steps and standing in front of the door to the Infirmary. To one side was a lighted compu-interface—one of the few accessible outside the guards' station. Not that it mattered—the interface was covered in thick plasti-glass so the prisoners couldn't break the security shield around it. Even if they could have broken through, it was supposed to be impossible for even the most genius hacker to get into the system.

Except it seemed that Lathe had found a way in.

Going into the Infirmary, he returned with one of the battered trustee tablets. After typing in a series of commands, he frowned.

"We got here just in time, the cold air is set to start blowing in about two minutes." He tapped some more. "There—I've set it to scan my ID tag before the climate control comes on. As long as I stand in front of the interface with my tag in its sights, it will just keep scanning and scanning and never turn itself on...I hope, anyway." He looked grim.

"Thank you," Ari said. "I'll go get Jak and be right back. Just... just wait for me, all right?"

"I won't leave until you're back," Lathe promised and she knew he would keep his word.

"Thank you, Lathe," she said again, daring to put her hand on his arm. "I know I don't deserve your help after...after what I did but—"

He cut off her words by leaning down and taking her mouth

in a hot, breathless kiss. When he pulled back, he looked down in Ari's eyes, his turquoise gaze troubled and intense.

"Just come back to me, little one," he growled hoarsely. "I don't like sending you down into the lashers' den all by yourself. Be careful, be quick, and come back alive."

"I...I will," Ari promised breathlessly. Could it be that he still cared for her? That he still felt something under the anger? But she had no time to think about that now. She had to get Jak and get out of here.

"I'm starting the override now." Lathe turned to the climate control interface and shifted so that his prison ID tag was squarely in view of its sensor. "Go," he said, speaking over his shoulder. "Hurry, Ari—I don't know how long this will last."

The words, *I love you,* hovered on the tip of her tongue but Ari swallowed them back down again. Kiss or no kiss, she was certain the big Kindred didn't want to hear that right now.

"I'll be back soon," she said instead. Then she turned and took off at a run. It was going to be a race to get Jak out and get back in time—a race she would either win or die running.

# FORTY

I *need the torch—the one in Stubbins' tool box,* Ari told herself as she ran. The wiring would be simple to fix but in order to get Jak's cell door open, she would also have to cut through the massive padlock that kept him in. And the blowtorch she'd seen in the Spice Lords' tool box was the only way she could think to do that.

The question was, how could she get to it?

Ari had no idea but she sent up a prayer as she ran lightly through the darkened corridors of the prison.

*Please, Goddess of Mercy—help me do what I came to do. Help me rescue my brother and get both of us out of here alive!*

There was no answer but she felt a warm surge of confidence and put on a burst of speed. Soon she found herself under the stairwell where Stubbins held court every day.

The faded red toolbox was sitting squarely in the middle of the folding table where Stubbins had no doubt left it. He had often told Ari there was no need to hide it or lock it since no one could touch the tools inside unless he contributed his own DNA to help them.

For a moment, Ari could see him vividly—licking his thumb and pressing it to the end of a hammer or a wrench or any of the other hundred tools in the box and then passing it to her.

*His DNA,* she thought as she opened the massive tool box and looked inside. *I need his DNA to activate the torch or I'm getting nothing but an almighty big shock. Please Goddess, help me find a way.*

The hand-held blow torch was lying in the top compartment looking insolent.

*Touch me if you dare,* it seemed to say. *But you'll never get me —not without Stubbins.*

Ari searched frantically around but there was nothing to help her. No way to get the torch. She was just about to reach into the box, hoping that maybe a tiny bit of the Spice Lords boss's DNA might still be clinging to the touch button, when she heard a voice.

**"Look again, daughter. Look for what you need."**

Ari jumped and looked around but there was no one there—she was alone under the stairwell. Who had spoken to her? The voice had been warm and powerful and strangest of all *feminine.* But she was the only female here in BleakHall so who—?

Just at that moment her eyes swept over the top of the folding table again and she saw something she was *certain* hadn't been there before—something that made her heart leap up in her chest.

Lying in a small metal ashtray was the burnt, chewed stub of a nico-stick and the end still looked slightly damp.

Exactly what she needed.

*How is this possible?* Ari wondered. She knew Stubbins was always extremely careful to take the stubs of his nico-sticks with him and flush them down the toilet at the end of every day for exactly this reason—so no one could use his DNA to get at the tools. Yet, here one was, just as though it had been waiting there for Ari.

*Though I know it wasn't here before,* Ari told herself. *It's like it suddenly just appeared.*

Still, she was overjoyed to have it now, however it had gotten there.

Tweezing the blackened stub between thumb and forefinger, she picked it up and said a silent prayer that there was enough of Stubbins' saliva left on it to activate the torch. If not, she was going to have to come up with some other way to free her brother.

Holding her breath, she pressed the chewed end of the stub to the bottom of the torch's bottom. Nothing happened.

*Well nothing is supposed to happen until you add your own DNA,* Ari reminded herself nervously.

Licking her thumb, she pressed the small black button on the bottom of the torch, adding her own DNA as well. There was a momentary pause in which her heart started to sink...then the handle of the torch changed from red to blue, indicating that the tool had been designated to her.

*Yes!* Ari grabbed the torch triumphantly. What else? She still had the small socket wrench and the screwdriver from earlier but maybe she would need a bigger weapon? She hoped not but it was best to be prepared.

Finding the largest wrench she could—one as long as her forearm and incredibly heavy—she used the nico-stub to activate it and grabbed it as well. Then it was time to go and Ari ran as fast as she could while carrying the heavy tools.

*Jak, here I come!*

---

Lathe stood impatiently in the dim corridor just outside the Infirmary, making sure to keep his ID badge in view of the climate control's system's view-window. Behind the unbreakable plastiglass a small red circle was spinning around and around, indicating that the system was scanning...scanning...scanning. Lathe just hoped it would stay in the loop he had programmed for it long enough for Ari to come back.

*I shouldn't have kissed her...and I shouldn't have let her go alone!*

But what choice did he have? The override wouldn't work for any ID tag but his and since the tag had been surgically implanted in his skin, there was no getting it out. Not right now, anyway. He just had to hope and pray that his override would last long enough for Ari to get her brother and get back to safety.

*I should have insisted that she come with me by herself—we could always come back and get her brother later.*

But that was by no means a certainty. And even if it had been, he'd understood why Ari didn't want to leave her brother behind. He wouldn't have left Thonolan if he'd been in a similar situation.

*Oh Thonolan...little brother,* he thought, grief rising up in him suddenly. *If only I could have saved you. If only I could avenge you...*

Taking the Yonnites who ran this place to court and possibly shutting down or changing the management of the prison was a good and worthy task, but it wasn't really the revenge Lathe craved. He wanted to kill the one who had murdered his brother —kill him with his own hands and fangs. Unfortunately, he had never been able to find out exactly what had happened to Thonolan, even after he came to BleakHall. His brother had simply been found dead in his cell one morning and his body had been burned before anyone could claim it.

At least that was what the official BleakHall report said— Lathe had his doubts.

The thought that he couldn't even see his brother's body tormented him. He felt that he had never truly had the chance to say goodbye. And he...

A soft sound in the shadows to his right caught his ear. Lathe turned his head, looking alertly for the source of the noise. Was Ari back already? Was she—

"Hello, Medic," said a low, hissing voice. "What are you doing in the main part of the prizzon? I thought you and your little friend would be back in your zzell by now."

―――――――――

Ari took a deep breath and stepped into the tunnel where the lashers were kenneled. She had been through here several times before but always during the day, when the huge, scaly beasts were asleep. Now it was night time and—

*And they're **still** asleep,* Ari told herself firmly. *Everything will be okay. Lathe will keep the cold air from blowing and waking them up. And even if they did somehow wake up, you're protected by Lathe's scent. Everything is going to be just fine. So get down to the hole and set Jak free.*

She walked as quickly and quietly as she could, moving with increased confidence since she'd been through the tunnel before. But she soon found that this time wasn't like the other trips she'd made to the hole.

All around her, she could hear stirring—the sliding of scales over scales, the restless movements of animals about to wake.

*But it's still warm down here,* she thought desperately, even as she quickened her pace. Well, as warm as it ever seemed to get in the hole, anyway. Which to be honest, wasn't all that warm. Maybe the lashers were stirring because their bodies knew it was almost time to wake?

*Or maybe they're just hungry,* whispered a sinister little voice in her head. Ari shivered and tried not to listen to it.

*I'm protected by Lathe's scent,* she reminded herself. *They're afraid of him so they should be afraid of me too—right?* Or at the very least, it should make the huge creatures want to avoid her.

She hoped.

At last she reached the end of the tunnel and stepped out into the dim light of the hole. Going to her brother's cell, she stood on tiptoes and whispered through the bars as loudly as she dared.

"Jak? *Jak!* Come on—wake up!"

Her answer was a loud snore and the sound of Jak turning over restlessly. Ari cursed silently to herself. Her brother always had been a sound sleeper.

"Jak!" she hissed again. Stooping, she found a few small stones on the floor and tossed them through the bars of his cell, hoping to hit him. "Jak, come *on!*"

At last she heard him rousing and after a long moment, his sleepy face appeared between the bars.

"Ari? What are you doing here in the middle of the night?"

He blinked. "It *is* the middle of the night, right?" He frowned. "But it can't be—why isn't it cold?"

"It *is* the middle of the night but Lathe—Medic—is keeping the climate control system from blowing."

She was already making her way to the gray electrical panel and pulling out her tools as she spoke. She'd been working on the wiring for the door locks for some time—there was only one small wire still unconnected but she'd been saving it, trying to make the job in the hole last so she could see Jak as much as possible.

Now Ari connected the wire and listened with satisfaction to the sliding click as the automatic locking mechanism on all the cell doors cycled, first locking, then unlocking the doors, then locking them again. She jiggled the wire once more and they unlocked. Now she only had to cut the heavy-duty padlock on the outside of his door and Jak would be free.

Her brother was still peering owlishly through the bars of his cell at her when she returned.

"Ari, what are you talking about? How can Medic keep the cold air from blowing? What's going on?"

"What's going on is we're getting out of here tonight but we have to hurry," Ari told him, priming the torch and putting on the safety goggles that were attached to it. "Stand back a minute and don't look, Jak. I have to cut the lock off your cell and then we're out of here."

---

"I zzaid, what are you doing down here?" Mukluk demanded, coming out into the light. He had his pain-prod in one hand and was tapping it impatiently against his scaly palm.

Lathe froze. *Whatever I do, I can't let him move me! If the climate control stops scanning my prison ID, the cold air will start blowing. Have to stay right...here.*

"Medic? I azked you a quezztion!" The head of the Horvath guards was sounding more agitated by the moment.

"I forgot something in the Infirmary," Lathe told him, trying to sound bored and unconcerned, as though being out of his cell in a part of the prison where he didn't belong after lights out was nothing out of the ordinary. "So I came down to get it."

Mukluk's slitted yellow eyes narrowed and his forked tongue lashed.

"Liar! You are up to zzomething. I know it!"

He hit Lathe in the back with his pain prod, giving him an agonizing shock right in the kidneys.

Lathe roared with surprise and pain and went rigid as the electric current arced through his body.

*Gods...the pain!* It felt like a horse had kicked him in the back —a *big* one.

But he must not move. If he turned away, even for a second, the climate control system would finish its cycle and start blowing cold air to wake the lashers. He must hold still! Somehow he managed to keep his feet despite the pain and finally Mukluk removed the prod.

"What izz going on here? Why won't you move?" The Horvath sounded both angry and bewildered.

There was nothing Lathe could say so he kept his mouth shut. His nerves were still singing with pain and his knees felt weak from the high voltage. *Hurry, Ari!* he thought desperately. *I don't know how much of this I can take.*

"Anzzer me! What are you doing here?"

Mukluk shocked him again...and again.

Lathe's jaw clamped shut and his muscles went rigid and hard, his body spasming as the charges zipped through him, causing agony so great he could barely breathe.

"How can you zztill be zztanding? I have never zzeen a male take zzo much," Mukluk hissed as he withdrew the pain prod for the third time. "Not zzince that other male who also had fangzz."

"What?" Lathe whipped his head to the right to stare at the Horvath's scaly face. "*What* did you say?" he demanded.

"Oh, so now you zzpeak?" Mukluk's forked tongue swiped up to swipe across one yellow eyeball.

"Yes, I fucking-well speak," Lathe snarled. "Tell me what male you're talking about! Did he look like me but with blond hair and pale blue eyes?"

Mukluk shrugged, his scaly shoulders rolling.

"All you humanoidzz look the zzame to me. All I know izz that he had fangzz like yourzz. He wazz trying to get the other prisonerzz to rebell—to rize up."

That sounded like Thonolan. His younger brother had always been an idealist. He would have protested the unjust treatment at BleakHall—would have tried to get the other prisoners to stand with him. He had been charismatic too—Lathe was betting he might have convinced a fair number of the other inmates to rally around him which would have made him a threat to the Horvath guards and Mukluk in particular.

"What happened to him?" he demanded, standing rigidly still but turning his head so he was looking the big Horvath in the eye. "His name was Thonolan, what did you do to him?"

"Ah yezz, *Thonolan*," Mukluk mused, licking his other eyeball. "Yezz, that *wazz* hizz name."

"What did you do to him?" Lathe insisted again. "You bastard —tell me!"

Mukluk shrugged.

"He wazz cauzing trouble. Zzo I killed him—the zame way I'm going to kill *you*."

He planted the end of his pain prod directly between Lathe's shoulder blades and turned it up on full power.

Lathe gasped and clutched at his chest. It was as though a giant hand had reached in to grab his heart and squeezed it tight, constricting it so it couldn't pump...tightening until his lungs couldn't expand.

*Can't...breathe...* he thought disjointedly. *Heart...can't...*

Then everything went black and he slumped to the ground.

# FORTY-ONE

A ri felt the first blast of cold air swirling around her ankles just as she was cutting through the lock on Jak's door.

*Oh Goddess no—what's going on? Did Lathe get tired of waiting and decide to leave us here? Or did his override fail?*

But she didn't have time to worry about that right now. She was halfway done with Jak's lock and trying to concentrate on her work as the blue-hot flame of the welding torch cut slowly but surely through the tough, high-density metal.

*Focus Ari—focus...just get it done,* she told herself. But it would have been easier to concentrate if she didn't feel like she was being watched. There was an itching sensation between her shoulder blades and she started to have a picture in her mind—an image of large, yellow eyes...*hungry* eyes—staring at her from the mouth of the tunnel, waiting to see what she would do next.

Between her shoulder blades wasn't the only place she itched either. The small spot on the side of her neck, just under her left ear where Tapper's knife had nicked her in the kitchen earlier, was also itching fiercely. Absentmindedly, Ari reached up to scratch the spot with one hand while she continued cutting with the other, holding the blow torch steady as she did.

But when she scratched the itchy spot, she cried out in pain and nearly dropped the torch. The place where the knife had poked her was incredibly tender and painful—almost as though it was somehow infected.

Ari yanked her hand away and looked at her fingers—they were bloody and she could feel something warm and wet flowing down the side of her neck.

*Oh my Goddess,* she thought numbly. *Fresh blood. That's not good—not good at all.*

"Ari? Ari!" Jak's voice from the bars above was hoarse with fear. "Ari, watch out—the lashers are waking up and there's one right behind you!"

Ari heard a snuffling sound behind her and then a hungry-sounding growl. As the padlock on Jak's cell at last gave way and fell off with a metallic *clunk,* she turned to see a huge lasher with yellow eyes standing not three feet from her.

It was an enormous beast—its head as high as hers though it stood on four legs instead of two. Or did it?

As it shifted a bit, its massive shoulders blocking the exit from the hole, Ari caught a glimpse at its haunches and saw with a shock that the short black fur that covered its front half gave way to broad, shimmering iridescent scales, as wide as her hand, on the lasher's back half. Instead of paws tipped with long, razor sharp claws as it had in front, its body ended in a thick, muscular coil of tail with a spiked point on the end.

*It looks like something out of mythology,* Ari thought wonderingly. *Half feline, half serpent. How the hell can something like that even exist?*

But exist it did. The lasher took another step towards her, dragging its scaly, muscular back half on the metal floor with a sound like dry leaves rustling together. It sniffed the air, its muzzle wrinkling as though it wasn't sure it liked what it was smelling.

*And what **is** it smelling?* Ari thought wildly. *Partly Lathe's scent on me—that's for sure. His scent would probably be enough to make it leave me alone if not for the blood.*

The blood. She could feel it trickling freely down her neck now. She pressed one hand just under her ear, hoping to stem the flow but the pressure of her own touch was so painful she couldn't stand it.

"Ow!" She yanked her hand away instinctively, scattering blood droplets over the dirty metal floor.

"Ari?" Jak's voice behind her sounded panicky. "Ari, what are you doing? Don't you know these damn things are attracted to the scent of blood?"

"I didn't do it on purpose," Ari snapped. "I didn't know I was hurt until I scratched under my ear. I'm sorry."

"I thought Medic was supposed to keep the cold air from blowing so the lashers would stay asleep!" Jak snarled.

"He's supposed to be trying," Ari kept her eyes on the lasher as she spoke. "But he said that his override might fail. That must be what happened."

She hoped that was what had happened, anyway. She hoped Lathe hadn't simply decided to go without her. He wouldn't do that...would he?

Ari wasn't sure.

The lasher sniffed at one of the droplets and lapped it up with a long, black tongue. Then it made a rumbling sound in its throat —a *hungry* sound, Ari thought—and took another step towards her.

*Oh Goddess, I've made it worse,* she thought numbly. *So much worse.* Chilly air was rushing from the vents along the floor, freezing her feet and ankles but she barely noticed it. Her legs felt like they were made of pudding and her heart was pounding in her ears so loudly it was difficult to hear herself think. She wondered if this particular lasher was the one who had tried to get into Lathe's cell—the one that had been stalking her.

"Ari, I'm going to open the cell door and you run in." Jak's voice was soft but intense. "The cell doors open outward—that thing can't reach you in here with me."

"And then what?" Ari demanded in a shaky voice. "We're both trapped in the cell together? No, Jak—we have to get past it. We have to get out or we'll be stuck here until it's too late to go!"

"Then I'm coming out to help you fight it," he said, his voice steady and low.

"No—you'll only get yourself killed," Ari said sharply. "I have weapons." She held up the torch and nodded at her tool belt. "But you can't touch them because they're designated to me. Stay in the cell, Jak."

"But—" he began.

"Let me help."

The new voice yanked her attention away from the monstrous lasher for just a moment. Cutting her eyes to the right, Ari saw the Beast standing with his face pressed to the bars of his cell.

"Let me help you fight them...and take me with you," he said urgently. His mismatched eyes flashed gold and green in the dim lighting. "Cut the lock on my cell," he urged Ari. "I can help you."

"Don't listen to him, Ari!" Jak exclaimed. "He's a fucking murderer and sociopath—he's only out for himself."

"I may be a convict and a murderer but I have a sense of honor, little girl." The Beast's voice was low and serious and he looked gravely at Ari. "Let me out and I give you my oath as a Kindred I'll either help you fight your way out or die trying."

Ari looked at him more fully, her eyes going wide.

"You...you're a Kindred? But I thought you said you were a hybrid."

"I *am* a hybrid—half Beast Kindred and Half Blood Kindred. That's how I came by my name...and my fangs." He grinned, showing his fangs, shorter than Lathe's but no less deadly for all of that.

"Ari, don't listen to him," Jak insisted but Ari was staring at the big convict, her heart slamming against her ribs. She was remembering everything Lathe had told her—how the Kindred revered and honored women...how they always kept their word.

Should she take a risk and set the Beast free?

"Ari, watch out!" Jak gasped. "It's about to—"

Just then, with a roaring growl, the lasher lunged at her.

———

"Zzo, this other male with fangzz...he meant zzomething to you?"

Lathe opened his eyes to see Mukluk standing over him, his pain-prod held ready to deliver the killing blow. Since he was lying on his back, Lathe could imagine where the blow would be. His body couldn't take many more of the punishing electrical jolts. The last one had nearly stopped his heart—he could still feel it hiccupping unsteadily in his chest as though it was trying to find its natural rhythm.

*It'll only take one more jolt,* Lathe thought. *If he presses that thing to my chest and shocks me there, my heart will give out—for good this time. I wonder if that's the way he killed Thonolan?*

The thought sent a surge of anger through him, as strong as the jolts from the Horvath's pain-prod. And then he felt a swirl of chilly air eddying against his cheeks and a new thought intruded.

*Cold air...that's not good. Why? Something important...something I forgot...*

"You are too zzmart for your own good, Medic. I don't know how you managed to dizzable the climate control and delay it azz you did," Mukluk hissed, his forked tongue lashing. "But you will be going to the hole for it."

"The...the hole?" Lathe frowned. *Something about the hole—what was it?*

The Horvath guard hissed angrily.

"Yezz—the hole. *If* I feel merciful. Juzt now I think I might kill you after all."

The Horvath's hissing words brought back what his scrambled memory had been unable to supply and Lathe felt a sudden burst of horror.

*The Hole! The climate control...the cold air, it will wake the lashers—Ari! She's right down there in the hole, the middle of their den with only my scent to protect her!*

He had to get out of this alive—not just to avenge his brother but to save the female he loved—even if she didn't love him back.

"You'll never know how I hacked your system if you kill me," he pointed out, trying to keep his voice steady. "What if the override I put in BleakHall's system is set to go off every night at the same time? What if it's set to go off at a *random* time? You'll never know when the lashers might be sleeping instead of guarding the inmates as they're supposed to. You won't have a fucking *clue*."

He was taking a chance and he knew it—hoping to get Mukluk angry enough to want to question him without making the Horvath guard so enraged he just decided to kill Lathe on the spot. But it was all he could think to do.

For a long moment, the verdict seemed to hang in the balance. Lathe could see the Horvath's fingers tightening on the trigger of his pain-prod and the deadly metal tip of it hovered just over his chest, only about an inch from his heart. If Mukluk pulled the trigger—

At last the Horvath guard made a hissing sound of disgust and flicked his forked tongue.

"You will be punizhed for this, Medic. Punizhed and quez-ztioned mozt thoroughly until we get everything you have done out of you. I wizzh I had time to do it now. But the lazhers will be coming—get up."

"Not until you get that thing out of my face." Lathe nodded at the pain-prod.

With a hiss of annoyance, Mukluk pulled the deadly metal tip of the long, black rod back just a few inches. Not very far, but it was enough, Lathe estimated.

He prepared to make his move.

---

As the lasher lunged at her, Ari had the presence of mind to hold up the flaming blow-torch. But the torch hadn't been meant to use as a weapon. Its flame was short—no longer than an inch—and the lasher simply dodged her hand and aimed for her other side.

Without thinking, Ari pulled out the big wrench—the one she'd gotten in case she needed a weapon.

*Well I certainly need one now!* she thought numbly as she fumbled the heavy metal tool out of her belt.

There was no time to swing the wrench—the lasher was too quick. She was barely able to get it up between herself and the springing beast. But she had no idea if the security shock which kept the tools from being handled by anyone but the person they were designated to would work on a lasher.

*Please,* she thought. *Please, Goddess...*

It worked.

As the end of the wrench touched the short black fur of the lasher's muzzle, Ari felt a powerful jolt go through it. It probably would have been strong enough to knock a grown man down but the lasher was bigger than a man—and much more massive. It simply snarled and took a step back, its muzzle wrinkling in anger.

"Get me out of here," the Beast said urgently from his cell. "Before that thing fucking eats you up, little girl."

The lasher had retreated to the doorway of the tunnel, its yellow eyes glowing balefully in the dim light. Ari felt safe enough to move the few steps it took to get to the Beast's cell. Keeping one eye on the snarling, angry beast standing in the doorway, she began to burn through the lock on the Beast's door.

"Ari, no!" Jak protested, seeing what she was doing. "He'll kill us both as fast as the lashers will! Hell—he probably wants to leave our bodies for bait so he can get away."

For a moment his words almost made Ari pause...but then she

remembered again, Lathe telling her how Kindred always honored and protected women.

"I don't believe that," she said steadily, continuing to cut. "Lathe told me that Kindred protect females. I'm going to let him out."

"Thank you, little girl." The Beast's voice was a rough growl. "I swear you won't regret it."

*I hope I won't,* Ari thought, keeping one eye on the angry lasher as she continued to cut through the lock. *Or it will probably be the last thing I do!*

---

Lathe made as though to sit up and then kicked out, catching the Horvath guard in the shin and sending him toppling forward. He barely rolled out of the way in time as Mukluk came crashing down with a hissing howl.

The moment the Horvath was on the ground, Lathe elbowed him hard in the midsection and rolled again, getting out of the way of the lizard guard's long, muscular tail. He wanted to bite the bastard—he could feel the venom gathering in his fangs—but Mukluk was thrashing and he couldn't get a grip on any one part of the guard's body. Also, though he longed for revenge, it was no longer his primary objective—rescuing Ari was.

Grabbing the pain-prod, which had clattered to the floor when Mukluk fell, he gripped it by the handle and rammed it against the Horvath's side. Pulling the trigger, he felt a surge through the prod and watched with grim satisfaction as Mukluk's entire scaly body went rigid, jerking and seizing, dancing to the tune of the deadly jolt.

He didn't pull back until he saw the yellow eyes roll up in Mukluk's head. Then, when he was sure the guard was out, Lathe got to his feet. The cold air was swirling all around him, the temperature dropping fast, and he was afraid for Ari. She was down in the tunnel with the lashers and Lathe wasn't sure how long his scent would keep her safe.

Gripping the pain-prod hard, he started for the hole at a dead run, knowing that he was racing against time.

*Please, Goddess, don't let me be too late! Please let me save her one more time!*

---

As Ari finally finished cutting through the high-density metal lock and it fell to the ground, the big lasher was twitching its scaly hindquarters, obviously getting ready to pounce.

"Ari, run!" she heard Jak shout and then the cell door slammed open and the Beast emerged.

He was immense—much bigger than she'd guessed from his face with its mismatched eyes peering from between the bars.

*Goddess, he must be seven and a half feet tall,* Ari thought numbly. And then the Beast lunged forward to meet the pouncing lasher. With one massive hand, he caught the animal by the throat.

The lasher struggled and hissed, its muscular, scaly bottom half lashing frantically. Its long front claws dug bloody furrows in the Beast's arm and chest but he didn't even seem to notice.

"Die, you big bastard," he growled and Ari saw the tendons in his muscular wrist and forearm stand out as he squeezed the lasher's throat. It let out a final strangled roar and went suddenly limp in his hand.

Ari expected the massive Kindred to drop the lasher, but instead the Beast wrapped his other hand around the furry throat and twisted. There was a sickening cracking sound like a thick tree branch splintering and the lasher's head was suddenly hanging at an odd angle.

"Just in case," the Beast said. He looked at Ari with unreadable mismatched eyes and finally dropped the lasher in a heap at his feet.

For a moment her heart was beating right between her teeth. What would he do to her? Had Jak been right? Was she next to have her neck snapped?

"Stay away from my little sister, Slade." Jak was suddenly behind her, having finally come out of his cell even though Ari had told him to stay inside.

"I haven't been with a female in a long fucking time but I'm not interested in this little girl." The Beast's nose wrinkled. "She's got another male's scent on her so strong he might as well have stamped his name on her forehead. Or...someplace else." He raised an eyebrow at Ari and she found herself blushing.

"That's Lathe—he's a Kindred too," she explained. "He told me he has an escape route dug under the prison but we have to get to him first."

"Which means going through that tunnel filled with angry, hungry lashers." Jak sounded shaken. "How in the Hell are we supposed to do that, Ari? I can't touch any of your tools and you're bleeding—calling the damn things right to you. Slade might be strong but he can't take on fifty lashers at once."

"Oh no? Just watch me." The Beast—Slade as Jak called him

—rolled his broad shoulders and flexed his neck from side to side, like a man warming up for a fight. He turned to Ari. "You ever get the lights in the lasher tunnel fixed, little girl?"

Ari's heart sank. "No—I was saving it for last. I wanted to have an excuse to come down and see Jak as often as I could."

"Too bad." Slade shrugged. "It would have been better for you two if you could see what was coming. As it is, you'll just have to stay close to me."

"Are you going to fight them in the dark?" Ari asked, her voice wavering.

"Not dark to me, little girl." Slade grinned, showing his fangs again, and pointed to his mismatched eyes. "Kindred have great night vision. Now come on—we need to get out of here before someone sounds a fucking alarm. I'm not going back in the hole."

Ari exchanged a look with her big brother and Jak nodded silent agreement.

"All right," she said, taking a grip on the wrench with one hand and her still-burning blow-torch with the other. "Let's go."

---

Lathe smelled fresh blood as he came down into the subbasement —the same place he had found Ari crying earlier, before the meeting of the Mistresses. The memory made his heart fist in his chest, especially when he remembered how roughly he'd spoken to her.

Was it her blood he smelled now? Had the lashers torn her to pieces when the climate control system kicked on and began blowing the cold air that woke them?

"Ari?" he shouted, plunging into the mouth of the tunnel.

A low, snarling growl come back in answer. Lathe could see shapes in the darkness up ahead—one shape, actually—but it was moving too fast to distinguish and it was larger than Ari—*much* larger.

*What in the Seven Hells? Is that her brother? Gods, what a monster! How is she so petite if he's over seven feet tall?*

But the scent wafting from the tunnel was distinctly Kindred. Lathe frowned even as he ran forward. There was no other Kindred here in the prison, of that he was certain. If there had been, he would have taken steps to rescue them. In fact, the only male he knew of who was supposed to be kept down here in the hole was the dangerous prisoner the Horvath's had called 'the Beast' and his files had said nothing about a Kindred heritage.

A lasher launched itself at him from out of the darkness and Lathe batted it away with the buzzing pain-prod. It made a sound of pain—almost a yelp—and slithered off as fast as it could.

"Ari," he shouted, running forward. "Ari are you safe? Where are you?"

"Behind me, Brother—she's behind me," a deep, growling voice answered him. "Move out of the way, we're getting out of here fast."

"I'm okay, Lathe." Ari's voice floated to him from somewhere back in the dark tunnel. "There aren't many lashers left—Slade killed most of them."

They all ran out of the tunnel together and Lathe had a confused impression of one of the biggest Kindred warriors he had ever seen. The male was bearded and shaggy and had two mismatched eyes—one green and one gold. He was also covered in bloody scratches and bites, but he seemed well enough.

Behind him was a much smaller male with black hair and dark blue eyes like Ari's. And behind him—

"Ari!" Lathe caught her up in his arms and crushed her to him.

"I thought you'd left without us." She hugged him back, her voice filled with tears. "Oh Lathe, I thought..." Her voice hitched in a sob. "I thought you were so angry you decided to leave me here."

"Never," he swore fiercely. "I'd never leave you, Ari!"

Then he smelled the scent of blood on her again and held her by the shoulders so he could examine her.

"What happened? Where are you hurt?"

"I'm fine." She sniffed and dashed tears from her eyes. "None of the lashers got me—Slade killed them before they could get to us." She looked up at the huge Kindred with the green and gold eyes. "Thank you—you saved our lives."

"That's all right, little girl but do you mind if we save the celebration until *after* we're out of here?" He turned to Lathe. "I heard you have an escape tunnel dug somewhere in the prison. You mind pointing the way?"

"It's in the Infirmary," Lathe told him. "Let me just get it ready."

Tapping his prison ID, he gave the command he'd been holding off for as long as he could—telling the nanites to finish the tunnel as fast as possible. It was certain to trip the prison's alarms but at this point it couldn't be helped.

"Come on." He gestured for them to follow him. "We have to get going—we're going to have company pretty quickly and I'd rather be out of BleakHall before they find us."

They ran up through the subbasement and through the

prison. If there were any more lashers around, they made themselves scarce because Lathe saw neither hide nor hair—neither whisker nor scale might be more accurate—of a single one of them. He wondered how many the huge Kindred warrior called "The Beast" had killed in the tunnel. There had been multiple scaly shapes slumped unmoving in the darkness and the male certainly looked like he had been through a terrible battle.

Lathe was just grateful that the other Kindred had kept Ari safe. She was still armed with her tools but he knew very well that such weapons wouldn't keep back a hungry lasher for long, especially if it smelled fresh blood.

As they came around the hall leading to the infirmary, he braced himself for a fight. He was almost certain he hadn't killed Mukluk—although the Goddess knew he wished he had. If the head guard had assembled the other Horvaths and all of them were armed, it was going to be almost impossible to get through, even with The Beast at his back.

But when they got to the area outside the Infirmary, Mukluk was gone.

Lathe stopped short, frowning. Where in the Seven Hells had the lizard guard gone? And for that matter, where were the rest of the Horvaths that Mukluk should have called to help him catch the escaping prisoners?

Narrowing his eyes, Lathe peered into the shadows but he saw nothing. His frowned deepened—he didn't like surprises. Could they be in the Infirmary?

But when he opened the door, his work station was quiet. There were the familiar shelves with their meager supplies, his battered trustee tablet which he had used to hack the BleakHall system—with a little help from some extra nanites—and the cracked plasti-leather of the exam table.

Where were the guards? What was going on? Had Mukluk dragged himself off to a corner somewhere and died? Or maybe just passed out without alerting anyone else? That would be the best-case scenario but Lathe didn't hold out much hope for it.

"What's wrong, Brother?" the huge Kindred asked him. "Problems?"

"Not right now," Lathe said grimly. "But I'm betting we'll have some soon. Better be ready to fight."

"Oh, I'm always ready for a fight." The Beast grinned, showing short, sharp fangs. "You could say it's my specialty."

Lathe frowned. The Beast must be a hybrid—that would account for his massive size and mismatched eyes. He told himself he should have read the chart more carefully and gone down to examine the other male when he was first transferred into Bleak-Hall. He had almost left a fellow Kindred behind!

But there was no time for remorse now—they had to get out of here.

"Come on," he said, jerking his head towards the supply closet. "Let's go. We'll worry about the fight if—or more likely *when*—it happens."

# FORTY-TWO

Ari had to take a deep breath before she could make herself jump into the dark hole in the ground Lathe revealed when they got to the Infirmary supply closet.

"This is it? Looks kind of narrow." The Beast—or Slade as she was beginning to think of him—rumbled, frowning.

"I had the nanites dig it to my own dimensions," Lathe said. He glanced up at Slade, who was at least half a head taller and broader in the shoulders than he was. "Sorry, Brother—I didn't expect to run into anyone of your, er, size while I was here."

"It's all right." Slade sounded unconcerned. "I'll make it work."

"I'll go first," Lathe said. "Then Ari, then her brother—Jak, right?" He raised his eyebrows at the smaller man.

"Good to meet you." Jak gave him a wary nod. "I was in the hole when you first came and I've been there your whole stay, but I've heard all about you, Medic."

"It's Lathe," Lathe told him. "I hope to never go by 'Medic' ever again."

"Lathe, then. Thanks for looking out for my little sister." Jak held out a hand to him and Lathe clasped forearms with him briefly.

"You're welcome."

"And thank you, Slade." Jak turned to the Beast. "I misjudged you. I'm sorry about that."

The massive hybrid shrugged.

"I'm used to it. You don't get to be my size without everyone around you pissing their pants in fear of you. So I don't take it personal."

Jak nodded. "Got it. And thanks."

"Jak, you'll come after Ari and then the, uh Beast—" Lathe continued.

"Slade," Slade rumbled. "I'd like to drop my moniker too. It's just my combat name but I don't fight in the ring anymore."

"Slade—Brother, you'll bring up the rear. Are we all ready to go?"

"As we'll ever be—let's get out of here," Jak said fervently. "I never want to see this place again."

"Let's go then," Lathe said and dropped into the hole in the ground.

They heard his feet hit the bottom with a crunch of soil and pebbles and then he called up, "All right, Ari—it's safe. Come down!"

Ari bit her lip and hesitated for a moment, claustrophobia taking an icy grip on her throat. Down in the dark, crawling through a narrow tunnel with tons of earth overhead—could she do it?

Then Lathe's voice came drifting up again.

"Just jump, little one—I'll catch you."

*I can do it,* Ari told herself. *If Lathe is with me, I can do it.*

Taking a deep breath, she jumped.

Strong, warm hands caught her by the waist and set her gently on her feet.

"All right, little one?" Lathe murmured in her ear.

"Fine." Ari whispered back. She felt a little shaken and she didn't like being in a dark, confined space but she found that having the big Kindred near her really did help.

Jak jumped down next and then Slade shouldered his way into the cramped space. Ari couldn't see much but it appeared to her that both of his massive shoulders were scraping the sides of the tunnel. Slade didn't complain though, he just looked at Lathe.

"All present and accounted for, Brother," he said. "Let's move."

"It's a long way," Lathe warned them. "Follow me and just keep going, no matter what."

Ari thought later that for as long as she lived, she would never forget that nightmarish journey in the dark. She hung on to the back of Lathe's jumpsuit and Jak hung on to hers since neither of them could see in the dark like the Kindred could and all of them went as fast as they could over the bumpy, uneven ground. She couldn't use the blowtorch in the tunnel to see where she was going—Lathe said it would burn up the oxygen supply too fast. So Ari tucked it into her belt and tried not to mind that she couldn't see where she was going.

The tunnel had been dug for someone Lathe's size so at least it wasn't too narrow for her—Ari thought she would have gone crazy if it was. But every now and then she could feel the sides of the tunnel brushing her on one side or the other or some loose dirt would sift down onto her head and she would remember all over again that they were underground—buried with no way to get out except to make it to the end.

She tried very, *very* hard not to think about all the horror vids she'd ever seen about people being buried alive and just kept going, keeping a tight grip on the back of Lathe's jumpsuit. She had no idea how Slade was managing, since every step he took, both sides of the tunnel scraped his broad shoulders. Either the big hybrid wasn't claustrophobic or he was doing a better job controlling his fear than Ari was with hers.

At last, after what seemed like hours and hours, Lathe called for a halt.

It was pitch black so Ari ran into his broad back and then Jak ran into hers, making her feel even more crowded and claustrophobic.

"What is it? What's wrong?" she asked Lathe. Because though she couldn't see him, she could feel that he was making motions in the darkness.

'It's not done yet." His voice was flat. "I told the nanites to finish as quickly as possible but they haven't gotten through yet."

"You mean we're at a dead end? Stuck underground with no way to get out?"

Ari heard the panic in her own voice but she couldn't help it. *Buried alive,* whispered the voice in her head. *Just like that one vid you watched with the girl who was stuck in a cave-in and called and called for help but no one came for her and she died there and—*

"It's all right, little one." Lathe's firm voice in her ear cut into her panicked thoughts and made her feel a little better. "The tunnel's been sloping up for some time— we're only a few feet from the surface."

"Then let's finish the job ourselves," Slade rumbled. Ari heard the noise of him digging into the roof of the tunnel and then dirt pattering down all around her.

"Yes—do it," Lathe answered and then he was digging too. Jak joined in as well but there wasn't much Ari could do—she was too short to reach the ceiling. She closed her eyes and tried to pray.

*Please Goddess, let us get out of here soon. Let the end of the tunnel be close. Let us be all right. Please...please...*

There was no answer but a warmth seemed to fill her from the inside out and Ari felt better.

Then a big gust of fresh air came from overhead, startling her. Ari took a deep, gulping breath, suddenly realizing how hard it had gotten to breath in the small space.

"That's it!" she heard Lathe say excitedly. "We're through!"

"Are we?" Ari looked up, her eyes dazzled by the brilliant starlight overhead after being in the dark so long. "Are we really?"

"You zzertainly are," a hissing voice said in her ear and then a rough hand reached down and yanked Ari out of the tunnel by the collar of her prison jumpsuit.

"What a long way you've come," Mukluk said, shaking her and setting her on her feet with an arm around her neck. "And what a zzhame you'll only have to go right back again."

# FORTY-THREE

For a moment, everything was confusion.

"Let her go, you bastard," Lathe was shouting as he jumped out of the end of the tunnel. "You touch her and you die!"

"*Her* izz it?" Mukluk turned Ari around and stared at her more closely. With one scaly claw, he made a downward slicing motion, causing the buttons on her orange and blue jumpsuit to pop off and baring her breasts.

"Stop it!" Ari grabbed for the sides of her jumpsuit but the Horvath had already seen her.

"Zzzo, you *are* a female," he hissed, spinning her around and clamping a scaly forearm around her neck again. "I had my doubtzz about you. The way Medic protected you when it wazz known he wazzn't a lover of other malezz was highly zuzpiciouz. Now it makezz zenze."

"Let me go!" Ari gasped, struggling against the arm that held her. There were other Horvath guards there too—all of them armed with pain-prods. She supposed she ought to be thankful that BleakHall policy forbade the guards to use any kind of projectile or laser weapons but at the moment, when they were outnumbered and she was being held captive, it was small comfort.

"Touch her and die." Lathe's voice was deadly and his eyes were glowing red again—a sure sign he was going into Rage.

Jak was out of the tunnel too and shouting and behind him, the Beast was a huge, hulking menace. But it didn't seem to matter —there were fifteen guards at least—how could they overcome so many? Especially when Mukluk already had her as a hostage?

Suddenly the warm, feminine voice spoke to her again—the same one that had directed her when she was trying to get the torch out of the tool box.

***You know what to do, daughter,*** it murmured in her ear. ***Be brave—you will prevail.***

*Does she mean I should fight?* Ari wondered, looking around for the source of the voice. *Can I still use the tools I brought with me as weapons?* But she knew the jarring electrical shock which was so effective in keeping other inmates from taking the tools, didn't work on the Horvath guards. If it did, the Spice Lords could have led an uprising and taken over BleakHall.

*But just because I can't use their shock doesn't mean the tools are useless,* she thought.

Mukluk had her by the neck but her arms and hands were free. Surreptitiously, Ari began to feel along her tool belt. The heavy wrench was too big to swing effectively in a small area and the torch was too difficult to turn on without the Horvath notic-ing. That left the petite socket wrench and the screwdriver.

Remembering how she had punctured Gorn's eye with it, Ari

chose the latter. Carefully, she pulled it from her tool belt and held it at waist level. Catching Lathe's burning red eyes, she made a motion with it—letting him know what she intended.

The big Kindred's eyes widened and he made a short, sharp shake of his head. He seemed to be telling her not to try anything foolish. But Ari knew if she could just get away from Mukluk—or at least distract him—Lathe and Slade would have a chance at defeating him and the rest of the guards.

Taking a deep breath, she held the screwdriver tight.

*Goddess, be with me,* she prayed. For it must be the Goddess of Mercy whose voice she had been hearing—there was no one else she could think of that might speak to her so.

***I am with you, child,*** came the warm reply. ***I will give you strength.***

At once, Ari felt as though someone had given her an injection of adrenaline. Power surged through her and she pulled back her arm and stabbed down as hard as she could with the deadly little screwdriver.

On her own, Ari wasn't at all certain she could have even penetrated the Horvath guard's scales. But with the power of the Goddess behind her, she felt the point of the screwdriver pierce through the alien hide and drive deep into the flesh beneath.

The effect was immediate. Mukluk howled and let go of Ari to grab for his wounded leg. Spinning around, she used some of her newfound strength to execute a Ton-kwa roundhouse kick. Since he was bending down to reach for the screwdriver still lodged in his thigh, her blow caught him square in the face and the big Horvath went over on his back howling.

The other guards seemed stunned at first—they froze for just a moment, looking to see where the damage to their leader was coming from. Ari could see the surprise and uncertainty growing on their dim faces. Surely the great Mukluk couldn't have been brought down by the diminutive inmate he'd had such a firm grip on only a moment ago—could he?

That one moment of inaction was deadly—for the guards. At once, Lathe and Jak and Slade sprang forward, wading into battle with angry growls and cries. All of them had suffered at the cruel hands of the Horvath guards and now it was time to make the scaly bastards pay.

Of course the Horvaths were armed with pain-prods but Lathe had a prod of his own and he wasn't shy about using it. Jak was quick enough to leap out of the way and as for the Beast, well, getting shocked only seemed to make him angrier and more violent.

Ari shivered as she watched the immense hybrid roar in anger and lift one of the Horvaths over his head, bringing the alien guard down on one muscular knee like a man breaking a stick. There was a crunching sound and the Horvath gave a burbling cry and went limp, his spine bent the wrong way. Beside him, Lathe and Jak were fighting too—both of them had pain-prods now and they were using them to much better advantage than the dim-witted Horvaths.

Then Mukluk was up and running at Lathe, despite the screwdriver still lodged in his thigh.

"Lathe!" she screamed. "Watch out! Behind you!"

The big Kindred turned and when he saw who his attacker was, he seemed to grow even bigger somehow. Mukluk attempted to hit him with a pain-prod but Lathe batted it aside almost contemptuously. He seized the Horvath guard by the shoulders and head-butted him, his forehead knocking against the bony skull of the lizard guard in a way that made Mukluk howl with pain. But Lathe wasn't done with him.

"This is for Thonolan," Ari heard him growl. Then he opened his mouth and his fangs seemed to grow longer than she had ever seen them. In a sudden swift, savage move, he lunged forward and sank the shining white points into Mukluk's face, right on his scaly cheek.

The Horvath guard began to shake and shiver, his back arching and his forked tongue whipping the air like a wounded snake. When thin black foam began to seep from his mouth, Lathe dropped him and spat—then spat again as though trying to rid his mouth of a bad taste.

"Brother," Ari heard him say in a low, choked voice, "You are avenged."

When he turned to her again there were tears in his eyes—though if they were tears of sorrow or fury, she couldn't tell. Maybe both.

"Lathe," she whispered but it was clear he didn't hear her. He had a faraway look on his face as he swiped the tears from his cheeks.

"We've got 'em on the run now," Jak shouted, dragging her attention away from the big Kindred.

She had been transfixed by the sight of Lathe and Mukluk but now she looked around and saw that most of the guards were lying on the ground and the rest were running away. Apparently the loss of their leader had scared them off.

Lathe turned to her. His eyes were still red but Ari saw that his face was calm.

"It's finished," he said in a low voice. "Come on."

"Where are we going now?" Ari asked.

Lathe didn't answer. He swept her up in his arms and then they were running through the night, rushing into the dark forest where tree branches whipped her in the face and thorns tugged at the sleeves of her tattered jumpsuit.

*Going,* she thought. *Getting out of here. But where—?*

Almost before she could finish her thought, Lathe was sitting her down in a large, empty glade.

"What—?" she began to ask but then he slapped the empty air beside her. The slap produced a hollow metallic *thunk* and then, to Ari's amazement, a ship appeared out of nowhere.

"Nice shuttle," Jak said, coming up behind her. "Sleek."

"Thanks. It's fast too—that's what counts right now." Lathe pressed his palm to the side of the ship and the doors opened in response to his touch. "Everyone get in," he ordered. "We haven't got a minute to lose—there's going to be trouble on the Mother Ship and we have to warn them."

# FORTY-FOUR

Sylvan was working late in his office—something he knew that Sophia hated but was sometimes necessary—when he heard a knock on his door.

"Come in," he called, assuming it was one of his subordinate officers, come to give him some news. The door slid open and, as he looked up from his desk, he saw his sister-in-law, Olivia walk into the room.

"Oh, hello Olivia," Sylvan said, looking back down at his screen. "Is there a problem? Am I needed at the med center?"

Though he was the head of the Kindred High Council, he still tried to get to the med center and practice his doctoring skills at least twice a week. Healing the sick was his first career choice but he happened to have a talent for administration and leadership too—which was probably why the Goddess had appointed him to lead the Kindred of the Mother Ship. Sometimes Sylvan wished he was still just a regular doctor working every day at the med center—his life would have certainly been much simpler if he was.

"Commander Sylvan, I presume?" Olivia's voice broke into his musing and he looked up again, frowning when he saw that his sister-in-law was still just standing there.

"Well...yes. You know it's me, Olivia. Is everything all right with you and Baird? And little Daniel?"

"We are...well." Olivia still spoke stiffly and she was moving stiffly too, Sylvan saw with puzzlement. Was something wrong with her? Her blonde hair was smooth and tidy and her clothes were neat but her silver-gray eyes looked blank. As she approached his desk, her arms were stiff at her sides and she seemed to be holding something gripped in one hand.

For some reason, a chill went down Sylvan's spine. Something wasn't right here—he was sure of it. Acting on instinct, he rose from the desk and stepped away from his sister-in-law. Undeterred, Olivia came straight towards him.

"Olivia, are you well?" he asked, frowning down at her. "Do you want me to call Sophia for you? Or Baird?"

"I have something for you," Olivia raised her hand over her head, not answering his question. "Something from Mistress Hellenix."

"You do? But when did you meet *her?*" How could his sister-in-law have met the flamboyant Mistress from Yonnie Six? Sylvan took a cautious step towards her. "Olivia, is everything all right? You're acting...strangely."

Suddenly, Olivia rushed at him.

She was only a blur of motion—Sylvan had known her for years but he had never seen her move that fast. In fact, he had never seen *any* human move that fast. Only years of training as a warrior saved him as his instincts took over and he dodged out of the way just in time.

Olivia ran right past him but then she turned at once and headed for him again, her right arm upraised as though to stab him with whatever it was she was gripping so tightly.

Sylvan didn't want to hurt her so he ducked and dodged and managed to catch her by the wrists. At last he could get a good look at the thing she was holding.

In her hand was a long, sharp syringe filled with bright green fluid.

"Gods!" Sylvan gasped. "What is that? What's *wrong* with you, Olivia?"

"I must give you this." Her eyes were blank and though he was holding her firmly, she kept attempting to stab him with the syringe. Not only that, she was *strong*—as strong as another Kindred warrior at least, Sylvan thought. He had been joined to Sophia for a number of years and he knew a normal human female's capacity for strength—at the moment, his sister-in-law was far exceeding it. Though he was putting all his effort in to holding her at bay, he could barely keep her in place.

"Olivia!" he exclaimed, squeezing her wrist tighter. "Don't do this! Drop the syringe or I'll have to hurt you—you know I don't want to do that!"

"I must give you...I must give you..." Olivia repeated over and over, her arm trying to stab downward with the syringe.

Gripping her wrist tighter than he wanted to, Sylvan at last forced her to drop the syringe.

"What's in this, anyway?" he demanded as it clattered to his desk. "What are you trying to inject me with?"

"Mission failed," Olivia announced in that same, calm, flat tone. "Self-destruct sequence initiated."

"What?" Sylvan dropped his hold on her and took a step back. Her eyes...what was wrong with her eyes? They had gone from silvery-gray to bright, pulsing red.

Some instinct caused him to duck and then, to his horror, Olivia's head blew apart in large, bloody chunks.

"Goddess!" Sylvan gasped as she toppled over, fluid spraying from her neck. It didn't look like blood exactly—it was pink instead of red. But it was doing a pretty good job of coating his desk and walls with arterial spray. What in the Seven Hells was going on? The thing that had just exploded in his office couldn't be Olivia...could it?

Sylvan ran from his office and looked for the nearest viewscreen. There was one in the reception area just outside his door so he didn't have to go far. He called his brother's suite with shaking fingers, praying to the Goddess all the while that everything would be all right. He could have used a Think-me and bespoken his brother, of course, but he needed to see Baird's face. And more important, Olivia's.

"Yes, Brother?" Baird's face came on the screen in a moment. "Is everything well?"

"That's what I need to ask you," Sylvan said urgently.

"Well, we're all fine." Baird frowned. "What's this about?"

"Let me talk to Olivia," Sylvan said urgently.

"Why? Is something wrong in the med center?" Baird asked. Without waiting for an answer, he called to the other room, "*Lilenta,* Sylvan needs you."

"Is there something wrong in the med center?" Olivia asked,

echoing her husband's question. She was a nurse and since Sylvan was a doctor the two of them worked together often.

She came into the room and walked up to the viewscreen which Baird had mounted on the wall of his living area.

"Hi, Sylvan. What's wrong?" she asked, frowning. "I was just getting Daniel down for bed but if you need me at the med center Baird can take over. Honey, go in with Daniel for a minute could you?" she said to Baird.

He nodded and went into their son's room, leaving Olivia to peer at the viewscreen.

"Are you okay?" she asked.

"No...yes. I...don't know." Sylvan ran a shaking hand through his hair. Seeing his sister-in-law acting and talking so normally, he was more certain than ever that the thing that had exploded in his office couldn't have been a real person. But then, what in the Seven Hells was it?

"Sylvan?" Olivia leaned closer to the viewscreen, a look of concern on her lovely features. "What's wrong?" she asked. "You look like you just saw a ghost."

"I...I don't know what I saw," Sylvan admitted. "Will you please ask Baird to come to my office at once?"

"So it's *not* a problem in the med center?" Olivia looked at him doubtfully. "What's this all about, Sylvan?"

"I'll tell you when I know," Sylvan promised. "For now, please just ask Baird to come to my office."

Olivia still looked concerned but she nodded.

"All right—I'll send him. But, Sylvan...be careful, okay?" She gave a worried little laugh. "Sorry—I'm not sure why I said that. I mean, you're just in your office right? I'm sure you're safe there."

Sylvan reflected that he would have thought the same thing a moment ago.

"Thank you for your concern, kin-of-my-mate," he said formally. "But I am well—I just need Baird."

Olivia nodded and, as she ended the call, Sylvan heard her calling again for her mate.

Speaking of that, Sylvan wanted to check on his own mate. If a perfect clone or whatever it was of Olivia had been able to infiltrate the Mother Ship, who knew what else might be out there?

Taking a deep breath to try and calm his nerves, he bespoke Sophia.

*"Yes, honey?"* he heard her ask through their mental link. *"What is it?"*

Suddenly Sylvan knew he wasn't ready yet to tell her what had happened—he didn't want to worry her when she was alone with the twins.

*"I...just wanted to hear your voice,"* he sent back, trying to keep a mental guard between his chaotic thoughts and emotions and his mental link with her.

*"What's wrong? I can feel that something's going on with you."* Sophia's mental voice sounded like she was frowning.

*"I can't talk about it now—I just wanted to be certain you and the twins were safe,"* Sylvan sent.

*"Yes, we're fine."*

*"Good."* Sylvan breathed a sigh of relief. *"Then I want you to do something for me—go make certain the suite door is locked and don't let anybody in—even people you know. Even me—until I link with you again and let you know I'm right outside the door. All right?"*

*"Sylvan, what is this about? Is the Mother Ship under attack? What's wrong?"* Sophia demanded.

"No, we're not under attack—at least I don't **think** we are. This is just a precaution. I promise I'll explain as soon as I get back to the suite." He made his mental voice as soothing as he could. "Please just trust me, Talana and do as I ask—all right?"

"All right." She still sounded worried but perhaps a little calmer. "Just...be careful, Sylvan. As Head of the High Council you're vulnerable. And if anything ever happened to you—"

"It won't. I'm being careful—Baird is coming to join me now," he promised.

"All right. I love you—I'll always love you."

"I love you too, Talana."

As he broke the mental connection, the viewscreen in front of him flashed to life again.

"Commander Sylvan?" It was Commander Hrake, a Beast Kindred communications officer who reported directly to Sylvan. "Commander Sylvan, are you there? Please respond," he said, his golden eyes worried.

Sylvan gave the viewscreen access and accepted the call.

"Yes, Hrake—what is it?" he asked.

"Oh, there you are, Commander. I couldn't reach the viewscreen in your office for some reason," Hrake said. "I'm sorry to bother you but you have an urgent call coming in from a Commander Lathe. Will you take it?"

"Put it through." Sylvan nodded. He had been wondering how his fellow Blood Kindred was doing in BleakHall and sending up nightly prayers to the Goddess for his safety. If Lathe was calling him, it must mean that his mission was complete and he was coming home.

The viewscreen flickered and a harried-looking Commander Lathe appeared on the screen. He had blood on his face and there were other people crowding around behind him but he seemed well enough.

"Commander Sylvan," he said urgently, before Sylvan could say a word. "You are in grave danger. Mistress Hellenix of Yonnie Six put a contract out on your life. You have to take steps to protect yourself at once!"

"Thank you, but I believe the threat has already been neutralized," Sylvan said dryly.

Lathe ran a hand through his hair distractedly.

"You mean you were already attacked? Gods, I'm sorry, Commander! We had a hell of a time getting out of BleakHall and I thought—"

"We?" Sylvan interrupted him. "Did you find other Kindred prisoners there?"

"I found one at least. Commander Sylvan, meet Slade—he's a hybrid from—Gods...I don't even know where you're from," he said to another male who was sitting beside him in the passenger's seat.

"The Blood Circuit originally and more recently, Priux Prime. And of course, the hole at BleakHall." The male grinned at Sylvan. He was wild-looking with mismatched green and gold eyes, long brown hair and a full beard that badly needed trimming. "Pleased to make your acquaintance, Commander. Can I ask—does your Mother Ship have any Pairing Puppets on board?"

"Pairing Puppets?" Sylvan frowned at the question. Pairing Puppets were the life-like female androids that were used by unmated Kindred warriors to ease their sexual tension until they could find and align with a mate. "Well...yes we do," he said. "In the Unmated Males section."

"Perfect. Thank you." The male called Slade nodded.

"Appreciate that, Commander. I've been dreamin' of a sweet little Pairing Puppet to take the edge off for fucking months now."

"Well...you're welcome to use our facilities." Sylvan still didn't know what to make of the male. One of his best friends, Merrick, was a hybrid but this Slade seemed to be very unusual, even for his rare kind. Had he fought on the Blood Circuit and killed the wrong person? Was that how he'd ended up in Bleak-Hall? Or had he just angered the wrong mistress, like so many of the prisoners there?

"I also have two prisoners from Phobos with me," Lathe said, leaning in towards the viewscreen again. "A brother and sister—Lord Jak and Lady Arianna Blackthorn. Permission to bring them aboard the Mother Ship, Commander Sylvan?"

Sylvan's eyebrows rose almost to his hairline.

"How did a lord and lady from Phobos wind up in BleakHall Prison? Never mind." He waved a hand when Lathe started to explain. "If you trust them, I trust them. You're welcome to bring them aboard."

"Thank you." Lathe hesitated. "And...I'd like to have someone check them out in the med center. We've all been through a lot tonight—we could all use a thorough checkup."

"Report to the Med center as soon as you get here," Sylvan said. "But Commander Lathe, can you tell me anything else about the assassination attempt? There are some...troubling details I'd like to get clear."

"I'm afraid not." Lathe shook his head regretfully. "All I know is that it was planned by Mistress Hellenix of Yonnie Six. We were warned by her, uh, Kindred slave, Malik—he said that she believed if she got rid of you, most of the complaints against BleakHall would go away and she and the other Mistresses could continue making profit without anyone bothering them." He frowned. "In Malik's opinion, she was probably right."

"I see." Sylvan nodded. "All right. Well, send your coordinates and I'll have them fold space for you at once. We'll see you aboard the Mother Ship very shortly."

"Thank you, Commander Sylvan."

Just as Lathe signed off, Baird walked into the reception area of Sylvan's office.

"I heard that—who are we folding space for?"

"Commander Lathe—the Blood Kindred officer I sent to BleakHall—remember?"

"Oh, right—the Kill-all/Cure-all Blood Kindred." Baird nodded. "So he made it out all right?"

"He and several others, apparently. Including one of the largest hybrids I've ever seen who apparently has an itch to scratch. He already asked me if we have Pairing Puppets aboard," Sylvan said dryly.

Baird's black eyebrows rose and he snorted out laughter.

"Really? I guess if I'd been locked up in prison for the Goddess knows how long, I'd be in need of a little female companionship too."

"It seems he is—although from what I could see of him, he's in need of medical attention first. In fact, all of them look like they've been in a fight for their lives." Sylvan frowned. "I hate to ask, but could you bespeak Olivia and ask her to go to the med center after all? I need someone I can trust there to evaluate them when they come in and I'd like to get her opinion."

"Sure." Baird shrugged. "She can leave Daniel with Sophia and your twins."

"Oh, that reminds me." Closing his eyes, Sylvan bespoke his

own mate again, reassuring her that everything was all right and letting her know that she'd be watching their nephew for a little while.

*"Well you're certainly sounding calmer,"* she sent back. *"Is the danger over?"*

*"I think so."* Now that he knew the threat Mistress Hellenix had sent against him was neutralized and understood where it had come from and why, Sylvan felt a good deal more confident that things were all right. *"You should still be cautious,"* he warned his mate. *"And I'm sorry to ask you to watch Daniel as well as the twins by yourself."*

*"Oh, don't worry about it—Kara and Kaleb will love it. I can just hear them now—'cousin slumber party!' It's going to be a blast,"* she sent dryly. *"I'll go ahead and pop some popcorn right now."*

*"I love you—thank you for understanding,"* Sylvan sent with real gratitude. Even after years of marriage, he still felt like the luckiest male in the world to have gotten Sophia as his wife.

*"I love you too. Just be careful and come back to the suite as soon as you can. Oh—there's Liv at the door now. See you later, honey."*

Sylvan sent a burst of love and affection—the mental equivalent of blowing a kiss—and then closed the mental link and looked at his brother.

"Well?" Baird stared at him, frowning. "You wanna tell me what this is all about? Why did you need me to come up here? And why are you out here instead of inside your office?" He frowned. "And what's that pink sticky stuff on your clothes?"

"I'll show you," Sylvan said grimly. Come inside my office— but watch where you step. I'm afraid it's rather messy."

# FORTY-FIVE

The vastness of the Mother Ship was a little overwhelming for Ari who was used to her own quiet manner house on Phobos or at most, a Ton-kwa meet at one of the larger market towns. But even the largest market town on Phobos would have fit easily inside the confines of the Docking Bay where Lathe landed the Kindred shuttle they were flying in.

There was a nice blond-haired woman to meet them, however. She introduced herself as Liv and shook her head when she saw them.

"My goodness! Well, I can see why Sylvan wanted me to come check you all out," she said, looking them over. "Welcome home, Doctor," she added respectfully, nodding at Lathe. "If you don't mind my saying so, you look like you've had a rough night."

"I've had about six months of rough nights," Lathe's deep voice sounded tired to Ari—so weary that she wished she could put her arms around him and comfort him. But now that they were in the big, clean, modern ship where he belonged and she so clearly didn't, she didn't dare to touch him. Besides, she was still using both hands to keep her jumpsuit, which Mukluk had ripped open, closed.

Liv hustled them all off to the med center—which was apparently the Kindred version of a healing house—where healers and nurses of all kinds were bustling around.

Slade and Jak were taken to separate exam rooms, with Slade protesting all the way that he was just fine and all he needed was a quick shower and the directions to the Pairing Puppets—whatever *those* were. Which left Ari and Lathe standing beside Liv, who was deciding where to put them.

"I can look after myself, Nurse Olivia," Lathe told her. "But I'd like you to take special care of Lady Arianna for me. She has been through some very traumatic situations in the past several days."

"Understood, Doctor." Liv nodded. "I'll do the initial exam but do you want me to bring her to you when you're finished cleaning up so you can do a more thorough checkup yourself?"

For a moment Lathe and Ari locked eyes and she saw an unreadable emotion in those turquoise depths. Could it be regret? Sorrow? Or simply weary indifference after the night they had all endured? And why was he using her formal title now instead of just calling her 'Ari'?

"No," he said at last. "No that...shouldn't be necessary. When you're certain Lady Arianna is healthy and well, she and her brother can return to their home planet of Phobos. It won't be necessary for me to see her again."

"What—*ever?*" Ari burst out, unable to stop herself. "After everything we've been though at BleakHall together you're just going to walk away and *leave?*"

Lathe looked taken aback. But almost at once the surprise on his face smoothed away and a look of impersonal professionalism replaced it.

"BleakHall was another world. I think we're both aware of that. It's time to leave it behind and get back to our separate lives." He nodded at her formally. "I wish you a very happy and healthy future, Lady Blackthorn. May the Goddess bless you."

Then he turned away from her and left without a single backwards glance.

Ari stood staring after the big Kindred, her mind a mass of seething, conflicted emotions. Anger—how dare the big asshole tell her to have a nice life and just leave her standing here in the hallway? Disbelief—Lathe had fought for her—had gone into Rage for her—had *killed* for her. Could he really have lost any and all emotion for her so quickly?

But what Ari felt most of all was despair.

*Never,* whispered a desolate little voice in her heart, *I'll never see him again. He doesn't want me anymore and there's nothing I can do to change that.*

"Oh, honey..." The nice nurse, Liv, shook her head and put an arm around Ari's shoulders. "That was...rough."

"He left." Ari's voice sounded thick and disbelieving in her own ears. "I can't believe he just *left.*"

"I'm betting there's a story behind all this." Liv squeezed her shoulders comfortingly. "Come on—why don't you tell me all about it while I get you checked out?"

Numbly, Ari allowed herself to be led away. At the far end of the med center she could still see Lathe's broad back, clad in the

BleakHall trustee jumpsuit of striped blue and green. He was standing there talking to what she assumed must be another doctor but he didn't even seem to notice Ari looking at him. After a moment, he finished his conversation, turned the corner and was gone.

As she caught her last glimpse of him, Ari's vision doubled... then trebled and she realized she was crying.

Liv seemed to notice it at the same time because she steered Ari into a small room and helped her sit on an exam table covered in a soft, blue drape.

"It's all right now, honey," she told Ari in a low voice. "We're in private now—just let it out."

The way the nice nurse was helping her hide her grief reminded Ari of Lathe holding her in the Rec Yard, shielding her from the eyes of the other inmates as she sobbed her heart out. His strong arms around her...the warm fragrance of his skin...the low soothing words he'd used to comfort her...

*And now he's gone,* she thought desolately. *Gone and I'll never see him again. Ever.*

It was all too much. Ari collapsed on the table, sobbing as if her heart would break—as if it was already broken and there was no mending it ever again.

---

Lathe's heart was sore and proud as he made himself walk away from her. He told himself he was giving Ari what she wanted— her life back. Now she could go back to Phobos with her brother and never think of him again.

As he intended to never think about her.

*Liar,* whispered a little voice in his head. *Even now you can't get her out of your mind.*

He tried but he couldn't seem to put Ari's stricken face out of his mind. Still, he was sure he would forget her in time. And despite her words, Ari was probably already on her way to forgetting him.

After all, she had never really loved him the way he had foolishly allowed himself to love her.

*I was a means to an end,* Lathe told himself. *Protection from Tapper and the other violent inmates...a way to rescue her brother... a way to get out of BleakHall. That was all I ever was to her.*

Of course some of that might be slightly unfair—after all, Ari hadn't known that he had a way out of the prison until he told her. So she couldn't have been using him as a means of escape.

*Well she used me enough,* Lathe argued with himself angrily. *She got me to fall in love with her and let me believe she was something she wasn't. Just like Talsa did! And besides she doesn't love me—she never did.*

Feeling justified, he left the med center for his own suite. He had much to tell Commander Sylvan and plenty of incriminating vid-feed stored in his prison ID tag but that could all wait. It had been a hell of a long time since he'd had a decent night's sleep and he intended to get one now...and then get back to his normal life as soon as possible.

A life that didn't include Ari.

# FORTY-SIX

"It's all right, honey—just let it out. It's okay." Liv stood by the sobbing girl and rubbed her trembling back and shaking shoulders, feeling helpless. Poor little thing—Liv really didn't know her but she seemed completely heartbroken.

Was this all about Doctor Lathe? He had always impressed Liv as withdrawn and somewhat aloof but extremely competent. Thanks to his unique gift as a Cure-All, he had a one hundred percent success rate with his patients. But he didn't lean on his natural abilities too heavily—he was also one of the most knowledgeable physicians Liv knew. In fact, aside from Sylvan and Yipper, the little Tolleg surgeon who lived aboard the Mother Ship, she couldn't name another doctor she trusted more.

He also would have been the guy she would think was least likely to have a tortured romance. But if the girl sobbing her heart out on the exam table was any indication, he had certainly gone out of his way to break character.

"Do you want to talk about it?" she asked Ari when the girl finally seemed to have sobbed herself out.

"N-no. Not...not right now, anyway." Ari looked up at her with wet, wounded eyes. "It's still too...too fresh. But is there any way..." She hesitated for a moment.

"What is it, hon?" Liv urged her. "Go on—ask for anything you need and I'll do my best to get it for you."

"I just...I'd really like a shower," Ari said in a small voice. "I just went through a long dirty tunnel to get out of a prison where I was afraid to do more than wash in the sink." She looked at her fingernails which *did* appear to be full of dirt. "I feel so *grimy*."

"Of course you can have a shower," Liv told her. "You're in luck—I believe this is one of the exam rooms with a full bathroom in it. Come on."

She helped Ari off the table and led her to the small bathroom with its sink, toilet, and shower stall. After showing her how to work the Kindred appliances, and making sure she was steady on her feet, Liv left, leaving the door cracked open behind her just in case Ari needed anything else.

As she came out of the bathroom, there was a knock on the door and a familiar voice said, "*Lilenta?* You in there?"

"Right here." Liv drew the privacy curtain, blocking the bathroom from view and went to the door. "Is everything okay?" she asked when she opened it and saw her husband's wide, golden eyes.

"Fine. It's just...Sylvan wanted to see you."

Baird stepped back, revealing Sylvan, who was waiting behind him with a troubled look on his face.

"Oh, hi, Sylvan," Liv said. "If you're wondering about the patients from Dr. Lathe's ship, I put the two males in exam rooms six and seven for Dr. Brike to examine and I have the girl, Lady Arianna, here with me. I just..."

But her words trailed off when Sylvan came up to her and took her by the shoulders. He leaned down, peering into Liv's eyes, seeming almost to examine her for some reason. Then he shocked her completely by giving her a crushing hug.

"Sylvan?" she gasped, barely able to breathe in the big Blood Kindred's embrace. Sylvan was a wonderful brother-in-law and an excellent doctor but he wasn't usually this demonstrative. Also, there was a kind of unwritten rule that mated Kindred didn't touch women other than their wives. If they did, the woman's husband was likely to get very upset. But Baird just stood there watching with solemn eyes as Sylvan embraced her.

At last he released her and Liv could breathe again.

"What was *that* for?" she asked, looking up at him, wide-eyed.

"I'm just...so glad that you're all right, kin-of-my-mate." Sylvan's pale blue eyes were suspiciously bright and his deep voice was slightly choked.

"I don't understand." Liv shook her head. "What in the world is going on?" She looked first at Sylvan and then at Baird. "What's wrong?" she demanded.

"Tell you later, *Lilenta* when we know more about it," her husband rumbled. "For now—"

But then the three of them heard a gasp and a clatter followed by an audible *thump* from the bathroom.

# FORTY-SEVEN

Ari swam back to consciousness to see three pairs of worried-looking eyes bending over her. One pair was silvery-gray—those belonged to the nice nurse called Liv, she was sure. The second pair of eyes was pale, wintry blue. And the third pair was pure gold and looked almost animalistic.

She blinked up at them, realizing as she did so that she was wet and naked except for a large towel someone had wrapped around her. She was also back on the exam table, she saw as she looked around.

"She's coming around," Liv said to the man—*no, Kindred—he has to be Kindred,* Ari thought—with the pale blue eyes. "Maybe she just fainted from exhaustion."

"Or hunger," said the Kindred with pale blue eyes. Wasn't he the one Lathe had called on the viewscreen during their ride to the Mother Ship? Ari tried to place him. Commander Sliver? Commander Sylpan? What had Lathe called him?

"Uh, I hate to contradict you two since you're in the medical field and I'm not," the other Kindred—the one with the bright gold eyes—rumbled. "But what about *that*? Do you think it could have anything to do with why she fell out?"

He was pointing at her, Ari saw. Pointing at the side of her neck, right under her ear. As soon as she realized that, she felt a dull throb of pain coming from that area.

*That's where it hurts,* she thought groggily. *I touched it in the shower and it hurt so much everything went black. What is it?*

"Oh my God, what *is* that?" Liv echoed her thoughts, a worried look on her pretty face. "I didn't notice it before because of her hair but now I can't *unsee* it."

"It looks infected." Commander Sylvan—that was his name, Ari remembered suddenly—sounded grim. "I'll have to clean it out and then we'll need a biopsy."

He started to reach for Ari but she jerked away from his hand instinctively.

"No," she begged faintly. "No, please. It hurts...hurts so much. Please, don't...don't touch."

"Olivia, please get me a sedative," Commander Sylvan said. "And a numbing agent as well."

"Right away." Liv bustled away and was back in a moment. "All right," she said to Ari. "This is only going to sting for a minute and then you won't feel anything at all."

Something sharp pricked Ari's arm before she could protest and then she found herself floating off again.

---

She had strange dreams while she was under—a number of

people came into the exam room. Commander Sylvan worked on the side of her neck with a sharp looking instrument. Liv the nice nurse held a little blue basin for him and when he was done, the basin was filled with some kind of blackish, oozing liquid that, even in her half-conscious state, Ari thought looked disgusting.

As they worked, they talked.

"...some kind of poison."

"...never seen corruption this advanced on a patient who was still mobile. No wonder she fainted."

"...eaten through several layers of tissue. I'm afraid it's quite close to some very important blood vessels."

Ari didn't think they knew she could hear them or they wouldn't have spoken so freely. The things they were saying probably would have frightened her if she could have felt frightened. But just at the moment, she seemed to be floating on a cloud, utterly weightless and she couldn't make herself feel any emotions at all—not even about Lathe when she thought of him.

All right, that wasn't exactly true—she did still feel a dim sense of sadness and loss when she thought of the big Kindred and she had a vague idea that these cloudy emotions would solidify into something truly awful if she wasn't floating.

But that was something she would have to deal with in the future, when whatever it was they had given her had finally worn off. For now she could only lay inert on the exam table and let herself be worked on.

"All right," she heard someone say after what seemed like a long time...and no time at all. "I think she's stable. It should be safe to let her sleep."

There was a faint pressure in her arm and everything slowly faded to black.

When she woke up again, there was another strange person staring at her. He had long floppy ears and big, soulful brown eyes. He looked like some kind of animal to Ari but there was definite humanoid intelligence in his gaze. He was looking under the bulky pad of white bandages someone had placed on the side of her neck and shaking his head doubtfully.

"This is very bad. Yes it is, yes it is!" he told Liv in a high, piping voice.

"I know, Yipper." Liv looked worried. "Is there anything you can do? Sylvan says he's out of options."

"I will have to think. Yes I will, yes I will." The little *man? person?* looked upset. "What kind of poison was it?"

"We don't know. But look...her eyelids are fluttering. Lady Arianna?" Liv called, putting a hand on Ari's arm. "Honey, can you hear me?"

"Just...Ari," Ari croaked through dry lips. "So...thirsty."

"Oh, of course. Here—do you want to sit up? I have some water."

"Yes... please," Ari whispered.

Liv raised up the bed she was in, getting her into a sitting position and then helped her sip some water. Ari felt about a hundred percent better afterwards although the side of her neck was still strangely numb.

"What happened to me?" she asked Liv, feeling much more able to talk now that her mouth wasn't so dry. "All I remember is feeling an awful pain in my neck and falling down in the shower."

"Yes, you gave us quite a scare. I never should have left you alone." Liv looked remorseful. "I should have seen that you had something wrong with your neck too."

"I do?" Ari put a hand to the side of her neck instinctively. "I mean, I knew it hurt and it was bleeding when I was in the hole—it almost got me eaten by Lashers. If I hadn't let the Beast out of his cell—"

"Whoa—hold on." Liv put up a hand to stop her. "I want to hear the whole story—it sounds fascinating. But first I need to know how you hurt your neck in the first place. Did you cut yourself on a piece of rusty metal or—"

"Rusty metal? No...no, it wasn't rusty." Ari swallowed hard, remembering the bright silver glitter of Tapper's blade as he held it under her ear. What the hell had been on that knife?

"*I got it from a poisoner,*" she remembered him saying. "*It's deadly, it is.*"

At the time Ari had thought nothing of his words—she'd been too busy trying to stay alive. But now they came back to her with sick clarity. Was Tapper going to reach out from beyond the grave and kill her after all?

"I...I got poked with a knife," she whispered, looking down at her hands. "By a man who wanted to rape me. But Lathe...he stopped him."

"Oh, honey..." Liv squeezed her hand consolingly. "I'm so sorry. But...do you know if there was something on the blade? Or maybe you got something—some germ from the prison—in the cut afterward?"

"I don't know." Ari shook her head. "He said...the man who was trying to...to..." She took a deep breath, trying not to feel Tapper's hot, rancid breath on her cheek again...trying not to hear his screams as Lathe fed him feet-first into the meat grinder. "He said he got the knife from a poisoner on...I think he said on Chathm Prime. He said..." She grimaced. "He said it was deadly."

"Oh dear. Oh dear, oh dear, oh dear. This is bad news. Yes it is, yes it is." The little person whom Liv had called, "Yipper" was shaking his head again, his long ears flopping. "The Chathm system is known for its deadly poisons," he said, sounding both worried and sorrowful. "Now I am quite certain—there will have to be considerable excision and restructuring."

"What?" Ari demanded. "What does that even mean?"

"Lady Arianna...Ari..." Liv squeezed her hand harder. "I'm afraid you had a malignant cyst on your neck. By the time Doctor Sylvan got to it, it was...well, it was pretty big."

"How big?" Ari felt a sick kind of curiosity. It was almost like they were talking about someone else entirely—someone who had nothing to do with her.

"About like this." Liv held up a closed fist. "It was black, too. That's why I didn't see it right away—it blended right in with your hair."

"Black?" Ari had a vague memory of the Kindred Doctor working on her neck and Liv holding a little blue pan filled with goopy, vile-looking black liquid.

"It's all cleaned out now," Liv hastened to assure her. "But I'm afraid the effects of whatever poison you were given have spread. And if we don't do something very soon, they're going to spread even more."

"I can excise from here..." Yipper poked a spot just above the top of Ari's ear and then drew an imaginary line down to just above her collar bone. "To here. And apply a prosthetic. Yes I can, yes I can. I will try to make it as natural looking as I can—especially the ear."

"But what about the blood vessels?" Liv asked anxiously. "Sylvan said her jugular and carotid are both affected."

"I can build her new ones. Yes I can, yes I can." Yipper nodded his head, his long ears flopping. "It won't be easy but—"

"All new blood vessels, a fake ear, *and* you want to make the whole side of my neck a prosthesis?" Ari interrupted, feeling panicked. "Are you sure that's my only option? Has anybody asked Lathe what he thinks? He's a really good doctor too, right?"

"Well...no, nobody has asked him," Liv said carefully. "But I think Doctor Sylvan believed the corruption from the poison is too far advanced—"

"It might not be though. It might not, it might not!" Yipper exclaimed excitedly. "I don't know why I didn't remember the Cure-All. Maybe because he has been gone for so long from the Mother Ship. But one bite from him—"

"No, wait—I changed my mind," Ari said hastily. She well-remembered the cold expression in Lathe's eyes the last time he had looked at her, as well as the way his bite made her feel. She couldn't bear to have pleasure from him that way knowing that he felt nothing for her. It would kill something inside her—something that was already almost dead.

"Why not, honey?" Liv asked. "If Yipper thinks there's a chance—"

"I don't want him to think I'm just using him, all right?" Ari burst out. "That's what he already thinks—that I was only with him in BleakHall because he could protect me. But I didn't mean to do that—I wasn't faking how I felt. I was just so afraid almost every single minute..."

She tried to swallow past the lump in her throat and felt tears stinging her eyes as she struggled to continue.

"So many awful things almost happened to me and Lathe kept talking about how he hated liars and I was afraid if I told him what I really was he would hate me too and throw me out of his cell. And then he found out when Tapper tried to...to rape me and he was so *angry*..."

She choked up, unable to help it. The events of the past week seemed like a nightmare to her now—a nightmare that was still somehow going on even though she had finally gotten to safety.

Liv rubbed her arm comfortingly.

"Listen, Yipper, I think you'd better go so Ari and I can talk," she said to the little surgeon. "I'll let you know what she decides soon."

"Very well but don't wait too long, please." Yipper's big brown eyes were worried. "The corruption is halted for now, yes it is, yes it is. But there is only so much we can do to stop it and it will continue to grow if the area is not healed or excised."

"I understand." Liv nodded. "But right now I think Ari needs to talk her way through this before she can make a decision."

"I will go and speak to Doctor Lathe in the meantime so he can be ready, yes I will, yes I will," Yipper declared.

"No!" Ari sat up in bed and grabbed for his hairy little arm. "No," she said again urgently. "I want your word that you won't tell him *anything*."

Yipper looked confused.

"But if he can help you..."

"No!" Ari exclaimed again. "He never wants to see me again and I refuse to be dependent on his charity."

The little surgeon shook his head in a baffled way.

"Do you know, sometimes I think I understand human emotions and then I find that I was wrong and I do not understand them at all. No I don't, no I don't," he said mournfully. "Sometimes I think it was easier to work with the Dark Kindred. They were...simpler."

"Just let Ari and I talk for a while and then we'll make a decision," Liv said gently. "I know you just want to help, Yipper, but it has to be Ari's choice what treatment she gets."

"Very well, very well." The little surgeon left, still looking upset and Liv turned to Ari.

"All right, hon, as my best friend Kat would say—spill. Go ahead and get it all off your chest so we can work through this thing together."

Ari started slowly...talking about how Jak had been taken by slavers, then sold to Yonnie Six, then sent to BleakHall. Then she explained the solid-holo device and the transport bubble she had hidden in her prison ID tag.

"Wow—it's ugly but useful," Liv remarked, staring at the tag in surprise as Ari activated the bubble for a moment. She couldn't show Liv the solid-holo because her power source was depleted but Liv made her promise to let her see as soon as she got it powered up again.

"And Yipper can remove that for you as well," she added. "It looks surgically implanted but I'm sure now that you're out of BleakHall you don't want to keep it as a souvenir, right?"

"I *would* like to have it taken out," Ari said and sighed. "He might as well do it when he's replacing the entire side of my neck and head."

"You know, before you go that route we really should at least let Doctor Lathe *try* healing you," Liv said softly. "He really does have an amazing success rate."

"No," Ari said stubbornly. "You heard him—he never wants to

see me again." Tears threatened and she had to sniff them back. "I just can't believe he'd act like that. After everything we went through..."

"Tell me more," Liv urged gently. "Tell me the whole story. I think you need to get it off your chest."

Ari went on, telling Liv how Lathe had taken her under his wing from the first. And how quickly feelings had grown between the two of them.

"He even told me he was falling in love with me," she confided to Liv. "And he couldn't...couldn't understand why because he thought I was male." She hung her head. "I should have told him then what I was—I should have shared my secret with him. But he had been going on and on about how he hated liars and people who misrepresented themselves. Apparently there was some girl who wanted a job on the Mother Ship and she tried to use him to get it but she was already engaged?"

She looked at Liv, hopeful that she might have more information but the nurse only shrugged.

"I'm sorry, hon—I don't know about that. Doctor Lathe hasn't been aboard the Mother Ship that long and he's always been an intensely private person. If some girl kicked him to the curb, he probably never said a word about it to anyone. That's the kind of guy he is—he keeps it all inside."

"Well, he let it all out with me," Ari said softly. "It seemed like he did, anyway. He was so warm and protective and gentle with me...right up until he didn't want me anymore," she ended in a whisper.

Liv frowned. "I think this sounds like a bad case of wounded pride. He doesn't like it that you fooled him so thoroughly and

made him think he was in love with another guy when he probably sees himself as straight as a board."

"He's definitely not a lover of other men," Ari said. "But for a
while I made him question that and I think…" She sighed. "I think
he just can't forgive me for it. I tried and tried to apologize but he
just wouldn't accept my apology. I think he thinks I was just using
him for protection but honestly, it was so much *more* than that."

"So how do you really feel about him?" Liv asked. "I can see
how upset this is making you—are you just bothered because you
don't want Lathe to think badly of you?"

"No, I'm upset because I *love* him!" Ari clapped a hand over
her mouth. Oh Goddess, had she really just said that out loud?

*You said it all right—and you meant it too,* whispered a little
voice in her head. *You're madly in love with him and you have
been for a while—probably from the minute when he held you and
let you cry out on the Rec Yard.*

"I love him," she said again, testing the words and hearing the
ring of truth in them. "I *do*."

"Just now figuring that, are you?" Liv asked dryly, a little
smile playing around one corner of her mouth.

"You know…I thought about it some at BleakHall but it was so
scary and violent there I felt like I barely had room to breathe.
Out here in the free world I can see…" Ari cleared her throat. "I
guess I can really see what I lost."

"I wouldn't say he's lost for good," Liv said. "Maybe just really
thoroughly pissed off you made him question his entire sexuality.
That tends to be pretty hard on the male ego, no matter how
progressive a guy is."

"No…" Ari shook her head mournfully. "No, he's gone, Liv.
He'll never want anything to do with me again and I guess…I

guess I don't blame him. It's my fault he left...and my fault he's never coming back." Her voice sounded choked and wrong in her own ears and her eyes stung as she spoke.

"Honey, don't blame yourself that way." Liv put an arm around her and squeezed her shoulders. "You were incredibly brave to go into that hell hole all by yourself like that. Of *course* you were afraid to tell your secret. Listen..." She looked Ari in the eyes. "I've never been to prison, thank God, but I *know* what it's like to feel helpless and vulnerable in an all-male environment. I was kidnapped by the Scourge back when the All-Father was still in power and if my husband Baird hadn't traded himself for me..."

She shook her head and Ari saw that her eyes were bright.

"Sorry." Liv sniffed. "It was a long time ago but I still have nightmares about it occasionally—standing there naked with the All-Father and his minions all around and feeling completely alone...totally isolated."

"That's it—that's *exactly* how I felt." Ari nodded. "But I never meant to fool Lathe in the first place. *He* came up to *me*. He told me..." Her throat felt thick. "Told me he couldn't ignore my cries for help. And he said my scent drew him to me."

"Yeah, that sounds like a Kindred." Liv nodded knowingly. "Sometimes I think they find their mates through their noses way more than their eyes."

"His scent was pretty amazing too," Ari admitted. "His bonding scent, I mean."

Liv's eyebrows went up.

"His body released his bonding scent for you?"

"Uh-huh." Ari nodded. "Is that unusual? Or do Kindred do it for every woman they're interested in?"

"Listen, hon—the bonding scent is the big guns. It doesn't

come out until *'the one'* shows up—the woman the Kindred wants to mate with for life," Liv said, frowning. "I forgot to ask you, but did you ever dream of Doctor Lathe? You know—before you met him?"

Ari nodded. "I dreamed of his eyes. They're so vivid you know—such a gorgeous turquoise." She sighed.

"And did he dream of you?" Liv asked, still frowning.

"He said he did," Ari admitted.

"So you were Dream-sharing *and* he was making his bonding scent for you and he *still* walked away?" Liv shook her head in evident amazement. "He must *really* be mad at you."

"That's exactly what I've been saying," Ari pointed out. "He's angry with me. So angry he can't forgive me."

"It's a lot to consider." Liv took a deep breath and pressed her hand gently. "Thank you for telling me all this, Ari. It sounds like you've been through some really awful traumatic experiences and I know it couldn't have been easy to talk about."

"Thank you for listening to me." Ari took a deep breath. "It really helped to talk. I think I've made my decision—I'm going to let that little Yipper guy do what he said and give me a whole new neck. Does he do good work?" She looked at Liv anxiously.

"Oh yes—he's the best," Liv assured her. "But tell you what, why don't we get you a nice warm bath to relax you and then a good supper and you can sleep on it tonight and make the final decision in the morning."

"Do I have that long?" Ari asked anxiously. "I thought this poison stuff—this corruption—was spreading."

"We've been able to slow it down a lot," Liv promised her. "You can have a night to think about it—this is a really big thing to decide. You need time to make up your mind."

"My mind is already made up." Ari raised her chin stubbornly. "Lathe hates me now—and if he doesn't want anything to do with me, then I don't want anything to do with him."

"That would be great if you weren't still crazy in love with him," Liv said softly. "Am I right?"

Ari hung her head. "It doesn't matter if I love him," she said in a small voice. "He doesn't love me back."

"Well...let's just get you a bath and some supper and a good night's sleep," Liv said soothingly. "Things might look different in the morning."

Ari didn't see how they would. She was determined not to bother Lathe or even let him know she was sick in any way. As far as she was concerned, they were out of each other's lives forever.

No matter how much it hurt to know she would never see him again.

# FORTY-EIGHT

Lathe was in a debriefing meeting about his time in BleakHall with Commander Sylvan when Nurse Olivia knocked twice and then stepped into Sylvan's office.

For some reason the head of the High Council looked suddenly anxious and his eyes widened slightly. He sat up straighter in his chair, his body tensing.

"Olivia? Is that you?" he asked in a low, hoarse voice.

"Of course it's me." Olivia—who was the sister of Sylvan's mate—frowned. "I'm sorry to interrupt but can I please speak to Doctor Lathe?"

"Well, we were about to wrap things up, I believe." Sylvan rose and nodded graciously. "Do you need privacy for what you have to say? Would you like to use my office?"

"I think that would be a very good idea. Thank you." Olivia spoke to Commander Sylvan but she was looking at Lathe and her eyes were flashing. He thought uneasily that she looked angry for some reason which was totally out of character for her. She had always been an excellent nurse to work with—very cool and calm under pressure and extremely professional and knowledgeable.

"Thank you for your time, Commander Lathe. I'll let you know if we need you to testify before the Yonnite Sacred Seven but I believe the vid evidence you brought back should be more than sufficient," Sylvan said. Then, nodding and giving Olivia one last unreadable look, he left them alone in his office.

Olivia didn't waste any time. She marched right up to Lathe and slapped him hard across the face.

"Ow!" Lathe took a step back, his eyes widening in surprise. "What was that for?"

"You," Olivia said succinctly, "Are being a jerk."

"What?" Lathe was still stunned by her behavior. She had never been anything but consummately professional before. He just couldn't believe she had struck him. "Nurse Olivia," he began but Liv shook her head.

"Oh, no—I'm not here to talk to you Nurse-to-Doctor. I'm here to talk to you as a woman talking to a man. Do you have any idea how brave Ari had to be to do what she did? To walk willingly into that horrible place filled with murderers and rapists knowing she could be killed or raped herself at any minute if anyone found out what she was—that she was really a girl? Do you have *any idea?*"

"Of course I do!" Lathe protested. "BleakHall is a horrible place for *everyone*. I should know—I spent six months there."

"But maybe a little *less* horrible for someone who knew they could defend themselves?" Olivia put a hand on her hip. "Think about it, Lathe—when was the last time you felt truly vulnerable?

You're a seven-foot-tall Kindred warrior with deadly, poisonous fangs. You can take on just about anyone who comes for you. But how would you feel if you were Ari's size? She's *tiny*—five-foot four at most. And she put herself in terrible danger to save her brother, even knowing anyone and everyone she met in BleakHall could and *would* want to hurt her."

Lathe frowned uncomfortably. "Yes, I understand that."

"Maybe you understand here." Olivia reached up and poked him in the forehead with one stiff finger. "But I don't think you get it *here*." She poked him in the abdomen which made Lathe wince. "You don't understand that gut feeling of fear because you don't *have* to," she continued. "Of *course* Ari was afraid to tell you her secret—she thought you'd be angry with her and kick her out of your cell to be raped and murdered. Or maybe that you'd hurt her yourself when you found out she was a girl."

"I would never have done that! *Never*." Lathe growled. His surprise at Olivia's behavior was beginning to wear off, leaving anger and defensiveness in its place. "I never laid a hand on her," he protested.

"Think about it though, Lathe," Olivia said, glaring up at him. "Ari saw you kill multiple men while you were there. One of them she said you put through a freaking *meat grinder*. I can only imagine how horrible *that* must have been to watch."

"I was in Rage," Lathe muttered. Feeling put on the defensive, he added, "The male was trying to hurt Ari. Trying to rape her. Just the thought of him doing that..." He couldn't finish—his jaw clenched and he shook his head. "He died too slowly," he said, his voice deep and furious, even in his own ears. "After what he tried to do, he deserved his fate and more."

"All right, I know you were killing in self-defense and in Ari's

defense," Olivia said patiently. "But the point is, you're a moun-
tain of muscle *and* she saw you commit multiple violent killings.
Of *course* she was frightened of you—too frightened to tell you
the truth."

"I...said things to her. Did things when I thought she was
male that I never would have...never could have..."

"I understand that must have been hard on your ego," Olivia
said, frowning. "It would be hard on any straight male. But the
fact is, Ari didn't *intentionally* make you think you were into guys.
That was the conclusion you drew yourself when you found yourself attracted to her. And then you freaked out because you
thought for about two seconds you were gay."

"I have no problem with two males being together," Lathe
protested.

"Right." Olivia put a hand on her hip. "As long as one of them
isn't *you*."

"Why are you here?" Lathe demanded, angrily. He had an
uncomfortable feeling that everything she was saying was true
and it didn't exactly put him in the best light. "Did Ari send you?"

"Oh no—she doesn't even know I'm here," Olivia told him.
"She thinks you hate her now—that you want nothing to do with
her—so she's determined not to bother you. So determined that
she's decided to undergo a massive head and neck reconstruction
surgery rather than ask you for your healing bite."

"What?" This was more shocking to Lathe than even her slap
had been. "What are you talking about?" he asked urgently.
Seizing Olivia by the shoulders, he peered into her face. "Did
something happen to her? Is she injured? Where is she?"

To her credit, Olivia didn't keep him in suspense or try to
draw out the tension to punish him.

"She's in the med center and she's in stable condition," she said quietly. "She was apparently cut by a knife owned by the same guy you put through the meat grinder. Topper, was it?"

"Tapper," Lathe said absently. "Gods, I *knew* I smelled fresh blood on her! Why didn't she tell me she was hurt?"

"She didn't know how bad it was herself, I don't think," Olivia said. "But Lathe...the knife was poisoned."

*"What?"* The news got worse and worse! "What are you talking about? I thought you said she was in stable condition," he demanded.

"She is," Olivia assured him. "For now. But the corruption from the poison is going to keep on growing if it isn't excised or healed. Those are Yipper's words—not mine," she added.

Lathe nodded. He trusted the little Tolleg surgeon's opinion implicitly.

"And does he think that my bite could heal her?" he asked.

"He thinks it's worth a try but Ari isn't having it," Olivia said bluntly. "As I said, she thinks you hate her."

"Gods..." Lathe raked a hand through his hair. "Nothing could be further from the truth. But she made me believe—"

"I know," Olivia interrupted. "She made you believe you were gay."

"No, damnit—I wasn't going to say that!" Lathe blew out a breath in frustration. "I was *going* to say, she made me believe that she *loved* me the way...the way I love her." He could scarcely get the words out and he couldn't meet Olivia's eyes when he said them. "When I know that she doesn't," he added in a low voice.

"I think you'll find you're wrong about that if you'll just talk to Ari." Olivia's voice was suddenly and unexpectedly gentle after the scolding she had given him.

"I'm sorry but...I just don't believe that to be true." Lathe took a deep breath. "But of course I'll heal her if I can. Even if she doesn't care for me, I would never knowingly let anything bad happen to her if I could stop it."

"You two met under really bad circumstances," Olivia said softly. "But I believe the Goddess put you together. Why else would you have been Dream-sharing? Why else would your body make your bonding scent for Ari?"

"I don't know." Lathe shook his head. "It doesn't make sense. Nothing in my life has made sense since my brother died. I just wanted to avenge him and instead I met Ari and we got...entangled."

"Just go talk to her tomorrow," Olivia urged. "Get her to let you heal her—or at least try." She smiled. "If what my sister, Sophia, tells me about a Blood Kindred's bite is true, that should go a long way towards bringing you back together."

Lathe felt the blood rush to his face, thinking of the way Ari had reacted to his bite in the past. He cleared his throat.

"As I said, I don't believe she feels for me as...as I feel for her. But I will try to get her to let me heal her. If I can."

"That's all I ask," Olivia said calmly. She bit her lip. "I'm sorry I slapped you. I just thought you were pushing her away because of your wounded pride."

"That was part of it," Lathe admitted. "But I would bond her to me in a heartbeat, pride or no pride, if I thought she really wanted me to. If I thought she felt as I do."

Olivia smiled at him and headed for the office door.

"I think you might be surprised. Just keep an open mind and come visit her tomorrow morning around eleven. I'll be sure she's ready for you."

"Thank you, I'll be there," Lathe said gravely as he saw her out the door. He didn't for a moment think that Olivia was right in her assessment of the situation. But he was grateful to her for informing him of Ari's condition.

He just hoped she would let him try to heal her.

# FORTY-NINE

"Oh Liv, is that you again?" Ari called from the bathroom as she heard the door to her exam room open. The privacy curtain was up so she couldn't see her friend. "Thank you so much for the new clothes you brought over. I feel *so* much better dressed than wearing that awful gown. You were right—nobody can feel normal in a hospital johnny."

She looked at herself in the viewer, twirling slightly from side to side to see the pretty red dress swirl around her thighs. It was a bit big on Ari but that was fine. The lacy white underwear Liv had sent with the dress fit fine but the stranger upper garment— Liv had called it a bra—didn't work at all. Which was just as well since the slightly too-large top of the dress had a tendency to slide off her shoulder on one side, which would have shown the lacy straps.

Ari was content to go without it, though the thin red fabric *was* a bit clingy around her breasts and nipples. It felt good just to be wearing something pretty again. The new outfit was the most feminine thing she'd put on in ages—a vast improvement over the awful blue and orange striped prison jumpsuit. In fact, the dress was so pretty she could almost ignore the layer of white bandages that covered the side of her neck.

Almost.

She still had her prison ID implanted in the hollow of her throat, but Yipper could take that out when he did the other surgery. Ari had been wearing it so long she barely even noticed it anymore.

"I know you've come to try and make me change my mind," she continued, as she turned to leave the bathroom. "But I've decided to let Yipper do what has to be done. I just don't think that Lathe wants anything to do with me and I won't—" She trailed off abruptly when she opened the privacy curtain and saw who was standing there.

Not Liv at all, but Lathe.

"Hello, Ari," he said in a low voice. He was wearing what Ari had come to think of as the "Kindred Uniform"—a long-sleeved shirt made of some heavy satiny material and black leather trousers tucked into high black boots. Over this he was also wearing a white doctor's coat. The pale blue of the shirt brought out the turquoise of his eyes and the look on his face was quiet and serious.

"Lathe!" Ari put a hand instinctively to the side of her neck, trying to hide the ugly white bandages. "What...what are you doing here?"

"I came to ask your forgiveness," he said quietly. "And to ask if you'll let me try to heal you."

"Heal me? Who told you I needed healing?" she demanded.

"Do you?" Lathe took a step towards her, his eyes scanning over her body and then back up to her neck.

Ari wondered if he thought she was pretty in the new red dress and then got angry at herself for wondering it.

"I'm fine," she said, lifting her chin defiantly. "So you can just...just go."

"Not until I at least examine you." He took another step forward, his hand outstretched. "May I?"

Ari bit her lip. She knew what he would see if he lifted the bulky white bandages because she had dared to peak under them herself.

What she had seen had almost made her cry.

A web of ugly black lines radiated out from the spot under her ear where Tapper's knife had nicked her. They ran like rivers of midnight water up the side of her face and over her scalp as well as down her neck, all the way to her collar bone in the front and her shoulder blade in the back. Slowly but surely the corruption was spreading. She would probably have to go under the knife today before the affected area got any bigger.

"Please, Ari," Lathe murmured when she didn't answer him. "Please let me see."

"It...it's really ugly," she said at last in a low, choked voice.

"Nothing about you could ever be ugly to me." Lathe's voice was slightly hoarse. "Please, little one...trust me."

The use of his old nickname for her took Ari by surprise and put her off her guard.

"Well..." She shrugged. "I guess it couldn't hurt for you to just *look*."

"Thank you for trusting me. Will you sit on the bed, please, so

I can examine you?" He indicated the high hospital bed and Ari went and perched on it. Doctor Sylvan had ordered some kind of 24/7 numbing treatment for the pain so she didn't even flinch when Lathe reached up and pulled the bandages aside.

Ari waited unhappily to see a look of disgust on is face but his expression was carefully neutral. At last he nodded and replaced the bandage.

"Well?" Ari couldn't stand it anymore. She needed to know his opinion of her situation.

"It is...a bad case of corruption," Lathe admitted. "Possibly the worst I've ever seen."

"So you can't heal it, right? Doctor Sylvan didn't think you could."

"I don't know if I can or not," Lathe said honestly. "But I would like the opportunity to try."

"You don't have to," Ari said quickly. "I mean I know...know how you feel about me."

"Do you?" Lathe gave her a penetrating look. "You know, somehow I doubt that. Will you let me try to heal you? It is, after all, my fault you were wounded in the first place."

"*Your* fault?" Ari looked at him incredulously. "You're kidding, right?"

"Of course not." His eyes glowed briefly. "I should have protected you from getting cut in the first place. My honor *demands* that I heal you."

Ari bit back a sigh. She'd been hoping that he might talk as he had that night in the cell—say that he had feelings for her. That he wanted to heal her because he loved her.

*Stop wishing for the impossible,* she told herself angrily.

"Lathe, it wasn't your responsibility to protect me," she said at last.

"I disagree." He frowned. "But no matter whose fault it was, since you're aboard the Mother Ship where I am a doctor, it *is* my responsibility to heal you."

Ari bit her lip.

"I don't...don't understand why you even want to try. You were going to leave and never see me again. You hate me for lying to you."

"I could never hate you, little one." There was rough tenderness in his voice as he reached to cup her cheek. "Please, Ari—let me at least *try*."

"Well..." Ari looked up at him uncertainly. "Do you...do you really think you can?"

"I don't know," Lathe said honestly. "Normally my essence can heal almost anything but whatever poison Tapper used was like nothing I've ever seen before. I studied the chemical composition from your biopsy—it's uniquely effective and *very* aggressive. But if I have even the slightest chance of being able to heal you, well...that's a chance I need to take, little one."

His use of the sweet nickname at last melted Ari's uncertainty.

"All right," she said in a low voice. "But not here. There are all kinds people going back and forth outside the door and you know how it is for me when you...when you bite me." She felt the hot blood rushing to her cheeks. "I can't...I might not be able to keep my voice down."

"Yes, I understand." Lathe nodded gravely. "Would you like to go somewhere more private? My suite perhaps?"

"Yes, I...I guess that would be okay. At least I'm dressed to go out." Ari nodded down at the red dress she was wearing.

"Yes, so I see." Was there a hungry note in Lathe's deep voice? "You look lovely," he murmured. "And *extremely* feminine."

"Well it helps that I'm not dressed in a baggy blue and orange striped jumpsuit," Ari pointed out, trying to lighten the tension that had somehow grown up between them. "Which is all you've ever seen me in."

"You looked beautiful even in the BleakHall jumpsuit," Lathe said quietly. "Always beautiful to me, Ari."

"Thank you." Ari looked down at her hands. "Um, should we tell anyone we're going?"

"I'll inform Nurse Olivia on our way out of the med center," Lathe murmured. "She can note in your chart that we're trying an 'alternative treatment method' away from the exam room."

*Alternative treatment method—right...* Ari shivered again when she thought of the incredible, overwhelming pleasure his bite brought her. Was she crazy to be agreeing to this? Surely he was only offering to try and heal her because he felt guilty. Probably letting him give her such intense pleasure—letting him make her come—was only going to make her feel worse when he inevitably turned his back on her and walked away again.

But Ari couldn't help it—even though she knew it was a bittersweet pleasure that would end all too soon, she couldn't help wanting to be with the big Kindred one more time. To feel his hands and mouth on her body—even if it was just to sink his fangs into her flesh.

*I want to be with him just one more time,* she told herself as Lathe ushered her out of the exam room, one large hand at the small of her back. *It doesn't matter if I'll never see him again after that. I just want to be with him.*

Resolutely, she pushed every doubt and worry she had over the situation out of her head and let Lathe lead her out of the med center to his suite.

# FIFTY

L athe's living quarters were bachelor-neat with no paintings or art work on the walls and no decorative touches around the room. Ari wasn't much for knick-knacks or frou-frou like fancy throw pillows but she thought it *could* use a woman's touch. For instance if *she* lived here the walls wouldn't be bare. She liked to have pictures and artwork to look at when she was thinking in the lab—it inspired her creativity.

Then she caught herself and realized what she was doing— imagining how it would be if she and Lathe lived together as a couple.

*Don't be stupid, Ari,* she told herself. *You're only here so he can try to heal you in private—that's all. So you might as well stop mentally redecorating his home in your head—it's never going to happen.*

"Please, have a seat." Lathe gestured to a large, comfortably looking couch built to Kindred proportions sitting in front of a fireplace. But instead of wood or logs, the bottom of the grate appeared to be filled with large blue crystals.

"Thank you—do you build fires a lot? Aren't the fumes produced difficult to vent in a space ship?" Instead of sitting, Ari went to examine the silver mesh screen in front of the fireplace with interest.

"I wondered the same thing when I first came to the Mother Ship," Lathe admitted. "But actually, it's a clean-burning flame that produces only heat and light—no fumes of any kind. See those crystals? They're Denarian fire rocks—all you have to do is apply a spark and..." He pressed a button on one side of the mantelpiece over the fireplace and the crystals caught at once and began emitting blue and green and gold flames.

"Oh!" Ari exclaimed in delight. "That's *fascinating*. I wondered how it was practical to have a fireplace in a space ship but that makes perfect sense."

"All the suites have them," Lathe told her. "Apparently the Earth females find them..." He cleared his throat. "Romantic."

"I can see how they might think that." Ari shrugged, trying to look unconcerned and went back to sit on the couch. "For myself, I was just interested in the mechanics of it. I love to know how things work."

"Is that how you became an inventor?" Lathe raised an eyebrow and went to sit beside her. "How you came up with your, uh—what did you call it? Your solid-holo projector?"

"Oh yes, the look/touch." Ari felt the warm blood rising in her cheeks. "Lathe, I just want to say again how sorry I am about... about what I made you think about me *and* about yourself. I never meant to lie to you—"

"It's all right." He raised a hand to stop her. "I am over my wounded pride."

"Um...you are?" Ari raised her eyebrows at him in surprise.

Lathe nodded. "I was recently reminded that as bad as Bleak-Hall was for me, it must have been doubly terrifying for you. I don't blame you for being afraid to tell me the truth about yourself."

Relief washed through her.

"Thank you," she said earnestly. "Thank you for accepting my apology."

"I'm sorry it took me so long," Lathe said seriously. "I'm afraid I can be a bit...stubborn at times."

"I am too," Ari admitted, remembering how determined she'd been not to even let him try to heal her. Speaking of the healing though... "Should...should we get started?" she asked Lathe. "I mean, with you, um, biting me?"

She could feel the blood rising in her cheeks as she spoke. Goddess, it was really embarrassing but just the thought of having those sharp fangs sinking into her flesh again was already making her feel wet and hot between her thighs.

"Yes, that *is* why we are here." He nodded and then frowned. "I just have to find the right place to bite and inject my healing essence."

"You...you're not going to bite my neck are you?" Ari asked, trying to keep the quaver out of her voice. "Doctor Sylvan has prescribed some numbing cream for the, uh, injured side but I still don't like the idea of getting bitten there. And the other side of my neck is really tender too." She hoped that didn't mean the corruption was spreading but she was afraid it did.

"Hmm..." Lathe frowned. "That presents a unique problem.

"I *had* intended to bite the unaffected side of your neck—there are plenty of big blood vessels there to carry my essence straight to your heart and circulate to the rest of your body."

"Isn't there anywhere else you can bite instead?" Ari asked anxiously.

"Well..." He sighed. "There is but you might not like it."

"Just tell me," Ari said. "Where else could you bite me?"

"The second-best place would probably be on your inner thigh area—the inguinal crease," Lathe spoke reluctantly. "The femoral artery is located there and it's very large and fast-flowing —it should be able to handle the amount of essence I'll need to inject you with."

Ari's heart started beating faster.

"So...you want to, uh, bite me between my legs?" She couldn't help remembering the last time he'd been between her thighs, when he was covering her scent with his own.

"Not directly between your legs," Lathe hastened to assure her. "Just at the place where your thigh meets your torso." He cleared his throat. "You could, of course, keep your undergarments on. And I would promise not to do anything...improper."

*Like licking my pussy until I pull your hair and moan?* Ari thought dryly but didn't say. The very idea of saying it out loud made her feel nervous and hot.

"O...okay," she managed to get out at last, then she realized he was watching her with those gorgeous turquoise eyes of his, waiting for an answer. "I guess as long as you...as you promise not to...not to do anything improper."

"Of course not," Lathe said seriously. "So then...should we begin?"

As he spoke he removed his white doctor's jacket and slipped off the couch, kneeling at her feet Clearly he was waiting for her to let him in.

"Oh, um..." Blushing so hard her face felt hotter than the fire, Ari took the unspoken hint and obeyed, parting her thighs.

Lathe moved between her legs and lifted the flirty red skirt of her dress but for a moment he just sat there—staring not at her panties but at her face.

"Thank you, Ari," he murmured. "Thank you for trusting me."

"You...you're welcome," she whispered.

He nodded. "Now spread your legs wide for me and just relax. I promise not to take too long."

Ari did as he said. Leaning back against the plush back of the big leather sofa, she parted her thighs, trying not to think about what had happened the last time she'd been in this position for him.

"Just relax," Lathe repeated softly. He ran his big, warm hands up her thighs, making Ari shiver as his gentle touch seemed to set her on fire. "Gods, you're lovely," he murmured as he touched her. "Forgive me—I know that's not very professional of me to say but I can't help it. Your skin is so smooth and soft."

"Th-thank you," Ari stuttered, feeling hot and cold all over at the same time. "I...I don't mind you, uh, saying that."

"Thank you." Lathe sighed. "Now look...here is where I'm going to bite you."

He drew an X with his fingertip, just at the crease where her torso met her right leg. "I'll need you to spread even wider to let me in. Can you?"

In answer, Ari opened her thighs even wider. This was embarrassing because she could feel her pussy lips parting with the movement, opening like a flower under the white lace panties Liv had given her to wear with the red dress. Could Lathe see her pussy parting for him as she opened her legs? The panties *were* fairly sheer.

*I should be all right as long as I don't start getting wet,* Ari told herself uncomfortably. *If these panties get soaked he's going to see **everything***.

Well hopefully that wouldn't happen. After all, Lathe had promised to make this quick, she reminded herself as he bent to nuzzle at her inner thigh. He opened his mouth and she thought he was about to get started. But instead of biting, he flattened his tongue and licked from the bottom all the way up to the top of her thigh.

"Hey!" Ari protested, jumping a little and feeling her heart skitter in her chest. "I thought you were just going to bite."

"I am." Lathe looked up at her, an unreadable expression in his eyes. "But I must prepare the site first. What I am doing is drawing the blood vessel I need to pierce to the surface. It's much easier that way."

It didn't *feel* easier to Ari and she thought uncomfortably that she could feel herself starting to get wet. But hopefully he would hurry up and just get it over with.

But rather than rush the experience, Lathe seemed determined to take his time and lick and suck every inch of her inner thigh.

"Lathe," she whispered at last. "When are you going to—"

At that moment, he bit—all four points of his fangs sinking into the tender flesh of her inner thigh at once.

At once Ari felt the pleasure overtaking her...overwhelming

her...rolling her over like an unexpectedly huge wave at the beach.

"Oh!" Unable to stop herself, she grasped for him, her fingers finding his thick, dark hair. Her back arched and a moan that sounded suspiciously like his name left her lips. There was a warm tingling that ran from her pussy, all the way up to her neck and Ari writhed under him, overcome with desire.

It seemed to go on and on but at last, Lathe sat back, panting. His eyes were heavy-lidded with desire as they traveled from the spot between her thighs...up to her flushed face...and back down again.

"Oh!" Ari whispered, slumping back against the sofa. She felt like she'd been in the process of getting electrocuted by pleasure and someone had just cut the current. "That was...amazing. It felt so *good.*"

"I'm glad my bite gives you pleasure, but I'd like to see if it worked," Lathe murmured. Rising, he bent to examine the wounded side of Ari's neck again, lifting the bandages to have a look.

What he saw made him purse his lips and shake his head.

"Let me guess," Ari said with a sinking heart. "It didn't work."

"Not completely, no. But I believe it is *starting* to work," Lathe said. "The webwork of corruption is definitely shrinking. I think if I bit you again, injected more of my essence..."

"All right." Ashamed of her own eagerness but unable to help herself, Ari spread her thighs for him a second time, welcoming him in. But when she looked down at herself she almost shut them again.

*Oh my Goddess—look how wet I'm getting!*

It was true—the white lace panties were now thoroughly

soaked with her juices. The sheer material had turned transparent and was clinging to her swollen pussy lips. Ari could even see the little pink pearl of her clit poking out between them, as though begging for attention.

She started to close her legs but Lathe stopped her, his hands on her thighs.

"What's wrong, Ari? I thought you wanted me to bite you again."

"I do but it's just..." She shifted in embarrassment. "I can't seem to help uh, reacting when you bite me."

"Reacting?" He looked down at her see-through panties and understanding dawned on his face. "Oh, *reacting*," he murmured. "Gods, yes—I see what you mean. Always so wet, my *numalla*."

"I...I'm probably ruining the nice panties Liv gave me to wear," Ari whispered, her cheeks feeling flushed with a strange mixture of shame and desire. She liked the hot note she heard in Lathe's deep voice and the way he was looking at her made her heart feel like it was beating right between her thighs.

"If that bothers you, you can always take them off," he offered in a soft growl. "Would you like to do that, Ari? Do you want to take off your panties before I bite you again?"

Goddess, that deep, warm tone he was using and the half-lidded look of lust in his turquoise eyes made her feel so hot she could barely breathe. Not to mention that his bonding scent had come out to play. The warm, rich, masculine fragrance coming from him seemed to do things to her insides, making her feel molten from the waist down.

"If...if you don't mind," she whispered. "I mean if it won't bother you to bite me so close to..."

"To your sweet, wet pussy?" he growled softly. "No, of course it won't bother me, little one. Would you like some help to take them off?"

"Yes, please," Ari murmured. She lifted her hips and Lathe obligingly reached for the sides of the panties and pulled the soaked lace down her legs, leaving her completely bare.

"That's good," he said softly, spreading her thighs again with his hands and leaning closer. "Goddess, your scent is so sweet! Are you ready for me to bite you again, Ari?"

Ari nodded. "Yes, please. I...I want you to."

Feeling almost drugged with lust, she allowed him to spread her wide again. But she couldn't help the moan of desire that came from her throat when she felt his rough whiskers brush against her sensitive pussy as he pressed his face to her inner thigh.

"Relax now sweetheart and let yourself come when I bite you," Lathe instructed. "That will speed up your heart rate and carry my essence to where it needs to go."

"Yes, Lathe," she moaned but the words were barely out of her mouth before he bit her again.

As the four sharp points of his fangs sank into her flesh a second time, Ari cried out and bucked her hips in pleasure. Lathe had instructed her to let herself come but it was like telling her to let herself breathe. There was no way to stop it—like a wave at the ocean it rolled her over and she went with it helplessly, swept out like a bit of driftwood in the tide.

She felt the tingling in her neck again but the rest of her body was so alive with pleasurable sensations she could barely notice it.

"Lathe!" she moaned. "Oh Goddess, yes—that feels so good...*so good!*"

He didn't let up again until she'd come three or four times, her pussy clenching helplessly even though he wasn't even touching her there.

*Goddess, so good but I feel so empty,* Ari couldn't help thinking. *Need something...something inside me. Something deep and hard...*

But Lathe was still being careful not to touch her intimately, except for the side of his face which was rubbing against her as he bit her inner thigh. The rough whiskers felt good—almost *too* good to her over-stimulated pussy. She moaned and edged away from him a little just as he finished and sat up.

"How do you feel, little one?" he murmured, looking up at Ari. "Did you feel the healing that time?"

"Some," she whispered. "The pleasure when you bit me was so intense it was hard to concentrate. "I felt so..." she looked down at herself and bit back a gasp. Her pussy was more wet and swollen than she had ever seen it—her outer lips coated and shiny with her juices which were beginning to spill out over the brown leather couch cushion. "Goddess! Now I'm going to ruin your couch!" she exclaimed.

"You won't ruin it," Lathe promised her. "But...if it bothers you I can help clean you up. As I did our last night at BleakHall," he added. "When I covered your scent."

"You mean...clean me with your..."

"With my tongue, little one." His voice was a soft, lustful growl. "Yes, it would be my pleasure to give your soft little pussy a tongue bath if you feel that your juices are a little too messy."

"That's...that's very kind of you," Ari whispered breathlessly. "If...if you really want to, I don't mind."

"I would love to taste you again," Lathe growled. "And since the healing compounds in my essence are also present in my saliva and other body fluids, it would be most beneficial."

"Well if it's part of the treatment then I guess we should definitely do it," Ari murmured. Heart pounding, she spread her legs wider. "Come clean me up, Lathe," she murmured. "Give me a tongue bath like you promised."

A low groan of desire rose in his throat as he pressed between her legs for a third time and wrapped his arms around her thighs.

Ari gasped as he split her wide and then cried out as she felt his hot tongue lapping her pussy fiercely, starting at the bottom and gliding eagerly to the very top of her slit, as though Lathe wanted to capture every drop of her honey along the way.

"Gods, you taste so sweet," he growled, after the first pass. "But your pussy is still so wet, my *numalla*—I'm afraid I'll have to keep licking."

"That's all right," Ari assured him. "I...I don't mind. You can lick me as much as you want to, Lathe."

The big Kindred took her at her word. Cupping her ass in his hands, he raised her to his mouth like a thirsty man drinking from a bowl of water. Ari couldn't help remembering how he'd told her that Kindred *needed* to taste their mates this way—needed to lick the honey from their pussies and make their females come again and again.

She tangled her hands in his hair once more and pressed up to meet him, eager to take the pleasure he was giving, eager to open herself for him completely. Lathe lashed the sensitive, swollen bud of her clit with his tongue and then sucked it into his mouth, circling it slowly until she cried out and twisted in his hands, so over-stimulated it felt like she might leave her body and start flying.

"Lathe!" she moaned. "Oh Goddess, yes...right there...right *there*. Don't stop—I'm so close...so *close*."

At that moment she felt two long, strong fingers sliding into her pussy, filling her exactly the way she needed to be filled. With a low cry, she felt herself tipping over the edge yet again—but this time her pussy had something to grasp when the orgasm hit her.

*Feels so good,* she thought deliriously as he pressed deep inside her. *So, so **good!***

But though it felt good, it wasn't *exactly* right. She needed more somehow—not just his fingers. She needed something thicker, something longer...

Lathe stayed with her, riding out her orgasm until she collapsed, panting on the couch.

"Oh, Goddess..." Ari's voice sounded weak in her own ears. "That was...that felt amazing, Lathe."

"But did it help your healing? I need to check your throat." Carefully he withdrew his fingers and licked them clean. Then he lapped gently around Ari's pussy—not to stimulate her again but simply to clean up her juices, just as he had promised. "Gods, I love your taste," he murmured as he finished and stood to look at her neck. "Hmmm..."

"Well?" Ari wanted to see the look on his face but since he was peering at the side of her neck, the angle was wrong. "Is it all right? Did it work?" she asked anxiously.

"Not...completely." Lathe sounded frustrated. "At least the bandages can come off now, though. Come see for yourself."

He helped her off the couch and led her to a bathroom—what the Kindred called a "fresher" she remembered—to look at herself in the 3-D viewer.

Ari bit her lip when she saw how wide her pupils had dilated and how flushed her cheeks were. The red dress was askew, one shoulder drooping so low it was barely covering her breast. She started to pull it up but Lathe stopped her.

"No, you need to see the results of the healing." Peeling the bandages off carefully, he pointed to the exposed side of her neck.

Ari let out a little gasp. The ugly black webbing of corruption was almost completely gone. Except for a small spot under her ear, no bigger than a large coin, nothing remained of the evil black lines that had covered her neck.

"That's amazing, Lathe," she breathed, turning her head from side to side to admire the healing. "You can barely see it at all now!"

"But it *is* still there." He sounded frustrated. "And it needs to be eradicated completely or it *will* grow back."

"What can we do?" Ari met his eyes in the viewer. "Just keep, uh, doing this as treatment every time it starts growing again? Letting you bite me and make me come?"

"Well, that would require you to stay aboard the Mother Ship." Lathe's voice was carefully neutral. "I thought you intended to return to Phobos."

"I don't have to go right away." Ari was careful to keep her tone casual as well. "I mean, Jak already runs the family business by himself. He wouldn't mind if I stayed on the Mother Ship. At least for a while."

"I'd love to have you stay," Lathe said quietly. "But the physician in me doesn't want to settle for an incomplete healing. There is *one* other thing we could try. But you might not want to when you hear what it is."

"Tell me," Ari said curiously. "I was going to let Yipper dissect the side of my neck—whatever it is, it can't be worse than that."

Lathe took a deep breath as though trying to think how to say what he had to say.

"Remember when I told you the healing compounds in my body are present in my saliva and other body fluids as well as in my essence?"

Ari nodded. "Yes—so?"

"So they are particularly concentrated in my semen—my seed," he murmured. "Of course, injecting my essence into your bloodstream via my fangs is the most direct route to get the healing compounds where they need to go, but they *will* find their way to the area that needs healing no matter how they enter your body. And since the compounds in my seed are so concentrated—"

"Yes," Ari said, before he could finish the explanation.

Lathe frowned and lifted her chin to look into her eyes. "You realize I'm talking about fucking you, little one? About filling your soft little pussy with my cock and coming deep inside you?" he growled.

"Yes," Ari whispered again.

Though he had already given her multiple orgasms, she suddenly felt weak in the knees with need. Standing on her tiptoes, she pulled him down for a sweet, breathless kiss. He tasted of her own secret flavor which only made her want him now.

"Yes, please," she told him when the kiss finally broke, holding his eyes with her own. "I want you to fill me. I want you inside me, Lathe. *Deep* inside."

He voiced a low growl of approval.

"Gods, little one. I didn't know you wanted it that badly."

"I do." Ari felt shame and desire rising inside her. "I was

thinking that when you were...were using your fingers on me," she told him. "Thinking that I needed something longer...something thicker..."

"I think we can manage that," Lathe growled softly. Then his face grew serious. "There is one thing though—I want you to know I'll be careful not to bite you at the same time I fill you with my seed. That would form a bond between us so I'll be cautious with my fangs while I'm inside you."

Ari felt her heart sink but she only nodded. She wished with all her heart that they could bond but apparently it wasn't to be. If this was the one and only time she could make love with the big Kindred then she would take what she could get.

"All right," she whispered. "Can...should we go get started?"

Lathe rumbled a laugh. "Eager, aren't you little one?"

"Yes," Ari said simply. "I...I can't describe it, Lathe but I feel so...so *hungry* inside for you. Hungry to be filled." She looked up at him. "Does that make sense?"

"Perfect sense because I'm hungry to fill you—to feel you all around me," he murmured. Stooping, he picked her up in his arms and carried her out of the bathroom, taking her back to the couch.

He settled on a broad cushion with Ari in his lap and she wiggled against him, feeling something hot and hard pressing against her ass.

"Aren't you forgetting something?" she asked, raising an eyebrow. "How can you get to me with your trousers in the way?"

"That's easily fixed." Reaching between them, Lathe unfastened the trousers and pulled the black leather open, revealing his long, thick shaft.

Ari bit her lip when she saw the size of it. She'd only seen him hard once, when she sucked him in the Rec Yard. But somehow she seemed to have forgotten how huge he was. Now that she was preparing to make love with the big Kindred, she had doubts about whether she could take him or not.

"Wow." She laughed uneasily. "I know I told you I needed something bigger than your fingers but this..." She nodded at his shaft and shook her head doubtfully. "I don't know, Lathe. I've only ever had sex twice before and you're *way* bigger than either of the guys I was with."

"You're a *numalla*," he murmured confidently. "That's one reason we Blood Kindred love a female who makes a lot of pussy honey—it helps her to allow a Kindred-sized shaft to slide in easily. And I promise to go slowly, Ari. Unless you've changed your mind?" He lifted an eyebrow at her in question.

"No." Ari shook her head firmly. "No, I want to do this. Let's just...take it slow, okay?"

"As slow as you need to," Lathe promised. "In fact, I'll let you take the lead. I'm just going to sit here while you do what you want with me."

"Hmm, I think I like that." Ari felt a surge of power. She liked the idea of taking control. Rearranging herself in his lap so she was straddling his lean hips and facing him, she lifted the short red skirt.

Lathe groaned softly when her pussy came into view again.

"Gods, look how wet you are again, little one! Can't wait to feel that soft, hot little pussy wrapped around my shaft."

His hot dirty words gave Ari a surge of desire...and of confidence as well.

*I can do this,* she told herself. *I can take him—I'm a numalla.*

Taking a deep breath, she raised up and took his hot, hard shaft in one hand, loving the way it pulsed in her fingers. Then she fit the broad, flaring crown to the opening of her pussy and bit her lip as she started to push down, feeling herself stretching around him.

"Relax, sweetheart," Lathe told her urgently, rubbing her hips gently as he watched what she was doing. "Just relax and let me in. You're wet enough...you can take me."

To her surprise and delight, Ari found he was absolutely correct. After the broad head breached her entrance, she felt another thick inch slip easily inside her. And then another and another—it was as though her body really was hungry for his— longing for Lathe to fill the aching emptiness inside her with his cock. Though she could feel her inner walls stretching to accommodate him it was a good, pleasurable kind of stretch—there was no pain, just the feeling of being more full inside than she ever had been before.

"Gods, little one, so beautiful," Lathe groaned as she sank slowly down on him, taking more and more of his thick hard shaft inside her. "So beautiful and so brave to take me all the way inside you...to open your soft little pussy and let me in."

"I...I want you inside me," Ari whispered breathlessly. "I need you, Lathe—need to feel you all...the way...in."

As she spoke the last word, she felt him bottom out inside her, the broad head of his cock pressing hard against the mouth of her womb in a deep and intimate kiss.

"Oh, Goddess, Lathe," she moaned. "In me...you're in me so deep."

"You feel so good around me, little one," he growled. "I told you, you were wet enough to take me, my sweet *numalla*."

"Mmm...it feels even better than I thought it would." Ari put her hands on the big Kindred's broad shoulders, steadying herself, trying to get used to having him inside her. She'd never felt like this before—so opened, so completely full. But it was a wonderful sensation—made doubly so by the fact that it was the man she loved who was filling her.

*But he doesn't love me back,* she remembered sadly. *He's still just trying to heal me. That's all.*

Well, she couldn't do anything about that—right now she would have to take what she could get. And if she only had this one chance with Lathe, then she would take it and make the most of it.

"I'm ready," she told him, looking into his eyes. "Fill me with your seed and heal me, Lathe."

His eyes were heavy-lidded with desire.

"My pleasure, little one. Just let yourself be open so I can fuck you...so I can make love to your sweet little pussy."

Ari felt a surge of lust at his hot words and spread her thighs a bit wider, trying to get him even deeper into her pussy. Gods, she loved the feel of him inside her!

"Yes, Lathe," she murmured and braced herself on his broad shoulders, ready for him. "Make love to me—I want you to."

---

Lathe loved how bravely she opened herself for him, how deeply she took him into her tight little pussy. Gods, she fit like a warm velvet glove all around him—squeezing and milking, almost as though her body knew that it needed his seed to heal and was trying to urge him to give it up.

But Lathe intended to make this last. If it was his one and only time with Ari, he didn't intend to rush an instant of it. Gods, he loved her—he wished they could have more than this once together. But he knew he shouldn't be greedy. At least the Goddess had granted him one time with her—he wanted to make it count.

"Get ready, little one," he murmured, looking into her lovely dark eyes. "Going to fuck you now—going to fill you with my cock and come deep in your sweet little pussy."

"Goddess, Lathe," she whispered breathlessly. "I love when you talk like that!"

Lathe could tell she meant what she said because he could feel her wet inner walls pulse around him as she spoke—squeezing him even tighter with pleasure.

"You like when I talk dirty to you, little one?" Taking a firm grip on her hips, Lathe pulled almost all the way out of her and then thrust back in, giving the mouth of her womb a hard kiss with the head of his cock. "You like when I tell you what I'm going to do to you?"

"Yes!" Ari's long eyelashes fluttered almost closed, a moan of pure pleasure drawn from her throat at his deep thrust. "Goddess, that night at BleakHall when you talked to me about how you'd make love to a woman...the things you said...and then when you told me to make myself come...I was *so* turned on," she murmured breathlessly.

"Turned me on too," Lathe admitted in a growl. "Though at the time I couldn't understand why I'd want to talk so to another male. I told myself it was just your feminine scent driving me crazy."

As he spoke, he stroked into her...setting up a slow, steady rhythm he knew would drive her wild.

"I...I should have told you then," Ari confessed, her fingers tightening on his shoulders as he filled her over and over. "Oh, yes! Gods Lathe, I've thought about it so often..."

"I don't know what I might have done if I found out you were a female that night," Lathe mused, rolling his hips to drive deeper into her. "Probably would have gone down on you right there and lapped your sweet pussy all night."

"Mmm...I was imagining you doing that—doing all the things you said you liked to do when you made love to a woman," Ari admitted, rolling her hips to join his rhythm. "I think that was part of the reason I wanted to...to suck you in the Rec Yard," she admitted. "I told myself it was to prove to everyone we were a couple and prove to you that you should let me stay in your cell but really, I was thinking about all the hot things you said in the back of my head."

"Gods, I was so conflicted about letting you do that," Lathe growled and gripped her hips more tightly. "But I couldn't seem to help myself. Watching your soft pink lips wrap around my cock was just too much."

Just the thought of it made his balls tighten and he knew he was getting close.

"Ari, sweetheart," he murmured as he continued to thrust up into her. "Do you think you can come for me one more time? It would help carry my seed and my healing compounds deep inside your body if you could."

"I think so," she whispered and then gasped as he thrust deeply into her. "I just...I need a little help, Lathe."

"With pleasure, little one."

Finding the tight little bud of her clit between her plump pussy lips, he began to stroke around it with the pad of his thumb, circling the little pink pearl over and over as he continued to drive his cock up into her.

"Lathe..." Ari gasped, gripping his shoulders. "Oh Goddess that feels...feels amazing!"

"You *look* amazing," he told her in a low growl. "So ripe and wet, your little pussy all spread open on my cock while I fuck deep inside you and claim what's mine."

"Yours?" Ari's eyes opened wide and she stared at him uncertainly. Lathe knew he should stop himself but he couldn't—he felt too strongly for her to hold back anymore.

"Yes, *mine*," he growled, looking into her eyes. "Mine because I want you, to care for and protect. Mine because *I love you*, Ari."

Her breath caught in a moan as she met his gaze.

"Oh, Lathe, do you really mean that? You love me?"

"With everything in me." He kissed her fiercely, taking her mouth with his as he continued to thrust deeply into her and stroke her clit with his thumb.

When he finally let her go, Ari looked at him with shining eyes.

"I love you too, Lathe," she moaned as she rode him, working her hips to take him deep inside her soft little pussy. "And I never want to be without you. Tie me to you forever—bite me and bond me."

Her words galvanized something inside him—shocked him to his very core with possessive desire.

Growling hungrily, he pulled her down and Ari gladly bared her throat for him. As he thrust up into her one final time, Lathe sank his fangs into the unmarked side of her neck, injecting her with his essence as he spurted inside her and filled her with his come.

Ari cried out, her back arching as she came too. Her pussy clenched around his cock, tight and sweet and wet and exactly what he needed. Lathe found himself coming again, shooting spurt after spurt of seed deep in her swollen pussy, giving her what they both needed so badly, tying her to him forever even as he healed her completely.

"*I love you, Ari,*" he told her, sending the words through the new link they had formed as he bonded her to him. "*I love you so much and I'm never letting you go.*"

EPILOGUE

"So you're the one who told Lathe I was sick?" Ari laughed at the guilty look on Liv's face.

"Well, yes—I admit it. But what was I supposed to do—just let the two of you go your separate ways and be miserable the rest of your lives?" Liv's silver-gray eyes opened wide in protest. "Besides, it was Yipper you made promise not to say anything—not me."

"I guess that's technically true. But I wouldn't have cared one way or the other—Lathe and I are together now and that's all that matters." Ari grinned happily. It seemed that lately, ever since she and Lathe had bonded, she had a joy bubbling up inside her that just couldn't be controlled. It manifested itself in the form of a silly grin that wouldn't go away, no matter how hard she tried.

"Look at you—you're *glowing*, doll." Kat, Liv's auburn-haired friend laughed at her. It was her living area they were sitting in, along with Sophie and Lauren and some of the other Kindred brides who Liv had introduced her to. Because Kat was married to Twin Kindred, her suite was slightly larger—and slightly noisier too, with all three of her sons running around.

Not that Ari minded. She secretly hoped that she and Lathe might have a son soon too. They had certainly been trying often enough lately.

"I can't help myself," she said in response to Kat's remark. "I'm just so...*happy.*"

"We can tell," Lauren, who was Liv and Sophie's cousin, said dryly. "If you grin any wider the ends of your mouth will meet in the back and the top of your head will fall off."

"She's got the 'just-bonded' glow, that's all," Liv said, as they all laughed at Lauren's prediction. "I remember how it is—you just can't get enough of each other. Isn't that right, hon?" she asked Ari.

"That's about right," Ari agreed, grinning again. "Gods, I'm sorry—it's like my mouth is stuck this way. I swear my cheeks hurt from smiling so much."

"That sounds like a good problem to have to me," Liv said. "But how does your brother, Jak, feel about you staying aboard the Mother Ship with Lathe?"

"Oh, he was a little disappointed but I think he knew I was about ready to get out on my own. I couldn't stay in Blackthorn Manor all my life."

"Blackthorn Manor—it sounds like something out of a Jane Austin novel," Sophia sighed.

"It's really no big deal," Ari protested, feeling her cheeks get hot. "I wasn't exactly a lady out of a historical romance vid. I just spent all my time up in my lab inventing and fiddling."

"I heard you're going to be working in the tech division here aboard the Mother Ship," Liv said. "They're lucky to have you."

"I'm lucky to be here," Ari said seriously. "Honestly if it wasn't for Lathe, I would still be stuck in BleakHall prison. I'd probably be dead by now," she added soberly.

"Oh no—there went the smile," Lauren exclaimed. "Quick, think about your new man and get it back."

Ari gave a self-deprecating little laugh. "I'm sorry. It's just...I still have nightmares about that place sometimes. I think I probably will for years to come."

"It takes time to get over traumatic life events," Liv said quietly. "But I'm sorry to hear you're having nightmares."

"It's okay." Ari shrugged. "I wake up and Lathe is beside me, waiting to comfort me. I guess you could say he's still protecting me from BleakHall, even though we're long gone from it."

"What about that other guy you brought back from BleakHall —the big hybrid Kindred with the green and gold eyes?" Sophie asked.

"Oh, you mean The Beast—I mean, Slade?" Ari asked. "I don't know, actually."

"Oh, didn't you hear, doll?" Kat leaned forward confidentially. "He got into some trouble down at the Pairing Puppets house."

"He *what?*" Liv, Lauren, and Sophie all said at once.

Ari said, "What *is* a Pairing Puppet anyway?"

"Pairing puppets are these kind of...android-type things— female robots that the unmated Kindred can use to, uh, blow off steam, if you know what I mean, until they find a mate," Liv explained.

"So what kind of trouble did he get into?" Lauren asked. "Did he break one of the puppets?"

"Not exactly." Kat's blue eyes were dancing with anticipation —clearly she loved a good story. "He actually had sex with a Pairing Puppet that *wasn't* a puppet."

"What?" Liv asked blankly. "What does that even mean?"

"Apparently a couple of the girls on one of the tourist groups that come up from Earth were feeling adventurous," Kat said. "They decided it might be fun to 'try out' a Kindred warrior with no one being the wiser. One of them chickened out but the other girl ended up with the hybrid—with Slade."

"Oh my God, but didn't they know the risks?" Sophie asked. "You could get bonded by accident to a complete *stranger*."

"I know." Kat giggled. "Can you *imagine?* It was lucky for her that hybrid Kindred usually can't form a bond."

"Merrick did, though," Liv said. "He's another hybrid Kindred we know," she explained to Ari. "But bond or no bond, I've seen that guy—I imagine she got the ride of her life."

"I know," Sophie exclaimed. "He's even bigger than Merrick and Merrick is *huge*. I can only imagine how sore she was the next day. She'll probably be walking bow-legged for a week!"

"Anyway, she ran away from the Mother Ship afterwards and now Slade can't find her." Kat shrugged. "That's what I heard, anyway. I think he's pretty upset over what happened—he was looking for a no-strings-attached night with a Pairing Puppet and he got a real-live girl instead."

"Speaking of female androids, did Sylvan ever find out about the android me that came after him?" Liv asked.

"What?" asked several voices and Liv had to explain about

the attempt on Sylvan's life by the robot-version of herself which had been paid for by Mistress Hellenix of Yonnie Six.

"I had a heck of a time prying the story out of Baird," she said. "He and Sylvan were *really* upset. To be honest, I was too—I don't know why Mistress Hellenix would pick *me* to make a killer robot clone of!"

"Maybe because you and Sylvan work together," Sophie offered. "I'm just glad she didn't model the assassin robot after *me*. Poor Sylvan still jumps whenever Liv walks in the room. I would hate it if he had that reaction with me."

"Now I start every conversation with him, 'Hi, Sylvan, it's the real me,'" Liv explained with a little grin. "It doesn't seem like it was a very *good* clone though. Sylvan said it looked exactly like me but didn't act or talk like me at all."

"Do you think Mistress Hellenix made the robot herself or had someone else make it?" Lauren asked.

"Lathe thinks she had someone make it—someone with connections to Uriel Two," Ari spoke up. "He said that Malik—the Volt Kindred warrior that Mistress Hellenix keeps as a slave—talked about her having an artifact in her collection that might help him regain control of his home world...which is Uriel Two."

"But I thought it was completely controlled by AIs now—artificial intelligences?" Sophie asked.

"It is but apparently that's the reason Malik is hanging around with Mistress Hellenix. I guess he's trying to get his hands on that artifact—whatever it is. Or maybe she has ties to Uriel Two because of it? Something like that." Ari shrugged.

"Well he might not be able to hang around with her much longer," Kat said. "Isn't Sylvan going to bring her up on charges before the Sacred Seven—the Yonnie Six version of the High Council?"

"Yes, but the Yonnites think men are lower than dirt," Liv pointed out. "Who knows how far the case will get since the plaintiff is a male."

"Sylvan has thought of that," Sophie said. "He's hired an excellent female attorney to take the case. She's thoroughly conversant with human and Kindred law and as soon as she's had a little time to bone up on Yonnite law, they're taking the Bleak-Hall Yonnites to court."

"I hope they can make some changes," Ari said in a low voice. "There are some terrible things happening in BleakHall and not everyone who's locked up deserves to be there."

"Case in point—you and your brother," Kat said seriously. "But tell us, doll—was it worth going to prison to meet the love of your life?"

"Of course it was," Ari said, smiling. "It was a terrible time but if I hadn't gone to BleakHall and gotten trapped there, I never would have met Lathe. All my happiness now is due to the sadness and terror I went through at BleakHall. I wouldn't trade it for the world—even if I do still have nightmares."

"Well, like you said, you have Lathe to wake up to and to hold you tight when that happens." Kat reached over and patted her hand. "The Goddess knew what she was doing when she put the two of you together."

"Yes." Ari nodded. "I'm sure she did."

For she was certain now that it hadn't been the Goddess of Mercy but rather the Kindred Goddess who had spoken to her and helped her during their escape from BleakHall. She had felt the same, warm feminine presence when she and Lathe had visited the Sacred Grove and a soft voice had whispered in her ear, ***"Daughter, you are home."***

*Yes,* Ari thought. *I'm home—here with the man I love and all my wonderful new friends. I'll live out my days on the Mother Ship as a Kindred bride with Lathe and thank the Goddess every day for my good fortune.*

She smiled again, contentedly and let the rest of the conversation wash over her. She had a long, healthy, happy life with a man she loved to look forward to and as many friends as she could wish for. In fact, there were only two things troubling her.

First, who exactly had made the assassin robot and how close were their ties to Uriel Two? And secondly, she couldn't help feeling bad for poor Slade. He had saved her life down in the lasher tunnel and had fought bravely with no thought for his own safety when they were getting free of BleakHall. What exactly had happened between him and the girl he had believed was a Pairing Puppet? And would he ever find her?

Sending a prayer to the Goddess for the big hybrid, Ari decided she would ask Lathe if they could have Slade over for dinner one night. It was the least they could do after he had helped them escape the nightmare prison. She only wished she could see him as happily settled as she and Lathe were.

But maybe he would be...someday in the future.

# THE END?

Of course not—I think you know what's coming next. Read on for a sneak peek at Slade's story, *Bonded by Accident,* coming soon to my Kindred Tales series. And look for Malik's story in Kindred 23, also coming soon. (As long as no one else pops up and demands to have their story told first like Ari and Lathe did. Characters can be so pushy sometimes! ; )

Hugs and Happy Reading to you all!

Evangeline (in August 2018)

## LEAVE A REVIEW

If you've enjoyed this book, please take a moment to leave a review. Good reviews are like gold for an author—they let other readers know it's okay to take a chance on a new series. Plus they give me the warm-fuzzies. : )

Thanks for being such an awesome reader!

Hugs and Happy Reading,

Evangeline

---

**And now, here's a taste of *Bonded by Accident*, available September 8 at the Aliens & Alphas Bookstore...**

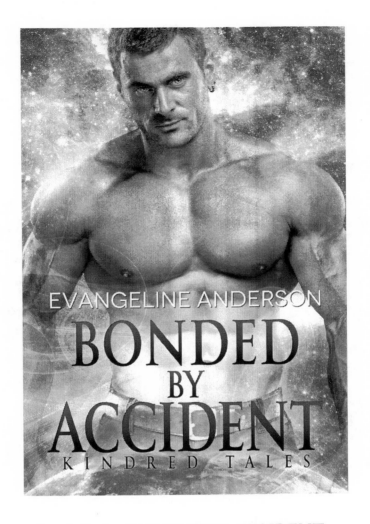

Sneak Peek at BONDED BY ACCIDENT—
A Kindred Tales Novel

**A hybrid warrior, born of both worlds, belonging
to none
Seeking to end his sexual torment without breaking
a vow
A girl from Earth with an itch to scratch**

**Looking for no-strings-attached sex
But when you make love with a Kindred, things get complicated
What are Brandi and Slade going to do now that they are...
*Bonded by Accident?***

Slade is an ex-slave, an ex-con, and a widower who has made a vow never to love another woman since his mate died tragically. But after his escape from BleakHall Prison, he finds he has a desperate need for female companionship. How to scratch his itch without breaking his vow? Easy--visit the Pairing Puppets aboard the Mother Ship--female-looking androids without emotions that help unmated Kindred males relieve their urges until they can find mates.

Brandi Dixon is a single mom with a difficult life. She and her daughter live in a double-wide trailer in small-town rural Florida. Brandi longs for a man but she's picky and doesn't want to bring home a string of "temporary daddies" for her daughter like her mom did to her when she was growing up. Then her cousin wins tickets to tour the Kindred Mother Ship and tells Brandi there's a place where she can have hot, no-strings-attached sex with a Kindred warrior. Brandi wouldn't normally do such a thing but she's desperate--it's been a three year dry spell and she *needs* a man--even if it's only for a single night.

Posing as a Pairing Puppet, she gets picked by Slade for a night of passion. But imagine her surprise when, after the best sex of her life, she hears the big Kindred's growling voice *inside* her head!

Now Brandi is freaking out and Slade is pissed off that he

broke his vow. Yet neither of them can deny the animal attraction that keeps drawing them together. When Brandi's daughter, Emmie, gets herself into terrible danger, Slade is the only one who can help. Will Brandi let the huge Kindred warrior into her life? You'll have to read BONDED BY ACCIDENT to find out!

# CHAPTER ONE

S lade was horny as hell, but it wasn't his fault.

Being locked in solitary in a super-max prison with no female contact for five years will do that to a male. And of course, the eroto-lust stimulant his old mistress had given him, in an effort to make him fuck her brains out, didn't help either.

Slade shifted uncomfortably on the exam table, hearing it groan beneath his considerable muscular bulk. Even for a Kindred warrior, he was on the big side. At seven and a half feet, he was taller than most of his kind and a look at his eyes revealed the reason why. The right eye was like melted gold and the left was a brilliant green.

Slade was a hybrid—half Blood Kindred and half Beast Kindred and he had both the fangs and the mating fist to prove it.

Not that anyone had looked at his mating fist in a good long time...

Just thinking that...imagining sinking balls-deep in some willing female and letting the fist swell within her had him hard as rock under the too-tight orange and blue striped BleakHall jumpsuit he wore.

Slade shifted again, trying to ease the pressure, trying not to think about finding a female to ease his need.

Of course, he didn't want a *real* female, Slade reminded himself as a pretty little human nurse bustled into his room and started taking his vitals. She was as gorgeous as a Rathian *gorna-flower* in bloom, but so tiny she looked likely to break if he so much as looked at her wrong. Why were all these human girls so damn *small*?

But even if the little nurse hadn't been too small and skinny for his taste, there were other factors holding Slade back from making a move. One, the little human female smelled strongly of another Kindred. Doubtless she was bonded to one of the males who worked aboard the Mother Ship—that made her strictly off limits.

And second and more important, Slade had taken a vow.

Not a vow of celibacy or chastity exactly—more like a vow that he wouldn't be with a real woman again. Not after Cinda. Though it had been nearly six years since she died, her memory was still fresh in Slade's mind and he sure as hell didn't intend to cheat on it.

Not with a real woman, anyway. Which was why he was *extremely* eager to get off this damn exam table and go find the Pairing Puppet House which he knew was somewhere in the Unmated Males section of the Mother Ship.

Pairing Puppets were female androids the unmated Kindred

males used to relieve their needs until they could find the female the Goddess had for them and form a bond with her.

Only hybrids couldn't bond with anyone. He hadn't even been bonded to Cinda, though they had been together for five years. Even without the mental connection most Kindred shared with their mates, and despite the fact that both of them were slaves, it had been a beautiful relationship.

Right up until the time his old master had sold her...

Slade tried to push the memory out of his mind. Cinda was gone—dead by her own hand. The old master was history too—Slade had made sure of that himself. And as for the mistress he'd been sold to—the one who had bought him right off the chopping block—well, she'd gotten rid of Slade as soon as it was evident he wasn't going to service her the way she wanted to be serviced. But not before she'd given him the eroto-lust stimulant to try and convince him to fuck her.

Slade closed his eyes, remembering the angry look on her thin, pretty face when he'd refused her advances...

"What's wrong with you, slave? Did I not save you from death after you killed your old master? Have I not given you good food and a fine, thick mattress to sleep upon? And am I not beautiful?"

"I'm grateful for the food and the place to sleep and of course, for my life, Mistress," Slade had growled. "And sure, you're pretty. A little on the skinny side but hell, I guess that's the fashion here. But sorry—I'm not gonna fuck you."

"Such crude language!" his mistress had sniffed. "Then again, your crudity is part of why I bought you. Along with your...other attributes." She eyed the bulge in Slade's leather slave trousers greedily. "All I'm asking is that you service me—**not** fall in love with me. So get started immediately—or else!"

Slade had thought privately that there was no way he'd ever fall in love with a skinny, stuck-up female like her. She wasn't even remotely his type. But even if he had been interested in her, he wasn't going to break his vow.

"Sorry," he'd told her. "I can't. Also, I won't. Ask me anything else. You want me to fight for you—be your champion in the ring? I spent years in the Blood Circuit—I can win a hell of a lot of credit for you. Or I can help out around your house—fix anything that gets broken. I'm good with my hands."

"I already *have* plenty of credit and I have no need of a male who's good with his *hands*. I bought you because I was assured you were good with *other* things," his mistress sniffed. "I've a mind to see how that huge knot at the base of your shaft feels inside me. You *will* service me or pay the price."

"Sorry Mistress but threats don't exactly make my dick hard," Slade growled. "In fact, they tend to have the opposite effect."

"We'll see about that." The mistress had motioned to her personal physician, who had been standing by and watching the entire show with a completely neutral expression on his face. Maybe he saw his mistress threatening males into sleeping with her all the time, Slade had no idea. But for whatever reason, he didn't seem the least bit fazed by the conversation.

At the nod from the mistress, the physician had darted forward and jabbed Slade in the arm with a needle.

"Hey!" Slade hadn't expected that—he'd been keeping his eye on the angry woman who had bought him. He reached for the little physician but the male had already danced out of range and was standing safely in the mistress's shadow. "What the fuck was that?" Slade demanded, looking down at his arm where a single ruby droplet of blood welled, just above his elbow.

"Eroto-lust enhancer." The mistress sounded pleased with herself. "We'll see how long your resistance lasts once the chemicals hit your system. You'll be **begging** to service me then—begging to sheathe that enormous shaft inside me and give me what I bought you for."

Then she had turned on her heel and left.

To his distress, Slade had indeed begun to feel the effects of the enhancer not long after. His shaft seemed to be always hard, his thoughts constantly preoccupied by sex.

But Slade was a stubborn son-of-a-bitch—he refused to give in.

He jerked off on a regular basis to try and keep the lust contained and used meditation to clear his head—as much as he could anyway—a fact which baffled his mistress.

"How has he been able to resist the effects of the enhancer?" she demanded of her physician after Slade refused her yet again. "It cannot be that he is controlling his lust through self-pleasure. You *assured* me that only sheathing his shaft in a female would ease his need!"

"Forgive me, Mistress." The little physician had bowed and groveled. "I do know what is the matter. I *know* the serum is effective—I injected it into one of your other breeding slaves and his lust could scarcely be contained."

"Yes, I *know*—which is why half my female slaves are now pregnant," the Mistress snapped. "Yet this one resists—how?"

"Maybe because you're not my fucking type," Slave growled. He was damn tired of standing there, watching them discuss him like he wasn't even in the room. Like he wasn't even a real person —which as a slave, he wasn't. Not to his mistress, anyway. He was just a way to scratch her itch but by now Slade had decided he would be damned if he'd go anywhere near her.

His mistress wasn't one to give up easily though. She liked to get her money's worth.

"You *will* service me," she'd told Slade. "Or I will have you thrown in prison. I'll say you raped me and since you've already got a murder charge from killing your previous master, that will mean an instant life sentence." She'd leaned forward, hands on her hips, her blood-red nails *tap-tap-tapping* against her sharp hip bones. "Think of that, Slade—you'll be spending the rest of your miserable existence in a place with *no* females at all. And you know the lust enhancer I had my physician give you won't ease until you sink your shaft into a warm, wet cunnie. Do you *really* prefer years of torment over servicing me?"

"Fuck yes," Slade had growled. "I told you, Mistress—I took an oath not to be with another female after the one I loved died. All your drugs and threats won't change that. So leave me the *fuck* alone!"

The mistress had stared at him for a moment, white dents of fury on either side of her long, aristocratic nose, fingers tapping at her bony hips. Then she'd turned on her heel and strode out of the small slave-hut where Slade was kept.

The next people to walk through his door had been a heavily-armed contingent of peace keepers, arresting him for aggravated rape of one of the ruling class—a charge that did, indeed carry a life-sentence.

Slade was charged, tried, and convicted all in one day. After all, it wasn't like a lowly slave could afford a solicitor to argue for him in court.

From there, it was a short trip to the local prison. Where Slade, unfortunately, got into several fights and had to kill to defend himself. After twisting an attacker's head completely off during a particularly brutal battle, he had gained the charge of "mutilator" to add to his other charges of murder, rape, and arson. It was then that the powers that be decided to transfer him to BleakHall—a triple max pen owned by the man-hating mistresses of Yonnie Six.

Slade had never believed he would get out of there. Solitary had been a bitch but he'd resigned himself to a life of it...until a chance to escape came up. Slade grabbed it with both hands and didn't let go until he'd gotten to the Kindred Mother Ship.

Where he was told they had Pairing Puppets.

The android girls weren't real, Slade reasoned, so it wouldn't really be breaking his vow to Cinda to be with them. And maybe sinking his shaft into one of the artificial girls would finally quell the effects of the eroto-lust enhancer. He'd been living with the constant overwhelming sexual need caused by the drug his mistress had given him for six years by now and he was damn tired of being horny all the time and not being able to do anything about it.

*Well, I'm going to do something about it now,* he thought, shifting on the exam table again. He even knew who he wanted to do it with. For the last several months, he'd been dreaming of a Pairing Puppet with big brown eyes—a girl with a pretty face and a full, curvy figure. Wide hips, big breasts tipped with ripe, juicy nipples just made to be sucked, and a sweet little pussy able to accommodate his larger-than-average shaft were all just waiting for him.

Slade knew the girl of his dreams was a Pairing Puppet because in all his dreams he saw her in the Pairing Puppet house, surrounded by others of her kind, all ready and waiting to accommodate the unmated males of the Mother Ship. As soon as he got off this damn exam table and away from the med center, he was going to go and find her.

Or a puppet that looked like her, anyway. He knew he couldn't really expect to find the *exact* Pairing Puppet he had been dreaming of. But hell, one with a full figure and brown hair and eyes would be good enough for him.

When he found her, he was going to sink his shaft deep in her willing pussy. But first he was going to drop to his knees and lap her long and hard between her thighs. He hadn't tasted pussy in over six years which was a damn shame since in Slade's opinion, there was no finer flavor in the entire fucking universe. He...

Slade realized that his thoughts were going in circles. Damn it, he had to get out of here! He had to scratch the itch that had been driving him crazy for the last six years. Then maybe he could think straight again and wouldn't have to walk around with a constant hard-on.

Finally, after years of torment, relief was in sight.

"All right, Mr. Slade," said the little human nurse, interrupting his circular thoughts. "Now that I've taken your vitals, Dr. Brike will see you for a more thorough exam."

"Don't need to be examined," Slade growled. "I'm perfectly fine."

"I'll be the judge of that." A Blood Kindred doctor in a white coat came into the exam room as the nurse left. "Now then, it appears you've just come in with my colleague, Dr. Lathe, from BleakHall prison. Knowing the reputation of that place, I expect you'll be physically run down—possibly even malnourished." He was studying a tablet as he spoke but when he looked up at Slade's massive, muscular bulk his eyes widened. "Well," he murmured, making a note on the chart. "Perhaps *not* malnourished then."

"The only thing I'm starved for is sex, Doc," Slade said bluntly. "I've been locked up for six years now with no female companionship, if you know what I mean. If you'll just point me the way to the Pairing Puppets I'll be healthy and happy both."

"Well..." The doctor's pale blue eyes widened. "Direct, aren't you, Brother?"

Slade shrugged his broad shoulders.

"It's the only way I know to be. Now could you point me in the right direction, please? I've got a six-year itch that needs scratched."

"I'm afraid the Pairing Puppets' House is closed for the evening," the doctor said, frowning.

"*Fuck*," Slade growled in frustration.

"Not until tomorrow, I'm afraid," the Blood Kindred doctor said dryly. "I'll tell you what—I'll check you out of the med center and get you assigned to a guest suite for tonight. Why don't you rest and shave and shower—get a good hot meal and a good night's sleep. Then you can be at the Puppet House first thing in the morning when they open to, ah, scratch your itch."

It sounded like the best offer Slade was going to get.

"All right." He sighed. "I've waited six years—I guess I can wait another six hours."

"That's the spirit." The doctor clapped him on the shoulder.

"Now let's get on with this exam. I have to look you over before I can release you and have you assigned a suite."

With a resigned sigh, Slade submitted to the exam. He would take the doc's advice. A hot meal of decent food, a shave and a shower—not to mention a good night's sleep on something besides a mattress thinner than a *bergrath's* shadow—would be welcome after so long in the hole at BleakHall.

And tomorrow he would find her—the pretty little Pairing Puppet of his dreams. The one with wide hips and big brown eyes.

She was waiting there for him—Slade just knew it.

---

**Want to read more of Slade's story?**
**Of course you do! I have exciting news for you—this book will be available two weeks earlier than it's scheduled Amazon release at my new webstore which will be opening September 8, 2018.**

The new store, Aliens and Alphas, will have many of my backlist titles for those of you who have been reading my work from before my Kindred days, as well as all my new books as they come out.

I'll be able to offer coupons and discounts that I can't do at other major retail chains and there will be one-click shopping once you set up an account. Basically, it's going to be freaking awesome. :D

Be looking for my next newsletter about the new store to find out how you can win prizes, get new books early, and get deep discounts when you visit Aliens and Alphas to get my books.

HAVE YOU HEARD ABOUT *Evangeline's* BRAND NEW ONLINE SHOP FOR READERS?

# ALIENS *AND* ALPHAS BOOKSTORE

GET *exclusive book releases*, *special box sets* AND *reissues of old favorites* YOU CAN'T FIND ANYWHERE ELSE.

**LAUNCHES SEP 8, 2018**

## LAUNCHES SEPTEMBER 8, 2018

Visit my new online shop for readers at
https://shop.evangelineanderson.com/.

**The Aliens & Alphas Bookstore offers you exclusive (pre-)releases like BONDED BY ACCIDENT, special box sets, and reissues of old favourites like that you can't find anywhere else.**

Every month you can vote for your favourite out of print titles to be brought back in front of readers!

Sign up for the Aliens & Alphas VIP list to never miss a release, get exclusive sneak peeks, discounts and so much more.

# THEY ARE
# COMING BACK...

GET *reissues*
OF OLD *favorites*
EXCLUSIVELY AT

**ALIENS AND ALPHAS**
**BOOKSTORE**

# BRIDES OF THE KINDRED GLOSSARY

**AllFather**—the evil head of the *Scourge,* a race that are the byproduct of a failed genetic trade. The *AllFather* is one of the Old Ones and has the power to reach into a person's mind to harvest emotional pain and trauma. He lives for the fulfillment of the *Scourge Prophesy.*

**Ancient Ones**—beings which live in the *Deep Blue*—the darkest and most inaccessible part of the Rageron jungles. They are sentient but not related in any way to the Kindred. Each *Ancient One* has two forms—a bipedal form which resembles a human or Kindred and a beast form which can be deadly and they can change between forms at will. The Ancient Ones predate even the First Kindred and revere the *skrillix* plant, which they guard jealously.

**Bespeak**—to contact someone mentally using a *Think-me*

device. It is considered rude to bespeak someone you don't know intimately.

**Beast / Rager Kindred**—come from Rageron—a jungle planet full of beautiful but deadly flora and fauna. They have dark hair, golden eyes, and hot tempers but their most defining characteristic is the mating fist. The mating fist is an area at the base of the *Beast Kindred*'s shaft which engages fully only during bonding sex with his chosen mate. When engorged it swells to keep the *Beast Kindred* and his bride locked together until she is completely bonded to him. This ensures sex that is both extremely long lasting and multiorgasmic for both partners.

**Blackness which Eats the Stars**—another name for the *Hoard* or *Grimlax*, an ancient enemy of the Kindred. These beings have no souls and so are considered demonic by the Kindred.

**Blood Fever**—a condition suffered by unmated females on Tranq Prime, the home world of the *Blood Kindred*. *Blood Fever* or *Burning Blood*, as it is often called, is caused by a parasite living on the icy world that affects only women. The parasite—found in the *fleeta* or blood beetle—reacts with a compound in the Tranq Prime water supply to cause the fever. Symptoms include chills, the feeling of the blood heating in the veins, and increased coloration of the nipples and inner sex. If the fever is not treated in forty-eight hours, it will result in death.

Once a Kindred male has had a female's blood, he forms a natural antidote to *Blood Fever* which he can pass on by sharing body fluids with her. The most effective way to get the antidote into the female's system is for a Blood Kindred to bite her, thereby injecting it along with his essence. However, it is also possible to pass along the healing fluid through sex.

*Blood Fever* used to be very common on Tranq Prime which is what prompted the cold, proud natives to initiate a genetic exchange with the Kindred in the first place. A recent vaccine has nearly eradicated the disease, however, and the original inhabitants of the ice bound planet have little reason to continue the trade. A faction calling themselves Purists are against any further trade with the Kindred.

**Blood/Tranq Kindred**—are blond with pale blue eyes and come from Tranq Prime where ice, snow, and arctic-like temperatures are the norm. To combat the severe weather conditions, the *Blood Kindred* have higher than normal body heat with double the human amount of red blood cells. They have developed specific biting rituals to share their supercharged blood and take the blood of their mates during their own version of bonding sex. They have a set of double fangs located where a human's canine teeth would be. These fangs do not develop fully or become sharp enough to pierce flesh until a *Blood Kindred* is with a woman he wishes to mate and bond with.

**Bonding Ceremony**—a wedding-type ritual which takes place after the *Claiming Period* if the bride chosen by a Kindred warrior has allowed him to have bonding sex with her and joined her mind to his.

**Bonding Sex**—the extra step a Kindred warrior takes to bind his bride to him permanently during intercourse. For the *Beast*

*Kindred,* it is the use of the mating fist. For the *Blood Kindred,* bonding sex means sex during penetration. *Twin Kindred* bind a bride to themselves by entering her and coming in her at the same time.

**Claiming Ceremony**—a sort of engagement service that takes place when a bride is first claimed by a Kindred warrior. He declares his intentions toward her and she vows to obey the laws of the *Claiming Period.*

**Claiming Period**—women who are drafted are required to go up to the Kindred Mothership and spend a thirty day "claiming period" with the warrior who has chosen them. If, at the end of that time, they have managed to resist the charms of their Kindred mate, they are allowed to go back down to Earth and resume their normal life. However, if they succumb to their Kindred male's seduction, they are mated for life and must move to the Kindred ship to live, leaving everything else behind and seeing their family and friends on Earth only infrequently. Of course, many women are unwilling to give everything up at the drop of a hat, draft or no draft. But the Kindred have a secret weapon—devotion to their female's pleasure and attention to detail during incredibly hot sex.

**Claming Period Rules**—The *Claiming Period* lasts for four weeks during which the Kindred warrior attempts to seduce his chosen bride and she tries to resist him:

*The Holding Week:* the Kindred warrior may hold his bride.

*The Bathing Week:* the warrior and his bride bathe together and he is allowed to massage her with scented oils and make her come.

*The Tasting Week*: the warrior is allowed to perform oral sex on his bride.

*The Bonding Week*: sex is allowed but it is completely up to the bride whether she will take things a step further and allow bonding sex which is a special and specific process to the three different types of Kindred males. (Most women have given in well before this point but a few do resist.)

The only way out before the claiming period is up is a breach of contract. This can happen if the Kindred warrior does not strictly follow the rules and tries to skip forward in the order of allowed events or by breaking one of the rules laid down by the Kindred High Council. These rules—mostly to do with restrictions on communication with Earth—are for the safety of everyone aboard the Mothership and are nonnegotiable. Ignorance is no excuse for breaking them and will result in immediate termination of the claiming period.

**Convo-pillar**—A half inch long insect which resembles a brightly colored caterpillar. *Convo-pillars* were genetically engineered by traders on the fringe colonies around Rageron to translate alien languages by communicating via thought waves to their wearer's brain. They have been outlawed by the Kindred High Council because their notoriously unreliable translations cause more conflicts than they solve.

**Dark Kindred** —also known as *Enhanced Ones*—this faction of the Kindred race broke off centuries ago when there was a shortage of viable females to call for brides. Vowing to overcome their sexual urges, the *Dark Kindred* made a genetic trade with the cyborg-like residents of Zeaga Four who are ruled by a group

482   BRIDES OF THE KINDRED GLOSSARY

of sentient machines called the Collective. Since all emotion is prohibited on Zeaga Four, the organic inhabitants get emotion damper implants to keep them from committing Feel-crime. Anyone found guilty of Feel-crime without a special dispensation from the Collective may be summarily purged.

**Deep Blue**—the darkest and most inaccessible part of the Rageron jungles

**Dream Sharing**—occurs when a Kindred warrior's mind aligns with that of his bride and they begin to see each other's day to day activities and memories in their sleep. However, the alignment of the two (or three in the case of the *Twin Kindred*) minds can take several forms and is not limited to sleep.

**Fireflower Juice**—an alcoholic beverage made from the Fireflower plant native to Rageron. It resembles milk in appearance but has the flavor of honey, vanilla, lavender and blueberries.

**High Councilor**—the rightful ruler and defender of the Kindred home planet, First World. Only the *High Councilor* may sit upon the throne of wisdom and see with the eye of foreknowledge. Without a *High Councilor* in place, First World and the rest of the Kindred race cannot be adequately protected against the evil machinations of the Hoard.

**Hoard**—an ancient enemy of the First Kindred also known as the *Grimlax* or the *Blackness between the Stars*, they are evil, demonic beings with ravenous appetites and a desire to conquer, devour, and destroy every living thing in the universe. They are divided into tribes with the lowest echelon being the most numerous and primitive. The elite or upper echelon tribes are more sophisticated and intelligent but also much more dangerous. They are notoriously manipulative and able to change their appearances using a technique called "shadowing" to look like anyone or anything they choose.

**The Kindred**—a race of genetic traders who have traveled the universe for centuries looking for viable matches to expand their gene pool. Since a genetic anomaly ensures that their population is ninety-five percent male, they are specifically looking for women.

The three genetic trades the *Kindred* have already made have resulted in three very specific types of men. But though they take on some of the physical characteristics of the race they are trading with, the *Kindred* gene always ensures three things: physical prowess, extremely large and muscular body structure, and undying loyalty to the female of their choice.

**Krik-ka-re**—a Scourge tradition in which the mind life of one being may be traded for or ransomed by another.

**Kusax**—a special knife made from the tainted metal at the core of the *Scourge* home planet. One scratch can be deadly as it infects the wounded person with a soul poison which ensures a slow, agonizing death.

**Law of Conduct**—the Kindred law which says every warrior is responsible for the good behavior of his bride and gives him the right to punish her—within reason. Often the "punishment" is sexual in nature and some brides become serial offenders simply to experience their Kindred warrior's particular form of discipline. ; )

**Luck Kiss**—a kiss performed by the best man and maid of honor at a Kindred *Bonding Ceremony* in order to bring the happy couple good luck.

**Mate of my kin**—the way Kindred warriors refer to the brides chosen by their brothers. It is analogous to the English term sister-in-law.

**Marks of Possession**—the *Scourge* way of marking a female as their mate. The *Marks of Possession* include a close-fitting collar, piercings in the nipples and clitoral hood, and a brand on the inner hip or the top of the buttocks. *Scourge* with Kindred blood also desire to scent-mark their mates but they require the traditional marks of their kind to really feel bonded to the female of their choice.

**Mother of All Life**—the main Kindred Deity, a kind and benevolent goddess whose teachings include respect and reverence for all things female.

**Numala**—a *Blood Kindred* name which means "liquid pussy." It refers to a female who produces more than the regular amount of lubrication when aroused. *Numalas* are much prized by the *Blood Kindred* and sought after as mates because they are more likely to be able to accommodate a *Blood Kindred* warrior's larger than average cock.

**Psychic-Knife**—a torture device developed by the *Scourge* that is able to break the mental and emotional bond between a Kindred and his bride.

**Rage**—*also* **Protective Rage** *or* **Berserker Rage**—a state of altered consciousness that comes over a Kindred warrior when his bride is threatened. It floods the bloodstream with endorphins and causes such intense anger and aggression that a Kindred in this state becomes a killing machine who will die to protect the woman he has claimed.

**Sacred Grove**—an area of green and purple trees that houses the temple of the *Mother of All Life*. The Kindred Mother ship has been equipped with an artificial green sun like the one on their home world in order to allow these holy trees to grow and flourish.

**Scourge**—a genetic trade gone wrong, these menacing outsiders have twisted desires and sexual needs fierce enough to frighten away even the most adventurous. Their need to dominate and possess their women completely has led to a strange prophesy that they must fulfill...or die trying.

**Scourge Prophesy**—"One of two, alike and yet different—the double fruit of a single womb from the third planet of a yellow sun. She shall be marked with a white star between her breasts." These words were spoken by Mee'ah—the last living female of the *Scourge* race who was believed to be a great seer. The *Scourge* are a dying race, forced to create new members in test tubes and artificial wombs because they have no females. Yet, because they have some of the same genetic characteristics as the Kindred they are able to create only male children and each new generation is weaker than the last. The prophesy refers to the woman the *Scourge* believe will be able to mate with the *AllFather* and bear only daughters to rejuvenate their race.

**Skrillix Plant**—also known as the *Pain Vine*. This plant is found only in the heart of the Rageron jungles called the *Deep Blue*. The brilliant crimson berries of the *skrillix* are said to cure many illnesses, including stasis sickness and can also dissolve an improperly placed or artificial soul bond. The thorns are said to be as poisonous as the berries are helpful. One prick from a *skrillix* thorn can give waking nightmares, forcing the victim to relive painful memories. When minds are linked by the juice of the berries, these visions can be shared with others who can witness them via a chemically induced neural link.

**Take-me**—an animal native to Twin Moons that has been domesticated by the Kindred for transportation aboard their ship. The *Take-me* has green fur and two heads, one on either end. Each head has three purple eyes. The *Take-me* has the unique features of being to expand and compress its mass which makes it ideal for storage. Because they originally lived in caves, most *Take-mes* stay very contentedly in small dark areas in the Kindred food prep areas where they live off the scraps and leavings of their master's meals. They can eat almost anything except banana peels which they are allergic to.

**Tharp**—an animal that looks very much like a thin fur blanket which can be worn as a garment. *Tharps* are cultivated on Tranq Prime and prized for their ability to multiply their host's body heat and keep them warm in even the most frigid conditions. A *tharp* can be worn by only one person— as a neophyte or youngster it imprints upon a host and will slowly starve if parted from them. *Tharps* are intelligent and capable of limited movement. They live as long as their host and subsist only on body heat, needing no other form of sustenance to survive.

**Think-Me**—a thin silver wire worn around the temples which facilitates mental communication between people who already have an intimate connection.

**Touch-U**—a flat black mat-like animal native to Tranq Prime which the Kindred have adapted to be a home health appliance. The *Touch-U* is capable of giving a gentle massage or an all-out erotic experience depending on which button is pushed.

**Twin Kindred**—come from Twin Moons—a world of vast, stormy oceans dotted with craggy but beautiful islands. True to their namesake, *Twin Kindred* always come in pairs. The brothers are not identical, however. There is always a light twin and a dark twin. These labels refer not just to skin, hair, and eye coloring but to the twin's moods and perceptions of the world. The dark twin in the pair is usually more moody and withdrawn while the light twin takes a substantially brighter view of life. The twins are closely linked and able to sense each other's emotions. They cannot be separated by long distances or for long periods of time without severe pain. They must also share a woman, linking her into their mental and emotional exchange for very intense ménage sex.

**Urlich**—a type of dog bred by the *Scourge*. At maturity they are modified with machinery to heighten their sense of smell and intelligence which results in a cyborg-type animal. Once in pursuit of whatever scent has been programmed into their brains, the *urlich* are utterly single minded and incapable of stopping until their prey has been cornered and captured.

**Wave**—a Kindred cooking appliance which emits thousands of finely collimated beams of heat to cook food in under a minute.

**Zichther**—an animal native to the jungles of Rageron, the *zichther* resembles a small bright blue teddy bear in appearance until it opens its mouth and reveals three rows of incredibly sharp, shark-like teeth.

# KEEP UP WITH YOUR *favorite* SERIES...

**COUGAR-VILLE**   **BORN TO DARKNESS**   **BRIDES** *of the* **KINDRED**   **KINDRED TALES**   **ALIEN** *Mate* **INDEX**   CyBRG Files

# ...AND JOIN MY *newsletter* TODAY

## SIGN ME UP!

Sign up for my newsletter and you'll be the first to know when a new book comes out or I have some cool stuff to give away. Don't worry—I won't share your email with anyone else, I'll never spam you (way too busy writing books) and you can unsubscribe at any time.

As a thank-you gift you'll get a free copy of BONDING WITH THE BEAST delivered to your inbox right away. In the next days I'll also send you free copies of CLAIMED, book 1 in the Brides of Kindred series, and ABDUCTED, the first book in my Alien Mate Index series.

http://evangelineanderson.com/newsletter/

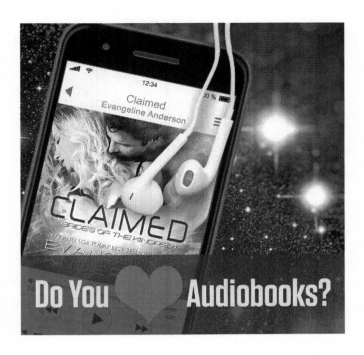

**You've read the book, now listen to the audiobook.**

My Kindred series is coming to audio one book at a time. Sign up for my audiobook newsletter. Besides notifications about new audio releases you may also get an email if I'm running a contest with an audio-book prize. Otherwise I will leave you alone. : ).

http://evangelineanderson.com/audio-newsletter/

# ALSO BY EVANGELINE ANDERSON

Below you'll find a list of available and upcoming titles. But depending on when you read this list, new books will have come out by then that are not listed here. Make sure to check my website for the latest releases and better yet, sign up for my newsletter to never miss a new book again.

---

### Brides of the Kindred series

CLAIMED (Also available in Audio)

HUNTED (Also available in Audio)

SOUGHT (Also Available in Audio)

FOUND (Also Available in Audio )

REVEALED (Also Available in Audio)

PURSUED (Also Available in Audio)

EXILED (Also Available in Audio)

SHADOWED (Also Available in Audio)

CHAINED

DIVIDED

DEVOURED

ENHANCED

CURSED

ENSLAVED

TARGETED

FORGOTTEN

SWITCHED

UNCHARTED

UNBOUND

SURRENDERED

VANISHED

IMPRISONED (coming soon)

BRIDES OF THE KINDRED VOLUME ONE

Contains *Claimed, Hunted, Sought* and *Found*

BRIDES OF THE KINDRED VOLUME TWO

Contains *Revealed, Pursued* and *Exiled*

BRIDES OF THE KINDRED VOLUME THREE

Contains *Shadowed, Chained* and *Divided*

BRIDES OF THE KINDRED VOLUME FOUR

Contains *Devoured, Enhanced* and *Cursed*

BRIDES OF THE KINDRED VOLUME FIVE

Contains *Enslaved, Targeted* and *Forgotten*

BRIDES OF THE KINDRED VOLUME SIX

Contains *Switched, Uncharted* and *Unbound*

*All Kindred novels are now available in PRINT.*

*Also, all Kindred novels are on their way to Audio, join my Audiobook
Newsletter to be notified when they come out.*

## Kindred Tales

*(The Kindred Tales are side stories in the Brides of the Kindred which stand alone outside the main story arc.)*

MASTERING THE MISTRESS

BONDING WITH THE BEAST (Also Available in Audio)

SEEING WITH THE HEART

FREEING THE PRISONER

HEALING THE BROKEN (*a Kindred Christmas novel*)

TAMING THE GIANT

BRIDGING THE DISTANCE

LOVING A STRANGER

FINDING THE JEWEL

BONDED BY ACCIDENT (coming soon)

## Born to Darkness series

CRIMSON DEBT (Also available in Audio)

SCARLET HEAT (Also available in Audio)

RUBY SHADOWS (Also available in Audio)

CARDINAL SINS (coming soon)

DESSERT (short novella following *Scarlet Heat*)

(Also in Audio)

BORN TO DARKNESS BOX SET

Contains *Crimson Debt, Scarlet Heat,* and *Ruby Shadows* all in one volume

---

### Alien Mate Index series

ABDUCTED (Also available in Audio)

PROTECTED (Also available in Audio)

DESCENDED (Also available in Audio)

SEVERED (Also available in Audio)

*All Alien Mate novels are now available in PRINT.*

---

### The Cougarville Series

BUCK NAKED (Also available in Audio)

COUGAR BAIT (Also available in Audio)

STONE COLD FOX (Also available in Audio)

BIG BAD WOLF (coming soon)

---

### The Swann Sister Chronicles

WISHFUL THINKING (coming soon)

BE CAREFUL WHAT YOU WISH FOR (coming soon)

---

**The Institute series**

THE INSTITUTE: DADDY ISSUES

(Also available in Audio)

THE INSTITUTE: MISHKA'S SPANKING

---

**The CyBRG Files with Mina Carter**

UNIT 77: BROKEN

UNIT 78: RESCUED

---

**Stand Alone Titles**

ANYONE U WANT

BLIND DATE WITH A VAMPIRE

BLOOD KISS

CONFESSIONS OF A LINGERIE MODEL

COUGAR CHRISTMAS

DEAL WITH THE DEVIL (Also available in Audio)

EYES LIKE A WOLF

HUNGER MOON RISING

PLANET X (Also available in Audio)

PLEASURE PLANET

PURITY (Now available in Audio)

SHADOW DREAMS

SPEEDING TICKET

STRESS RELIEF

TAKE TWO

THE LAST MAN ON EARTH

THE PLEASURE PALACE

THE SACRIFICE (Also available in Audio)

WHEN MR. BLACK COMES HOME

---

**YA Novels**

THE ACADEMY (Now available in Audio)

# ABOUT THE AUTHOR

Evangeline Anderson is the *New York Times* and *USA Today* bestselling author of the *Brides of the Kindred, Alien Mate Index, Cougarville* and *Born to Darkness* series. She is fourty-something and lives in Florida with a husband, a son, and two cats. She had been writing erotic fiction for her own gratification for a number of years before it occurred to her to try and get paid for it. To her delight, she found that it was actually possible to get money for having a dirty mind and she has been writing paranormal and sci-fi erotica steadily ever since.

You can find her online at her website
www.evangelineanderson.com

Come visit for some free reads. Or, to be the first to find out about new books, join her newsletter. She's also got a mailing list for updates on audio books.

Made in the USA
Middletown, DE
21 September 2023

38964709R00302